She looked defia░░░░░░░░░░░░░░░░░░re just trying to th░░░░░░░░░░░░░░░░░

"That's ridiculou░░░░░░░░░░░░

Her blush deepene░░░░░words tumbled out in a rush. "Am I that dangerous?"

That was a hell of a question, he thought. His eyes moved over her flushed cheeks, her mouth, the curves of her breasts and hips in that damned dress, and he felt his self-control beginning to slip.

"You think you understand," Max said coldly, "but you don't."

"Don't I?" Carly's eyes were bright. "I'm just wondering if I get any say in this. Because if I do, I'd much rather be brazen. Frankly, Max, it is not my hand that I want kissed."

Trust Me

MELANIE CRAFT

An AOL Time Warner Company

WARNER BOOKS EDITION

Cover design by Diane Luger
Cover illustration by Sandy Haight
Cover photo by Franco Accornero
Book design by Giorgetta Bell McRee

Warner Books, Inc.
1271 Avenue of the Americas
New York, NY 10020

Visit our Web site at www.twbookmark.com

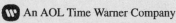 An AOL Time Warner Company

Printed in the United States of America

First Paperback Printing: November 2003

10 9 8 7 6 5 4 3 2 1

This book is dedicated to the
Mercer Veterinary Clinic for the Homeless.

Founded in 1992 by students at the University
of California at Davis, the Mercer Clinic provides
free veterinary care to the companion animals of
the homeless. Royalties from this book will be
donated to support the Mercer Clinic.

Acknowledgments

My thanks to the following people:

Mitch Douglas at ICM and Beth de Guzman at Warner, for their guidance.

Kira Craft for tea and sympathy during rewrites.

Joyce Higashi for organizing my life and letting me pretend that I'm the one doing it.

Lizzie Brumble Schwartz for unflagging friendship across many years and miles.

And most of all, Larry Ellison, who didn't write this one either, but who was an integral part of the process. My love and gratitude for his support, patience, humor, and willingness to praise first drafts.

Trust Me

CHAPTER 1

———— ◆ ————

"You're not what I expected," said the man. He was handsome, with steely eyes that matched his suit, and he was as out of place in the tiny veterinary clinic as Carly Martin, D.V.M., would have been in a Fortune 500 boardroom.

His gaze moved over her, and he nodded thoughtfully. "But now that I see you, it makes sense. That wholesome girl-next-door look must work wonders on lonely old men."

Carly sighed and pushed the reheat button on the coffeemaker. It was clearly going to be one of those days. The man, whoever he was, had bypassed the receptionist and cornered her in the staff room, where she had gone to change into a clean lab coat and gobble a few bites of cold pizza for lunch. He had walked in unannounced, set his briefcase on a chair, then dared to call her Charlotte, which was the most reliable and efficient way to get things off to a bad start.

Morning at the clinic had begun with the frantic arrival

of Gigi Beeson, society doyenne of San Francisco, whose pug had just consumed a five-carat emerald earring. Carly had used an endoscopic forceps to retrieve the jewel, and the small dog was going to be fine, but after dealing with Gigi's hysterics and a yowling, barking waiting room full of increasingly impatient clients, Carly wasn't so sure of her own chances.

And now there was a stranger blocking the doorway, saying things that made no sense. If he was a random lunatic, he was the best-dressed lunatic she had ever seen. A heavy silver watch was his only ornament, but Carly had spent two years caring for the pampered pets of San Francisco's elite and knew money when she saw it. That suit was Italian, tailored to an expert fit over his broad shoulders, and his shoes and belt together were worth more than her entire wardrobe. Men like him did not wander the streets looking for veterinarians to accost.

"Okay," Carly said, trying not to think about the state of the waiting room. "You have exactly one minute until I take my coffee and go back to work. Please explain what you're talking about, and how you know my name."

The stranger regarded her coolly. "Your name is just the beginning. One word from me, and my people will dig up things about you that even your mother doesn't know. Yet."

Carly didn't know whether to be amused or annoyed. "You're threatening me?"

"Damn right," the man said. "The day you decided to fleece Henry Tremayne was the day that you messed with me, lady. And that was a very big mistake."

"Henry! What does Henry have to do with this?"

The man's mouth curved cynically. "Not bad," he said.

"Not bad at all. The startled surprise, the innocent, mystified look . . . You're almost convincing. Have you been practicing, or have you done this before?"

The novelty of the encounter was wearing off. "Look," Carly said. "I'm tired, my feet hurt, and my afternoon is booked solid. I don't have time to stand here listening to you, so would you please get to the point? Who are you?"

"My name is Max Giordano. I'm the executor of Henry Tremayne's will."

"What?" In an instant, Carly forgot her sore feet and the overcrowded waiting room. "Oh, my God, Henry isn't . . . ?"

"No. He isn't. He's alive, albeit barely. There was an accident, and he hasn't regained consciousness."

Carly pressed her lips together, trying to recover her composure. She did not want to cry in front of this forbidding man, but the news was overwhelming. Henry, barely alive? He was nearly eighty, but he had always seemed ageless to her, and he had been fine just yesterday afternoon, when she had stopped by to see him. Technically, of course, it wasn't Henry who she was visiting, but the latest addition to his ever-changing menagerie. This time it was a three-week-old kitten, abandoned in a dumpster on the other side of town. Henry's reputation as a willing caretaker for any creature lost or unloved had brought the baby, special delivery, to his doorstep. Carly had left him sitting in his favorite red velvet armchair, his white head bent as he fed the tiny cat with an eyedropper.

She cleared her throat, blinking hard. "What happened?"

"He fell down the stairs and fractured his skull. He's in the ICU at Hopkins Memorial."

"Is he going to die?"

"At the moment, I have no idea."

"And you . . . ? You're his lawyer?"

"No," Max Giordano said. "I'm his grandson."

Max's day had started at 5 A.M., when he had been awakened by the most shocking phone call of his life. He had stumbled into the shower and blasted himself with hot water in an attempt to clear his mind and process the incredible news: Henry Tremayne—who wasn't even supposed to know that Max existed—not only knew about him, but had left him in charge of the entire Tremayne trust.

In the year that Max had spent planning his first face-to-face contact with his only living relative, he had never imagined that it could happen in such a way. Henry, pale and unconscious in the hospital bed, his frail body violated with tubes and monitors, had looked more dead than alive. Max had spent the next hours sitting alone in the visitors' lounge, clenching a Styrofoam coffee cup and staring through the window into the chilly, gray light of the new dawn.

It was easy to brood in a hospital. The cold sterility of the place, with its utilitarian white walls and steel-framed furniture, magnified the horror he felt as he realized how close he was to losing the grandfather he had yet to meet.

Eight o'clock brought a meeting with the Tremayne legal team, confirming what had been said on the phone. Fourteen months ago, Henry had quietly rewritten all of his legal documents to name Max as his primary heir and successor trustee.

Fourteen months. The timing couldn't be a coincidence. His grandfather had learned of his existence shortly after Max had hired an investigative firm to track down the family of the father he knew almost nothing about. Henry's lawyers were close-mouthed on the subject, but it was obvious to Max that someone at the firm had leaked—or, more likely, sold—the information to Henry. Had his grandfather even believed the story at first? To suddenly be told, almost forty years after the fact, that his son Alan had fathered an illegitimate child only days before the car wreck that killed him . . . well, that wasn't the kind of news that you mentioned casually over lunch. Max had spent many nights staring up at the darkened ceiling over his bed, trying to come up with a reasonable plan for dropping such a bomb on an unsuspecting old man.

Little had he known that the announcement had already been made. It was lawsuit material, but at the moment, Max had a more immediate problem to deal with, in the form of a woman named Charlotte Martin.

She was staring at him, obviously stunned. "You're Henry's grandson? I didn't think he had any family at all. Aside from the pets, that is."

"Rich, old, and alone," Max said. "The perfect target."

She stiffened. "I think you'd better explain yourself."

He was pleased to see caution darkening her eyes, replacing her earlier carelessness. She wasn't feeling so confident. She didn't know what to make of him, or the threat that he represented, which was exactly as he had intended. Confused and on the defensive, she would be easy to read. She could cling to the innocent, self-righteous role if she wanted to; it would make no difference in the end.

It was time to get this over with. "You've been mentioned in my grandfather's will."

"Yes," she said matter-of-factly.

Max looked curiously at her. This was an abrupt switch. He had expected wide eyes, trembling lips. *What? Dear Henry thought of me? How kind. How unexpected. How much?*

"You're not surprised, Ms. Martin?"

"Give me some credit," she said. "Anyone with the brain of a hamster could have guessed that you were leading up to that. Why else all the jabs about old, rich men? But I'd like to know what you're doing here, talking to me about your grandfather's will while he's still alive. Do Henry's lawyers know about this? Because if they don't, then you have absolutely no right to—"

"The lawyers were the ones who called me," Max replied. "And I wasn't using the word 'will' in the technical sense. My grandfather's estate is actually held in something called an inter vivos trust, which means that all of his assets are under the care of a person called a—"

"Trustee. I know what a trust is. My brother is a tax attorney, and he just helped my parents set one up. You should have just said so, instead of assuming that my entire understanding of estate planning comes from the daytime soaps. So you're actually Henry's trustee, not his executor. Fine. What does that have to do with me?"

Max opened his mouth, then closed it again. This wholesome-looking veterinarian might be an unlikely femme fatale, but she was smart enough to cause trouble if he wasn't careful. "Henry Tremayne has given you custody of the animals in his estate," he said, his eyes never leaving her face as he waited for her reaction.

She blinked. "All of them? My goodness."

"You will be their caretaker in the event of his incapacitation, and their owner upon his death. They may be placed in qualifying homes, the criteria for which are outlined in a special document, but they must never be abandoned, euthanized, or given to a shelter."

He pulled a slip of paper out of his suit pocket, and consulted it. "The sum total of the animals is . . . twenty-three cats, eleven dogs, two birds, and an iguana. Are you willing to accept custody under these terms?"

He had intentionally avoided telling her that the pets were only the first part of Henry's bequest. It was his chance to erase the Charlotte Martin problem in one quick stroke, thanks to a trick in the wording of the legal documents. If she refused guardianship of the animals, then she would forfeit everything, and he had the disclaimer statement sitting in his briefcase, ready for her signature. He waited, concealing his impatience. There was no way that she could possibly agree to this part of Henry's plan. He knew, from having questioned the lawyers, that she lived in a tiny basement apartment with barely enough room for one animal, much less thirty-seven. She had to refuse. She had no choice.

His heart leaped as she began to shake her head.

"No," She said. "I don't think—"

Max seized the word. "No?"

"No," she repeated, more firmly now. "It's twenty-two cats, and definitely no iguana. Henry found homes for the Persian and the yellow tomcat, then adopted the new kitten, and Oscar—the iguana—died weeks ago."

She shot Max a chilly look. "Died of old age, I should

add, in case you're planning to accuse me of murdering him."

Max put a hand to his forehead and discovered that he was perspiring. The clinic was hot, or maybe the day was finally getting to him. "Answer the question. Do you, or do you not accept custody of these animals?"

"Of course I do," she said, but a wrinkle furrowed her brow. "It's the least I can do for Henry, after everything that he's done for me. I just wonder . . . I can't bring them to my house . . . and the cost of feeding all of them . . ."

She stopped herself and squared her shoulders. "Well, I'll figure something out," she said. "Henry loves his animals, and he's been a good friend to me. I accept."

Frustration gripped Max. What was this woman thinking? How could any sane person agree to be his grandfather's zookeeper? Her response proved that she already knew what else was included. "I'm sure this isn't news to you," he said, "but you'll receive a generous income from the trust to cover care of the animals."

She exhaled softly. "That will help."

Max paused, hoping to catch impatience in her expression as he delayed the real news. But she didn't betray a thing.

"There's more," he said finally.

Charlotte Martin looked surprised. "Something else?"

"Yes. Something else." Max narrowed his eyes at her. He had hoped that things would not get this far, but she was turning out to be more adroit than he had expected. There was no way to delay the inevitable next step, but he reminded himself that it was only a preliminary defeat. The real battle was only beginning.

He took a deep breath. "My grandfather has given you the Tremayne mansion."

"What!"

Carly reached back to grab the edge of the counter as her knees went wobbly. "The house?" she said, her voice sounding thin and squeaky to her own ears. "Henry left me his house?"

"No." Max Giordano shook his head. "A *house* is a little building with a picket fence. My grandfather left you a mansion with an estimated value of 20 million dollars. He left you his castle, for God's sake, and he's under the impression that you'll turn it into some kind of stray animal rehabilitation center. I assume that you know what he's talking about."

"Oh, my God. He was serious about that?"

Max nodded grimly, and she stammered, "I mean . . . it was something that we chatted about, yes, but never in detail, and he never said anything about putting *me* in charge of it. It was just an idea. I never thought . . ."

"Really. You never thought. Oh my." He widened his eyes in disbelief at her shock. "Well, guess what, Ms. Martin. I find that a little hard to believe. I'll bet that you've been thinking about this for a long time. It must have taken some work to insinuate yourself into Henry Tremayne's life and brainwash him into making a gift like this."

Carly stared at him, finally understanding what had brought this man into her clinic with both fists swinging. Because of her, Max Giordano was not going to inherit a significant portion of his grandfather's estate, and he was angry about it. This was all about greed, and the ugliness of it appalled her. Who would have guessed that gentle, eccentric Henry Tremayne could have produced a grandson like this?

"Henry and I are friends," she said. "I make house calls to take care of his pets, and that's all. Your accusations say a lot more about you than they do about me."

"Sorry, Doc, but I wasn't born yesterday. Old men don't casually leave mansions to pretty young female *friends.*"

"They do if they have no one else," Carly exclaimed. "Where have you been? I've known Henry for two years, and I've never seen you or heard a single word about you. Just the fact that you think he's a gullible old man who would fall prey to some . . . temptress . . . is ridiculous. He's one of the sharpest people I know, old or young. Have you ever so much as spoken with your grandfather, or are you just showing up now to collect his money?"

Max Giordano paled slightly, and Carly hoped that her question had hit a nerve. She glared at him. "When was the last time that you visited him?"

"You don't understand the situation."

"No? Explain it to me, then. When was the last time you called him? Just to say hello. I'm curious."

Max remained grimly silent.

"I think I do understand," Carly said, nodding. "And I'm not surprised that Henry never mentioned you. You had better pray that he recovers, Mr. Giordano. Your grandfather is one of the kindest and most caring people I've ever met, and if you've missed your last chance to know him, you'll have lost more than you can ever imagine."

It wasn't nice, but she hadn't intended to be nice. She

wanted to slap him verbally, to see if he was capable of feeling even a flicker of shame over the way he had neglected his grandfather. Any kind of guilty reaction would have satisfied her, but what she saw was astonishing.

A shadow crossed his face; dark, naked, and saturated with a grief so great that every healing instinct in Carly's body cried out in sudden sympathy.

And it was gone as quickly as it had come. Carly blinked, feeling as if a ghost had just flitted by and touched her with one stroke of a spectral finger.

"Mr. Giordano?" she said hesitantly, regretting her harsh words. For all his abrasiveness, he apparently was no stranger to pain, and she was suddenly ashamed to have added to it.

He simply reached for his briefcase, giving no sign that he had heard her. "One of the lawyers will meet you in front of the mansion at six," he said. "You'll be given the keys then, and you can come and go as you please. For now."

"For now?"

"Don't get too comfortable, Ms. Martin. You're only the temporary guardian of the animals and the mansion. If my grandfather recovers, this will all have a very different ending. And believe me, in the meantime, I'll be watching you."

CHAPTER 2

———————•❖•———————

The hills of San Francisco's elegant Pacific Heights district were one of the last parts of the city to be touched by the rays of the evening sun. Golden springtime light dappled the roof of the Tremayne mansion, illuminating the dark slate tiles and gloomy gables, which would have looked more at home in the midst of a perpetual thunderstorm. Henry's house was a Gothic wonder in a neighborhood of Victorian gingerbread, and it stood high on the highest hill around, bordered by a stone wall that gave the estate the look of a fortress. The combination of house and grounds covered an entire city block, and Carly knew from Henry's stories about his childhood that the property had once been even larger.

The Tremayne family had been in San Francisco since the nineteenth century, and Henry's own father—an old-fashioned rogue given to legendary gambling binges and surprisingly good investment decisions—had built the house with the fortune he made from his shares of the Comstock Lode, won in a gin-soaked all-night game of poker. Or so Henry claimed. He liked to tease her, and he knew that she was susceptible to believing any wild yarn as long as it was delivered with a straight face. It was just as likely that his father had been a sedate church elder in the grocery business.

The wrought-iron gate was open, as always. Carly had never seen it closed, and from the look of the hinges, it would take a strong man and a blowtorch to close it. She turned her VW into the driveway and headed uphill toward the house. It was a familiar route by now. She had been making weekly visits to Henry and his menagerie for two years, ever since the day her business partner Richard had buzzed her on the clinic intercom to tell her to take the call holding on line one.

"There's a weird old guy on the phone. He says he's got a sick raccoon."

"A raccoon? He shouldn't be handling a wild animal. Has he been bitten? You'd better give him the number for Animal Control."

"No, no. It's not wild, it's a pet." Richard sounded appalled by the idea. "It ate some spoiled tuna, and now it has indigestion, or something. He wants a house call. I told him you'd go."

The "weird old guy" had turned out to be Henry Tremayne, calling with his usual lack of pretension. His regular veterinarian had retired and moved to Florida, he told her, his enunciation as elegant as his grammar, and he did not care for the fellow's successor. He was looking for someone new, but he was having a bit of trouble finding a doctor who was willing to come to the house. Would she be so kind? He would certainly compensate her for the trouble.

At the time, Carly was fresh out of her small hometown of Davis, California, and the Tremayne name meant nothing to her. After a brief conversation, she had decided that he seemed like a nice old man, harmlessly eccentric, and had taken his address and promised to stop by later that afternoon.

When his directions led her to the foot of the driveway leading up to the towering Tremayne mansion, she had checked and rechecked the numbers on the gate against the ones in her notes, convinced that she had made a mistake. Finally, she had worked up the nerve to drive up the hill and approach the front door.

Looking back on it now, she found it hard to imagine that there had ever been a time when she hadn't spent Wednesday afternoons sitting with Henry in the solarium, drinking tea from the antique silver service and making genteel conversation. He was a great fan of both pets and poetry, and had spent most of her first visit reading to her from T. S. Eliot's *Old Possum's Book of Practical Cats*. On her second visit, he had presented her with her own copy, a first edition. At the time, she'd had no idea of what it was worth, and later, when she found out, Henry had only laughed when she tried, red-faced, to return it.

Richard had been shocked when he realized what kind of client he had tossed away, and he had insisted on making the next trip to the mansion all by himself. But Henry took an immediate dislike to him, and the next week Richard grudgingly told Carly that he was too busy to waste his time on house calls.

Carly had met Richard Wexler when he lectured at the University of California in Davis on the use of lasers in veterinary surgery. He was thirty-five then, ten years older than she, and somehow her postlecture questions had turned into a discussion over dinner at the nicest restaurant in town. They dated through her last year of school, and as graduation approached, Richard had stunned her by suggesting that she join him as a partner in his San Francisco practice. She had been over the moon with delight, and had completely ignored everyone who warned her that mixing romance with business was a recipe for disaster.

Carly grimaced. She hated to remember her own dewy fantasies of gazing into Richard's eyes as they worked together, tenderly ministering to the sick and wounded creatures of the city. At least she hadn't married him, she thought—not that he had asked.

He was a brilliant and tireless surgeon, happiest when he was in the operating room involved in some complex procedure. His practice, though physically small, had one of the best-equipped facilities in the Bay Area, and other veterinarians regularly referred cases to him. He would have been welcomed onto the faculty of any vet school in the country, but he was a cowboy, not a team player, and academic life would not have suited him at all.

But Richard's surgical strength was also his weakness. He had no patience for weepy pet owners and the hand-holding and explanations they required. He knew what had to be done, and he wanted to do it, not to stand around explaining himself to nonprofessionals. Carly had been sure that she was just what he needed. She could be the nurturer and the comforter, the link between his high-tech skills and their anxious clients, and becoming a partner in his established practice would immediately give her the kind of security that would otherwise take years to build.

They had signed an agreement to take reduced salaries for a five-year period, reinvesting their profits in the business during that time. Richard kept a controlling interest, which was fine with Carly, who could not have afforded to buy an equal share anyway. She was flattered and grateful that he had chosen her as a partner despite her inexperience. It was a risk for him, but she saw it as a testament to his belief in her.

The first few months had been the bliss that she had imagined. But as she gradually settled in, and her momentum began to fade, she began to see that Richard's practice, and Richard himself, were actually very different than she had believed.

At first, Carly made excuses for the things that felt wrong. If Rich always seemed to be pushing the newest and most dramatic procedures, even when she thought that a noninvasive approach would be better, she told herself that it was his confidence that made him so aggressive. And if he dismissed her when she questioned his judgment, she reminded herself that he was the expert, and it would be better for her quietly to watch, and learn.

So she did. And by the end of their first year together, she had learned that she was no longer in love with Richard Wexler, and that she did not even particularly like him. They had nothing in common, including their opinions on how to run a veterinary practice. He was the most gifted surgeon that Carly had ever known, but he was also egocentric and had no tolerance for any ideas but his own. His clients were wealthy professionals who could afford the whopping charges that he ran up and seemed to consider the size of the bill a measure of the quality of care. At first, Carly had tried to meet with some of Richard's clients to explain her views on their options, but she usually found that they did not want to listen. They wanted the instant results that he could deliver, and even when they arrived undecided, they quickly fell into the thrall of his brash self-assurance.

"Just like I did," Carly muttered, parking her car in the top semicircle of driveway in front of Henry's house. Rich had somehow mesmerized her, and the spell hadn't begun to dissolve until she started to see him every day. By then, of course, it was too late.

She hadn't been surprised when he flatly refused to release her from their contract, though she didn't know whether his motive was malice or money. Whatever the case, he had her legally hooked. If she broke the agreement and left, she would forfeit every cent she had invested, and that was much more than she could afford to lose.

So the business relationship, at least, had endured. Carly had gritted her teeth through months of postbreakup unpleasantness when Richard refused to speak to her except in icy monosyllables. They had eventually come to an uneasy truce, but even with almost three years to go before she could pull out her 30 percent of the equity, Carly had no illusion that she and Richard would ever be friends. The clinic was doing well, though, and it was some comfort to know that the partnership had at least been a good financial move. By the time that she was free to leave, she would have enough money—with a little help from the bank—to open her own practice, and there would be nothing that Richard could do but scowl as she waved good-bye.

Three years to go. It wasn't really so long, although

there were days when it felt like an eternity. But she had no other option—or, rather, she hadn't had one until that afternoon, when Max Giordano delivered his incredible news.

Carly stepped out of her car and turned to look at the gigantic stone mansion. There were knots in her stomach. After Max had left the clinic, she had spent the remainder of the day trying to focus on her work, but she felt as if she had been hit by a hurricane, and conflicting emotions still battered at her like ocean waves. If what Max had said was true—she couldn't quite believe that there hadn't been some mistake—then Henry Tremayne had given her a gift that was incredibly, overwhelmingly generous. It was impossible not to want such a gift, but at the same time, it was also impossible to want something that would only come about through Henry's death. It was a strange, sad frame for such a magical picture, and thinking about it made Carly feel queasy. She hoped she would be allowed to see Henry at the hospital. Even if he couldn't hear her, she wanted to hold his hand and tell him aloud that she loved him.

She heard the purr of a car engine and turned to see a gleaming black Jaguar sedan cruising up the driveway. It was exactly six. The Jag slowed to a stop beside her battered VW, looking somewhat like a spaceship landing next to an oxcart. Carly squinted curiously, trying to see through the tinted windows. It seemed out of character for Henry, with his dislike of nouveau-riche flashiness, to have employed a hotshot Jag-driving attorney.

The car door opened, and a familiar gray-suited figure stepped out. Carly instinctively crossed her arms against her chest. "You told me that a lawyer would be meeting me," she said.

Max Giordano slipped off his mirrored sunglasses. "I reconsidered."

Apparently, he'd meant it when he said that he would be watching her, Carly thought. If she had been less tired, or less upset about Henry, she might have been amused by all of the melodrama, but as it was, she simply found him offensive. "Why, are you afraid that I might try to steal the family silver without you here to keep an eagle eye on me?"

"No. The lawyers and the insurance company have detailed records of everything valuable in the house. If anything disappeared, it would be easy to trace."

"Oh, for . . ." Carly began hotly. "You can't actually think that I would try to—"

"Steal the silver? I doubt it. You have the house, after all. And enough money to buy much more modern furnishings."

That does it, Carly thought. She pointed at him. "You're on the verge of becoming the new owner of thirty-five pets, Mr. Giordano. And since I don't think you would enjoy getting dog hair all over that nice suit, you'd better give me the key before I really get mad."

Silently, he handed her a single brass key on a cheap metal ring, an incongruous match to the ornate front door. Carly's hands were shaking as she fumbled at the lock. She had always prided herself on her ability to deal calmly with rude and unreasonable people, but this man was testing her limits.

The door clicked, and swung open into an arched entrance hall. A crystal chandelier hung from the vaulted ceiling, over the wide mahogany staircase that rose grandly to the second floor. Carly paused on the threshold.

"Just like that?" Max said, from behind her. "That's it?"

"What's it?"

He looked incredulously at the door. "No security system? Just a single dead-bolt lock?"

"That's Henry for you," Carly said. "He doesn't believe in newfangled technology."

"An old man, living alone in a forty-room mansion, and he doesn't even have an alarm?" Max looked upset. "That's crazy. No neighborhood is that safe. What if someone had tried to break in here?"

"I never said that he doesn't have an alarm."

Distant barking had begun with the creak of the opening door, and it was quickly getting louder, echoing through the dark house. Moments later, Henry's "alarm" erupted into the hall in a wriggling, welcoming mass.

Dogs of every shape and color surrounded them, jumbled together like a crazy wolf pack. Two retrievers butted happily against Carly's legs, a beagle paused by the foot of the stairs and howled, and a border collie, a corgi, and a Yorkshire terrier ran in circles, barking furiously.

"My God," Max exclaimed, as the rest of the pack pushed through the doorway toward him. "This has to be more than—"

His sentence ended in a sudden, strangled sound. Carly turned and saw that Lola, the Great Dane, had pinned him against the outer wall of the house, her huge paws on his shoulders. On her hind legs, she was almost as tall as he was, and she gazed soulfully into his eyes, wagging her tail.

"Meet your grandfather's security system, Mr. Giordano," Carly said, grinning. "They seem to like you. I can't imagine why."

Lola licked Max's nose, and he choked, turning his head from side to side, trying to avoid the large pink tongue. "Get this dog off me!"

Carly was suddenly enjoying herself very much. "So," she said. "Tell me. Would you try to rob this house?"

Max ignored her. "That does it," he growled, raising his hands against Lola's furry chest. "Down, dog. Down! I mean it."

Lola dropped down onto all fours and leaned comfortably against Max's legs as he wiped off his face, scowling. "Some watchdogs," he said. "What do they do, lick burglars to death?"

"You never know," Carly said. "Lola doesn't usually take to people like this. Henry rescued her from an abusive home, and she's actually very shy."

" 'Shy' would not have been my first choice of adjectives," Max said, brushing short brown hairs off of his jacket. He slanted a sideways look at Lola.

"Maybe she likes the way you smell. Do you have a dog?"

"*Me?* No."

Carly hadn't thought so, but it would have been one explanation for Lola's unusual behavior. Some abused dogs became aggressive, but the Great Dane tended toward the other extreme. She was skittish, frightened of almost everyone, and had a way of seeming to shrink into herself that was oddly touching in an animal her size. Her reaction to Max was a good sign, Carly thought. She was starting to relax around strangers. Henry would be delighted.

Max Giordano's behavior was another surprise. When people really disliked animals, they tended to make awkward, abrupt motions around them, and to use more force than was necessary. But in spite of Max's obvious distaste for the dog, his hands had been gentle as he pushed her away.

Interesting, Carly thought, mentally filing away the observation. She walked into the entry hall. "I'm going to go feed this pack," she said over her shoulder. "Are you coming in to supervise? Or are you just planning to search me before I leave?"

Max didn't answer. She turned to glance at him and saw that he wasn't even looking at her. He was staring into the house, and the remote expression on his face made her wonder if he had heard her.

"Hello?" she said. "Are you coming inside?"

He blinked and focused on her. "In a minute," he said. "You go ahead."

Carly shrugged. "Suit yourself."

The pack of dogs followed her down the hallway, milling happily around her legs as they sensed the possibility of kibble. The kitchen was at the back of the house, connected to a series of large pantries that had once been the domain of numerous proper butlers and well-starched maids. Ceiling-high glass cabinets still displayed the Tremayne china, complete with hand-painted gold monogram. It was a service for fifty, but it had been a long time, Carly thought, since the old house had seen such a crowd. Of people, that was. Now all the staff rooms—in addition to the formal dining hall and the solarium—were occu-

pied mostly by four-footed creatures. Cats were everywhere: reclining on the kitchen shelves, curled up on the
brocade seats of the ornately carved dining chairs, draped
over the padded wicker solarium furniture. A caged parrot
greeted Carly with a screech, and a white cocker spaniel,
too old to bother with greeting visitors at the door, snored
under Henry's favorite chair.

Despite the crowd of pets, the house seemed oddly
dark and empty, and Carly wondered what had happened
to Pauline, Henry's live-in housekeeper and general aide-
de-camp. The short, efficient woman had been running
Henry's life for years, and it wasn't at all like her to disappear in the face of a crisis. Had Max sent her away? Not
if he knew what was good for him, Carly thought ominously, making a mental note to find out. If Max Giordano
was under the impression that he could just march in and
start taking over, he was wrong. Dead wrong, and she intended to tell him so. It was the least she could do for
Henry.

CHAPTER 3

———◆·◆———

Taking over was foremost in Max's mind as he stared down the hallway after Charlotte and the dogs. Taking over was his natural response when faced with a situation that begged for someone to step in and make order out of chaos, and in his opinion, thirty-five pets in a crumbling mansion that had just been willed out of the Tremayne family forever was chaos at its worst.

It seemed to Max that the first thing he could do for his grandfather was to save the old man from the consequences of his folly. Ms. Martin had played him beautifully with her idea about turning the house into an animal shelter; but if Henry had been lonely enough to fall prey to a clever young woman, then the current disaster was as much Max's own fault as anyone's.

When was the last time you called him? Just to say hello? Her words had been haunting him all afternoon. He had been waiting for just the right time, and he had waited too long. But Henry was still alive, and there was still hope.

Let him live, Max thought. *Let me know him. Let me say the things I meant to say. Give me another chance, and I'll do it right this time.*

He had intended to follow Charlotte into the house, but he found himself hesitating. The castlelike doorway would have been forbidding even without the two reclining stone gargoyles that flanked the path. They seemed to be eyeing him suspiciously, and he had the same cold, anxious feeling in his stomach that he'd had a year ago, when he made his first trip to see the house where his father, grandfather, and great-grandfather had all lived.

From the public sidewalk, Max had stared up at the mansion on the hill. It was larger and more imposing than he had ever imagined, and every one of its Gothic arches seemed to rise skyward with the grand and solid security of old money.

That was just after his thirty-eighth birthday. His company had gone public the year before, and his stock holdings had made him a millionaire many times over. By any account, he was a success story, and he knew that he had every right to march up to the front door of the mansion and announce himself. But he didn't. He got back into his car and sat there, silently watching as the sun went down. He had achieved more than he had ever believed possible, but this was another league entirely, and as he stood in the shadow of his own father's home, Max Giordano felt like an impostor. He had a new car and a custom-made suit, but he was still nothing more than the unwanted bastard kid from Brooklyn.

That was when he swore to himself that the mansion would belong to him one day. No matter that it was dark, depressing, and completely opposite to his own modern, clean-lined taste. To him, it was beautiful. It bore his right-ful name and his rightful history. It was the legacy of the family he had been imagining since he was a child, and someday he would step forward and claim it.

Max jammed his hands into the pockets of his pants, turned his back on the open front door, and walked toward his car. When he entered the Tremayne mansion, he thought, it would be at Henry's invitation. He would step through that door as a member of the Tremayne family, acknowledged by his grandfather's own voice. Until then, he would wait.

It was not long before Charlotte Martin returned, somewhat the worse for wear. Her shirtsleeves were rolled up, and a lock of hair had been pulled partly out of her braid. It flopped sideways on her head, like a strange alien antenna.

Max had been leaning against the side of his car, con-templating the house. Now he straightened up and frowned at her.

She sighed. "What now?"

"Your hair."

She reached up to check. "Oh," she said. "Elvis."

"Elvis is dead."

"Not the singer. The cat. Big black tom—he hides in high places and jumps onto people's shoulders when they aren't looking. He got me from off the top of the refriger-ator while I was feeding the dogs. I'm surprised that you didn't hear me yell."

She pulled off the elastic band that held her braid to-gether and shook her head, letting loose a mass of wavy auburn hair. Max eyed her as it tumbled around her shoulders. She was pretty, he thought, in an artless kind of way. Her lips were full and expressive, and her eyes were an indeterminate blue, a stormy-sea shade. They widened, slightly, quizzically, and he realized that he was staring.

She looked coolly back at him. "Ready to search me?"

"I don't think that'll be necessary," he muttered, unsettled by the idea. He imagined running his hands over her body, feeling her curves through the faded, snug-fitting jeans and blue cotton shirt. It was an unexpectedly erotic thought. She had a kind of healthy softness, like a fifties pinup, that made her seem very touchable.

He caught himself. Was she being deliberately provocative? It would benefit him to remember that this was a female who knew exactly what she was doing. He preferred elegant, immaculately dressed women, and if Charlotte Martin had managed to engage his imagination while wearing dog-hair-covered Levi's, then he was clearly dealing with an expert.

"Well," she said sweetly, "how nice to hear that we've built such a sense of trust together, Max. Now that we've gotten that out of the way, I have a few questions for you. First of all, where's the kitten?"

"What kitten?"

"The baby! He's only three weeks old, and he needs to be fed every four hours." She looked suspiciously at him, as if he were some kind of monster who ate very tiny cats. "He's gone, and so is the basket he sleeps in."

Ah, that kitten. Max nodded. He knew that kitten. It had caused a stir in the hospital at 7 A.M. when it arrived, in a basket, under the arm of a very short and very determined woman named Pauline. "The kitten is with the housekeeper," he said.

"Good," Charlotte said. "Which brings me to my next question. Where is the housekeeper? If you sent Pauline away, let me just warn you—"

"Pauline is asleep in my hotel suite. And so is the kitten, I assume."

Her mouth dropped open. "What?"

"She was the one who found Henry at the bottom of the stairs yesterday evening. She called the paramedics and gave him CPR."

"Pauline knows CPR?"

"Apparently so," Max said. It didn't surprise him, judging from what he had seen of the woman that morning. Only five feet tall but built like a tank, Henry's housekeeper had marched into the Intensive Care Unit and all but mowed down the nurse who stood between her and the ward itself.

"Don't you talk to me about immediate family, missy," she huffed at the startled woman. "I've lived with that man for twenty years, and that makes me as immediate as they get. I want to see my poor Henry right now."

But the nurse was resolute, and just then, Pauline caught sight of Max. She stopped short, staring at him as if he were a ghost.

"You," she said. "They called you, then. I never thought you'd come."

"I came," Max said.

"You have the Tremayne eyes," she declared, reaching out to clasp his hands. He stood stiffly as she looked him over, his mind teeming with the questions he had been saving for so long. But it was not the right time for questions. The housekeeper was exhausted, running on nervous energy, unable to let herself stop and recover from the events of the night. Max had guessed that sending her back to the mansion would only send her into a greater frenzy of anxiety, so he had put her in a cab, handed her his room key, and all but ordered her off to sleep at the Ritz-Carlton.

Charlotte Martin gave him an odd, curious look. "Well," she said, finally, "that was a kind thing to do, sending her to your hotel. A day of rest will be good for her, although if I know Pauline, by now she'll have reorganized the Ritz's housekeeping department and presented her new, improved plan to the manager in charge."

"I believe that," Max said.

"She'll probably be back here before dark. I guess I'll leave her a note before I go."

"You aren't staying?"

"There's no reason to stay. The pets are all settled, and they'll be fine until tomorrow morning. I'll be back then, of course." She hesitated. "If you think I should stay, I'd be glad to, but . . ."

"That's your decision, Charlotte. Not mine."

She winced. "Please don't call me that. Nobody calls me that, not even my parents, and they named me in the first place. I'm Carly."

Max shrugged. "The key is yours," he said. "I'm sure that you'll want to move in at some point."

She looked troubled. "Right now, I really don't think . . . I mean, Pauline and I can make sure that everything runs smoothly until Henry comes home, but I can't even consider the idea that he might . . . not recover."

"I hope you're not going to try to tell me that you don't want the house."

Carly dropped her gaze, reddening. "No, I . . . I'd be a

liar if I told you that. Henry's gift would help me in . . . a lot of ways. But I can't think about that. I don't want to. I want Henry to get well, and that's the only thing I can focus on right now."

Her face was clouded with distress, and Max wondered if any of it was genuine. "It's not easy, is it," he said softly.

She looked up, startled, and he saw a flash of hope in her eyes. She had interpreted his tone as sympathetic.

He continued. "I don't like games. I think it would be simpler if we were honest with each other."

He enjoyed the warm rush of anticipation that coursed through him. The sooner they had the conflict out in the open, the sooner she would see that she was totally out-gunned. If they were enemies, he thought, then let it be known to them both. He had already felt the insidious allure of this woman, and it was time to clarify the terms of this encounter.

"I think it's time we talked business," he said.

Carly glared at him. "Oh?"

"My great-grandfather built this house in 1890. Henry was born here, and so was my father. This house has always belonged to the Tremayne family. I want it back, and I'm prepared to make you an offer right now."

"Don't you think you're being a little premature?" Carly asked icily. "I can't sell you a house that doesn't belong to me."

"I want you to sign an agreement stating that when— *if*—you become the legal owner of the mansion, you will sell it to me."

"You're forgetting that your grandfather has a plan for his house."

"To turn it into an animal shelter?" Max narrowed his

eyes. She was playing with him. That wasn't Henry's plan, it was hers. It had to be. "For God's sake . . ."

"The Tremayne Center for Animal Rehabilitation," she said. "Nonprofit, supported by Henry's foundation. It would be a structured version of what he's been doing all along. It's his dream. How could that happen if I sold his house to you?"

"Look," Max said, "an animal shelter in the middle of Pacific Heights is not a feasible idea. Maybe my grandfather didn't know about zoning laws, or the city health code, but let me assure you that I—"

"I wonder about that," Carly interrupted. "You might want to have a talk with Henry's lawyers before you decide that you know more than he does. He has a slew of special permits from the city, and I wouldn't be surprised if he's already arranged the whole thing."

Max could not read a thing on her face. It almost sounded as if she actually wanted to go ahead with Henry's crackpot notion. He had assumed that it had been just a ploy to gain his grandfather's sympathy, but what if Carly Martin was serious? No, he thought. It wasn't possible. She was just trying to strengthen her own bargaining position.

"It seems to me," Carly continued, "that if Henry had wanted you to have his house, he would have arranged it that way."

"It seems to *me*," Max replied, gritting his teeth, "that his judgment was clouded. Mine is not. Here's my offer, Carly. I will give you two hundred thousand dollars, just for signing an agreement giving me an option on the house. If my grandfather recovers, and changes his trust, the money is still yours to keep. And if he dies, I will buy the house from you. For five million dollars. Cash."

"You said that the house is worth twenty million."

Max smiled. Now they were back on track, he thought. "Yes," he said. "It is worth twenty. But five is a lot more than nothing, which is what you'll end up with if this goes to court."

"Court!"

"My lawyers will prove that Henry Tremayne was under your undue influence when he set the terms of this trust. It could take years of litigation, and it will cost you hundreds of thousands of dollars. The press will love it, believe me. You'll be front-page news. Your whole life will become public entertainment."

"Why would you do that to me?"

"I'd rather not," Max said honestly. "I would much rather make it easy for both of us. Think about it. You would have no pets, no crumbling old mansion to worry about. I'll take it all off your hands and give you a fair cash settlement. You'll be rich, with no strings attached."

"I see," she said, and blinked hard. Her lips were pressed tightly together, and Max was startled to see tears glimmering in her eyes. Her reaction made no sense to him. He had expected her to jump at his offer of quick-and-easy money. Was she crying over the fifteen million she had just lost?

"Carly," he said. "Be smart. You know that you can't afford to fight me in court."

"I could find a lawyer to take the case."

"No doubt. And you might even win. It isn't very likely though. Would you risk everything just to keep this old house?"

"Maybe," she said.

"Then you're a fool," Max exclaimed. He wanted to shake her. Why would she want the Tremayne house? She had no reason to care about it, and the idea of a nonprofit animal foundation was too absurd to be believed. "Listen to me. I am not bluffing. I have a team of world-class lawyers, and I will use them to ruin you if you force my hand. Do you understand?"

"Yes," she said a low voice. "I understand perfectly."

"Good. Then we have a deal."

She stood, staring at the ground, silent for so long that he began to feel restless.

"Carly? We have a deal?"

Slowly, she looked up at him, her face pale but for two red spots burning high on her cheekbones. "No," she said. "We don't. Not now, not ever. Come at me with your world-class lawyers if you want to, Max Giordano, but in the meantime, you can take your suspicious mind and your fair cash settlement and go straight to hell!"

CHAPTER 4

————•◆•————

Carly was still seething at eight the next morning as she drove into the hospital parking garage. She had just come from Henry's house, where she fed the animals and played a quick game of ball with the dogs on the back lawn. Henry had a crew of local teenagers on his payroll, who came over daily to exercise the dogs and do chores, and between the kids and Pauline, who was back and running at full throttle, everything at the mansion seemed to be under control.

But Max Giordano haunted her mind like a particularly nasty poltergeist. The previous day's encounter replayed itself endlessly in her thoughts, filling her with frustrated anger. It was no help that now, long after the fact, she was finally coming up with clever and withering responses to his ugly accusations.

Oh, so you think I'm after Henry's money, she imagined herself saying haughtily, calmly, her gaze impaling him like a knife blade. *That must make me seem like quite a threat to your own plans, Mr. Giordano.*

But no, she had gotten upset and flustered and ended up telling him to go to hell. How trite was that? She wished that she had the verbal acuity to fend off his barbs. It was her own fault, she thought. He could bait her all he wanted, but she didn't have to respond. And she wouldn't, if she ever saw him again. She wouldn't get angry, she wouldn't try to explain herself. She would just be coldly polite, then turn her back on him and let him feel her dignified contempt.

The elevator doors slid open, and Carly stepped into a hallway of shiny linoleum, with walls so white that they glowed in the fluorescent light. The ICU reception area was cheered slightly by two baskets of orange day lilies on either side of the long curved counter.

"I'm here to see Henry Tremayne," she said to the young woman behind the desk. "He was admitted on Wednesday night."

The nurse nodded. "Are you a family member?"

"No," Carly said. "I'm just a friend. May I see him?"

"I'm sorry," the woman said. "But we only allow immediate family into the ward. Mr. Tremayne still hasn't regained consciousness."

"How is he doing?"

"He's a fighter," the nurse said kindly. "He's hanging on. Have you talked to his grandson?"

"Today? No."

"Mr. Giordano had a meeting with Dr. Sheaffer this morning."

"Max is here? Right now?" Carly felt a flash of alarm. She had intentionally come early, hoping to avoid him.

"Yes. And the meeting must be finished, because he's just over—"

"Actually," Carly said quickly, "I should go. I'm on my way to work, and I don't want to disturb him."

"Oh, but he's just behind—"

Carly hurried on. "I brought something for Henry, and maybe you could put it by his bed for me . . ." Her voice trailed off as she suddenly realized that the woman's eyes had focused on a point just past her shoulder. Her heart sank. Too late.

". . . behind you," the nurse finished.

"Good morning, Dr. Martin," said a cool, familiar voice. "You're up early."

Carly turned slowly, warily, to face Max Giordano. Judging from his immaculate suit and still-damp hair, he had made it back to his hotel to shower and change, but the dark weariness around his eyes suggested that he had slept little, if at all.

"What's that?" he asked, nodding toward the object that she held clenched in her hand.

Silently, Carly handed it to him. It was a tiny porcelain figurine of a robed man. A bluebird perched on his shoulder, and two bear cubs tumbled in the grass at his feet.

Max turned the figurine over, examining it. "This is for my grandfather?"

Carly thought of her resolution to turn her back on Max, but she had also resolved to be coldly polite, and it didn't seem polite to turn her back on someone who had just asked her a question.

"It already belongs to him," she said. "I gave it to him for his birthday last year. It's Saint Francis of Assisi—he's the patron saint of animals. He watches over them, and protects them, like your grandfather does. Henry says that it's his good-luck charm, and I . . . thought that it might reassure him. If he wakes up, that is . . ."

She bit her lip, embarrassed as she realized that she was explaining herself again. It was a sentimental bit of foolishness, and it didn't take any great insight to see that Max Giordano was not a sentimental man. No doubt he would scorch her with a caustic comment any moment now. She tensed, waiting.

But the comment never came. Max frowned down at St. Francis, running his thumb thoughtfully over the figurine's tiny head. He looked up, unexpectedly meeting her eyes. Carly stood uncomfortably as he studied her.

Finally, he nodded. "Thank you. I'll put it by his bed."

He turned away. Carly watched as he opened the frosted glass doors and walked through them into the short corridor that led to the ward. The doors closed behind him, and Carly exhaled shakily. She had been holding her breath.

"Are you a doctor?"

The nurse behind the desk was speaking to her. Carly turned. "Sorry, what?"

"Didn't he call you 'Doctor?' If you're a doctor, the rules are a little different. Maybe we could arrange for you to visit—"

Carly shook her head. "I'm not a people doctor. I'm a vet."

"Oh!" The young woman laughed. "Okay. Can I ask you a question? I have the sweetest little terrier, only eight months old. She already knows how to sit and shake, and she heels like a dream."

"That's great," Carly said automatically. The doors were still closed, but they seemed to be looming toward her, like a frightening white portal that could regurgitate Max at any moment. *If I leave right now,* she thought, *I can get away before he comes back.*

"The thing is," the nurse continued, "she's been scratching like crazy lately. What do you think is wrong with her?"

"Fleas," Carly said. Did she hear footsteps, or was she imagining things? The doors opened, and Carly jumped, but it was a bearded man in scrubs and a lab coat, not Max. The man glanced briefly at her and walked over to wait for the elevator.

"Fleas," the nurse exclaimed. "Oh, no. I hope not—I don't want to have to shampoo all the carpets. You know, I did look, but I didn't see any on her."

"It could be allergies. Have you changed her diet recently?"

"No . . . but I did take her to a new groomer last week, and now that I think about it, that place just didn't seem clean to me."

The elevator chime sounded, and the doors slid open. Carly imagined that Max had left Henry's bedside and was now walking through the ward on his way back to the desk. Any second, she thought, he would be there.

"She might be having a bad reaction to one of the products they used. Here." Carly scrabbled in her bag for a clinic card and pressed it into the woman's hand. "I have to go. But I'd be glad to take a look at her. Give me a call, or just bring her in."

The elevator doors were closing as she rushed forward, barely catching the narrowing opening in time. She jumped on, breathless, getting a strange look from the bearded man, who probably thought that she had just escaped from the mental ward.

She tried to relax as the elevator carried her down to the lobby. What was it about Max Giordano that unnerved her so completely? He was a rotten person, sure, but she had never turned and fled like that in her entire life, not even when she was thirteen and Mary-Louise Rattner had threatened to beat her up in the girls' locker room.

It didn't make sense. She wasn't afraid of him, exactly. But her knees had gone weak when she had felt herself being measured by his silent gaze. Something about Max made her want to prove herself to him. She winced at the memory of the hope that had passed through her as she stared back at him, a sudden, furtive desire for . . .

For what? Approval? Warmth? From that guy? *Ha,* she thought. *Not likely.* She didn't even want to think about what it meant to be hoping for approval from a man who clearly hated her. And whom she hated right back. The psychological implications were not pretty.

By the time that she reached her car, she had decided not to think about it. She had already devoted far too much mental energy to Max Giordano. Better to forget all about him and get on with her life. She buckled herself in, turned the key in the ignition, and was rewarded with a sad chugging sound, then dead silence.

The meeting with the neurosurgeon had provided Max with plenty of information, but not the kind that he wanted.

"I can't tell you what will happen," the doctor had said. "And I don't want to give you false hope, Mr. Giordano. The trauma fractured the base of your grandfather's skull and caused what's called a subdural hematoma, which basically means bleeding under the protective membrane that covers the brain."

"How bad is it?" Max asked, steeling himself.

"We were able to clean things up pretty well. There was still some active bleeding, but we found the ruptured vessel and evacuated the lesion. He's being monitored for any increased intracranial pressure. Things look fairly stable, but to be honest, at his age, he's not going to heal like a younger man might."

"When is he going to wake up?"

The doctor raised his hands slightly. "I can't answer that. The CT scan shows some bruising to his brain stem, which is the part of the brain that controls the vital body functions like breathing, blood pressure, and consciousness."

Max felt sick. "You're telling me that he has brain damage."

"Yes, but that term has a very wide range of implications. Brain damage, per se, occurs in every traumatic head injury. The real concern is the extent and the location of the damage. If your grandfather were twenty years younger, I'd feel more optimistic. Frankly, I think it's a miracle that the fall didn't kill him."

"He's a strong old man," Max said. *So they tell me.*

The doctor nodded. "Let's hope so."

More than anything, it was Max's own lack of control that maddened him, made him want to pace the halls of the hospital, burning off energy by doing something, anything. He wasn't accustomed to being useless in a time of crisis, and while he could tolerate entrusting Henry to the best neurosurgeon on the West Coast, it was an entirely different matter to be forced to wait helplessly while his grandfather's life trembled in the hands of Fate.

After the meeting with the doctor, Max had had a sudden overwhelming need to get away from the hospital, to escape the disinfectant smells, the harsh lights, and the anxiety that simmered inside him.

He was on his way out when he saw Carly Martin at the nurses' station. Her back was to him, but it was impossible to mistake that auburn hair, or the curves of her body as she leaned forward to speak to the nurse.

Checking up on Henry's condition, no doubt.

Or so he thought, until he confronted her. Instead of the syrupy concern he had expected to see, her face was written with lines of uncertainty and worry. She could barely look at him, and when she did, she faced him with the awkward defensiveness of a child.

And then there was the business of the little statue. Max set the figurine on the table by Henry's bed, placing it carefully so that his grandfather would see it if he opened his eyes. He stared down at St. Francis's porcelain head, wondering for the first time if there was more to this situation than he had assumed. Was it really just a simple case of an opportunistic young woman and a lonely old man, or could Carly be genuinely emotionally attached to Henry? Could she even be—Max's chest tightened in an unexpectedly strong reaction to the thought—in love with him?

It happened, he told himself. Some women were attracted to much older men. Maybe it was a father-figure thing, some need to feel pampered or protected. Could that be the truth of the matter? He sincerely hoped not. It would make the situation a little more palatable, but would also create more problems than it solved. He knew how to deal with a con artist, but if he actually had a troubled young woman on his hands . . . Max shook his head. That would be very bad. He did not know how to fight a subtle and gentle fight. An emotional angle would complicate everything.

When he returned to the nurses' station, there was no sign of Carly.

"Where is she?" he asked.

"The vet? You just missed her. She took the elevator down."

Max strode toward the elevator and pushed the down arrow. She had disappeared quickly, but not so fast that he couldn't catch her before she left. And if she did manage to slip away, he knew exactly where to find her.

What he hadn't expected, as he walked out of the elevator into the busy lobby, was to see Carly making her way back into the building.

She hurried through the crowd, looking stressed, and when she spotted him she stopped in her tracks and put a hand to her forehead.

"Great," she said, as he approached. "Just great. This is really not my day."

"That was a quick escape," he said.

"Thank you. Now, will you please go away? I need to find a phone book. Unless you happen to have jumper cables in your Jaguar. My battery is dead."

"You left your headlights on?"

"No," Carly said flatly. "I left the interior light on. One of the doors wasn't closed all the way."

"That shouldn't be enough to drain a battery."

"It was enough to drain mine. I need a new one, and I haven't gotten around to buying it. This is what I get for procrastinating. Now I have to call a tow truck, and I'm already late for work."

"I'll drive you. You can deal with the car later."

"What?" She looked stunned, then wary. "Why?"

"Because you're late," Max said. "And because I'm headed that way."

That wasn't actually true, but he wanted to talk to her. This new idea about her possible relationship with his grandfather was very disturbing, and he wanted more information.

"Come on," he said, as she stood there, unconvinced. "It'll take half an hour to get a tow truck here, and it's already eight-fifty."

"I know! My first appointment is in ten minutes." She took a deep breath. "Okay, fine. You can drive me to work. But this is very strange, coming from you, and don't think I haven't noticed that."

She sat silently in the passenger seat as Max pulled out of the parking lot. He glanced over at her and saw that she was staring out the window, her face expressionless.

"You all right?" he asked.

"Fine," she said.

Max didn't believe it. The hospital visit had clearly upset her, and the more he thought about it, the more he wondered if he had misjudged the whole situation. The pain in her eyes yesterday when he had broken the news about Henry, the passion in her voice when she had called his grandfather "one of the kindest and most caring people" she had ever met . . . Was she acting a part, as he had assumed then, or did she genuinely love Henry Tremayne?

And if she did, what did that mean? Who, exactly, was Carly Martin? He knew a little bit about her life, but nothing whatsoever about her mind. He looked speculatively at her, letting his eyes travel over her profile, noting the tiny lines at the corners of her eyes as she squinted in the sunlight. He guessed that she was not quite thirty; young, but old enough to understand that a person's age often matters less than what is in their soul.

What if there had been some kind of May-December romance? If Carly had been Henry's mistress, she might very well feel entitled to the house. God forbid, she might even want to keep it, for sentimental reasons.

He was going to have to uncover the truth.

CHAPTER 5

——◆·◆——

The Union Street Veterinary Clinic was in the heart of San Francisco's trendy Marina district, and had the sky-high property taxes to prove it. Carly had once suggested to Richard that they sell their small building and relocate to another area, where they could have more space for less money. It seemed like a good idea to her, since they had a loyal clientele who would follow them, but Richard had vetoed the idea. He liked the prestige of being in an exclusive section of town, and the latitude it gave him to inflate prices to suit the local market.

Max pulled the car smoothly up to the curb, stopping in the red zone in front of the clinic, and turned off the ignition.

Carly glanced at him. They had exchanged only a few words during the drive, mostly because she had answered him in monosyllables, not trusting the sudden truce. She didn't know what he was up to, and it made her nervous.

"Thanks for the ride," she said, reaching for the door handle.

"You're welcome. If you don't mind, I'd like to come in and use your phone. My cell phone battery is dead."

Carly frowned, suspecting that he was up to something. But she couldn't come up with a good reason to refuse such an innocuous request. If she was lucky, Max would move in and out of the clinic without any drama. "Okay," she said. "Come on in."

To Carly's relief, the waiting room was empty, which meant that her nine o'clock client was running even later than she was. The front desk was also empty, and the jingle of the bell over the front door brought Nick, one of their veterinary technicians, from the back. When he saw that it was Carly, he waved briefly.

"I thought you were the Taylor cat," he said. "Dr. Wex is waiting for her."

"Where's Michelle?" Carly asked. "Max, the phone is right there. Push the line one button before you dial."

"She's sick," Nick said. "I'm the front and back office today. Something's going around."

"I guess so. Rich was out yesterday. Well, don't you dare catch it, Nick, whatever it is. I need you."

He grinned. "People who take herbs never get sick. Let me know if you want some."

Carly shuddered. The last time she had been on the verge of a cold, Nick had talked her into swallowing a dropperful of some foul, cloudy brown substance that had been so bitter that her tongue had gone numb in self-defense. Since then she had stuck resolutely to conventional medicine.

With a curious glance at Max, Nick excused himself. Carly hung up her coat and went around to the wall of client records to pull the chart for her first appointment. She was paging through it when Richard appeared. He was scowling, and Carly was surprised to see that his right hand was bandaged.

"You're late," he said.

Out of the corner of her eye, Carly saw Max pause in his dialing. "I'm sorry," she said quickly. "I left you a message on the voice mail. You didn't get it?"

Richard shook his head. "No, I didn't get it. Michelle called in sick, then you didn't show up. What was I supposed to think?"

"If you had checked the messages, you would have known."

"I've got a tumor removal and two hip replacements today, and you think I have time for secretarial work? I don't even get a lunch break." Richard seemed to notice Max for the first time. "Who's that?"

"That is Max Giordano," Carly said. Max replaced the receiver and stepped out from behind the desk to gaze down at Richard, who was several inches shorter. "Max, meet Richard Wexler, my partner."

Richard squinted at Max, his eyes darting over Max's tailored suit, his silk tie, his watch. "Don't I know you?"

"I doubt it," Max said. He hadn't missed Rich's not-so-subtle assessment of his net worth.

"Huh," Richard said, unconvinced. "You look familiar. Are you sure we haven't met somewhere?"

Carly cut in. "Rich, what happened to your hand?"

He was still frowning at Max. "I got bitten. That yellow Lab. The Palmer dog. It's nothing."

"When did that happen? You weren't in the office yesterday."

"It was the day before yesterday. You were off making house calls, so you missed it. Does it matter?"

It wasn't a real question, so Carly didn't bother to answer. Richard was very proud, and she supposed that he felt foolish about the wound, as if it proclaimed incompetence. He wasn't a bad animal handler, but he tended to be impatient. The high-strung retriever was notorious for snapping at everyone, but Richard was the type to take it personally.

Carly sighed. It was good that she had introduced Richard and Max, she thought dryly. Maybe they could go out for a beer and compare notes on how to make her miserable. No doubt Rich would be delighted to hear about Max's plans to ruin her life in court. Unless, of course, that meant more work at the office for him.

Max was regarding Richard with a kind of cool curiosity akin to that of a cat watching a large bug crawl up a wall, and Carly was glad that he didn't know that Rich had once been more than her business partner. He wouldn't care, but she would. It was a matter of feminine pride.

The bell jingled as the front door swung open to admit a woman struggling with an oversize cat carrier and a folded baby stroller. A whimpering toddler clung to her skirt. It was a welcome interruption, and Carly hurried forward to help.

"Thanks, Dr. Martin," the woman said, as Carly took the heavy carrier. Two resentful cat faces glared at her from inside. "Sorry we're late. The sitter didn't show up."

The toddler staggered forward, fell down with a bump, and began to cry. Carly hauled the carrier past Richard and Max, settled cats and client into Exam Room Two, then came out to grab the charts for the two Siamese. She needed a pen, she realized, and turned toward Michelle's desk.

Richard had gone back to his office, and Max was on the phone again. He had taken off his suit jacket and slung it over the empty chair, and Carly could see the powerful lines of his shoulders under his crisp white shirt. His black hair was short, cut to a perfect edge against the back of his neck, and she suspected that it was never allowed to get even slightly shaggy or uneven. He was perfectly, corporately, groomed every time she had seen him, and she wondered what his idea of relaxation was. A suit in a lighter shade of gray, maybe.

He was leaning against the edge of the desk, his body blocking the drawer where Michelle kept the pens. Carly touched his arm to get his attention, startled as her fingers met the hard curve of his biceps and felt the heat of his skin through the thin cloth.

There was a subtle scent of cologne lingering close to him, a smoky fragrance that mingled with the warm, male scent of his body. She felt a fluttery sensation in her chest when he turned to look at her, and found herself suddenly shy. She focused on his chin, where she could see the faint dark shadow of beard beneath the skin.

"Excuse me," she said, pointing to the drawer.

Max stepped back against Michelle's filing cabinet, but the phone cord was short. She could feel his eyes on her as she reached in to grab a pen. She slid the drawer closed and backed up awkwardly.

He replaced the receiver, a very slight, thoughtful frown touching his forehead. Carly wondered if she looked as flustered as she suddenly felt.

"Well," she said. "Thanks again for the ride. Are you going back to the hospital?"

"Later."

"You'll let me know . . . if anything happens."

It was as much of a question as a request, and when he didn't answer immediately, Carly felt her stomach tighten.

"Max," she said. "Please."

He was silent for a moment longer, then, abruptly, he nodded. "I'll let you know."

That afternoon, Carly had her hand on the doorknob of Exam Room One when she heard Richard say her name. She turned, and saw him beckoning to her from the open door of his office.

"What?" she asked, walking toward him. "I have a client waiting."

Richard's eyes were alight with excitement. "That guy this morning, didn't I say that I recognized him? I knew I'd seen him before. It's been bugging me all day, and I just got it. He was in *Fortune* magazine last month. I've still got the issue."

"Rich, I really need to—"

"He cofounded a sales automation software company that Syscom acquired in March. I've got the article right here."

"Max is a computer guy?" Carly asked, astonished. She would never have guessed that. He seemed smart, but not in an engineering sort of way.

"Yeah, right. When was the last time you saw a computer guy in a suit like that? No, he's all about sales and marketing. His partner was the techie, some guy from

MIT, but Giordano bought him out a few years ago. Do you know how much he's worth?"

That explained the shoes, Carly thought. And the car. But the revelation that Max was genuinely wealthy in his own right raised puzzling new questions.

She had assumed that it was either need or greed behind Max's anger at losing the chunk of his inheritance represented by the Tremayne mansion. But if Max was no trust-fund grandson, living at the edge of his income, waiting to inherit Henry's money, why threaten her with a protracted court battle for ownership of Henry's house? It was prime real estate, indeed, but it took only one look at Max's personal style to feel sure that a towering Gothic mansion was not his ideal home environment. He couldn't possibly want to live there. Even she didn't want to live there. Did he hope to raze it and use the land? Or was he some kind of control freak, with an ego that insisted that he be his grandfather's sole heir?

"What was he doing here?" Richard was asking her.

"Using the phone."

"Yeah, I saw that. But why was he here? He's not one of our clients."

"He drove me to work," Carly said, and had the pleasure of seeing Richard's eyes widen with shock as he made the obvious assumption. She didn't bother to correct him.

"I have to go," she said, noting with satisfaction that Rich had turned the sickly beige of unbaked bread dough. In the time since their personal relationship had ended, Richard had brought his girlfriends into the office. Women apparently loved the image of the macho Porsche-driving animal doctor with a heart of gold.

"You're dating him?" Richard was ogling at her as if she had grown a second head. "Max Giordano? You? How did *you* . . . ?"

Carly assumed a lofty expression. "Rich," she said, "I really don't feel comfortable discussing my private life with you. Now, if you'll excuse me . . ."

She turned and left him there, feeling his stare on her back all the way down the hall.

It wasn't a lie, exactly, Carly told herself later. The clinic was closed, and she was in the lab, cleaning up. She never actually *said* that she was dating Max, after all. Was it her fault that Richard had jumped to conclusions?

He had been in surgery most of the day, so she hadn't seen much of him, and even during his breaks he barely said a word to her. Several times, though, she had caught him watching her covertly, as if he were reassessing her value. Carly just ignored him and went about her business, finding the whole situation too absurd to be offended by Richard's inability to understand how she, of all people, could have bewitched a multimillionaire.

Even if it had been a lie by implication, even if she should, morally, have corrected Richard, what did it matter? It was a little fun at no real expense. For all she knew, she would never cross paths with Max again. He had no reason to come to the mansion, and running into him at the hospital this morning had been sheer coincidence. He had promised to contact her with any news about Henry, but it was hard to know if he really meant to do it. Assuming that Henry recovered, it was likely that she had seen the last of Max Giordano.

"Carly."

She looked up. Richard stood in the doorway. "Your friend is here," he said flatly.

Carly blinked. "What friend?"

"You have more than one rich guy driving you around?"

"Max?" Now it was Carly's turn to be stunned. "Max is here? Where?"

"In the waiting room. You'd think he would send a car service to get you, but no, he comes personally, in the brand-new black Jag."

His hands were jammed into the pockets of his lab coat, and Carly realized that it was envy glazing his eyes. Envy of Max: of the car, the *Fortune* article, and the golden glow of wealth.

Carly quickly tossed her dirty lab coat into the hamper and scrubbed her hands under the tap, surprised that Max had come back. What did he want? Was it about Henry? It had to be. There was no other reason for him to seek her out.

She instinctively smoothed her hair, checking it in the shiny metal surface of the paper towel dispenser. Richard watched her, and she knew that he had attributed her haste and confusion to romantic excitement.

"Hurry," he said sarcastically, as she stepped past him and out the door of the lab, blotting her still-damp hands on her jeans. "You don't want to keep *him* waiting."

CHAPTER 6

———— ◆ ————

M ax looked at his watch and saw that it was six-fifteen, two minutes later than it had been the last time he checked. The clinic waiting room was quiet, but he was restless, filled with the same sense of humming anticipation that preceded an important business meeting. He had spent most of the day at Syscom headquarters in Santa Clara, then returned to the city in time for a run along the Marina. The steady, pounding rhythms of his feet and heart had been exactly what he needed to clear his head, and by the time he reached the base of the Golden Gate Bridge, he knew what to do about the Carly Martin problem.

It was now painfully clear to Max that he had handled things in exactly the wrong way. He had expected a fight, and had immediately taken the offensive, believing that Carly would back down when she saw what she was up against. But she hadn't backed down. And the more time he spent with her, the less he understood her. He had always had a sixth sense about what made people tick, but he could not figure out what motivated this woman. That was the trouble, he thought. It was very difficult to plot a winning strategy unless you knew what your opponent wanted.

Making an overt enemy out of Carly Martin had been a tactical mistake, but not one that couldn't be fixed. He needed to win her over, to charm her until she relaxed her defenses. Only then would he be able to read her accurately enough to plan his next move.

Six-seventeen. Max drummed his fingers against his thigh. He had a seven-thirty dinner reservation for two at Mistral, the best French restaurant in the city, which had been no small coup for a last-minute call on Friday night. His assistant had spoken with the manager, after which a table had miraculously become available. It still gave Max a certain conqueror's pleasure to watch his own name open doors. Now the only hurdle—and it could be a tall one—would be in getting Carly to accompany him.

He heard her light footsteps hurrying down the hall, then she appeared in the waiting room, looking more worried than wary.

"What's wrong?" she asked. "What happened?"

"Nothing," he said.

Her expression turned to confusion. "Then it's not Henry?"

"The last time I checked, which was an hour ago, my grandfather's condition hadn't changed."

"Oh," she said. "So why are you here?"

Max affected surprise. "Because you need a ride," he said, as if it should be obvious. "Did you think I was going to leave you stranded?"

Carly stared at him. "I didn't think about it. I never

assumed that you would . . . I mean, I was just going to take the bus back to pick up my car."

"No need. I took care of it."

"You took care of what?"

"I had a mechanic replace your battery, then move the car to Henry's house. It's waiting for you there."

Carly held up one hand, as if stopping traffic. "Wait a minute. Let me get this straight. While I was at work, unaware that anything unusual was happening, you had my car fixed and moved?"

"Right."

"But . . . you don't have a key!"

Max shrugged. "Your VW is not what I'd call high-security."

"I don't believe this," she said. "This is crazy. You can't just take someone's car out of a public parking lot."

"For the right price, you can."

"That's illegal," Carly protested, then stopped herself. "Which isn't to say that I'm not grateful."

"You're welcome," Max said.

Just then Carly's partner, Richard, strolled into the room. "You kids still here?" he said coolly.

Kids? Wexler appeared to be in his late thirties, which made them roughly the same age, Max thought. Carly said nothing, and Max ignored the intentional belittlement. He had already written Wexler off as a self-important fool, and he didn't intend to waste his time on the man now.

"As a matter of fact, we were just leaving," Carly said, taking her coat from the rack. "Ready, Max?"

Max nodded and stepped forward to hold the door for her. Carly tossed a brief good-bye over her shoulder and sailed through the open door with a sudden queenly bearing that surprised him. He caught a whiff of her fragrance as she passed; the subtle, seductive scent of shampoo, body lotion, and warm skin, mixed together into a delicate feminine perfume. It was instinct, not choice, that made him turn his head to look after her.

And when he turned back, it was instinct that sent a chill to his gut when he saw Richard Wexler staring at him with a dark resentment that seemed to strip away everything else around them.

Richard composed himself as soon as he realized that Max had read his expression. Confronted, he ducked his head and made a show of shuffling through chart folders.

"Don't know where I put that damned file," he muttered. Max waited silently, watching the other man.

It didn't take long for Richard to realize that Max wasn't going to go away. He looked up. "You're still here?" he exclaimed too loudly. "Why? Is there a problem?"

"You tell me," Max said.

"I don't know what you're talking about," Richard said. "I thought you were leaving."

"I thought we might have something to discuss. Do we?"

"No."

"Fine," Max said. "Good night."

He shut the clinic door quietly behind him, and walked out into the cool evening air, putting Richard Wexler out of his mind. He had more important things to focus on. Once he had established some sort of truce with Carly, he intended to ask her a few casual questions about her relationship with Henry. He would give the impression that he was grudgingly willing to listen to her side of the story.

And then, he thought, he would slowly, slowly allow her to believe that she was winning him over. As she relaxed and became more confident, she would also become less cautious. If he handled things correctly, she would tell him everything he wanted to know and never realize that she was playing right into his hands.

As she waited for Max, Carly examined the petunias that she had planted around the Japanese maple tree in front of the clinic. They had been trampled again, their bright flower heads crushed and muddied, and their green leaves turning a sad crispy brown in spite of her diligent care. It was no wonder. The maple was a favorite marking spot for their canine clients, and no normal flower could withstand the daily chemical attack.

Carly frowned down at the plants, wondering if there was such a thing as a dog-resistant flower. It was a shame, she thought, that she couldn't plant a patch of those plastic ones that the old-time pranksters wore on their lapels, the kind that squirted you when you got too close.

She was giggling as Max approached.

"What's the joke?" he asked, opening the passenger door for her.

"Nothing important," she said. "What kept you? Don't tell me Richard is trying to solicit you as a client."

Max shook his head. "Just a brief discussion."

"About what?" Carly felt a flicker of alarm. Could Richard have said something about their old relationship?

"Small talk," Max said. He closed her door and came around to the driver's seat. Carly scrutinized him as he slid behind the wheel and started the engine, but she could read nothing from his face. Fretfully, she gnawed her lower lip. It would be just like Richard to drop some reference to their affair, trying to make himself look important by insinuating that Max was getting secondhand goods. And if he had done that, Max might realize that she had led Richard to believe that they were dating.

Damn. She had never been a good schemer; she suffered from an overly active guilty conscience.

"Are you hungry?" Max asked suddenly.

Hope warmed Carly. This was a good sign. Questions about her appetite were not what she would expect from a man who had just discovered that she was masquerading as his girlfriend.

"A little," she said cautiously. "Maybe. Why?"

"I want to take you to dinner. There's a French place, Mistral. Do you know it?"

Carly sat up straighter in the soft leather seat. First, Max Giordano had spontaneously fixed her car, and now he was asking her to dinner? What was going on? This was getting stranger by the minute.

"I know about Mistral. But I've never been there. It's way out of my . . . neighborhood." She cleared her throat. She had been about to say "price range." Not to mention that lowly veterinarians had to make reservations about five years in advance.

Max looked amused. "You don't eat out of your neighborhood?"

"With a car like mine," Carly said, "it's smarter to stay close to home."

"I see. Well, tonight you don't have to worry about that."

Maybe not, Carly thought, but the idea of having dinner with Max Giordano gave her plenty of other things to worry about. "Well," she said, "I appreciate the offer, but I really don't think it would be a good idea."

"No? Why not?"

She blinked, unaccustomed to such forthrightness. "Because I don't . . . I . . . uh . . ."

"Afraid that you might be on the menu?"

A reluctant smile cracked her face. "Actually, yes. You're being very friendly today. It's making me nervous."

"How about if I tell you that I've declared a cease-fire? I behaved badly yesterday, Carly, and I owe you an apology. I spent last night thinking about the situation with you, Henry, and the house, and I realized that I've been overlooking the issue at the center of all of this."

"And that would be . . ."

"That my grandfather wants to leave you his pets and his house because you're important to him. Because he trusts you. His wishes should matter more to me than my own . . . personal feelings. I think it's time that I conceded."

"What a sudden change of heart," Carly said slowly. Max had his sunglasses on, obscuring his face, and as she stared at his strong profile, she wasn't quite convinced. His sudden thaw seemed a little too abrupt.

"You don't believe me," he said, and the corners of his mouth curved up as if he were amused by some private joke.

"Not entirely. This new Max seems out of character. Did you ever see the movie *Sybil*?"

He laughed suddenly, the chuckle erupting out of him with a surprising openness. "If I promise that I don't have a split personality," he said, "will you come to dinner?"

Carly hesitated. Yesterday had made it obvious that she shouldn't get involved with this man. But today, common sense didn't carry its usual weight. She knew that she was going to agree to have dinner with him, and she knew that it was a bad idea, but strangely, she didn't care. In fact, she was enjoying the odd, breathless edginess that he sparked in her.

"They make a fantastic *boeuf bourguignon*," Max said.

"I'm sure they do," Carly said. "But I'm a vegetarian."

His eyebrows rose. "Really. How admirable. I like the concept, but I don't think I could live without an occasional rare steak. Don't you ever get the urge to sink your teeth into something bloody?"

Carly blanched. "No."

Max grinned. "It hits me right after I close a big deal."

"Sounds symbolic."

"I'm sure it is. The primal hunt and kill, disguised as modern business. When did you stop eating meat?"

"In vet school. I realized that it was sort of hypocritical to spend all day healing certain animals, then to go home and make dinner out of others." She shrugged. "It's a personal thing. But you don't have to worry, I don't moralize, and I won't make faces at your steak."

"Then you're accepting my invitation."

His voice was even, but Carly thought she heard a note of satisfaction. He was definitely up to something, and while she didn't know what it was, the shiver of curious excitement inside her promised that it could be a very interesting evening indeed.

CHAPTER 7

C̲arly wanted to go back to her apartment first, and Max knew by her brief hesitation that she didn't want him to come inside. But good manners won, and she awkwardly invited him in to relax while she changed her clothes. Curious about the reason for her reluctance, and aware that the apartment would offer some clues about her, Max accepted.

"It's kind of messy," she said, fumbling for her keys outside the front door. "I was in a rush this morning."

She lived in a converted basement apartment on the edge of the Haight-Ashbury district, which had been famous years ago as a hub of sixties counterculture. It still retained a certain seedy charm, if you liked ragged Victorian houses with dreadlocked teenagers lounging on the front steps.

A Frisbee flew out of nowhere and skidded across the hood of Max's car.

"Sorry, man." A lanky person of indeterminate sex, wearing a rainbow-colored T-shirt, came to retrieve it.

He—Max assumed that it was a he—paused to survey the Jaguar. "Dude, that's some car."

"Thanks," Max said.

"Yeah," the person said. "It's like, very capitalistic. Very 1980s."

"Damn right," Max said, and Carly giggled.

"I don't think that was meant as a compliment," she said. "You must not be from around these parts."

"Capitalism has been good to me," Max growled. "I was building a company while that kid was sucking his thumb and learning to be self-righteous."

Carly's smile grew, but she didn't answer.

Her apartment was tiny, with low ceilings that made Max feel too tall, and he was surprised by the frugality with which it was decorated. A colorful crocheted blanket covered the worn sofa, and the few battered pieces of furniture in the living room were solid and of good quality, but not old enough to be antique. A desk in the corner was piled high with books; paperback mysteries mixed in with veterinary journals.

"It's not big, but it's home," Carly said, and Max glanced at her, detecting an artificial brightness to her tone.

"It's cozy," he said, privately curious as to why a young professional like Carly would choose a neighborhood and apartment like this, when she certainly could have afforded better.

"It was a good deal," she said. "I'm hardly ever here, anyway." A quick frown flitted across her face, as if she knew that she sounded defensive. "Can I get you something to drink? I have water, and . . . water. Sorry. I was planning to go to the store, but I—"

"Water sounds fine," Max said. "Thank you."

She brought him a glass, then disappeared into the bedroom to change, promising to be quick. Max sat down briefly but felt too restless to stay on the couch. He stood up and began to explore the room. He picked up a tattered copy of *Dog Fancy* magazine and paged through it, glancing at the photos with mild distaste. He put it down and wandered toward the window, which was barred for security and surrounded by built-in shelves, their edges thick and blunted by too many layers of cheap white paint. A stubby little potted fern sat there, struggling toward the light. Next to the fern was a row of framed photos. There was Carly, in cap and gown, flanked by a beaming couple, who were clearly her parents. And there she was again, a gangly teenager in this picture, on a lawn with her parents and seven other children.

Max squinted curiously at the photo, noticing that the kids ranged from a tall red-haired young man to a dark-haired, almond-eyed pair of Asian toddlers. There was no family resemblance among the group as a whole, but the camera had captured a sense of loving familiarity that suggested otherwise.

Interesting, Max thought, replacing the picture, trying to ignore a sudden tightening in his throat at the sight of those joyful, innocent faces. Those kids, whoever they were, had never spent a moment worrying about where they would sleep that night or where their next meal was coming from. They were among the blessed, and probably didn't even know it.

"Oh, you found my family."

Max turned to see Carly standing in the doorway of her bedroom. His eyes widened at the sight of her. She was wearing a long dark skirt in some kind of loose, gauzy material, and a snug, cream-colored sweater. Her hair was in a low ponytail, and tiny gold hoops gleamed on her earlobes.

The transformation was impressive, but Max had had plenty of practice in keeping a poker face. He looked away, motioning toward the pictures. "The whole group is your family?"

"Every last one of them," she said, walking toward him. Lifting the lawn photo, she gazed at it fondly. "This is an old one. I was about fifteen here, so this was right before Josh went off to college. It was the last time we all lived at home. Mom and Dad had a houseful, didn't they?"

"Josh is the tall boy?"

"Right, he's my oldest brother. He's a hotshot stockbroker. Then there's Jeannie and me and Amanda, Chris, Kevin, and the twins, Anna and Alex. They're thirteen now." She sighed. "They're growing up so fast."

"You have an unusual-looking family."

Carly chuckled. "Every shape and size. I'm the third child. My parents wanted a houseful of kids, but Mom had a very difficult pregnancy with me, so when I was two, they decided to start adopting."

Max had suspected as much, but hearing her confirm it raised a wave of emotion inside him. The feeling did not result as much from discovering that an average-seeming couple like Carly's parents had taken on the awesome responsibility of adopting five children, as it did from the simple feeling of normalcy that the photo conveyed. It was completely at odds with his own dark, turbulent memories of the foster homes he had passed through as he struggled to reach eighteen. Some had been benign, merely doing him no harm, and others had left scars that he still carried.

There had been a time when he had dreamed of a family like Carly's, of sane discipline, warm affection, and of people who valued him for more than the monthly government check he brought them. After a while, he had stopped believing that they were out there at all. Apparently, he just hadn't been one of the lucky ones.

Carly set the photo back on the shelf. "We should go," she said. "I need to stop at Henry's house and feed the pets. We should have gone there first, but I wasn't thinking clearly. It's going to take me a while to get into the habit of this."

Max shook off the dark cloak of melancholy that was closing around him and looked down into Carly's clear blue eyes. "We can easily call Pauline and have her take care of it."

"Friday is Pauline's night off," Carly said. "Anyway, that's not her job. She and Henry have an agreement. She doesn't do windows or pets."

Max frowned, swallowing the protest that came to his lips. He hadn't planned on another visit to the house so soon, and didn't like the idea much at all. Being there had a strong emotional impact on him, and that night he needed a clear head. But there was a stubborn look on Carly's face, and he sensed that the issue wasn't up for discussion.

Well, there was certainly no reason that he couldn't handle standing in front of the damned house for fifteen minutes while Carly went inside and took care of business.

"Fine," he said, looking pointedly at his watch. It was after seven. If they missed their dinner reservations and ended up jammed into the crowded restaurant bar while they waited for a table to open up, the mood would be ruined. He would have to keep a close eye on the time. "Let's go."

When they arrived at the house, there were four large, white sacks piled like carcasses around one of the stone gargoyles. Only his horned head and the curled lump of his tail were visible, and Carly thought that he looked annoyed by such disrespectful treatment.

"Great," she said. "The dog food arrived."

Max prodded one of the sacks with his toe. "This is all dog food?"

"Believe it or not, this is a short-term supply. I noticed this morning that we were getting low, so I phoned all the bulk suppliers in the area, figured out who had been handling Henry's account, and asked them to make an emergency delivery. They let me have it on credit, which is a good thing. Do you have any idea how much it costs to buy two hundred pounds of kibble?"

Carly unlocked the front door and gestured down at the sacks. "Help me carry these inside, would you?"

He frowned. "Inside?"

"Yes. That's where the dogs eat, so that's where we need it."

There was an odd expression on Max's face as he stared at the open doorway. "Right now?"

What was the matter with him? "Right now," Carly agreed. "It's dinnertime."

But still, he didn't budge. "The delivery people should have hauled it in. That's part of their damn job."

"Well, they didn't," Carly said. "I'll try to arrange that for next time, but right now, we have four large sacks that can't walk, and I need you to help me carry them."

He didn't answer, and his face was as immobile as stone. Carly found herself getting irritated. "What's the matter? Are these big bags too heavy for you? Been spending too much time behind a desk, Max?"

That snapped him out of it. "Hardly," he said. He shot a hard, almost defiant look at the house. "You want me to bring in the food? Fine. You got it."

He reached down, grabbed one bulky sack, and slung it over his shoulder as easily as if it were a feather pillow. She blinked, taken aback, as he strode past her into the darkened entry hall. He stopped and turned to look at her. "Where do you want it?"

Carly swallowed. "Kitchen. Please."

"Fine. Where is it?"

"Next to the solarium."

"And where is that?" Max asked coldly.

"In the back of the house, right where it's always been . . ." She paused, startled. "Max, haven't you ever been here before?"

"No," he said, and started down the hall, leaving her standing in the doorway, surprised and concerned, her mouth filled with unvoiced questions.

She caught up with him just outside the kitchen. Her arms were wrapped awkwardly around a heavy sack, and as she was supporting it on her raised knee, attempting to free one hand to turn the knob, the kitchen door suddenly opened inward.

Carly squawked, lost her balance, and pitched forward through the open doorway. The bag of food hit the floor with a crunchy thump, and a second later, so did she.

"Ouch." She looked up from her inelegant position on the kitchen linoleum to see Max gazing down at her.

"Sorry," he said, offering her a hand. "I didn't know you were there."

"That's good. I'd hate to think you did it on purpose." His fingers closed around hers, and she felt his strength as he pulled her easily to her feet.

"About that desk-job joke," she said, brushing herself off. "I didn't mean it. Nobody would ever mistake you for a weakling."

"Or a three-martini CEO? I've made a point of avoiding that."

"Yes, I can see. What do you do, lift weights?"

"Only when there's no dog food around."

His expression hadn't changed, and it took her a moment to realize that he was being dryly humorous. She smiled at him and bent to pick up the fallen sack.

"I'll get that," Max said. "This is my job, isn't it?"

Carly hoisted the bag, staggering slightly under the weight. "You're looking at a woman who lifted an eighty-pound Rottweiler onto an X-ray table today. When I say help me with the dog food, I don't mean do it yourself, I mean help me."

"Eighty pounds?"

"Well, maybe seventy," she amended breathlessly. "He was only a year old. And one of the technicians might have given him a little boost from the back. You know how it is."

Max lifted the bag from her arms. "Find something else to do. I'll handle the food."

Carly, feeling a twinge in her lower back, didn't argue.

She had left the dogs outside in the fenced backyard while she was at work, and when she opened the kitchen door, she found them all sitting eagerly on the porch, having heard activity in the kitchen and surmising that it was dinnertime.

They looked faintly disappointed when, instead of letting them in, Carly stepped outside and closed the door behind her.

"Soon," she said, to the array of wagging tails and curious stares. "Ten minutes. I don't think Max needs another dose of you guys right now. You can be a little overwhelming to people who aren't used to pets."

Henry's back lawn had been carefully landscaped for privacy, and the artful, though overgrown, border of trees and shrubs girdling the expanse of grass almost disguised the fact that a city street lay just beyond the hidden fence. It was a dog paradise, complete with a small pond for splashing, and judging from the condition of the dogs' coats, there had been a lot of splashing that afternoon.

"You're a mess," Carly said sternly to the group, and was met with several wide grins. She threw a tennis ball for them for a while, then checked back into the kitchen and found all four bags of food stacked neatly in the pantry. There was no sign of Max.

He still hadn't appeared by the time the dog pack was crunching happily at their bowls. Was he waiting for her in the car? Carly was puzzled. Either he disliked dogs more than she had thought, or something strange was going on. She considered it as she walked back down the long hall. It seemed unbelievable that he had never been in Henry's house before. What kind of bizarre relationship would keep him from ever visiting his grandfather, yet leave him as the old man's trustee?

To her surprise, Max was not waiting in the car, or anywhere out in front of the house. Carly called his name, but there was no answer, so she went back inside. She walked through the entry hall into the huge, echoing living room. The velvet drapes were closed, as they usually were, and the room was dim until Carly flipped the switch that illuminated the central chandelier. Glittering crystal light fell in ripples over the ornate furniture, but the room was empty.

She frowned, walking forward. "Max?"

There was light coming from the dining room, through an opening between the tall wooden doors. She called again and heard the creak of old floorboards, then his voice.

"In here."

The dining room drapes were open, and the evening sunlight streamed in to illuminate the heavy mahogany table and chairs. Max was standing silently in front of a wall of framed oil portraits, and the tension in the set of his shoulders warned Carly to approach cautiously.

"What's going on?" she asked.

He didn't look at her. "Pauline was right," he said. "I do have the Tremayne eyes."

Astonished, Carly followed his gaze to a picture of Alan Tremayne, Henry's son. In the portrait, he was standing in front of one of the old oak trees in the backyard. He looked young, like a college student, with long light brown hair and sideburns, in the style of the early sixties. Alan had been killed in an accident, many years ago, and that was all Carly knew about it. Henry did not talk about his personal life, preferring to focus their afternoon discussions on neutral subjects like literature and animals, and Carly had never pressed him. She had always sensed a sadness underlying the old man's courtly manner.

"I never knew that Alan had a son," she said.

There was no humor in Max's tight smile. "Neither did Alan."

"But Henry—"

"Found out about me a little more than a year ago. After I hired an agency to find him. Someone got greedy, I guess. How's that for a confidential investigation? Those people are supposed to be the best in the business."

"That's pretty bad. But it did bring you and your grandfather together, so maybe—"

"Actually," Max said, "it didn't. I've never met Henry Tremayne."

Carly stared at him. "But if you knew about him a year ago, and he knew about you, then why haven't you met?"

"Why do people ever make the wrong decision?" Max asked harshly. "We screw up our lives and wonder why everything looks so damn clear in retrospect." The room was quiet for a moment, then he exhaled heavily. "I don't know. It never seemed like the right time to impose myself on him."

"But I wonder why Henry never—" Carly stopped herself. For anyone who knew Henry Tremayne, the answer was obvious. "Of course," she said, thinking out loud. "He was waiting for you to come to him. That would be his style. He's too polite to force his way into anyone's life. He knew that you had found him, so he was waiting . . ."

Max winced, and Carly wanted to bite her tongue off. This, then, was the darkness she had sensed yesterday in the clinic when she had confronted him with accusations of neglecting his grandfather. No wonder he was suffering silently. Something, a reason that she couldn't have imagined, had kept him from contacting his grandfather, and now he knew he had waited too long.

"Why weren't you ready, Max?" she asked, putting a gentle hand on his arm. He seemed hot under her fingers, as if there were a fire smoldering just under his skin. He stiffened when she touched him, but didn't pull away. "You were the one who searched for him. What made you stop? When you found him, didn't you want him?"

Max turned on her. "Want him!" he said hoarsely. "My own blood? He's the only family I have left. I've been wanting him since I was a kid. He just didn't have a face or a name until fourteen months ago. But then, when I learned who he was . . ."

"He's your grandfather. What else matters?"

"It's not that simple. What was I supposed to do, show up at Henry Tremayne's door, almost forty years after the fact, and introduce myself? 'Hi, Grandpa. You don't know me, but I'm the product of Alan's affair with a boozed-up cocktail waitress. He would have provided for me, I'm sure of it, if it hadn't been for that drunk-driving accident. Aren't you glad to have me as a reminder of how much your boy liked to party?' "

Carly knew that the anger in his voice was not directed at her, but still, she felt it sharply. She took a deep breath, rocked by the turbulence around him, and reached out again.

"Max, you need to believe me. That's not how Henry would see you. You don't know him yet, but—"

"I know enough about him," Max said. "And I know this: Long-lost relatives of rich old men tend to be looking for love of the green paper variety. I'm no damn fortune hunter, and I'm not going to let myself look like one."

"You?" Carly said incredulously. "You couldn't."

"I could. He's too rich."

"But so are you," she said, then blushed when he raised his eyebrows at her. "Richard mentioned something about your company. What I'm trying to say is, how could anyone possibly think of you as a fortune hunter? You have plenty of money."

"Not enough," Max said. "Not yet."

CHAPTER 8

❖

"Max Giordano?" Jeannie Martin-Schwartz paused over the bag of groceries she was unloading and considered the name. "Nope. Never heard of him."

"Good," Carly said. "That makes it easier."

"Why, who is he? Oh, Carly, get the baby. He's making a break for it."

Nine-month-old Nathan Martin-Schwartz was on all fours, doing a fast crawl toward the back door, which stood ajar.

"Hold it, kid," Carly said, picking up her small nephew and turning him in the other direction. The baby paused, looking puzzled, and Carly tickled his foot. "Max Giordano is Henry Tremayne's grandson. I had dinner with him last night."

"Oh, that sweet old guy with all the pets. How's he doing?"

"Not well. He fell down the stairs and hurt his head on Wednesday night. He's in the hospital." It was Saturday morning, and it seemed incredible to Carly that so much could have happened in so little time. She hadn't said a word to anyone about Henry's trust, and she didn't intend to. She preferred to think that he would be fine, which meant that she was really only pet-sitting until he came home.

"Who's his doctor?" Jeannie asked. She was an ER nurse by training, but she had quit before Nathan was born. "I hope it's Bill Sheaffer. He's the best."

"I don't know. Listen, Jeannie, I was thinking of bringing Max to one of the infamous Martin family Sunday dinners. Not tomorrow, that would be too soon, but maybe next week."

"Oh?" her sister said innocently, but there was a gleam in her eye.

"No, no," Carly said. "It's not like that. He's just a friend. Well, he's not even a friend, actually. He's more of a case study. I think it might do him some good to hang out with a family for a while."

Jeannie made a face. "That depends on how much family he can tolerate. Is he up to it?"

"I don't know. It could be a disaster. He's a bit prickly, but I don't think that he's a bad guy at heart. I think he's just lonely. I think he needs—"

"Hold it," her sister interrupted. "Lonely? Needy? I've heard this before. Is this another one of your lost-soul boyfriends? I thought you were over that. Loser men aren't kittens, and you can't just adopt them."

"Richard wasn't a lost soul," Carly said. "He didn't need me at all, and you can see how well that worked out."

"That's not how you told it at the time. I remember those stories about his rich family in Beverly Hills, and how nobody paid any attention to him when he was growing up. How he would wake up with nightmares about his father yelling at him, and you would have to sit up with him until he went back to sleep. We were all misty about him—until we met him."

"Come on," Carly protested. "Richard's an incredibly talented and dedicated surgeon. He's actually very emotionally fragile."

"Breaking up with him was the smartest thing you've done in years. And you can't let yourself go ricocheting back into your old habits. Do you remember Paul the tormented poet who would write you mournful haiku right on Mom and Dad's front door? In black permanent marker?"

"He took his art very seriously," Carly said.

"So did Dad, by the fourth time he had to repaint. And what about that guy who burst into tears right in the middle of Eric's birthday party? Then locked himself in the upstairs bathroom and threatened to jump out the window?"

"He had self-esteem issues. He was working on it in his therapy group."

Jeannie snorted. "All I remember is that the party went downhill after the rescue squad showed up with a net."

Carly winced. "Low blow, Jeannie."

"This is for your own good, little sis. You're not so young anymore, you know. There's no time to waste on another emotional charity case."

"Thanks a lot! Twenty-eight is hardly over the hill. And Max Giordano is not an emotional charity case. He's an interesting and complicated man, and I think that it would be good for him to get out into the country for an evening with a nice group of people."

"Twenty-eight is a good age to get serious and to look around for a man who is stable and reliable. Isn't your biological clock telling you anything?"

"No," Carly said. "I'm too busy working to be worrying about reproduction."

"It's all Richard's fault," Jeannie said, setting down a can of stewed tomatoes with a thump. "He's taking advantage of you. It's not fair."

"Jeannie, please." Carly had heard the same argument many times before, and she wasn't in the mood to deal with another one of her sister's indignant monologues.

"It's true, Carly, and you know it. That place is making plenty of money. So why are you broke all the time?"

"Rich isn't paying off student loans like I am, and he owns a much larger share of the clinic than I do. It's perfectly fair."

Jeannie snorted. "Well, he'd have a lot less income without you. And he acts like he's doing you some favor. It's just wrong."

Carly sighed. "Do we have to talk about this right now?"

Jeannie looked contrite. "No, of course not. I shouldn't be nagging you about money when you're worried about Henry. What's his status, exactly?"

"He's not conscious yet, but he's stable. Max told me that they have a whole team of doctors and therapists working with him. I'm sure he's getting the best care that money can buy."

"Hmm. He's . . . eighty? Is that right?"

"Yes, but he's always said that he comes from healthy

stock. His father and grandfather both lived to be almost a hundred."

"Just the same, Carly," Jeannie said gently, "I think you had better prepare yourself for the possibility that he may not recover. Eighty is pretty old, and even if he comes from a long-lived family, it's no guarantee that he's going to do the same."

"I don't like to think about it," Carly muttered. Just the idea of Henry dying, and what that would mean to everyone, raised such a tumult of emotion inside her that she couldn't let herself consider it.

"I know," Jeannie said. "I'm sorry, honey. I'm sure they're doing their best for him. If he makes it through the first week, he's got a pretty good chance of long-term survival. Of course, the degree of recovery is the issue. Even if he doesn't die, it doesn't necessarily mean that he'll be . . . hmm. Well, we won't talk about that now, either. Maybe he'll pull through."

"I hope so," Carly said.

"I do, too. And if Henry's grandson can handle total chaos with a bunch of lunatics, I say bring him to dinner. He might enjoy it. Although, of course . . ."

"What?"

"Well, I can just see Mom and Dad trying to be sly, asking him significant questions about marriage and babies and his future plans regarding both."

Carly shuddered. "Yikes."

"So you might want to brief them first."

"Good idea," Carly said vigorously. "Very good idea."

Self-control.
It was the most basic and the most formidable weapon

in a man's arsenal, Max thought as he pushed his way into the fifth mile of his run on Ocean Beach. The ability to control anxiety, or anticipation, pride or anger, and to proceed without the distraction of emotion was what separated the winners from the losers. He had spent many years cultivating his own self-control, and he had a record of wins to show for it.

So, what the hell had happened to him last night?

He and Carly had missed their dinner reservation after all, not that it had mattered. The head waiter at Mistral had been fawningly helpful and ushered them to a table right away, despite the fact that they had arrived almost an hour late. A damned hour late to dinner, and why? Because he had gotten snarled in the very net that he had tried to throw at Carly Martin. How ironic that he, of all people, would have gotten so caught up in the rising flood of his own half-assed hopes and fears that he would find himself spilling his guts to some woman he barely knew!

It was that house, he told himself. That house had too much symbolism attached to it. Being there had thrown him off-balance, and he stayed that way for the rest of the evening. He had managed to regain his outer composure, at least. But that was as far as it went, and as a result, he'd had an exquisite gourmet dinner that he hardly tasted, and a bland conversation with Carly that had accomplished nothing at all. The evening had faded out with a pathetic fizzle and the awkwardness of an eighth-grade date, and Max went back to his hotel early, thoroughly disgusted with himself.

A flock of gulls scattered in front of him as he continued down the beach, sucking in deep breaths of the damp sea air. Blood beat a hot rhythm in his temples, and he ran until all he could feel was the ache in his lungs and the burn in his muscles. He gave himself up to the pain, welcoming the too-brief respite from thought.

Back at the Ritz, hot and exhausted, Max left his car with the valet and strode into the lobby, nodding to the staff as they greeted him. They all knew him by then. His driver's license still said New York, but he had been living in his suite at the hotel for the past few months while he worked at Syscom, getting his company through the transition period. The Ritz was starting to feel as familiar as his Park Avenue apartment ever had.

Aware of several curious glances directed at him, Max squared his shoulders as he walked, meeting every gaze until the other person was the first to look away. It was a trick he had learned long ago, to give the appearance of confidence back in the days when he had needed to fake it. It annoyed him that even now, on a deep, childish level, wearing sweaty workout clothes into the lobby of San Francisco's most exclusive hotel still stirred up that old fear of not looking right, of tipping off the in-crowd that he didn't belong.

To hell with it, Max told himself. *I might look like a slob, but at least I look like a rich slob.*

The message light on the phone was blinking when he entered his suite. He stripped off his windbreaker, sat down at the desk, and pressed the button for his voice mail.

"Max? It's Carly. It's . . . um . . . about noon, and I'm at the house. I'll be here for a while, so . . . give me a call if you get this message, okay? I just found something that I really want to show you."

Max frowned. The house? He didn't have Carly's home number, so she must have meant Henry's house. He wondered what she was doing at the mansion for "a while" on a Saturday afternoon. Playing with dogs, combing cats? Shouldn't she be out enjoying the day? What did Carly Martin do when she wasn't caring for four-legged creatures? He picked up the phone and dialed.

Pauline answered on the second ring. "Oh, Mr. Max, it's you. Are you coming for lunch?"

Max hadn't planned on it. "Carly left me a message about an hour ago. Is she still there?"

"Oh, she's still here," Pauline said dourly. "I didn't expect to be fixing lunch today, but now that I am, I hope you'll join us."

"Thanks," Max said. "But I—"

"It's vegetable soup, and I made it myself. I would have made my famous chicken soup, but Miss Martin doesn't eat chicken. Now, I don't think that's healthy. A person needs protein, and I told her so, but she seems to think that she knows best." The housekeeper sighed. "I'm sure that you eat chicken, Mr. Max."

"Yes," Max said. "I've been known to."

"Good. I'll make a batch of soup just for you, and you can take it back to the hotel. Although you really should be staying here. If Henry knew that his own grandson was sleeping in a hotel with all this space right here in the house, he would be very upset."

She made a disapproving noise. "I should tell you that the hospital still won't let me see your grandfather. I suppose that just because I've lived with him for twenty years and devoted every waking moment to his comfort, I shouldn't expect any special treatment. Someone really should speak to them about it."

It was clear to Max who that "someone" was. "I'll see what I can do," he said.

"That would be very good of you," Pauline said. "You really should come over. Miss Martin has something she wants to show you, and . . . what?" She paused, and Max heard muffled voices in the background. When the house-keeper came back on the line, her voice was frosty.

"Miss Martin would like to speak with you herself," Pauline said. "I'll go out and cut some flowers for the table, since I'm sure you want privacy, and I'd hate to intrude. I just hope that the soup doesn't burn while I'm away."

There was another pause, then he heard Carly's voice.

"Max? Hi. Are you really coming for lunch?"

"Do I have a choice?" Max asked. "Is Pauline still there, or did she actually leave?"

Carly chuckled. "She left. Quite a powerhouse, isn't she? She's a bit opinionated, but once you get used to her, you realize that she's got a heart of gold. I keep trying to get her to call me Carly, but she'll have none of it."

Her voice was light and smooth, threaded with humor, and Max found himself picturing the way her eyes crinkled at the corners when she smiled. He cleared his throat. "She said that you have something for me?"

"Right," Carly said. "That's why I called. It's not urgent, but it's important. I think you'll want to see it."

"What is it? You're being very obscure."

"I don't mean to be. It's just that after last night . . ."

Max felt himself tense. "What about last night?"

"Well," she said, "I was thinking about what you said,

and then this morning, when I stumbled across this book, I knew right away that you should see it. It's part of what you . . . need."

What did Carly think he needed? Psychoanalysis, probably, after the scene he had made. Max tapped his fingers on the desktop, hoping that she wasn't planning on giving him some kind of self-help manual.

"What is it, Carly?" he asked again.

"It's an album," she said. "More than a year of photos and press clippings, all the way up to last month's *Fortune* article. It's all about you, Max, and he saved everything. He must have been so proud of you."

"I wasn't snooping," Carly asserted later, after Max had arrived at the house and submitted to being fed Pauline's soup. "Obviously, I consider Henry's personal papers completely off-limits. But I was in the library, looking for one of the cats, and this was just sitting there, open, on Henry's desk. I saw your picture, and as soon as I realized what it was, I knew that you should see it."

Max nodded. "Thank you," he said briefly.

Henry's lawyers hadn't told Max anything more than the terms of the Tremayne trust, leaving him to find his own answers to the questions that plagued him. How Henry had learned about Max, what he knew about his grandson's life, and what he thought about it all . . . The timing of the documents seemed to answer the first question. And now, a partial answer to the second—and perhaps the third—was being offered.

He and Carly were sitting in the solarium, looking out over the back lawn, where the dogs were chasing each other in circles, fighting for possession of a battered stick.

Light streamed through the tall windows, each topped with a stained-glass panel that cast rainbow glints into the room. Bushy green plants grew in ornate urns all around them, and among the normal varieties of houseplant, Max saw several terra-cotta pots of what could only be catnip, judging from the reactions of the felines who dropped by for a nibble.

One blissful tabby hopped into Max's lap and began to knead his thighs with her paws. He lifted one hand to brush her away, but she immediately settled down into a fuzzy lump and went to sleep, her purrs rumbling gently against his skin. He frowned down at her.

The album, a red leather-bound book, sat on the table in front of him. He had not yet touched it.

Carly followed his gaze. "I thought you might want to take it back to the hotel," she said. "But if you want to look now, alone, I'll go and—"

Max shook his head. "No. Not now. I'll wait."

He still felt unsteady, and he did not want to risk another episode like the one the previous night. Over the phone, Carly had described the album as containing photos of him in locations from New York to San Francisco. He had been photographed in restaurants, in hotels, in cars, and on the street. They were the kind of pictures that a private eye would take with a long lens, she said. Max didn't know why he was so astonished to learn that his grandfather had been investigating him in turn. It certainly made sense.

But how much had Henry's hireling uncovered over the past year? Only Max's adult life, or did the scrapbook also tell the darker story of his teens? Were the foster-care documents in there? The truancy reports? The arrest records for breaking and entering, for petty theft? None of that information would have been difficult to dig up. Max's stomach clenched as he imagined his grandfather paging through that red book, thinking about him, judging him.

The suspense was gnawing at him, but he did not touch the book. It was not the time. Not in front of Carly, or anywhere near her. He wondered why she had brought the album to his attention. It seemed to be a simple gesture of kindness, but she had no reason to be kind to him. On the contrary, he could think of several reasons why she might have it in for him. She could have brought out the album in an attempt to provoke him into another emotional outburst, hoping to use it against him. Or she might be attempting to gain his trust, thinking—wrongly—that she could charm him just as she had charmed his grandfather.

She smiled at him, and he gazed back at her, letting his eyes move critically over her, as if she were a statue or a painting. Her hair was smoothed into its usual braid, and in the sunlight, her blue eyes matched the floral print on her cotton sundress. She lacked only a wide-brimmed hat and wicker basket filled with roses to look like a casting director's idea of Girlish Innocence.

"What are your plans for the afternoon?" he asked.

"Oh," she said. "I don't really have any, I guess."

Perfect. He wanted to talk to her, and this wasn't the place to do it. He hadn't missed the ever-so-slightly ajar kitchen door, or the flicker of motion behind it as Pauline hovered just beyond, listening in on the conversation. *God help me,* Max thought, *if I'm ever that old and bored.*

"Actually," Carly amended, "I do need to run over to

the clinic. One of the cats has an abscess on her foot, and I want to pick up some antibiotics."

"I'll take you there."

"Max, you don't have to drive me around."

"I know that. But I want to. If you don't mind."

"Mind?" A tinge of color touched her cheeks. "No, I don't mind."

CHAPTER 9

———◆———

During the drive to the clinic, Carly began to get the feeling that she had imagined the previous night's encounter in the Tremayne dining room. It wasn't that she suddenly expected Max to confess all of his innermost thoughts to her, but it seemed to her that sharing such a raw and honest moment was a strong step toward forming a friendship. They should have been more relaxed around each other, but instead, things seemed to have taken a step backward. The dark fissures that had opened up in him had been resealed with a seamless veneer of poise and politeness that kept the conversation flowing smoothly but left Carly feeling disturbed.

Even so, Max was good company when he wanted to be, and she fell quickly into the lure of his charm. They chatted as he navigated the city streets, then, somehow, the subject of love came up. Carly had jokingly referred to her first flame, a sophisticated "older man" of ten, whom she and her nine-year-old friends had chased around the playground threatening to kiss.

"Did you catch him?" Max asked.

Carly grinned. "I was bigger than he was, so it wasn't much of a contest. That was technically my first kiss, except that he was struggling so hard that I actually bit him on the chin."

"And then you lived happily ever after?"

"No. That was the high point, unfortunately. He went off to private school, and it was years before I saw him again. By then, he had purple hair and a motor scooter, and the magic was gone."

Max chuckled, and she felt a warm pleasure at the sound.

"Sounds like it wasn't meant to be," he said, downshifting as they approached a stop sign. Carly noticed his fingers as he gripped the gearstick. His hands were strong and square, like working hands. Only the cleanly groomed nails and lack of calluses marked them as belonging to a businessman.

"And what about the real thing?" Max asked casually. "Have you ever been in love, Carly?"

She shot a sideways glance at him. It was a strange question, unexpectedly personal, and something about the studied nonchalance of his voice suggested that he had a reason for asking. But what could it be?

"I don't know," she said cautiously.

"You don't?"

"No. It's more complicated when you're an adult."

A sudden, anticipatory tension in Max's body made Carly realize that he had found her answer very interesting, and an alarming possibility presented itself. Had Richard indeed said something about their involvement? Or had Max guessed, and was trying to get her to confirm it? It was not a pleasant thought. But why would Max care about her old relationship? What interest could he possibly have in her personal life . . . unless it was the same curiosity that she felt about him, the urge to know him on a level deeper than the outer self he presented to the world.

Could he actually be thinking of her that way?

"Complicated," he repeated. "How?"

Anxiously, Carly squeezed the edge of her seat. "Sometimes people enter relationships for the wrong reasons," she said. "Looking for the wrong things."

"And what were you looking for, Carly?" Max asked quietly. "Security? Someone older and more experienced to take you under his wing?"

He knew. Humiliation burned through her. He knew, and the only way he could have known was through Richard's idiotic male posturing. Damn Richard, damn his ego! What warped version of the story had he given to Max? He had probably painted her in his usual colors, as a Goody Two-shoes who didn't have the sophistication to handle an adult relationship. She could see him, winking at Max. *Just a warning, buddy. Guys like us have to stick together.*

"Security was part of it," she said. If Max already knew everything, at least she could try to set the record straight. "I was just out of school, and I didn't know if I could make it on my own. I thought I loved him." She sighed. "I have this problem with idealism. Rose-colored glasses, that kind of thing. I end up wasting a lot of time because of it."

Max looked skeptical. "The age gap didn't bother you?"

"Age gap," Carly said. "I never really thought about it.

If anything, I guess it helped. All the guys my own age were just getting started, but he was well established. He seemed very glamorous then, and I was in awe of him. I didn't know him very well. Anyway," she added, "It was a huge mistake, but by the time I figured that out, it was too late."

"What do you mean, too late?"

"Too late to leave. I couldn't afford to walk out. I didn't have any choice but to stay in the arrangement and wait until—Max, good grief! What's wrong?"

He had recoiled sharply. "Stay in the *arrangement*?" he repeated.

"Well, yes. I had to."

"And wait until when?"

"Until I can get my money. It's a long story."

"Really," said Max, with a sudden chill in his voice. "It sounds very simple to me. Let me see if I understand you. You fell out of love and wanted to leave, but instead you decided to wait around for the big payoff?"

"I suppose you could put it like that," Carly said slowly. "But it wasn't much of a decision—I mean, I had to stay. If I'd quit, I would have lost everything I'd invested up to that point."

She looked curiously at Max. There seemed to be something wrong with him. He looked almost ill. "It would have been foolish to leave," she explained, "just because my feelings had changed."

"Foolish," Max repeated.

"Well, yes. It wasn't an ideal situation, but I knew it would only be for a few more years. It hasn't been that bad, really. He can be unpleasant, but I've learned how to handle him."

Max's face darkened like a thundercloud. "I see," he said, staring stonily through the windshield.

Carly couldn't understand why he was suddenly so angry. She felt a flicker of guilt; was she being unfair to Richard? From the way that Max was scowling, she thought that she must have said something wrong. Maybe she did sound unkind. "He is a brilliant man," she amended. "That was what first attracted me to him. And I suppose I do owe him a lot . . ."

"Yes," Max growled. "You sure do."

So that was it. This was some kind of guy thing, with men defending their own. She felt rising annoyance. "Hold on," she said. "I think I deserve more credit than that. He would have had a really difficult time finding another partner who was willing to do the kinds of things that I—"

"My God!" Max exclaimed violently. The car swerved, and Carly braced herself, alarmed, as he quickly brought it back under control. "This is unbelievable. Please, spare me the details. I really don't want to know."

Carly stared at him. "Okay, I'm sorry."

"So am I," he said grimly.

They drove in silence, until Carly couldn't stand it any longer. "I just wanted you to hear my side of the story," she said. "I don't understand why you're so upset."

"I'm not upset."

"Something is obviously bothering you."

His fingers were tight on the steering wheel. "Look," he said finally. "I have no idea why you're suddenly being so candid with me, but I'll return the favor. You caught me by surprise. I had started to think that you were a different kind of person."

"Oh," Carly said, confused. "Well, I guess I'm just me."

"You should have stuck with your earlier approach. I would have been much more generous if you had convinced me that you loved him. But now—for some unfathomable reason—you're telling me that you don't, and that you've been willing to sell years of your life to a man that you find *unpleasant*."

"What else was I supposed to do?" Carly demanded. "I thought about walking away, but I couldn't. I can't. Maybe you don't understand what it's like to worry about money, but I'm still paying off student loans. And then there's rent, and insurance, and car repairs, and . . . and utility bills, and by the time I take care of everything, I'm happy just to be able to feed myself! That money is the only security I have. It belongs to me. I earned it."

"That's one way to look at it," Max said. "But I'll give you some advice, Carly. You might think that the money is worth it, but it isn't. And telling me all of this was a very big mistake."

"Oh," Carly said hotly. "That is so unfair. You have no right to judge me for being practical. I've had no choice. Not until now, with Henry's gift."

"The payoff, you mean?" Max said. "I guess it was worth it, then. I suppose that if you're going to sell your body, Henry Tremayne was the right man to pick. But tell me, Carly, are you available to anyone who looks like a potential gold mine, or do you restrict your *arrangements* to lonely eighty-year-olds?"

CHAPTER 10

———— ❖ ————

One look at Carly's face told Max that his cruel question had hit the mark. She sat as if stunned, her mouth slightly open.

"What?" she croaked, finally. "Henry?"

The light ahead turned green, and Max hit the accelerator with more force than necessary, his hand clenching the gearstick as the engine roared. Was this how it was going to be? After everything she had just admitted, did she think she had the right to be insulted and hurt by his judgment? He was fighting down a hot mixture of emotions, not the least of which was a sense of betrayal. To think that she had actually gotten him to the point of making excuses for her, imagining scenes of romance, of love, of—at the very least—honorable motivations for her affair with Henry. So much for the rebirth of ideals. He should have known better.

"Let me make sure I understand this," Carly said, her voice rising shrilly. "All this time, you were talking about Henry?"

"Who else?"

She made a noise that sounded strangely like a growl, and Max suddenly felt a sharp blow to his shoulder. He turned to see Carly, her face a mask of outrage, balling another fist and aiming it at him.

"You're disgusting!" she shouted, landing another blow. "You're a rotten, filthy-minded misogynist sicko!"

"What the hell are you doing?" Max demanded, swerving as she smacked him again. "I'm driving—"

Carly didn't even seem to hear him. "How could you think I was talking about your grandfather? About Henry Tremayne, my friend, whose pets I look after and who discusses world news and literature with me over afternoon tea!"

"Ouch, damn it," Max said, giving up on trying to handle city traffic with a madwoman in his front seat. He pulled the car to a screeching halt by the curb next to a small city park.

"I've had it with you, Max Giordano," Carly raged. "I was actually starting to like you, but I just changed my mind. You're horrible, and I never want to see you again!" She fumbled for the door handle.

"Hold it," Max said. "If that whole discussion wasn't about Henry, then who—"

"Richard, you idiot!" Carly shouted, opening the door. "I was talking about Richard." She slammed the door behind her and stormed away.

Max cursed under his breath, yanked the keys out of the ignition, and followed her. "Carly!"

She was well on her way into the park before he caught up with her. Head high, stride firm, she shot one furious sideways glance at him. "Go away!"

"The hell I will," Max said, keeping pace with her. "We're going to straighten this out right now. You were talking about Richard Wexler, your partner?"

Red spots burned hotly on her cheeks. "I just told you that, Sherlock."

"You and he were . . . involved?"

"Right."

"For how long?"

"Too long."

"That's what you meant when you said that you couldn't afford to leave your arrangement? You meant a professional arrangement?"

"No," Curly snapped, stopping in her tracks and turning on him, her words tumbling out in a rush. "I meant that I was sleeping with your grandfather, trying to milk that nice old man for every penny he's worth. That's what you've been waiting to hear, isn't it? Why even bother to wait, Max? As far as I can tell, I've already been tried and convicted, so why not just hang me right now?

"Obviously," she continued sarcastically, "I've been spending my nights scheming to get into Henry's will, so that I'll never have to work another day in my life. I'm sure you've noticed that I just hate my job. Can't stand animals, either. And all those years in vet school? Those sixteen-hour days I worked just to get myself through? Oh, those were for fun, not because I actually have a goal that I've been dreaming of since I was a kid."

She reached out with one emphatic finger and poked him in the chest. "And I'll tell you something else. To somebody with your bank balance, my life may not look like much, but you had better believe that I'm pretty darned happy with it, and all of your grandfather's money wouldn't do so much for me that I'd ever manipulate him or prostitute myself to get it."

Her eyes met his defiantly, and Max could tell that she was ready for him to argue. But he didn't. Instead, he simply waited, watching as she faced him expectantly, her lips compressed and her shoulders tense. He waited, as her quick and shallow breathing slowed, and the hard lines of her face slumped into wary uncertainty.

She took one more ragged breath, and Max could see that she was trying to bolster her own rage, to pull it around herself like chain mail.

"I've had enough of this," she said, and turned her back on him. "Good-bye."

He moved quickly, catching her by the arms and turning her around to face him again.

Carly gasped, and tried to pull away. "What do you think you're—"

"Look at me."

"What . . . ?" A flush crept over her cheeks as he held her. He stared down at her, trying to see the truth behind the startled blue shimmer of her eyes.

Integrity in others was the last thing that Max expected to meet when confronting the world. He had seen too many adjustable morals to have any illusions left about the inherent goodness of humankind, especially where money was concerned. But as he searched Carly's face and saw nothing but clear, unwavering honesty, his cynicism broke under the rising force of his instinct.

"I'll be damned," he said slowly, stunned. "You're telling me the truth."

There was a rush of release in saying the words, and also a strange feeling of vertigo as he understood their deeper meaning. Carly Martin was not his enemy. It was possible that she wasn't even his opponent. But if she wasn't any of those things, then who exactly was she?

Carly let out a shaky sigh. "Of course it's the truth," she said. She sounded as if she was trying to be stern, but Max felt her tremble under his hands.

"I don't know why Henry gave his house to me," she said. "Honestly, I don't. And this foundation that he wants me to set up . . . I don't know how to do it. I'm only twenty-eight, and I'm still learning how to be a vet. I'll do the best job that I can, but I can think of a hundred people who would be better at it than I."

"He obviously had a reason for choosing you," Max said.

"I've been thinking about it for days, and I can't come up with any reason except . . ."

"What?"

"Well, I wonder if he thought that he could rescue me, like he rescues his pets."

Max realized that he still had his hands on her arms. Her skin was soft under his fingers. He frowned, and let go. "Rescue you from what?"

"From my partnership at the clinic. He even offered me an interest-free loan to open my own practice, but the situation is so complicated . . . I haven't felt sure that I should take him up on it."

"Why not?"

"There are so many legal issues with Rich . . . What I was trying to say to you, before, is that our partnership is contracted for three more years, and I'd forfeit everything I've invested if I broke the contract."

"He won't let you leave?"

"Believe me, there's no way he'll let me pull out my money early. So, unless I decided to walk away from all of my savings, I'd have to get a lawyer, and go to court, and even so, I'd probably lose. I can't put myself through all of that. It's too stressful."

"No more stressful than staying where you aren't happy."

"Ha," Carly exclaimed. "You corporate big shots might be comfortable threatening people with court battles, but the idea makes me break into a cold sweat. I don't want to spend my time meeting with lawyers. I'm a vet. I want to do my job."

"I'm sure Wexler is counting on that."

"Maybe. But that's not even the point. Starting my own business is a huge step, and I'm not ready for it yet. I don't have enough experience. I didn't want to accept Henry's offer until I was sure that I would be successful enough to pay him back."

"I doubt that he would have made an issue of it."

"You know what? You're probably right. I probably could have taken his loan and spent it on a trip to Tahiti, and Henry would never have said a word about it. And that's the best reason I can think of for repaying him quickly, and with a fair rate of interest. Wouldn't you do the same?"

It was a rhetorical question. Her tone of voice clearly indicated that any decent person would impose limits on Henry Tremayne's generosity. She didn't even ask whether Max agreed, which he found interesting.

"Maybe not," he said deliberately, wondering why she was so sure of his integrity. "If Henry Tremayne wanted to be my knight in shining armor, I might let him."

"No, you wouldn't." Carly said immediately. "You couldn't."

Her conviction intrigued him. "Why do you say that?"

"Because of what you said last night. You're not a user, and the idea that you might be mistaken for one is unbearable to you. You're cynical, Max, and I think you've been hurt by the world more than once, but it didn't make you cruel, and you don't try to punish kindness just for existing."

Max was silent for a moment. He had no idea of how to respond to such a statement. He knew that most people would choose "ruthless" rather than "virtuous" as a one-word description of his character, but he would not have agreed with them. He had a handful of principles that he never knowingly compromised, and although he was not always nice, he did try to be fair. That, he believed, was what mattered.

"It will be a while before I earn my halo," he said dryly.

"No kidding," Carly said. "You have a bad habit of jumping to conclusions about people."

But the barb was tinged with gentle humor, making what could have been a criticism come off as a shared joke. It was a strange sensation.

"Anyway," Carly said, "I think Henry is still determined to save me. That's what this is all about."

"Do you need saving?"

"No, no. Really. I can handle Rich."

Max pictured the man in his mind, trying to see him from a female perspective, trying to imagine what Carly could possibly have seen in him. He was handsome enough, if you liked blond preppies.

He found himself imagining Richard and Carly as

lovers, and his stomach knotted as his mind offered up images of the preppie with his hands on her, his mouth covering hers, of Carly's body pressed against—

Enough! Max cut off the increasingly explicit picture. What was the matter with him? He had no idea where that little film had come from.

Carly looked curiously at him. "Are you all right?"

"Fine," he said, but the images were still there, stuck in his brain like burrs. They seemed to hover behind his eyes, mocking him. "Just fine."

CHAPTER 11

When Carly arrived at the clinic on Tuesday morning, Michelle was already at her desk, and her expression was grim.

"Dr. Wexler fired Nick," she said, without any preamble.

"What?" Carly put down her umbrella and stared at the receptionist. "What do you mean?"

"Yesterday, after you left. Nick was subbing for Tracey in the OR, and he must have done something wrong, because I could hear Dr. Wexler yelling all the way out here. Something about Nick having a bad attitude."

"He was *yelling*? Why? Did Nick say what happened?"

Michelle shook her head. "No. He was pretty upset, so he just grabbed his coat and took off."

"This is crazy," Carly exclaimed. "If Nick has a bad attitude, *I've* never seen it. Where is Rich?"

"Out back. I haven't said a word to him. The mood he's in, I figured he'd fire me, too."

* * *

Richard was outside in the tiny square of green that served as a yard, leaning against the back wall of the building and smoking a cigarette.

Carly didn't waste any time. "You fired Nick?"

Richard looked startled. "Who told you?"

"Do you think I wouldn't have noticed? What happened?"

"He has a smart mouth," Richard said defensively. "And I don't know where he got the impression that he can take time off whenever he wants it."

"Time off? Rich, I don't even know what you're talking about. Nick hasn't taken any time off."

"He was gone last Tuesday."

"He had an organic chemistry midterm the next morning! And you okayed it, remember? If you had a problem, why didn't you bring it up then?"

A flush of belligerence crept over Richard's face. "I never okayed any time off. Maybe he checked it with you, I don't know. You'd give the kid the day off for a hangnail."

"But . . ." Carly began, then stopped. She very clearly remembered talking to Richard about it. Rich had been in a good mood that day, and had agreed that Nick should take extra time to study. He had even told her to wish the young man luck.

Richard dropped his cigarette butt and ground it under his heel in one quick motion. "Don't forget," he said, "that I have the final say on everyone who works here. Everyone. Even you."

"Is that supposed to be a threat?" Carly asked, her temper rising. "Fine, Rich. Go ahead and fire me. We'll just annul that mistake of an agreement, and then you won't have to worry about my bad attitude, either."

"Yeah, you'd like that, wouldn't you," he muttered, staring at the ground.

"What's the matter with you?" Carly demanded. "You were yelling at Nick—"

He flashed her an angry look. "Why do you always take that kid's side? You weren't there. If you had been, you'd know that your technician is a flake. Yesterday he left a batch of antibiotics out of the cooler and destroyed it. That might not be a big deal to a groovy guy like him, but I'm the one who has to eat the cost. And this isn't his first screwup, either. He ruined a serum sample last week, and then had the fucking nerve to start arguing with me when I showed it to him." He raised his eyebrows at her. "Well? What do you say now?"

"That's . . . not good," Carly said, stunned.

"Damn right it's not."

"He's always been so reliable."

"Not anymore."

"He's . . . under a lot of pressure at school right now. He has a really heavy course load, and he's been staying up late, studying . . ."

"Yeah? Well, that isn't my problem. I'm not his dad. I told him last week that if he didn't shape up, he was out of here, but I guess he didn't believe me. Now he does."

Carly exhaled slowly. "It just sounds so strange," she said unhappily. "I've never had a problem like that with Nick . . . if anything, he's caught *my* slipups . . ."

"You're calling me a liar?"

"Of course not. I just wondered if maybe you make him nervous. He's not used to working with you, and—"

"And he doesn't ever have to work with me again."

"But Rich, we're understaffed! Even with Nick around,

I was spending too much time doing work that we should be paying someone else to do. You have Tracey to assist you in surgery, so firing Nick hardly affects you, but I can't work without a technician I trust."

"You have Pam."

Carly tried to control her frustration. "You know perfectly well that Pam isn't experienced enough to do complex lab work or X rays on her own. I don't have time to supervise her. I want Nick back."

"Forget it."

"Then I want a new technician."

"I'll look around."

A terrible suspicion began to take shape in Carly's mind, and she stared at Richard, searching his face. In the daylight, his tanned skin looked dull and coarse. Had he aged so much over the past few years, she wondered, or had her vision simply improved as she got to know him? The fine, sculpted facial bones were the same, as well as the molded nose and the sun-streaked hair, but the luster that she remembered was gone.

"What?" he asked, drawing himself up under her scrutiny.

Carly shook her head. "Nothing," she said. Richard was selfish, yes, and sometimes petty, but at the heart of it all, he was not malicious. It would be out of character for him to do something as profoundly evil as firing Nick in an attempt to provoke her into quitting. The young man had simply been a casualty of her partner's unpredictable temper.

She took a deep breath. "Give me your word that you'll get someone to replace Nick," she said. "This isn't a luxury, Rich, it's a necessity. If I can't keep up with my schedule, then we'll lose clients, and that means money."

"I said that I'd look around, didn't I?"

"Okay. Good. I'll post an ad—"

"No, I'll do it," he said, and Carly had to be content with that.

"Hello?" Michelle opened the back door of the building and looked cautiously out, clearly expecting to see one or more bodies bleeding on the ground.

"What?" Richard scowled at her.

"Dr. Wexler, your nine o'clock appointment is here," Michelle said formally, wearing her most neutral receptionist face. Carly noticed that he had been demoted from first name status as a result of the Nick episode. Richard didn't seem to care.

"Fine," he said. "I'll be there in a minute." Without looking at Carly, he pushed past Michelle and disappeared into the building.

"Oh, my poor Henry," Pauline sighed as she turned off the flame under the whistling kettle. "That poor saintly man. Did I tell you, Mr. Max, that he put my daughter through beauty school? She owns her own salon now, in Sacramento, and it's all because of Henry."

She poured hot water into a brown teapot, then covered the pot in something that looked to Max like a small patchwork quilt. He looked dubiously at the delicate china cup on the table in front of him.

"And when I needed an operation on my hip—I have terrible problems with my bones, you know—he wouldn't let me go to the HMO doctor. He said, 'Pauline, we can do better for you,' and he found me a famous surgeon. Then I thanked him and said that I couldn't do it because my insurance wouldn't pay for that fancy doctor, but I was sure that the HMO doctor was good enough for me. He wouldn't hear it, though, Mr. Max, and would you believe that he took care of everything? I never even saw a bill. And now my hip is as good as new."

She shook her head. "He never deserved to have something like this happen, never. Will he be all right, do you think?"

"I think so," Max said. He didn't have the heart to say otherwise.

"If you say so, then I'll believe it," Pauline said, and poured tea into his cup. "Some people might not be so glad about that, but I certainly am. Do you take milk or lemon?"

"Milk," Max said. He frowned. The way Pauline had just said *some people* sounded as if she had a specific person in mind.

"So," he said. "You wanted to talk to me about something?"

"Well, yes, I do, and I'm glad that I'm able to. I thought I might not have time, considering all the mess."

"Mess?"

"The mud," Pauline said. "I'm so busy cleaning up mud in the kitchen that I hardly have time to look after the rest of the house, which is a job in itself, you know."

Max nodded. He had come here directly from a series of meetings at Syscom headquarters, and the shift from software technology to kitchen mud felt a little too abrupt. He was not known around the office for his chattiness or his patience, and he now had to make a conscious effort to reach for the latter.

"I'm sure that you're wondering why there's such a problem with the mud," Pauline suggested.

"Yes," Max said. "I was."

"Well, it was never a problem before."

"Before?"

"Miss Martin wants the dogs to spend the day outside in the yard," Pauline said, with a dour look. "It seems to be her opinion that it's better for them to be out there instead of sleeping indoors in the sunroom during the afternoon, which is what they've always done."

"Isn't it good for them to be out in the fresh air?" Max could hardly believe that he was having this conversation.

"Well, maybe it is, and maybe it isn't. I'm just telling you that we've never done it that way before. And now, of course, some of those dogs spend the entire time rolling around in the mud, and then they come inside and make a mess that takes me hours to clean up."

"I see," Max said.

"Of course, Miss Martin is a professional, and she certainly knows more than I do. I've been taking care of this house for twenty years, you know, but I'm sure that it would be better if I just did what she thinks is best."

"I see," Max said again, and took a swallow of his tea. Apparently he had been called in to mediate a power struggle over who had control of Henry's house, and he couldn't think of anything he felt less like doing.

Casting his eyes around the kitchen, he noticed a cocker spaniel, so old that his white coat had turned a dingy yellow, sleeping on the floor of the pantry. "He's not outside."

"He is *too old* to go outside," Pauline said. "Samson never, ever goes outside, except to do his business in the morning and evening. I'm sure that Miss Martin would send even him out for the day, if it wasn't for his cracked rib. It hurts him to walk, poor dear."

"What happened to his rib?"

"Oh, I don't know," Pauline said. "Miss Martin noticed last week that he was limping. Those teenagers who come in to help, you'd think that they would see something like that, but no, they're just rushing in and out. I suppose one of the big dogs was rough with him. Bones break so easily when you're old."

"What about hiring someone to help with the cleaning?" Max suggested. "Now that there's all this extra mud."

Pauline looked shocked. "Bring a stranger into Henry's house?"

"Couldn't one of the teenagers help?"

"Well," Pauline said, "certainly not any of the boys, they're too wild. I can't imagine any of them working in the house, because they would just make a bigger mess, but I suppose that one of the girls might be able to help. I'd have to pay her extra, you know."

"I think that would probably be all right," Max said, fully intending to pay the extra salary himself if necessary. "But you'll have to talk to Carly about it. I'm not in charge of the house. She is."

"Yes, I know. Poor Henry was very generous to her. You know, Mr. Max, I wouldn't want to say anything bad about anyone . . ."

Wouldn't you? Max thought. It was obvious that Pauline didn't want Carly meddling in the affairs of the house, but he guessed that her feelings would mellow after she got used to the changes. But if they didn't, he hoped that she would find someone else to confide in.

Pauline took Max's silence as license to continue. "Well, I've been thinking about poor Henry's accident, and there's something that I just don't understand."

"What?"

"Well, Wednesday is the day that I do my errands, you know. I go to the grocery store last, because I have to come home right away so that the milk won't spoil. I always get back here between six-thirty and seven, then I put away the groceries." She paused, and her chin began to tremble. "Oh," she said, and fished a tissue out of the pocket of her apron and blew her nose. "Excuse me. I just can't help thinking that if only I'd been quicker that day . . ."

She shook her head. "I came in through the back door, and I could hear the TV in the sunroom, so I thought he was watching the news. He always sits in his chair and watches the news until seven. So why would he be off wandering around the house when the news was on?"

Pauline was clearly upset over this deviation from routine, but it seemed like a minor issue to Max, who could think of several hundred reasons why a man might go "wandering" around his own house.

"Maybe he had to go to the bathroom," Max said shortly, hoping she wasn't about to tell him that Henry's bodily functions were also on a strict schedule. He checked his watch, wondering how soon he could politely excuse himself.

Pauline looked mildly offended. "I'm sure that if he did, he would have used the powder room on this floor. His knees have been troubling him, you know. And if he wanted to go upstairs . . . I don't know why he would, but if he did, I don't see why he wouldn't use the elevator like he always does."

"Elevator?" Max said.

"Well, my goodness, you don't think that I go up and

down those steep stairs all day, do you? Henry doesn't either. He hasn't used the stairs in years. We have a little elevator that runs from the butler's pantry. It's been there since the 1930s and it is a bit slow, but very useful."

Max set down his teacup. It did sound strange, he had to admit. If his grandfather had arthritic knees and hadn't used the main staircase in years, why would he have chosen to use it last Wednesday? And how ironic that the decision would have led to an accident that had almost taken his life.

"He must have been feeling better that day," Max said. It was a weak explanation, but how could anyone know what Henry had been thinking? It occurred to Max that the minor details of his own life would probably look odd and inconsistent to a stranger who was trying to analyze them for meaning.

"I just don't understand it," Pauline said again. "I wish I'd been here. You should talk to Miss Martin and see what she has to say about all of this. Maybe she knows something."

"Why would she know anything?"

"Well, she was here, you know."

"No," Max said. "I don't know. What do you mean, she was here? When was she here?"

"The day of the accident. You didn't know that she was here that afternoon? Hmm." Pauline nodded as if he had confirmed something.

This was all news to Max, who was sure that Carly had never mentioned being at the house on the day of the accident. "What time was she here?"

"Oh, I don't know, exactly," Pauline said. "I never saw

her because I was out all afternoon doing my errands. But Henry was expecting her at about five-thirty."

"And you came home and found him when?"

"I came home just before seven, then I was in the kitchen for about twenty minutes. It takes a long time for me to put things away without anyone to help me, you know, so I didn't go looking for poor Henry until it was much too late. I didn't hear a thing, or I would have come right away."

"It's not your fault," Max said. "It's a big house. And for all we know, he could have fallen before you came home."

"I do wonder about that. It seems to me that if I had been here, I would have heard some noise from such a terrible accident. My hearing is very good."

Max was not surprised by this. He would have bet that she knew everything that happened within the Tremayne walls.

"And another thing, Mr. Max. If I had been here, and there was something that he needed from upstairs, don't you think that he would have called me to get it for him? I can't imagine what got into him to make him try to go rushing up or down those stairs."

Max shook his head. He had no answers.

"Maybe," Pauline suggested slyly, "Miss Martin would know."

"Maybe," Max said. He made a mental note to ask Carly about her visit that day. Apparently, she had been the last person to see Henry before he fell. Perhaps she knew something that could shed some light on his odd behavior.

CHAPTER 12

———— •◆• ————

After almost four months of living in San Francisco, Max had learned that there was no way to predict the local traffic patterns, other than to make one basic assumption: If it was daylight, then the Bay Bridge would be crowded. Today was no exception, and Max braced himself as Carly floored the gas pedal and deftly scooted her VW into the far-left lane, right behind the thundering wheels of a massive black semi truck.

"We're making good time!" Carly exclaimed loudly, over the noise.

Max resisted the urge to close his eyes. It was a testament to German engineering, he thought, that the rickety hatchback had not yet disintegrated into a jumbled heap of auto parts. Judging from the violence of the vibrations coming through the passenger seat, it was only a matter of time. He just hoped that it wouldn't happen while they were doing eighty in the fast lane.

It was Sunday, a rare fogless afternoon in the city, and as they sped across the bridge, he could see as far as the

Oakland hills. He had no clear idea of how he had ended up in Carly's car, headed north to Davis to have dinner with her family. He didn't think that he had ever actually agreed to go with her, but somehow it had happened, and now he was trapped. The invitation had surprised and confounded him, and despite Carly's efforts to explain that it was no big deal, that the Martins always had guests for Sunday dinner, he felt uneasy. He didn't understand why she had chosen him to be her guest. It wasn't as if he had been nice to her.

It was possible, he thought, that she was trying to put him under some kind of emotional obligation. They had not discussed the Tremayne mansion since the previous week, but if she was afraid that he still intended to take her to court, she might see this as a strategic move. If so, she could save herself the effort. He had intentionally put the topic on hold, and he was biding his time until there was a clearer indication of whether or not Henry would recover. If he did regain consciousness, there would be no need for a legal fight. And if he didn't . . . Max narrowed his eyes. Whatever happened, he would never allow his personal feelings about Carly Martin—whatever they might be—to keep him from doing what he had to do.

He shifted in the small seat, wishing for more leg room. Wishing, actually, for his own car. It didn't feel right to sit in anyone's passenger seat, and he missed the sleek, intimidating weight of his Jaguar. He hadn't been in a car like Carly's since he was sixteen, and that wasn't a time in his life that he cared to recall.

He opened his window, wanting to feel the wind on his face.

"Max," Carly said, "you aren't worried about meeting

my family, are you? This is just a casual thing. It'll be fun."

"I'm not worried," he muttered.

"You're being very quiet. Maybe I shouldn't have told you so much about them. I guess they do sound kind of weird."

"They sound fine," he said shortly. He frowned out the window, wishing that he hadn't come. He hated meeting new people, and he was annoyed that he had allowed himself to be talked into this. He had the edgy feeling of being a kid again, buckled into the front seat of yet another social worker's cheap car, on his way to yet another foster home. The old emotions were still tangible—hope and fear, clashing to form the dull alloy of resignation. The first night was always the worst, when he lay in the new bed, huddled in blankets thick with the smell of an unfamiliar house, listening to the night noises of strangers.

Whenever he met a new set of foster siblings, Max would look each one straight in the eye, daring them to stare back, daring them to say out loud what they already knew about him. But he wasn't the only hardened kid around, and it didn't always work.

We heard you got your mama's name cause you don't know who your daddy is. Your mama's a drunk. We heard she passed out in the store on her way to get another bottle.

Even now, as an adult, if he was caught in the wrong mood, meeting a roomful of new faces still brought on a cold sweat. But the difference was that now he had the talisman of wealth surrounding him, the strongest magic available for creating instant acceptance.

"My family is going to love you," Carly said firmly. He

glanced at her. Was it his imagination, or did her enthusiasm sound a little forced? He shifted in his seat again. Actually, he thought, her family would not love him. Not a bit. And that was fine with him. It was not a question of love, anyway. It was a question of respect. He definitely would have preferred to arrive in his own car.

Carly's parents lived about an hour's drive northeast of San Francisco, near the Davis campus of the University of California, where her father taught botany to undergraduates. They had an old ranch-style house on five acres of land that bordered a creek called Putah, and Max, who had never considered living anywhere that wasn't within walking distance of a Starbucks, was favorably impressed. They had olive trees and grapevines growing behind the house, and beyond the mowed and watered lawn area was a large meadow of knee-high grass speckled with native wildflowers.

"Nobody, and I mean nobody, touches my meadow," Mr. Martin said, as he walked Max through the field, pointing out—with a professor's enthusiasm for Latin names—the various plants he had raised from wild-grown seed. "It was a tomato farm back in '63 when we bought the place. Tomatoes!" He snorted. "The soil was stripped, a wasteland. You should see what they do to the fields here in the valley, son. Not that I have anything against agriculture. I like a store-bought vegetable as much as the next man, but the spraying, the spraying! Nature is resilient, Max, but by God, she has her limits."

Max's well-developed survival instincts had enabled him to pass judgment on the Martins within five minutes

of arrival. They were all crazy—but they were friendly.
Which was good, because there were a lot of them.

Carly had introduced him to the mass of adults, children, cats, and dogs present, and every introduction
seemed to be along the lines of: "This is Chris, who was
Dad's student, and dated Jeannie—my sister, that's her
husband Mark—but now he's married to Cathy, who went
to vet school with me, and their daughter—Heather, she's
thirteen—is best friends with my youngest sister Anna,
over there."

There was no apparent distinction between blood relatives, adopted relatives, in-laws and family friends, and
Max was taken aback by the noisy conviviality of the
group. It was difficult to get a word in edgewise, and he
didn't even try, preferring to listen and watch as he
processed the scene.

Rather than sticking by his side, Carly had turned him
loose as soon as they arrived, as if his welfare was now a
family responsibility. She did seem to be keeping an eye
on him, though, as if she feared that he might suddenly
become overwhelmed and bolt for the hills.

He watched her covertly, as well. She was in her ele-
ment, surrounded by her own people, and as Max saw her
laughing with her sisters at some private joke, he felt an
unexpected stab of envy. In the same way that his Jaguar
and his Park Avenue apartment were luxuries backed by
his bank balance, he thought, Carly's belief in the world's
basic goodness was a luxury backed by this group. They
had raised her to know that she would always be safe and
loved, and Max had the sudden feeling that no matter how
rich he became, Carly Martin's personal fortune would always be larger and longer-lasting than his own.

Dinner was potluck, served buffet style from a cluttered table set up on the lawn next to an arbor knotted with grapevines. Carly's thirteen-year-old sister Anna handed him a plate and trailed him as he approached the table. He cast an eye over the collection of food and picked up a serving spoon, about to break the crust of the nearest casserole.

"Stop!" Anna exclaimed suddenly. It was the first thing she had said to him since he arrived, although she had been hovering near him for some time, gazing at him with a fascination that he found unnerving.

Max paused, the serving spoon in his hand, and looked down at her. "What?"

"Put down the spoon," Anna said. "You don't want to eat that. Trust me."

The dish in question appeared to be an innocent mixture of baked pasta and vegetables. Max frowned. "Why not?"

Anna glanced from side to side and leaned toward him. "Carly made it," she said in a low, meaningful voice.

Max raised his eyebrows. "Is that a bad thing?"

"Oh, my God," Anna said. "How long have you known my sister?"

"Not long," Max said.

Anna nodded. "It isn't that Carly *can't* cook," she explained. "It's that she won't. Make normal food, I mean. And it's getting worse. Last week she brought this thing called 'nut loaf,' which was supposed to be like meat loaf, except—"

"No meat?" Max asked.

"Right. It was made with, like, soybeans, and peanut butter and stuff, and it had this tomato ketchup sauce—"

Max recoiled. "I get it."

Anna gestured toward the casserole dish. "That's called 'tofu surprise.' It's very, very healthy. Do you want to know what's in it?"

"No," Max said. He put down the spoon. "Thanks."

Anna smiled sweetly. "I didn't think so," she said. "Mark is almost done cooking the hot dogs. I'll bring you one when they're ready."

It took four folding dining tables, pushed together into a long, wobbly rectangle, to accommodate the group. Max was ushered into a chair directly opposite Carly's father, which, he was told, was the seat of honor. He soon learned that the "honor" involved being the designated audience for Professor Martin's steady stream of stories and bad puns. More than once, he caught Carly watching him with an expression very similar to the one he had seen on her face when Lola the Great Dane had pinned him to the wall.

None of it was remotely like anything that Max had experienced before. He had arrived expecting a variation on the usual theme, where he would sit politely, eat politely and—as soon as possible—leave politely, all the while fending off nosy questions about his family, his alma mater, his net worth, and his politics. But now here he was, dropped like a paratrooper into the wilds of a foreign country, surrounded by this huge, rowdy tribe of people who seemed to be too busy enjoying themselves to care where he'd gone to school or which fork he used for his salad. They told him jokes, brought him plates of food, and asked him for his opinions on everything from the stock market to whether or not lizards made good pets.

By all rights, he should have hated it. Their closeness

should have amplified his own sense of being an outsider, but, strangely, it had the opposite effect. The Martins were like a weird vortex of happiness, drawing him in, and as the evening lengthened, his resistance began to weaken. He began to relax—slowly, cautiously—in the warmth of their easy acceptance, and found that he was not having a bad time. They made him feel almost as if he belonged there, a part of their ragtag family group.

Belonged there? The thought was absurd enough to snap Max out his strange trance. He pushed his chair back from the table and folded his arms against his chest. *Illusion*, he said coldly to himself. *And it won't do you any good to forget that.* The Martins were not elegant people, but they had a refined social grace of their own. They were skilled hosts and knew how to make a stranger feel comfortable; but it would be an idiot's mistake to confuse the rituals of politeness with genuine acceptance.

His cell phone rang, sounding a sharp tone that turned a few surprised looks toward him. He reached for it immediately. He was not normally in the habit of answering calls in the middle of meals, but in this case, etiquette had to take a backseat to the possibility of news from the hospital.

It was Henry's doctor calling, and Max was glad for the excuse to leave the table. He stood up, and walked toward the Martins' olive grove to take the call.

CHAPTER 13

Carly caught Max's eye as he stood up, and mouthed *hospital*? to him. He nodded and walked away. He looked tense, she thought, but it was hard to infer anything from that, since he usually looked tense. She wondered if he had always been that way, and thought not. Darkness sat familiarly, but not naturally, on him, and Carly remembered the few times that she had seen him laugh. It was wonderful to watch his guarded expression lift like a theater curtain, flashing a glimpse of a very different Max Giordano in the wings.

"His grandfather is very sick," she said to the group at the table, for the benefit of anyone who didn't already know. The Martins were far too good-natured to be offended by Max's abrupt exit, but Carly didn't want anyone thinking that he was carelessly rude.

"I hope it's good news," Jeannie said sympathetically. It was clear that she liked Max, and that she had been pleasantly surprised when he had turned out to be nothing like the typical lost cause that Carly usually brought home.

Max wasn't a typical anything, Carly thought. He was being extremely quiet, but that was a normal reaction to a first encounter with the Martin family. Even so, there was an arresting intensity about him that drew the focus of the group. Carly hadn't missed the fact that her mother and sisters, all the way down to thirteen-year-old Anna, were practically flirting with him. It was harmless and cheerful, a gesture of appreciation for this handsome stranger in their midst, and Max had seemed flattered, though somewhat stunned by all the attention.

She looked toward the olive grove and decided to go and check on him.

He was standing under the canopy of branches, rolling a tiny green olive between his fingers.

"Hello," she said as she approached. "Do you like olives?"

He looked up. "I've never seen them on a tree. I thought they grew in jars."

His face was such a deadpan that it took Carly a few seconds to realize that he was joking. She smiled. "I'm sure you've seen an olive tree before."

"Nope. In my old neighborhood in Brooklyn, the only green plants were the dandelions in the sidewalk cracks. You wouldn't have liked it much."

"It doesn't sound like a very healthy environment for a kid."

He shrugged. "Kids adapt to almost anything. They're like little weeds themselves. If all you've got is a crack in the pavement, you put down your root and do your damnedest to bloom. You don't cry for things you don't know about."

"You do seem to be blooming."

He nodded. "I'm a tough weed."

"Was there news about Henry?"

"Improvement in his reflexes. They're falling all over themselves to warn me that it might not mean anything, but I get the impression that it's a good sign."

"Oh, Max, that is good news! I'm glad."

He frowned slightly at her. "If that's true, then you're a very unusual person."

"I like happy endings. What's so unusual about that?"

"Not everyone in your position would consider my grandfather's recovery to be a happy ending." He held up his hand. "I'm not being confrontational. I know that you care about him, and I'm actually beginning to believe that your saintly priorities are genuine. Unusual but genuine. I'm not going to apologize for being skeptical. You may be good at idealism, Carly, but I consider it a luxury I can't afford."

Carly smiled ruefully. "Some pair we are. You're suspicious and cynical, and I'm naive and dopey. I guess we could both stand to move a little more toward the center."

"Maybe. For the record, though, I don't think you're dopey."

She laughed. "You're not arguing with naive?"

"Live and learn. I'd call you lucky not to have gotten those lessons too soon."

He said it simply, but Carly heard something in his voice that reminded her of standing with him in Henry's dining room. *You don't know me, Grandpa, but I'm the product of Alan's affair with a boozed-up cocktail wait-*

ress. Those were not the words of a man who had enjoyed a sheltered childhood. She thought of the gray tomcat who lived in the tiny park across the street from her apartment. He had a torn ear, a knobby tail, and a body roughened from years of scrounging and fighting. She had finally convinced him to show up for a bowl of food in the evenings, but he kept a wary eye on her while he ate, and never let her touch him. She thought that perhaps he had some things in common with the man who stood before her. Max was a well-groomed stray, but fighting scars were not always so visible.

It was hard for Carly to imagine an existence like Max's: solitary as a satellite, without a single family tie. And he did not strike her as the kind of person who collected friends. What did you do without anyone to support you, to praise you, to love you?

He was running his fingers absently over the bark of the olive tree, and Carly could see by his expression that his thoughts were far away. His face was almost noble, she thought. The strong, square bones and long, slightly arched nose were as much old Rome as they were Brooklyn.

Someone who knew and loved Alan Tremayne might have found character in his face, but judging from what Carly had seen in the portrait, Alan had been a very average young man, with mousy hair and a face—perhaps already softened by alcoholism—that retained a child's lack of definition. He had the kind of generic fraternity-boy look that populated a thousand campuses, and aside from the eerily identical gray eyes, Max seemed to have nothing at all in common with his father. In every way that

Alan was bland, Carly thought, Max was fierce. She guessed that his mother had been a very beautiful woman.

But genes alone did not build a face like Max Giordano's. It was his own life that had added the angry pride, the guarded eyes, the . . . weariness? It was difficult for Carly to imagine weakness of any kind in a man who was so vigorously alive, but now that she was getting to know him better, she could sense something more subtle in him, something that seemed akin to a soldier's exhaustion after years and years of war. She didn't understand what Max's war was for, or why he felt a need to fight, but it seemed to her to be a deeply difficult way to live.

She had the sudden urge to reach for him, to take him in her arms and cradle his dark head against her. She wanted to stroke his hair and try to make him feel safe enough to realize that sometimes war was a choice, and not an inevitability.

But she stayed where she was. As she had learned from the gray tomcat, fighters and strays did not take kindly to sudden moves.

"Max," she said gently, "Henry is my friend, so of course I care about him. But I also care about you."

He looked coolly at her. "That's hard to swallow," he said. "You barely know me."

Carly nodded. "That's true. I don't know much about you, but even I can tell that you're badly in need of a family. I don't like the idea of you being alone in the world. It isn't healthy."

"If I'm going to have a family, Henry Tremayne is it," Max said. "Unless you're telling me that I should start one of my own."

"Well," Carly said, startled, "I didn't exactly mean—"

"It's the logical step at this point in my life. Unfortunately, I don't have a good candidate to play Eve to my Adam. My current girlfriend is not the maternal type."

"You have a girlfriend?"

"In New York."

"She didn't want to come out here with you?"

Max shrugged. "Nina's a well-known fashion editor. She wouldn't like it here."

"Oh," Carly said.

"Anyway, I didn't ask her to come."

"Oh," she said again, pleased.

"What about you, Carly? While we're getting personal, tell me about your plans to start a family."

"Me? I have a family."

"That's true. But you probably don't always want to be cuddling nieces and nephews. What about children of your own? Don't you want any?"

Carly was shocked by the question. "I want kids more than anything," she said. As the statement left her mouth, she knew that despite what she had asserted to Jeannie about being too busy to reproduce, it was the truth. She couldn't imagine any other way to live.

"And yet you're not married, either. It's been over a year since you ended your relationship with Wexler, but you don't even date?"

"I do so date," she said, stung.

"You spend your days taking care of other people's pets, and your nights . . . doing what? Imagining happy endings for Henry and me? What about your own happy ending?"

"Max Giordano, how did you manage to turn this around on me?"

His mouth curved dryly. "Years of practice."

Carly took a breath. "I maintain that you need a family, Max—and I actually do have an offer in mind."

That caught his attention. He looked sharply at her. "What offer?"

She felt her face getting warm. He thought that she was offering herself as his Eve. It was a startling idea, and, she had to admit, an appealing one. She tried to imagine what he would be like as a husband and father, with his fierceness channeled toward loving and protecting a tribe of his own.

"I . . . meant that I have a family to offer you. My family, I mean. They like you very much, Max. We adopt all kinds of people, in case you didn't notice, and we think that you should be an honorary Martin."

"I see," Max said, and was silent for a long moment.

Carly felt anxious. "If you want to, that is," she amended. "I'm not sure if being Martinized is an honor or a punishment, but it does come with a promise of regular meals, and there's always someone willing to come and fix a broken water pipe at 3 A.M., although I suppose that isn't too useful for someone like you."

Max held up his hand, and she stopped. "Thanks," he said, in an oddly flat voice. "But I'm past adoptive age."

"Oh, we don't think so," Carly said quickly. "We need you. Dad already has you slated to play bass broom in his jug band act for the Davis talent show. Me, I'm planning to be stuck in bed with a terrible flu that day, like I am every year."

Abruptly, Max cleared his throat and turned to look out toward the distant hills. Carly felt the withdrawal keenly and wondered if she had offended him. Maybe she had been too pushy; he was the kind of man who wouldn't appreciate being reminded of his weaknesses. Or perhaps it was that he didn't like her family, and she had put him in the awkward position of having to come up with a polite refusal.

She was about to apologize when Max turned back to face her. His eyes seemed strangely bright, almost luminous. "Why the hell are you doing this?" he demanded.

Taken aback, she could only stare at him. "Doing what?" she asked, finally.

"Being nice to me. Bringing me to meet your family. Telling me that you people want to *adopt* me. What is this, Carly? And don't give me any bullshit about caring about me. I want the truth."

"Okay," Carly said slowly. The truth was that she did care about him, not so much for what he had shown her, but for what she sensed was hidden in him. But such an apparently flimsy explanation was not likely to register with Max as the "truth" that he wanted. What, then, should she say?

"Do you believe in instinct?" she asked.

"Animal instinct?"

"The human version. Gut feelings."

"Yes. I consider that a basic survival skill."

Carly nodded. "So what would you say if I told you that my gut feeling tells me that you are not as bad a guy as you make yourself out to be?"

Max grinned unexpectedly. "I would say that any woman who got herself into a relationship with Richard Wexler should be very wary of her gut feelings."

"Very funny," Carly said coldly. "For your information, it was *ignoring* my instincts that got me into that mess, and I don't intend to make that mistake again. Look, Max. I like you. The Martins like you. I don't have any better way to say it, and you probably wouldn't believe me if I tried. Why are you looking at me like that?"

"You *like* me?" he repeated disdainfully.

"Is that so hard to believe?"

"Yes. What happens if my grandfather dies, Carly? What if we end up in a legal fight over his house? I might not turn out to be very likable at all. Would I still be an honorary Martin? My guess is no. So I would be more careful with my offer of family if I were you. You may not take it seriously, but I do."

"Oh, dear," Carly said. "Max, I understand what Henry's house means to you. And despite what you think, I don't want to take it away from you. But you need to understand what it means to me. This animal shelter is Henry's dream. If I sold the house and let your grandfather's dream die, I would be betraying his trust in me. Please don't ask me to do that."

Max folded his arms against his chest and looked away. He said nothing for a long time, and Carly grew restless. Finally, she braced herself. "There's something else I want to say."

He looked at her, eyebrows slightly raised, and she took a quick breath and continued. "I've been thinking a lot about this—yes, Max, I really have—and it seems to me that if Henry had known how important the mansion is to you, he never would have set up the trust the way he did. He probably thought he was helping you by not saddling you with that gloomy old house. It's the animal shelter that matters to him, not where it's located."

"What are you saying?" Max asked tightly.

"I'm saying that if Henry . . . doesn't recover, would you consider using some of your own money, along with Henry's endowment, to build and fund a new facility to be the Tremayne Center for Animal Rehabilitation?"

"And if I did that? You would sell me the house?"

"No," Carly said. "I would give it to you."

He stared at her as if she'd gone insane. "You can't be serious," he said.

She shrugged. "I am."

"I don't see what's in it for you."

"Are you kidding? A job running an incredible program like Henry's? My God, Max. It would be everything I ever dreamed of. Henry knew that."

"Most people dream of having 20 million dollars."

"Yes," Carly said patiently. "People dream of having 20 million dollars so that they can spend their lives doing exactly what they want. And I want to be a vet with my own practice. Anyway, it isn't as if I could just sell your grandfather's house and pocket the cash. The foundation has to go somewhere. Henry didn't really leave me a house, he left me a *job*. Isn't this making any sense to you?"

"No," Max said. He closed his eyes and reached up to rub his forehead as if it ached. "Maybe. I don't know."

"Well, think about it, at least."

He lowered his hands and exhaled slowly, almost angrily. "Think about it," he repeated. "*Think* about it? I have been in this world for almost forty goddamned years, and this is not the way it works."

Carly shrugged. "Maybe the world is bigger than you think."

He shook his head. "Happy endings," he muttered.

She smiled at him. "Why not?"

"Why not? That's a hell of a question to ask me, of all people. Don't get me started."

"Oh, Max," Carly said. She felt a mixture of sympathy and exasperation as she looked at him. It was almost as if she could see his mind working through all the possible ways that she could be trying to trick him. "There's no need to make a decision now. Are you having a good time here? You seemed to be enjoying yourself at dinner."

He looked startled by the question. "I'm fine," he said.

"Well then, why don't you accept the offer of family, at least. We won't revoke it. And I think that you and I can work out this issue of the house in a way that is acceptable to everyone."

"You think so," he said.

"Yes," Carly said seriously. "Remember, you and I both love Henry, and that means that we're on the same team."

Max's mouth curved disbelievingly, and he began to shake his head. "Carly . . ." he began, then stopped. He gazed at her, his eyes narrowed thoughtfully, and she felt him assessing her.

She stuck out her hand. "Don't worry. It will be okay. Friends?"

"Friends," he said slowly, as if he were testing the word. He reached out, and Carly felt his fingers close around hers. And then he stunned her by turning her hand over and raising it to his lips. The hot imprint of his mouth on her palm was a shock that shuddered through her body. It was like nothing she had ever felt before. Desire, as she had always understood it, was a pleasant but awkward feeling that sometimes appeared on its own and sometimes needed to be summoned up with a little willpower. But this was different. This was a tidal wave, an onslaught so overwhelming that she could only think of it as a force of nature.

He released her, and she pulled her hand back, curling it closed as if she had been burned. Her heart was beating fast, and her fingers retained the feeling of the curve of his jaw and the bristle of his skin. She looked down at her hand, then up at Max, speechless.

His eyes held hers. "Carly," he said, "if you really are who you seem to be, then I hope that this world never gives you a reason to stop looking for happy endings."

CHAPTER 14

————— ◆•◆ —————

"Zees cat, what can I do? He ees lunatique!" The French girl displayed her scratched and bleeding forearms to Carly. "I am supposed to care for ze children, not for zees animal stupide. I hate zees job."

The "animal stupide" was the fattest Persian cat that Carly had ever seen, weighing in at a stunning twenty-five pounds. Somewhere between the scale and the exam room, he had broken away from the young nanny, and—moving with astonishing speed for such a rotund creature—made a dash for freedom that ended with him wedged into the small corner space between the waiting-room couch and the magazine rack. It was a well-fortified position, and the nanny had spent the past ten minutes on the floor, cursing in French, alternately trying to coax and drag the growling cat out.

It was five-thirty, and the only other occupant of the waiting room was an elderly man with an equally elderly dachshund, neither of whom seemed fazed by the escapee drama.

"I queet," said the nanny tearfully. "I queet all of zees. I want to go home."

"No, no," Carly said. "It'll be okay. Here, sit down and let me try. What's his name?"

"Preencess."

"His name is Princess?"

"Oui." The nanny rolled her eyes and gave a dramatic Gallic shrug.

"That explains why he's so pissed off," Carly muttered, hunkering down to peer under the couch. "Kitty, kitty . . . ?"

Two unblinking eyes in a flat white face glared out from the shadowed corner. "Poor kitty," Carly said soothingly. "Poor nice kitty. Here, nice kitty, we aren't going to hurt you, but we do need to give you a checkup so that we can keep you healthy and . . . ow!"

"He ees a bad cat," said the nanny from behind her.

"He's a little upset," Carly said, sitting up. Thin lines of blood were forming on her wrist. "Well, so much for sweet talk. Michelle, will you buzz Brian in the lab and have him get the gloves and come out here?"

Brian was the new technician, Nick's replacement, and Carly was still astonished that the previous week's confrontation with Richard had actually produced results. After their argument, he hadn't said another word about the issue, and Carly had come to work on Monday morning resigned to the necessity of confronting him again. But before she could open her mouth, he had handed her three résumés as if the whole thing had been his own idea. Brian was the best of the lot; a shy kid with a bad complexion, an endearing smile, and several years of experience at the city SPCA. He had started that morning, and so far, things were working out well.

With Brian's assistance, Princess's checkup concluded smoothly, and Carly was washing her hands when she heard Michelle on the intercom. "Carly, there's a call for you on line one. It's Max Giordano."

Max. She hurried to pick up the receiver. "Hello?"

"You're putting in a long day," he said, and the sound of his voice was enough to make her heart give a little jump.

She glanced at the clock and saw that it was almost six-thirty. "I'm sorry," she said. "Are you at the house? It's been the usual chaos around here. I'm finishing up now, so I'll be there in about twenty minutes. The dogs must be starving."

"Nope. I fed them. The cats, too."

"You fed the pets?"

"Even lacking an advanced degree," Max said dryly, "I managed."

"Thank you," she said, surprised. "That was nice of you."

"Not so nice. They were giving me funny looks."

"Sad and hungry?"

"Speculative and hungry. Like they were calculating portion sizes if they divided me up."

She laughed. "That, I don't believe. You would be more likely to eat one of them."

"That's right. And they had better remember it."

"I was thinking about where we should eat," Carly said, trying to sound casual. After Sunday night, she had been trying to come up with a way to see him again without looking obvious, but he had saved her the trouble. On

Monday afternoon, he had called and asked if she was free for dinner on Tuesday. She was, and she had spent the time in between thinking of little else. She wouldn't have admitted it to anyone, but yesterday evening, she had cleaned her apartment, washed her hair, and stocked her refrigerator with everything that she needed to make Perfect Pasta Parmesan, on page 78 of her new Italian cookbook.

She took a breath. "It's getting a little late, though, so maybe we should just skip the restaurant. I could make us dinner at my place, if you don't mind something simple."

"Fine," Max said. "I'll meet you there. Twenty minutes, you said?"

"Um . . . give me thirty." It was a longer drive to her apartment from the clinic than from Henry's house, but if she hurried and took her secret shortcut, she could get back in time to jump in the shower and put on her new dress. She had found it that day during her lunch break, at a boutique just down the street from the clinic. Even on sale, it had been too expensive, but she had tried it on anyway, then had been unable to resist buying it. It was black, slinky, and sophisticated, sort of a New York look. It was exactly what she wanted, and she couldn't wait for Max's reaction when he saw her in it.

"Half an hour," he agreed, and to Carly, that statement held all the promise in the world.

As it turned out, the city was repairing a water main on Carly's shortcut, and by the time she navigated her way home, Max was waiting outside her front door. He was dressed casually, for him, in a lightweight gray sweater and black pants, and she felt a jolt of excitement as his eyes met hers.

"Sorry," she said, feeling suddenly shy, and painfully aware of her crumpled T-shirt and smudged makeup. "I forgot to tell you that I keep a spare key in the flowerpot."

"You have bars on your windows, but you keep a key in the flowerpot? That makes sense."

"The landlord put bars there, I didn't. I don't have anything worth stealing, as you've seen. Come on in."

Inside her apartment, he glanced around curiously. "It looks different in here."

"Does it?" Carly said innocently. It was a bad sign when a simple cleaning job provoked this kind of reaction. "Would you like something to drink?"

"Water."

"Fizzy or plain? There's also iced tea . . ." She stopped herself. Her refrigerator was now stocked with an assortment of drinks, and she suddenly wondered if she was overdoing it. The whole idea had been to make her offer to cook dinner appear spontaneous, but it didn't take a genius to notice that she was suddenly very prepared to receive a guest. *Well*, she thought, *so what? Men like it when women make the first move.* She had read that in *Cosmopolitan*, although she was afraid that it might only be true for the *Cosmo* cover models, who only had to smile in a certain way to give the impression that they were making a move. In her own case . . . well, it seemed a lot less certain. And the fact remained that she smelled like a farm.

She sighed and turned to Max. "Would you mind if I abandoned you for a few minutes? I'm going to shower and change. The kitchen is there—obviously—so just help yourself to whatever you want. I'll be right back."

She hurried into her bedroom and closed the door behind her. This was not how she had envisioned the beginning of the evening, she thought, frustrated. In her fantasy, there had been soft music, candlelight, and the enticing aroma of Perfect Pasta Parmesan to greet Max when he arrived. She had intended to open the door looking ravishing, or at least clean, then to slowly seduce him with food and conversation until he was overwhelmed by her feminine charms and unable to resist the desire to sweep her into his arms. That was how it was *supposed* to be, but thanks to Princess *le chat lunatique*, the Department of Public Works, and the general fickleness of fortune, she was locked in the bathroom while Max Giordano—who had most recently dated a sophisticated New York fashion editor—was probably sitting on her couch, wondering what the hell he was doing there.

This might be a good time, Carly thought dismally as she stepped into the shower, *to cut my losses*. She could climb out of the window and run away. Max would eventually get bored and leave, and then she could move on with her life and try to forget that she had ever been interested in the kind of man who could get a last-minute dinner reservation in San Francisco.

CHAPTER 15

Max was sitting on the couch, wondering what the hell he was doing there. Being in Carly's apartment made him feel as if the rest of his life took place in a different galaxy, rather than just across the city, and the sense of disassociation made him uneasy.

He drummed his fingers on his thigh and looked around. He had missed his run today, and his excess energy needed an outlet. He stood up, walked the five steps required to get to Carly's kitchen, and opened her refrigerator, looking for some kind of distraction.

By the time Carly reappeared, almost twenty minutes had passed, and Max was engrossed in chopping and adding fresh parsley to the pasta sauce now simmering on the old electric stove.

"You're cooking," she said, and it sounded like an accusation.

He looked up and did a double take. Her hair was loose, cascading over her shoulders, and she was wearing a short, tight, black dress made of some silky fabric that plunged low in the front, exposing the generous swell of her breasts. It was the kind of dress that invited the observer to imagine removing it, and it was such a startling contrast to Carly's usual style that Max found himself momentarily speechless.

She smiled shyly at him. "Even though we're staying here for dinner, I thought I would dress up a little."

Don't you mean undress a little? Max thought, and had to look away. The sight of her sent a shock of desire through him, and for some reason, that made him angry. Was she trying to provoke him? If so, she was doing a good job, but he didn't appreciate it. Taking Carly to bed would be playing with fire, and he was the one likely to get burned. Something strange and profound had happened to him on Sunday in the Martins' olive grove. Carly had looked at him with her clear blue eyes, and he had— for one brief moment—forgotten that he was alone in the world. It was like an old sports injury, so familiar that he no longer noticed the dull aching . . . until it stopped. And when it had resumed, not long after he had returned to his silent hotel suite, the new awareness was no blessing.

His fingers tightened around the handle of the wooden spoon. Carly's perfect little bubble of familial love would always protect her from the fallout of an affair gone wrong. He had no such buffer. With Nina, and the other women he had dated, he could handle the risk. But with Carly? He shook his head. No. Some things were better left alone.

"Is something wrong?" Carly asked.

"Nope," Max said flatly. "I hope you don't mind that I started dinner."

"Uh . . . no. Not at all. I see that you found everything that you need. It's sort of a Parmesan sauce you're making?"

"It *is* a Parmesan sauce."

"Right. Well. It's been a while since I went to the store, but I usually have the basic ingredients lying around. You never know when you might want to toss together some pasta."

Max didn't answer. She had apparently forgotten, but on the kitchen table, her copy of *100 Easy Italian Recipes* was bookmarked at page 78 with a grocery store receipt from the previous night.

"I didn't know you could cook," Carly said.

"I can't cook," Max said. "But I can put things together in a pan and stir. And then pour the results over a plate of pasta. It's a survival skill. Most men have it."

"Oh, survival. I see. It's not cooking, it's just stirring stuff in a pan. A macho thing, kind of like bricklaying."

"Right."

"Except for one thing . . ." A mischievous note crept into her voice. "When I came in, you were chopping parsley, and I saw you using the knife with both hands, doing that quick rocking motion . . . you know?"

"So?"

"So that's a chef move. Nobody who doesn't cook chops like that. You know exactly what you're doing. Somebody taught you your way around a kitchen, and I dare you to deny it."

He didn't. "My grandmother taught me. I also make a good lasagna, but she died before we got to the gnocchi. That old lady knew her gnocchi, too. Best I've ever tasted."

Carly didn't bother to hide her surprise. "When was that?"

"A long time ago."

"How old were you?"

"Eight. Ten. I lived with her on and off when I was a kid. My mother would leave me there for a few months at a time while she went off to do whatever it was she did. Drink, mostly. Then she would show up one day to pick me up, and they'd spend an hour screaming at each other. My mother kept threatening never to come back, but you can't argue with free child care."

"Oh," Carly said in consternation, and Max took note of the expression on her face. This wasn't even one of the bad stories, and he wondered how she would react to some of the uglier realities of his past. Better not to find out, he thought. She was indeed naive about some things—perhaps innocent would be a better word—and there would be nothing admirable in shattering her belief that the world was a basically good place.

"When did she die?"

"I don't know," Max said, and saw that he would have to explain. "Sometime before I turned twelve. I only found out she was gone when the social worker showed up."

"To tell you?"

She still didn't understand. "No," he said. "To take me. My grandmother wasn't around anymore, so my mother put me into foster care."

Carly quietly pulled out one of the wooden chairs beside the kitchen table and sat down. "I see," she said. "I didn't know that. I had the idea that you had lived with your mother the whole time."

"No. She couldn't handle me, especially when I got older. Christ, by then, she was drinking all the time, and she couldn't even handle herself."

"Who did you live with?" She looked anxious, as if it made some difference now.

"I ended up in a lot of homes. None of them lasted very long. I turned into a problem kid when I got into my teens, so it was as much my fault as anybody's." *In some cases*, he thought. *But not all.*

She seemed to sense that he was holding back. "I know a little about foster homes from our experiences with adopting my brothers and sisters. There are a lot of kids out there, of course, and I started to hear some of the stories . . ." A shadow crossed her face, and she looked sad. "Some of the situations were not as good as ours."

That was putting it mildly. "That's true," he said.

"Did something bad happen to you?"

"Nothing specific," Max said carefully, thinking of the afternoon he had spent huddled under a bed in a house in a nice suburb of New York City, listening to his latest foster father beat the hell out of his latest foster mother. He had knocked her to the floor, kicking her in the ribs and stomach as he screamed at her, and in between bouts, as she lay there curled up and sobbing, she had seen Max in his hiding place. Her eyes had dully registered his presence, then she had turned her head away. Not a word was ever spoken about it. If he were making a list of bad things, he thought now, that day would be on it.

"Max," Carly said suddenly. "You don't drink, do you?"

"Not unless I'm thirsty." The pasta water was boiling, and he added the noodles.

"I meant alcohol, wise guy. I can't believe it took me so long to notice. The other night, when we were at Mistral, I had wine with my dinner, but you drank Perrier. And you didn't touch Dad's homebrew, either. I thought that some kind soul had warned you against it, but I'll bet that you just don't drink."

"Considering my history," Max said, "it doesn't seem like a good idea."

She looked worried. "Of course. You must be very sensitized to . . . what do I call it . . . inebriated behavior. I hope that my family didn't offend you on Sunday. I know that some of them got a little tipsy."

"Your family didn't offend me. Even booze doesn't offend me. Uncontrolled, self-indulgent, self-destructive weakness . . ." He paused. "*That* offends me."

He could see that she found his vehemence disturbing. She said nothing, though, and Max found himself wanting her to speak so that he could argue.

"Well?" he said.

She blinked, surprised. "Well what?"

"You think that I'm judging my mother too harshly."

"I didn't say that."

"You didn't have to. It's impossible for someone like you to imagine a family as screwed up as mine, and so you're making excuses for her. You're thinking that weakness is something to be pitied, not despised. Am I right?"

"I wouldn't presume—" Carly began.

"Go ahead. I've already heard it all. Alcoholism is a disease, not a character flaw. She couldn't help it, so I shouldn't hate her for it, right? What if I told you that in my opinion, she could have helped it? That if thousands of other people can go sober, she should have been able to do it too?"

"She never tried?"

"She never succeeded, so I guess she didn't try hard enough."

Carly sighed. "Oh, boy."

"I guess it wasn't worth the trouble," Max added. He had no idea why he was talking to Carly like this. In fact, he didn't know why he was talking about his mother at all. There was a knot in his stomach, and he had the feeling that he should shut up, but he couldn't.

"I'll tell you," he continued, "the difference between you and me. It's a big one. You don't know what it's like to have nobody care whether you live or die. You can enjoy all of those emotional luxuries like compassion, and optimism, and pretend that you don't live in a world where people do terrible things to each other."

"Excuse me," Carly said. "Who are you talking to?"

"What?"

"It's hard to tell. The person you're talking to seems to be someone you've invented and accidentally mistaken for me."

Max put down the wooden spoon and folded his arms against his chest. "What is that supposed to mean?"

"It means that if you think back over the past few minutes, you'll remember that I haven't been arguing with you. I may not have had experiences as rough as yours, but I'm not such a baby that I can't face facts that are right in front of me. If you tell me that your mother chose to give you away to strangers rather than do the hard work of cleaning up her life, well, I believe you. And I'm sad about it. You were just a kid, and you didn't deserve the short end of the stick. But I do think that you're wrong about one thing."

"Really," Max said. "Please enlighten me."

"Compassion and optimism aren't luxuries. They're hard work. I think everyone has to make choices about how to live, and if those qualities are a part of my life, it's because I try to keep them there, not because I've been sheltered from harsh reality, or whatever it is that you think about me."

"I don't agree," Max said stiffly. "There's no way that someone with your life could possibly know what—"

"What do you know about my life? I treat stray cats when some sadist decides to set them on fire. I see dogs trained by ghetto gangs to be killers. Even the little things, like the idiots who come in asking me to declaw their cats. Do you know what it means to declaw a cat? It's not trimming their nails, it's cutting off the top joint of all of their toes. I won't do that, and so those people find another vet who will. You want to talk to someone about disillusionment? Talk to me. I'm telling you, Max, optimism is a choice, and you have to choose it, or you might as well just quit."

She looked squarely at him, daring him to argue. "Well?"

"Do you have a drainer for the pasta?" he asked. "It's ready."

She exhaled sharply. "In the cupboard. Look, Max, you can disagree with me if you want to, but you can't stand there and tell me who I am. It's not fair. And it's also a . . . a stupid excuse."

"Excuse? For what?"

"For telling yourself that you can't . . ." She stopped awkwardly, reddening. "It's just wrong."

"For telling myself that I can't what?"

She looked defiantly at him. "You finally figured out that I'm not some brazen Jezebel who seduces old rich men, so now you've decided that I'm a . . . naive child or something? I think you're just looking for an excuse to avoid actually knowing me. Why? Do I seem dangerous to you?"

That was a hell of a question, Max thought. His eyes moved over her flushed cheeks, her mouth, the curves of her breasts and hips in that damned dress, and he felt his self-control beginning to slip. Carly Martin was turning out to be dangerous in a way that made his first assessment of her almost laughable.

On Sunday, when she had dangled her friendship and her family in front of him—a tiny share of her world, sweet as candy—he had been shocked to realize how much he wanted it. He wanted it with a deep, desperate greediness, as visceral as the sexual desire he felt for her now. And these desires were connected to each other. He wanted her rarified world of siblings and children, barbecues and graduations, loyalty and safety. And he wanted to rip that dress off of her body, push her up against the wall, and lose himself in her, satisfying this fierce hunger. But he couldn't. It was not his life. The hot asphalt of Brooklyn would always be under his feet, one way or another, and he did not like games of pretend.

"You think you understand," he said coldly, "but you don't." She had no right to make either offer to him. Tossing crumbs to a starving man was not kindness.

"Don't I?" Carly's eyes were bright. "I'm just wondering if I get any say in this. Because if I do, I'd much rather be brazen. Then at least I might have a chance, which is more than I get with the nice-girl role. Frankly, Max, it is not my hand that I want kissed."

"Carly, for God's sake!" Max exclaimed. He turned away, unable to look at her, gripping the edge of the kitchen counter with one hand. He needed a minute to focus on something else. Anything but her. In just a minute, he would be fine.

But he didn't get it. She came forward and stopped right in front of him. "I'm not blind, Max," she said. "I saw your face when I walked into the kitchen. If I'm wrong about that, you'd better tell me."

"You're wrong," he said tightly.

He heard her quick intake of breath and felt her draw back. "You mean . . . that you don't . . ."

"I don't."

She was silent for a moment. "I see," she said finally. "If that's true, then why won't you look at me?"

"What?"

"Look at me," Carly repeated. There was something new in her voice. "And tell me again that I'm wrong."

He turned slowly to face her. Her lips were slightly parted, and her eyes seemed huge and wary. She was not as confident as she was pretending to be, he thought. But it didn't matter. He felt the heat of her body reaching out like a beacon, and knew that he was lost.

"Damn you," he said roughly, and pulled her into his arms. She stumbled, clinging to him as his mouth came down on hers. He raked his fingers into the silken sweep of her hair, holding her head as he kissed her. She felt smaller in his embrace than he had expected, and her softness made him feel too big, too strong, and too hungry, as if he could crush and consume her if he wasn't careful.

His mouth left hers and moved down to her neck, tasting the hollow between her jaw and throat. She was warm and sweet, like sunshine, or ocean breezes in the summertime. She moaned softly and arched her back, pressing herself against him. He could feel her breasts against his chest, and it was almost more than he could stand. He wanted her, God, how he wanted her. The fierceness of it was shocking.

"Carly . . ." he said, the word halfway to a groan. He slid his hands down, over the curves of her hips, his fingers gripping her rounded flesh, lifting her up, hard, against him. The next step, and the next, seemed as inevitable as the forward motion of time. Clothes would be pulled away, bodies meeting in frantic passion, and he would drive himself into her, demanding something, desperate for something that he could not name and did not know how to take. This was not lust, in the sense that he had always known it. This was something bigger, deeper, and much more treacherous. It was beyond his control. He had never known the feeling of craving a drug, of having a need so intense that denial felt akin to death. But now he thought that he did understand, and the awareness horrified him. A rush of adrenaline coursed through his body like a jet of fire, and his breath suddenly locked in his chest. He was drowning, he thought. He was underwater, and he could not breathe.

Abruptly, he released Carly. She made a soft, surprised noise. "Max?"

"My God . . ." he said raggedly, stepping back. His skin was cold, and it prickled all over.

"What's the matter?" Carly asked anxiously.

"I don't know." He shook his head, trying to clear it. He forced himself to take slow breaths. The hot flood of emotion inside him had switched abruptly from desire to panic, then receded, leaving him drained.

"Did I do something wrong?"

"No," he said. "Not you."

"Maybe you should sit down for a minute." The look on her face told Max something about the look on his own. He closed his eyes briefly, pained. The last thing that he wanted was to have her fussing over him. But he said nothing, and allowed her to lead him to the couch. He sat.

"Do you want a glass of water?" Carly asked.

"No," he said. "Thanks." His pulse was slowing down now, and he was starting to feel steady again. He hoped that she had not sensed the magnitude of his reaction. Nothing like that had ever happened to him before.

"Are you all right?" she asked.

"Yes," he said, more sharply than he should have. He modulated his tone. "I'm fine. Everything is fine."

She sat down next to him on the couch. For a few moments, they didn't speak. He could hear music from her upstairs neighbor's stereo leaking through the ceiling, and the creak of someone walking on the floor above them. He closed his eyes again, and had the sudden strange feeling that when he opened them, he would find himself in his grandmother's duplex in Brooklyn. It was the smell, he thought. Old buildings, on either coast, seemed to hold the same musty smell. Even an old woman's rigorous scrubbing couldn't banish it. It mingled with the aroma of the pasta sauce and made his head swim.

"Max? Is this about Nina?"

He opened his eyes. It took him a moment to process what Carly had said, because it was the last thing that would have occurred to him. "About Nina?" he repeated. "No."

"Oh," Carly said. "I thought that you might be feeling guilty."

That would have been one hell of an attack of conscience, Max thought. He shook his head. "Believe me. She and I don't have that kind of relationship."

"Okay."

He could see that she didn't really believe him, but he had no way of explaining to her what he himself did not understand. It was some comfort to his ego to know that she would not have asked about Nina if she had been fully aware of what had just happened to him. He had controlled himself well enough to keep her from seeing the extent of his sudden weakness, and that, at least, was good. Of all the things that he wanted from Carly Martin, pity was not one of them.

CHAPTER 16

—————◆—————

The Safeway market on Stanyan Street was half a mile from Carly's apartment, but the fog was light that evening, and the inconvenience of walking was nothing compared to the horror of having to find a new on-street parking space if she dared to move her car.

She crossed Haight Street at Ashbury, passing the busy ethnic restaurants and the neon lights of the psychedelic shops. Ragged street kids, many with dogs or cats on makeshift leashes, lounged in the doorways. The district, thanks to its countercultural heritage and—more practically—its cheap food and proximity to Golden Gate Park, had always been a gathering place for the homeless.

One girl, standing with a group of other teenagers, waved to Carly. Her hair was bleached to a white blond, and it glowed under the streetlights like a halo. A scruffy border collie was curled at her feet.

Carly stopped. "Edie," she said. "Hi. Where have you been?"

The teenagers, a motley group with partially shaved

heads and various body piercings, stopped talking and
stared at her, snickering. Edie ignored them. "Around,"
she said. "I've got a dog for you. Do you want him?"

Carly sighed. She had met the girl several months ago,
outside the Safeway. Edie had been in the parking lot, asking for change and carrying a black-and-white puppy
whose cough had immediately gotten Carly's attention.
She had brought the girl and dog back to her apartment
and done her best to doctor both of them, but her attempts
with the puppy had been much more successful. Edie had
refused to tell Carly anything more than her first name,
and she answered any questions about her life on the street
with withering sarcasm. Nonetheless, they had formed
some kind of bond, and every week or so, Edie showed up
at Carly's door, toting a foundling animal. Some of them
she gave to Carly, who did her best to find homes for
them, but others she took back. They already had owners,
she said. They belonged to her friends.

Strays and strays together, Carly had thought at the
time, troubled by the idea of animals being adopted by
people who could not even assure food and safety for
themselves. It hadn't taken her long to change her mind.
For a person living on the street, a dog or cat was warmth,
protection, love—all things that were otherwise in short
supply, and the homeless were often more devoted to their
animals than the average pet owner. When Carly discovered that it was not unusual for a street person to go without food in order to feed his pet, she had started collecting
and distributing the sample packs that pet food companies
regularly sent to the clinics in her area. Part of her foundation discussions with Henry Tremayne had involved the
idea of creating a clinic, like UC Davis's Mercer Clinic,

that would provide free medical care for the pets of people who could not otherwise afford it.

"Where is the dog?" Carly asked Edie. The black-and-white form on the sidewalk was the girl's own pup, now almost grown.

"In a safe place," Edie said. Carly looked curiously at her. It was hard to be sure in the lurid neon light, but there seemed to be a bruise on her jaw. She was thin, with the kind of jutting cheek- and hipbones that fashion models her age starved themselves to obtain. "You'll take him, right? He's in bad shape. Nobody wants him."

"He's too small," said a boy with stubby dreadlocks and a battered black leather jacket. "And ugly."

"Shut up, T. J.," Edie snapped. "*You're* too small, and you know what I'm talking about." Ignoring the snorts of laughter, she faced Carly. "Well?"

"Sure," Carly said. "Do you want to drop him off at my place? I'll be back there in an hour."

"No, I can't get him now. Maybe after the weekend."

Carly nodded. "Okay." She wanted to invite the girl to join her for dinner, but she knew by now that such a motherly suggestion would embarrass Edie in front of her group. She had learned that it was better to say nothing, but to make sure that she "just happened" to be preparing a meal whenever the girl dropped by. It was a transparent ruse, but Edie always accepted the invitation to come inside and eat, maintaining an aloof dignity that suggested that she was simply accommodating Carly's bizarre notion of having dinner at 11 P.M.

* * *

The call came on Thursday afternoon, while Max was sitting alone in a Chinese restaurant near Syscom headquarters, having a late lunch.

"Mr. Giordano?" It was Dr. Cooper, one of the neurologists on Henry's team of specialists. "I have good news. Your grandfather is showing some improvement."

"He's awake?"

"His eyes are open, and he's begun to show localized responses to stimuli."

"And in English, that means . . ."

"He's turning his head toward sounds. He is focusing his eyes and tracking objects. It's a good sign."

Max felt a jolt of anticipation. This was the call he had been waiting for. "Tell him I'll be there as soon as I can."

"Wait, I'm afraid I wasn't clear. You're welcome to come in, but I don't want you to expect too much. I understand that it sounds strange, but this is still a stage of reflex response."

"Reflex? What do you mean?"

"He's not conscious. It's what we call a vegetative state."

Max swore softly, under his breath, then was silent for so long that the neurologist finally said, "Mr. Giordano? Are you still there?"

"I'm here. That is a hell of a word to use, Doctor."

"I'm sorry. I didn't mean to upset you. That really is the standard term. But this is good news, despite how it sounds. The open eyes and the improved reflexes mean that his brain is healing."

"But he's not conscious at all? He wouldn't hear me if I spoke to him?"

"No. In this state, it's very unlikely that he has any awareness of present events."

"Unlikely. But not impossible?"

"Uh . . . no, not impossible, but I'd hesitate to suggest that your grandfather could—"

Max heard only the acknowledgment of possibility. "So he could be able to hear or see, just not to respond."

"There have been very few cases of people coming out of coma with memories of what was happening around them," the neurologist said disapprovingly. "And the odds of your grandfather's being aware are so small that I wouldn't—"

Max put down a twenty-dollar bill to pay for the food he had just ordered, and stood up, waving away the waiter's suggestion that they could pack the lunch for takeout if Max would just wait a few minutes.

"Doctor," he said into the cell phone as he walked out the door, "I consider my own life to be proof that predictions of the odds are not always accurate. I'll be there in an hour."

Henry had been moved out of the ICU the previous week, and into a private room on the neurological care floor. It was a slightly less stress-inducing environment, Max thought, or perhaps he was just getting used to the hospital. The smells and sounds didn't upset him as much as they had two weeks earlier, and he found that his daily visits were becoming an oddly comforting ritual. If there was nothing else he could do but show up and attempt to rack up points with Fate for his dogged dedication, he would do it. He wasn't a superstitious man, and he knew that his daily visits made no difference to anyone but him, but every time Max saw his grandfather's inert body and felt the sharp sting of guilt for having waited too long to come to him, he hoped that in some small way this could be the beginning of atonement.

Max was not emotionally prepared for the shock of seeing Henry's eyes open and gazing at him when he walked into the hospital room. A chill ran through him, even as he processed the less-encouraging signs: a slackness in the old man's face and an unearthly stillness that would not have settled around a sentient person. Or would it? Who was he to know whether there was awareness behind Henry's flat stare? He could only respond to the possibility, however small, that there was.

"Grandfather?" he said hoarsely, and approached the bed.

Henry's head turned slightly toward him, and his eyes seemed to follow. Reflex, the neurologist had said, but even so, Max found the response thrilling. He swallowed hard and sat down, reaching for the old man's bony hand.

"My name is Max Giordano," he said, not knowing how else to begin. They were alone in the room, although the presence of the many monitors made Max feel as if they were surrounded by a host of quietly humming robots. "I don't know if you can hear me, but if you can, I want you to know that I was wrong not to come to you earlier. I was wrong. I'm sorry."

His grandfather's eyes made him want to believe. Reflex or not, Max did indeed feel as if he were being watched, and it was a small step from there to thinking that maybe, just maybe, Henry was somehow present behind that pale gray gaze. The Tremayne eyes, Pauline had called them, and Max recognized them in his grandfather with the uncanny feeling of looking into a mirror. It didn't take the Tremayne eyes to tell him that this man was of his blood, but he was glad that the link was so physically obvious. In the many times that he had visualized his first meeting with Henry, Max had imagined himself telling the old man that he had every right to be suspicious of a stranger who claimed to be Alan's son. He had planned to offer to take a DNA test to set everyone's mind at ease. But now, after seeing the portraits at the mansion and looking down at the man in the bed, Max knew that it would not have been necessary.

"I never knew your son," he said aloud to Henry. "He was on his way to meet my mother when he crashed his car. He never showed up that night, but she thought that he'd just gotten tired of her and disappeared. She'd had a lot of men disappear on her, so I think that she was expecting it sooner or later."

He paused. "They had only been involved for a few weeks. She didn't know anything about him other than his name and that he was enrolled at Columbia. They usually met at the bar where she worked, or at her apartment, and I don't think that they ever had many personal conversations. When she found out that she was pregnant, she called the university looking for him, and that's how she learned that he was dead. They wouldn't give her any information about his family, though. She left a message with them, but she never heard anything. I wonder if you ever got it."

It was just one more unanswered question. Max had always preferred to think that the message had been lost rather than ignored. His mother had believed otherwise, assuming that Alan's rich family had wanted nothing to do with her or her child. It no longer made any difference, but Max thought that his mother had been mistaken. Henry did not seem to be the kind of man who would have rejected his own grandchild for the fault of being born out of wedlock to a woman of a different social class.

When Max had finally looked into the red album, he had found nothing to suggest that his grandfather had known about him earlier than fourteen months ago. And if the old man's own investigator had uncovered anything about Max's turbulent past, there was no evidence of it in the album. Aside from the fact that all the photos had been taken either with a long lens or from media sources, the album was the kind of collection of mementos that any parent or grandparent might treasure. The pages had spoken eloquently of Henry's pride and affection, and Max had found the experience so overwhelming that he had quickly closed the book and hidden it in a drawer of the desk in his hotel room. He had not looked at it since and could not even think about it without feeling a strange swelling ache inside himself. He did not know whether it was joy or pain.

His grandfather's hand was light and bony, and Max held it tentatively, as if he were carrying a bird. The silence was broken only by the sound of the monitors and the faint rasp of Henry's breath. He looked so small, Max thought. It was as if the threat was not that he might die, but that he might just disappear.

"I waited too long," Max said suddenly, his voice tight in his throat. "Too damn long. I hope that you never thought that I didn't want to know you, because I did. I waited my whole life for this, but then I waited too long. I don't know why."

He heard the sound of his own words in the air, and exhaled sharply, in a kind of harsh laugh. "No, that's not true. I do know. I wanted to be sure that you'd like what you saw. I don't know what it would have taken to make me decide that I was ready, but you took that problem right out of my hands, didn't you? So here I am. I'm not perfect yet, but I am here, and I'm not going away. I hope that's good enough for now."

It was getting dark outside by the time Max left Henry's room. He was drained and weary, and he was in no mood to deal with the woman who was waiting for him in the hall.

"Mr. Giordano. Hello." She stuck out her hand. She was trim and efficient-looking, with boyishly short gray hair. "I'm Joanna Melhorn. We met last week."

"Did we?" Max didn't remember. There were so many specialists working with Henry that he had stopped trying to know them all. She was wearing the ubiquitous white lab coat, so he had to assume that she was one of them.

His tone didn't seem to offend her. She smiled at him. "It is a bit overwhelming, isn't it? I'm a neuropsychologist. I work with several of Dr. Sheaffer's patients."

"Neuropsychologist?" The title wasn't one he had heard before, and it sounded ridiculous to him. "Does this floor require you to tack the prefix 'neuro' onto your job description before they'll let you off the elevator?" He was too tired to curb his tongue, and too tired to care that he was being rude.

Her eyebrows curved up, and she looked amused. "What an interesting question," she said lightly. "Actually, it is a real title. I have specialized training in disorders of the nervous system, and I do rehabilitation work with head trauma patients."

He made a point of looking at his watch. "What can I do for you?"

"Nothing. And I don't want to keep you. I'll be working with your grandfather, but I wanted to make sure that you know that I'm here for you, as well."

"Me?" Max frowned. "Why me?"

"Because a brain injury affects the lives of everyone in a family, not just the patient. An important part of my work is helping the whole family adjust to an event like this."

"I'm doing all right," Max said.

"I'm glad to hear that. But I hope that you'll call me if you have any questions or concerns."

"I have one now," Max said. "Is my grandfather ever going to be normal again? Or don't you know, either? *No Guarantees* seems to be the motto of this hospital."

Her bright face showed sympathy. "It's true. So many people seem to believe that it's better not to hope than to risk having hopes dashed. I don't agree. Understand the reality of the situation but don't give up hope, Mr. Giordano. We're doing everything we can for your grandfather. He's a good man, I hear. And clearly well loved."

Max nodded wordlessly, his throat suddenly tight.

"I hope they've caught whoever did this to him," she added soberly. "I do believe that there's a special place in hell for the kind of person who would attack a defenseless old man."

"It wasn't an attack," Max said. "Just an accident."

This seemed to surprise her. "What kind of accident?"

"He fell down the stairs."

"Really." There was a sudden edge to her voice. "What kind of stairs?"

"The main stairs at his house. Why?"

"Were you there? Did you see it happen?"

"No. No one saw it. He was alone. The housekeeper found him when she came home, and she called the paramedics."

"If no one witnessed it, then how do you know that he fell down the stairs?"

Max stared at her. "Because . . . it was obvious. He was found lying at the foot of the stairs. He fell."

She looked incredulous. "That's the official explanation?"

"What do you mean by official?"

"The police investigation," she said impatiently. "That was what they concluded? That he fell down the stairs?"

"There was no investigation. It was an accident. Would you please explain why you're asking me these questions?"

"I certainly will," she said. "My primary work is with the rehabilitation of brain-injured children. And it's a very sad fact of life that sometimes these injuries come about at the hands of abusive family members. I've been involved with enough of these cases to know which kinds of injuries are consistent with which kinds of accidents."

"What are you saying?" Max asked.

"I'm saying, Mr. Giordano, that something is very wrong here. A fall down the stairs causes injuries like broken bones, or broken teeth, or bruises on high-impact areas of the body—all the logical results of rolling and hitting the edges of a series of stairs. Your grandfather's injury is totally inconsistent with that. He has a depressed fracture at the base of his skull. That kind of trauma would only result from a single hard blow to the back of his head."

Max stared at Joanna Melhorn as her meaning became clear.

"That's impossible," he said finally. "He's been examined by a team of doctors. He's been in the hospital for more than two weeks, and you're trying to tell me that until this moment, no one noticed that his injury didn't match the alleged cause? You want me to believe that Bill Sheaffer just missed this?" He shook his head.

Her expression didn't change. "This is the first time I've heard about this *alleged cause*. I would be shocked if Mr. Tremayne's records said anything about a fall down the stairs. That would be a red flag to anyone here. Your grandfather's injury could be the result of a different kind of fall, if he went backward, and his head hit something hard on the way down. But it is beginning to sound to me, Mr. Giordano, as if you don't actually *know* what happened that night. Do you?"

"This is crazy," Max said, but he felt less confident than he had a few moments earlier.

She fixed him with an unwavering gaze. "I assumed that your grandfather had been mugged. With an injury like his, the first thing to rule out is assault, which should have been done when he was admitted. It's standard procedure. The doctors in the trauma center are required by law to notify the police when they see a suspicious injury."

"How do you know that they didn't?"

"Because," she said, "*you* would know if they did. Will you excuse me? I'm going to make a phone call. Have a seat over there in the lounge. I'll be right back."

Max walked over to one of the blue couches and sat down. He leaned forward, with his elbows on his knees, and stared down at his hands. The fluorescent light bleached his skin to a sickly beige, and he could see cookie crumbs scattered on the cheap institutional carpet. He sat, not moving, for almost ten minutes, until he heard her voice again.

"Mr. Giordano."

He looked up. "Well?"

"Well," she said. She was frowning, and she looked puzzled. She sat down, facing him. "The admitting physician did notify the police on the night that Mr. Tremayne was brought in."

"What? Why the hell wasn't I told about this before?"

"Because no report was filed. The records show that the woman who found him and called the paramedics—"

"Pauline," Max said. "The housekeeper."

"Yes. She was the one who told the admitting physician that he had fallen. I don't know if she specifically said that he fell down the stairs. Either way, the blunt trauma alone was enough reason to bring in the police."

"Let me make sure that I understand this," Max said. "Are you telling me that my grandfather did not fall? That someone *hit him* on the back of the head?"

"No. What I'm telling you is that he did not *fall down the stairs*. On the night that your grandfather was admitted, his head somehow came into contact with a fist-sized blunt object that was hard enough to fracture his skull. That kind of injury could have been the result of a fall, or of an assault. This is what Dr. Moore—the trauma center physician who admitted your grandfather—said to the patrol officer that night."

"Then why wasn't it investigated?"

Dr. Melhorn shook her head. "I can't answer that. The officer on duty must have thought that there was reasonable cause to believe that it had been an accident. It seems shockingly negligent to me, but I wasn't there, and I don't know the facts of the case. There might be more to it."

"Obviously, there *is* more to it," Max said. "If the admitting physician and the police agreed that my grandfather had an accidental fall, why should I believe you? You're the only one telling me that something else might have happened."

"I'm telling you what I see," she persisted. "I don't know Dr. Moore or the officer who took the statements that night, so I have no reason to think that they did anything wrong. But I've also been around long enough to know that things don't always run as tightly as they should. To me, this looks like something that should have been investigated, not ignored."

She sat quietly while he composed himself.

"I have no reason to believe that you know what you're talking about," he said finally.

She nodded as if she had expected such a reaction. "I'll give you the name of a forensic pathologist whom I trust absolutely. He testifies in court as an expert witness, and I strongly suggest that you ask him to review your grandfather's case. But I think he'll tell you exactly what I just did, which will then raise an important question. If a fall down the stairs did not cause your grandfather's injury, Mr. Giordano, you might—for your own peace of mind—want to find out what did."

CHAPTER 17

"So, it was right here that you found him," Max said.

Pauline nodded. They were standing in the arched entrance hall, at the spot where the sweeping flight of mahogany stairs rose toward the second floor.

"He was lying there . . . so still. Oh." She closed her eyes briefly. "It was terrible. I didn't know what had happened at first, I was so shocked. I ran to him, and he was unconscious."

"So you assumed that he had fallen down the stairs."

She looked at him as if he were dimwitted. "Well, of course. I'm no TV detective, Mr. Max, but I'm not stupid. He was right here at the foot of the stairs. How else could he have hurt his head so badly?"

"I don't know," Max said, and meant it.

She scowled at the staircase. "Terrible," she said again. "I don't know what he was thinking, trying to do something like that with his bad knees."

"So then, after the paramedics came, you went to the hospital with him."

"I certainly did! I wasn't going to let them take poor Henry away without me. Those ambulance drivers, my goodness. You hear such terrible stories about them . . ."

Max had never in his life heard a terrible story about an ambulance driver, but he didn't ask. "What happened when you got to the hospital?"

She shuddered. "All that noise, and then they were rushing him away, and I didn't know what was happening. I was so upset. And that doctor! He must have been right out of school. You know, Mr. Max, I have grandchildren older than he is. I didn't trust him at all. I thought that Henry should have someone more experienced, and I told him so, but it all happened so fast . . . I told them to call Dr. Goldblum, his regular doctor, but I don't think they did it right away."

"Did you talk to the police?"

"Oh, yes. I talked to an officer. He asked me what happened, and I explained to him about Henry's knees, and his dizzy spells, although I told him that he hasn't had one of those in a while, not since his doctor put him on those pills. It was his blood pressure, you know, and so I had been cooking him food without much salt, just like Dr. Goldblum told me to do; but Henry didn't like it very much."

She stopped for breath, and Max seized the chance. "Did you specifically tell the policeman that Henry had fallen down the stairs?"

Pauline pursed her lips. "Yes, I did, and to tell you the truth, Mr. Max, I think he could have been a bit more polite to me. I suppose that I'm just an old woman, and the things I have to say aren't of much interest to anyone, but if he is going to ask me questions, I do think that he should listen to the answers. He wasn't in the least bit interested in my description of the accident—"

"But you didn't see the accident," Max said. "Did you?"

Pauline looked disapprovingly at him. "That is exactly what the policeman said, and he interrupted me, just like you did, although in his case, it was done very rudely. He told me not to tell him about things that I hadn't actually seen, which was just ridiculous, in my opinion, because it was *very* clear to me what had happened, and I thought that someone should explain it to him so that he could put it in his report."

Max could only imagine how the average beat cop would have responded to Pauline's explanations, but he was not surprised to hear that the man had not been an empathetic audience.

"What kind of questions did he ask you?"

"He wanted to know if anything had been taken from the house, if I'd seen anything suspicious, which I suppose are the usual questions to ask, but it just proved that he wasn't paying any attention to what I was saying. So I told him that of course there was nothing like that, and how could there have been a burglar, with all of those dogs around? And Miss Martin knows to lock the front door when she leaves."

"So you told the policeman all of this."

"Yes. But his radio kept making noise, and I could tell that he was impatient. And then I realized, Mr. Max, that he didn't even know who your grandfather was! Can you imagine that? Not knowing Henry Tremayne? I lost my temper then and told him that Henry was a very important man, and that he was a personal friend of the mayor—

well, not this mayor, but the one before him—and so he had better make sure that everything was in order. He spoke with the doctor for a few minutes, and he left not long after that, and I'll tell you, Mr. Max. You'll never find anyone with more respect for our officers than I have, but I certainly wasn't impressed with the manners of that one."

Max exhaled slowly, thinking, trying to imagine the scene at the hospital that night. *I've been around long enough*, Joanna Melhorn had said, *to know that things don't always run as tightly as they should.* A crowded trauma center, a harried and inexperienced admitting physician, an overworked cop confronted with a hysterical housekeeper and an old man of no obvious significance, with an injury that could be explained away as the result of an accidental fall . . . To Max, it was looking more and more as if someone had dropped the ball that night.

"And then they sent me home," Pauline said darkly. "They told me that there was no reason for me to stay, and that there was nothing more that I could do for him. So *I* told *them* that I could certainly sit there in that lounge and pray. But then I went, because I knew that I had to feed the kitten. He was very small then, and he needed to be fed every four hours. I don't usually feed the animals, but there was no one else to do it that night. I just didn't feel right leaving poor Henry alone in that place, though. All those strangers! He's always been such a private man."

Pauline took a shaky breath and pinched her lips together.

"You did everything right," Max said. "You saved his

life. If you hadn't been there, he wouldn't have had a chance."

The housekeeper's chin began to wobble. She sniffed loudly and pulled the ever-present wad of tissues out of her apron pocket. "Oh, Mr. Max, that's kind of you to say, but if I'd just come home earlier, it would have all been different. I stopped to look at the magazines in the supermarket. I almost never do things like that, you know, since I truly believe that it's a sin to waste time. I should have come straight home. If I had, I could have gotten him whatever it was that he wanted, and he wouldn't have gone walking up those stairs, and none of this would have happened."

To Max's horror, she burst into a torrent of tears, and at that very moment, the key clicked in the front door lock, and Carly walked in, carrying a large bag of birdseed in her arms. She took in the scene before her in one surprised glance, then quickly plopped the bag down in the open doorway and rushed forward to wrap her arms around Pauline's heaving form.

"My goodness," she exclaimed, and the look she gave Max was faintly accusing. "What did you do to her?"

"Nothing," Max said. "We were just talking."

"It can't be nothing, look at her. Pauline? Pauline, calm down. It's me, Carly. Please don't cry. This has been a terrible time for you, I know. You've been so brave and strong. It's going to be all right, really it is."

Over the housekeeper's head, she turned to Max. "What on earth were you talking about that made her so upset?"

"I wanted more information on Henry's accident," Max

said, feeling defensive. "I didn't expect her to react like this."

"It must be post-traumatic stress disorder," Carly said. "You shouldn't make her relive that night; it's cruel. I'm sure that she feels responsible, somehow. It's her curse: She finds a way to feel responsible for everything. Pauline, let's go over there and sit down. Can I get you something? Is there something I can do to help you feel better?"

"Close the door," Pauline sobbed out, as Carly helped her toward the couch. "You're letting the bugs in."

An hour later, Carly was in the solarium, attending to a stubborn fur mat on one of the cats, when Max came into the room. She was surprised to see that he hadn't already left. He looked impatient, and she realized that he had been waiting for her to finish with the animals. She felt a flicker of anticipation, but then sensed from his expression that he was not about to suggest a last-minute dinner date.

"Is something wrong?" she asked, releasing the cat.

"I want to talk to you," he said, beckoning. Puzzled, she followed him into the library. He cast a suspicious look around the room, as if checking to make sure that Pauline was not lurking in one of the corners, then closed the double doors.

"Sit down." He motioned to the couch.

Carly sat, but Max remained standing, his arms folded against his chest. Something in his face seemed strange.

"Max," she said, "are you all right?"

"I'm fine."

"Aren't you going to sit? Come here. Relax." She patted the seat next to her on the couch and smiled at him. "If this is what a normal workday does to you, you should probably take more vacation time."

He took a seat in the armchair opposite her. "Carly," he said, "why didn't you tell me that you were here with my grandfather just before the accident?"

She blinked at him. "Was I?"

"Pauline told me that he was expecting you at five-thirty that day."

"Yes, I know. I do house calls on Wednesdays, and since Henry always needs me for something, I make a regular stop here each week. It's my last visit of the day, so I usually arrive between five and five-thirty."

"So it's true. You were here."

She found his tone disturbing. "I just said that."

"But you sounded surprised when I asked you about it."

"Well . . . the question was kind of out of the blue, Max. But it wasn't the part about being here that surprised me, it was what you said about my being here just before the accident. Do you mean that he fell right after I left?"

"Yes. Pauline found him at seven-fifteen."

"Oh," Carly said sadly. "I didn't know that." The revelation upset her for some reason, as if temporal proximity to the accident somehow made her responsible for it.

"When did you think it happened?"

"I don't know. Later, I guess. I never really thought about it." In her mind's eye, she could see Henry in his armchair in the sunroom, the tiny kitten in his lap.

"What time did you leave?"

"About six. No, it was a little after, because the news had started."

"Do you usually leave at six when you visit him?"

"No, usually we have tea after I check the animals, but he seemed tired that day, sort of distracted, so I thought that he probably wanted to relax and watch TV. He's so polite that he would invite me to stay even if he didn't really want me to, so I try to be sensitive to his moods. Max, why are you asking me all these questions?"

"I'm trying to get a better idea of what happened. So you're sure that you left at . . . what, six-fifteen?"

His explanation didn't satisfy her. "Pretty sure," she said. "I didn't want to keep him from his show. I guess that by the time I was in my car and driving away, it was probably as late as six-fifteen."

"Was anyone else here? Either while you were in the house, or when you were leaving?"

"You mean, like one of the teenagers?"

"Anyone."

She thought for a moment, then shook her head. "The kids come right after school, so they're all gone by five, at the latest. And Pauline was at the grocery store. She goes to the grocery store every Wednesday afternoon, because that's when they do double coupons."

"There was no one working in the yard? No gardeners, no repairmen, no one like that?"

"Usually those guys are done by that time of day. I didn't see anyone. I thought it was just Henry and me. Why? Did you learn something about the accident?" A shocking thought occurred to her. "Max," she said in a hushed voice, "you don't think that someone else was involved with the accident, do you? You don't think that someone pushed Henry down the stairs?" She couldn't imagine where he had gotten such an idea. "Who would do a thing like that?"

"No, I don't think that anyone pushed Henry down the stairs," Max said, but to Carly's great frustration, he didn't explain.

"But you wouldn't be interrogating me without a good reason," she persisted. "What is it? What happened today?"

"I'm not interrogating you. I'm just asking a few questions."

"Why?"

"Because I'm curious about that evening."

"Why now? What changed? What do you know that I don't?"

"Nothing."

"You can't expect me to believe that you're suddenly asking me these questions for nothing! Is this what was happening with Pauline when I walked in earlier? You made her cry. That wasn't very nice."

"I don't remember ever promising to be nice," Max said. He reached up to rub his forehead as if his skull itself ached.

Carly scowled at him. It wasn't fair, she thought. He wasn't the only tired one. She worked as hard as he did, and she was worried about Henry, too. This could have been a chance for them to take care of each other, but clearly, it wasn't going to be that way. She suddenly felt very tired of reaching out to him and meeting only resistance. If Max didn't want to talk to her, and wasn't even willing to sit near her, it seemed clear that there was nothing left for her to do but leave.

"It's getting late," she said. "Do you have any more questions for me, or am I free to go?"

His eyebrows lifted at her shrewish tone, and Carly immediately felt foolish. "No more questions," he said.

"Good." She stood up, avoiding his gaze, and turned toward the door. He said nothing as she walked away, but as her fingers touched the knob, she heard him rise from his chair.

"Wait," he said.

She turned back, quickly, hopefully. "What?"

"You need to check on Lola."

"*What?*"

"She has a sore ear."

Carly shook her head slowly. It was not quite what she had hoped to hear, and judging from Max's edgy stance and slight frown, it was also not quite what he had intended to say. He seemed, she thought, almost as unsettled as she was.

"Were you petting Lola?" she asked.

"How else would I know about her ear? You think she wrote me a note?"

"I thought that you didn't like dogs."

"I don't," Max said darkly.

The conversation had taken on a surreal feeling to Carly. "Okay," she said, "I'll check on her before I leave. Good night." She opened the door.

"Wait," Max said again.

Carly sighed. "You know," she said to the empty doorway in front of her, "I honestly don't have the stamina for this right now." She turned to look at Max. His shoulders slumped, and his skin had the ashy tone of exhaustion. "You look terrible," she said instinctively, concern softening her tone. "What on earth happened to you today? Can't you tell me? Maybe I can help."

He looked at her with dull eyes. "I'm fine," he said.

Carly knew that it would be useless to argue that point. "Of course you are," she said wearily. "You're always fine. Okay, Max. Suit yourself. I'll see you later."

CHAPTER 18

———— •◆• ————

Max had not expected another Sunday dinner invitation from Carly's family, and he hadn't gotten one, exactly. But on Saturday afternoon, he realized that Carly simply assumed that he would be accompanying her. It was strange to think that the Martins were expecting him, as if he really had been summarily adopted into their clan. But believing that would be deluding himself. The Martins were nice people, and charitable with their friendship. Thirty years ago, he had needed a family like theirs. But now? No. He was an adult, not a stray kid, and it was just . . . too late. The first visit had left him feeling raw all week, and he saw no reason to put himself through that again. He had pretended not to see the disappointment on Carly's face when he told her that he had too much work to do.

"They aren't normal," he said to Henry's still form on Monday morning at the hospital. "I don't know what they were thinking, expecting me to show up for another one of those ... things. They aren't my family. They don't even know me."

His visits to his grandfather had turned into semiconfessional monologues. Max would sit by the old man's bed and talk about everything from what he'd had for breakfast to his current venture-capital investments. That kind of rambling didn't come naturally to him, but neither did sitting quietly in the solemn and sterile atmosphere of the hospital room. Henry seemed awake enough to require something from him as a visitor, and Max entertained the hope that if he just blathered on and on, eventually the old man might turn to him and tell him to shut up.

So far, he had kept the conversation—if you could call it that—to neutral subjects, avoiding all of the things that weighed on his mind but didn't lend themselves to discussion.

On Friday morning, Max had phoned the District Attorney's Office to check the credentials of the doctor whom Joanna Melhorn had recommended. Confirmation had been immediate. Jerry Suzuki regularly worked with both the San Francisco police and the DA's Office, and he was considered the top forensics expert in the area. Suzuki had reviewed Henry's case over the weekend, and he agreed that Henry had not fallen down the stairs.

With typical professional reserve, Suzuki had been unwilling to speculate on what *had* happened, pointing out that while an attack certainly could have caused such an injury, so could an accidental fall in which the head contacted a hard, blunt, fist-sized object located close to the ground. The doctor suggested that Max check the area where his grandfather had been found for such an object.

But Max had already checked, and there was nothing

even remotely hard, blunt and fist-sized on the floor anywhere near where Henry had been lying. Even the carved
staircase banisters, entwined with wooden leaves and
vines, were delicately shaped, with no protrusions that
could have caused such an injury. Two round end tables
sat by the bottom of the stairs, displaying a motley group
of innocuous objects: books, decorative figurines, vases of
dried flowers.

A single hard blow to the back of the head.

If there had been an attempted robbery of the mansion,
and if someone had surprised Henry and hit him from behind, then why wasn't anything missing? It was impossible for Max to believe that Pauline's hawk eyes would not
have noticed a burglary. The stress and confusion of finding Henry, and the arrival of the paramedics certainly
would have distracted her, but she had been back in the
house for days, and if anything had been moved or stolen,
she would have said something right away.

Unless she had been involved. What did he really know
about Pauline, after all? She had been with Henry for almost twenty years, which would seem to eliminate her
from suspicion, but who was he to say that their relationship was as straightforward as it appeared to be? Max had
already seen that she had a controlling, possessive side,
and that she considered Henry and his house to be her personal property. It didn't take a detective to come up with
a handful of reasons why she might want to hurt or even
kill Henry Tremayne. Perhaps she needed money, and—
knowing that she would benefit from his will—she had
gotten tired of waiting for him to die. Or perhaps she had
learned that he intended to leave the house to Carly and

had gone into a jealous rage. Hell, maybe Henry had pissed her off by tracking mud into the kitchen.

And even if Pauline was not the type to bash someone in the head, it didn't necessarily mean that she was innocent. She could be protecting someone—a brother or a nephew who had come to rob the house at a time when she had assured him that Henry would be in his chair in the solarium, watching television. Perhaps Henry had heard a suspicious noise and gone to investigate. That would explain why he was in the front hallway and why nothing had been reported missing. With Henry comatose and Pauline involved with the plot, there was nobody left to report a burglary—with the exception of the pets, and they weren't talking.

And yet Pauline had been the first to mention something strange about the accident. If she was hiding her own involvement, then logically, she would never have called Max's attention to Henry's fall. She would be better served by not talking about it, by behaving more like the only other person known to have been at the mansion that evening. Carly.

That night, Max couldn't sleep. He lay in bed, staring up at the darkened ceiling, listening to the faint rumble of traffic on the city streets below. When he closed his eyes, he saw Carly as she had looked that night in her apartment, her eyes bright, her cheeks flushed, and her mouth soft and swollen from his kiss.

She sure as hell didn't look like the kind of person who would hit an old man in the back of the head. The money provided a motive, but that was not the same thing as evidence, and he was convinced that Carly Martin would not hurt a fly. In fact, he thought dryly, if she did accidentally hurt one, she would probably rush it into emergency surgery. He simply couldn't imagine Carly trying to kill Henry Tremayne. Or anyone, for that matter. She didn't even eat meat, for God's sake.

He exhaled, in a long, frustrated breath, kicking back the tangled bedcovers. The suite was air-conditioned, but he felt overheated and as restless as a feverish child. Ever since the night of their kiss, he had been plagued by memories of the feel of her body against his. He had hoped that the desire was transient and would fade away under the prevailing forces of time and reason. But if anything, it was getting stronger. More than once over the past week, he caught himself mentally following that kiss through to its natural conclusion. Carly was the kind of woman who would look beautiful in the morning, waking up next to him after a long, hot night of . . .

"Sleeping," he said sharply, out loud to the dark room. Dammit."

His judgment was in no way compromised by his physical attraction to Carly Martin, he told himself. Another man's might have been, but he had been around long enough not to make such a stupid, minor-league mistake. Hadn't he?

He lay there for another moment, thinking, and then sat up. He hadn't closed the curtains, and the yellow lights of the city cast a faint glow into the room. He got out of bed, walked to the desk, picked up the phone, and dialed.

It rang six times before a man's voice, foggy with sleep, finally answered. "Hello?"

"Tom. It's Max."

"Max? Everything all right?"

"I need you to do something for me."

The lawyer cleared his throat. "Hold on, let me just change phones." Over the long-distance line, Max could hear the rustle of bedcovers and the soft sound of a woman's voice. Belatedly, he remembered that on the East Coast, it was almost three in the morning.

A minute later, Tom Meyer was back on the line. "Okay. What's going on?"

"I want you to do two background checks for me. One on a woman named Pauline . . . something. She's Henry Tremayne's housekeeper. I don't know her last name."

"I'll get it. Who else?"

"Charlotte Martin. I want you to go ahead with a complete check on her. I need as much as you can dig up—personal, financial, everything. And I want it as soon as possible."

"Sure. I can get you the standard stuff—anything digital and public access—in a couple of days. If you want more than that, it'll take a little longer. I'll probably need until sometime next week."

"Fine. It's the nonstandard information that I want. I know that you have a knack for getting it—and I don't want to know how you do it."

Tom chuckled. "I have friends in the right places," he said. "I'll find out what I can. I'm not guaranteeing any of it to be admissible in court, though. Just so you know."

"I know. This is for my own use. Thanks, Tom. I'm sorry I woke you. Tell your wife that I'll delete your home number from my files."

"No problem. I'll call you on Friday with an update."

Max hung up. He walked over to the window and looked down over the glittering lights of the city. He had no specific reason to believe that Henry's accident had been anything but an accident, albeit a mysterious one. He pictured Carly again, looking at him with those big blue eyes of hers. *Call it insurance,* he thought. It wasn't that he didn't trust his instincts. He did. But he especially trusted them when they were backed up with facts.

When Carly's doorbell rang on Tuesday evening, her first thought was of Max. He had a business dinner that night at the UCSF research hospital nearby, and he said that he would stop by her apartment on his way back to the hotel. He wanted to talk to her about something, he said, but had given no indication of what that was. Carly spent the day trying to rein in her imagination; which kept presenting her with catastrophic situations, such as Max telling her that The Kiss had been a mistake, and that he hadn't been honest about the nature of his relationship with Nina.

The mysterious Nina had become a recurring theme in Carly's thoughts over the past few days. In Henry's red album, there had been two pictures of Max holding the arm of a slender blond woman in impossibly high heels, and the scenes had burned themselves into Carly's memory. They were action shots, taken in succession as Max and the woman were walking into a restaurant. Henry's photographer had captured Nina in profile, golden hair falling over the shoulders of her black coat like a blaze of sunshine. She was tall and very beautiful.

The doorbell rang again. "Okay, okay," Carly muttered, wishing that she had a glass of wine to steady her nerves.

But it was Edie, not Max, standing on the small concrete porch outside her front door. Carly concealed her surprise. She had forgotten to jot down a reminder that the girl would be coming over with her latest foundling, and it was pure luck that there was half a pizza heating in the oven.

"Hey," Edie said, in greeting. "I brought him. You want him inside, or out?"

She held one end of a braided nylon rope. The other end was attached to a tattered collar, which circled the neck of the most astonishingly ugly dog that Carly had ever seen. It was not actually clear that the animal was a dog, but Carly had to assume that it was, simply because she couldn't imagine what else it could be. About the size of a football, it was covered with matted tufts of gray-brown fur that obscured any sign of a face other than two pointed ears and a small black nose that looked like a mashed prune. Four stumpy legs stuck out of its squat body, but Carly was unable to discern a tail of any kind.

"Uh," Carly said, momentarily speechless. "Inside, I guess."

"He's okay. I named him Nero."

"After the emperor?" It seemed like a stretch to Carly.

Edie shrugged. "He can use all the help he can get." She leaned down and untied the rope from Nero's collar. With a motion that startled Carly, the dog shot forward into her apartment and crashed headlong into the side of the couch. He ricocheted backward, then turned and disappeared into the kitchen.

"He doesn't see too well," Edie said.

"He's housebroken?" Carly asked, hopefully.

"Yeah. He was at my friend's place, and he was fine. He doesn't like other dogs, though. Or cats. Or men. And sometimes he bites."

"Great," Carly said dismally.

"Not people," Edie clarified. "He only bites things. Table legs, mostly."

"Where did you find him?"

"In the park. Somebody dumped him there."

"Maybe he's just lost. I'll put up some signs and see if anyone calls."

"Don't kid yourself," Edie said. "He's not exactly a show dog, you know?"

It was not hard for Carly to coax Edie into joining her for pizza. The girl followed her into the kitchen, where they found Nero clamped on to the leg of Carly's small table. He was not gnawing on it as much as he was attempting—and failing—to crush it. His paws scrabbled on the floor as he increased his force, muttering and snuffling against the wood.

"Sorry about that," Edie said. She reached into her black canvas bag and pulled out a short, battered stick. She knelt beside Nero and seized him by the scruff of the neck. The dog froze, his jaws still locked on the table leg. "Neeero," she said coaxingly. "Puppuppup. Chew on this."

Nero growled, deep in his throat, but surprised Carly by releasing the table leg. Gently, Edie tapped his snout with the stick. There was a flash of crooked yellow teeth and pink gums as he seized it like a shark taking prey. He gave it a brief shake, then scooted under the table and settled down into a lump, the stick gripped firmly in his jaws. He looked to Carly like a small, badly stuffed cushion.

"It's a security thing," Edie explained. "He has an oral fixation."

Carly smiled. "Don't tell me that you've been reading Freud."

The girl's reaction was sudden and fierce. "Why, do you think I can't read? I know who Freud is. I'm not stupid."

"I don't think that at all," Carly said, surprised. "Do you like to read, Edie?"

"I go to the library sometimes. They don't hassle me now that I look sixteen, but they used to call the truant officer when I was there during the day." She grinned. "I tried to tell them that I'm home-schooled, but they didn't believe me. Wonder why?"

The answer to that question was obvious. Edie was wearing one of her usual outfits, a thrift-store polyester dress over ripped and grimy jeans, topped off with a battered fake-fur leopard-print coat. Her army-surplus boots were too big for her. Her eyes were ringed with black makeup, and her bleached hair was so pale and fragile that the ends were shattered, like spun sugar.

"How old are you?" Carly asked. The pizza was ready, and the spicy smell of food filled the kitchen. Edie watched her as she pulled the tray out of the oven.

"Fifty," Edie said. "I look good, don't I?"

"Very," Carly agreed, sliding a slice of pizza onto the girl's plate. She hadn't expected a straight answer. "How do you stay so young?"

"Sleeping in the park keeps me connected with nature." Edie looked mockingly at her. "You should try it."

"Is that where you sleep? In the park?"

"I sleep anywhere I want to," Edie said. "It's great to be me."

The shadow that Carly had seen on the girl's jaw last

week was indeed a bruise. The purple had faded into a dull greenish yellow, still vivid under Edie's translucent skin. Carly wondered what—or who—had caused it, but knew that it would be pointless to ask.

Instead, she gave Edie another slice of pizza. The girl had devoured the first piece in three bites, and was gnawing on the crust.

Between the two of them, they finished the rest of the pizza and leftover lasagna from the refrigerator. Edie's unwillingness to answer questions was not matched by a reluctance to ask them, and while they ate, she announced that she had been reading a book about animal diseases, and proceeded to quiz Carly on the symptoms of everything from distemper to leukemia. The longer they talked, the more obvious it became to Carly that Edie had basically memorized a first-year veterinary textbook.

"You know a lot about this," she said as she got up to put their dishes in the sink.

"I told you I'm not stupid."

"Have you thought about becoming a vet?" Carly asked.

"Sure," Edie said. "I'll pay for school with the money from my trust fund."

"You don't need a trust fund. There are scholarships and financial aid programs. That's how I paid for school. You could do it, too."

"Is that all you have to do to be a vet? Memorize things? Anybody could do that."

Carly ignored the gibe. "Some vet schools accept students out of high school for a six-year program. You would need to take the GED test. Do you know about that?"

"Yeah," Edie said, sounding sullen. "I could pass it if I wanted to. High school is for morons."

"And you would need to get some experience working in a hospital or a clinic."

"No problem. I'm such a wholesome American teen, it'll be easy for me to walk in and get hired anywhere." Edie stood up. "What a load of bullshit."

"I think that you could do it," Carly persisted.

"What do you know?" The girl looked angry. "You don't know anything about me."

"I've seen you almost every week for six months. I don't know where you sleep or what you do all day, but I do know that you're one of the most naturally gifted animal handlers I've ever met. And you're more than smart enough to make it through school—"

"You're easy to impress."

"It may be easy for you, but not just anybody can memorize a pathology textbook. I couldn't. I still need to look up half of the things that you just rattled off. If you wanted to surprise me, you did. You—"

The sound of the doorbell interrupted her. Edie was glaring at her. Carly took a short breath of frustration. It had to be Max, and his timing couldn't be worse. She didn't want Edie to leave, not just then, when they finally seemed to be on the verge of a breakthrough.

"There's ice cream in the freezer," she said, feeling as if she were trying to bribe a small child. It didn't seem possible that Edie would fall for it. But the girl made no move toward the door, which Carly took as a good sign. "There's chocolate. And strawberry, I think. Help yourself. I'll be right back."

CHAPTER 19

———————— ◆ ————————

Max had come directly from his meeting. His tie was loosened, but everything else was in perfect order, from his gray wool suit to the shine on his shoes. He looked to Carly as if he had just stepped out of a magazine or a movie, and she felt breathless at the sight of him. There was something absurd about having a man like that standing on her doorstep, next to the fish-shaped wind chimes and the scrawny geranium, but there he was, nonetheless, and despite her general anxiety, she was delighted to see him.

"Hi," she said. "Come in."

She was about to tell him that she was not alone, when she saw his expression change. She closed the door behind him and turned. Edie was standing in the kitchen doorway, staring at them, or more specifically, at Max. She was holding an open pint of ice cream in one hand and a spoon in the other.

"I can't find a bowl," she said.

"You have company," Max said. "Should I come back later?"

Carly hesitated, caught between conflicting desires. If she sent him away, there was a possibility that their discussion would be postponed until tomorrow, or later. She didn't think that she could stand the suspense. And there was nothing that she wanted more than to be alone with Max. But the situation with Edie was even more pressing, in its own way.

Carly made a quick decision. "Don't go," she said. "We were about to have ice cream. Edie, this is my friend Max Giordano. Do you mind if he joins us?"

Edie looked momentarily taken aback by the question, then shrugged. "It's your house, isn't it?"

"Thanks," Max said. He took off his jacket and draped it over the back of the couch. A slight frown touched his forehead, and Carly wondered what he was thinking. One glance at the girl spoke volumes about her situation. It was possible that Max, with his own troubled teenage past, might do a better job of communicating with Edie than Carly could.

Maybe. Carly looked warily at him. Or maybe not. It was also possible that he would have no tolerance at all for Edie's confrontational attitude. And if Edie sensed any disapproval from him, she was likely either to fight back or storm out, both of which sounded very bad to Carly.

She took a deep breath. "Max," she said, "I hope that you can vouch for me and tell Edie that I wouldn't be a bad person to see every day. I want her to come and work for me at the clinic."

Carly had been trying for dramatic effect, but the result was far beyond what she had intended. Edie froze in the doorway, her mouth dropping open. Her face flushed a dull red.

"You want to give me a *job*?" she asked slowly, incredulously.

"Yes." She had no idea how she was going to manage such a thing, but she intended to worry about that later. "I'll train you as a veterinary assistant. You can help me with exams and take care of the hospitalized animals. If you like it, I'll teach you how to assist in surgery and do lab work."

Edie's mouth pinched, and she looked from side to side, as if searching for an escape route. "You . . ." she began, then stopped. She took a breath.

"You're crazy!" she yelled, and threw the container of ice cream at Carly. It was not a good throw, and, fortunately, the pint was still frozen solid. Max stepped in front of Carly and deftly caught it before it hit the floor. He looked at the label and grinned.

"Chocolate," he said. "My favorite. Toss me the spoon, kid."

Furiously, Edie pitched it at him. He plucked it out of the air and calmly began to eat from the carton. Carly stared at him. This was strange behavior for someone who was usually so fastidious, and she wondered what he was doing.

"I'll pay you ten dollars an hour," she said to Edie, who was now glowering at Max and barely seemed to hear her. "And you'll get a raise after six months. It's the starting wage that we offer everyone at your level."

Edie turned on her. "You are so incredibly stupid that I can't believe you're real."

"I'm not stupid," Carly protested. "I really think you can do this."

"You think! I told you, you don't even know me. What kind of moron tries to hire somebody they don't even know? You—"

"I know you," Max remarked, taking another spoonful of ice cream. "I know all about you."

Edie stopped short. "Liar! I've never seen you before in my life."

"That doesn't matter," Max said. "Let me tell you about yourself. You stand outside the Safeway begging for money, but we both know what you're actually doing. You're selling your pride for small change. You can feel it every time some smug guy drives by and gives you a condescending look. You know you're smarter than he is, but he doesn't know that, does he? You sleep on the floors of strangers' apartments, or in doorways, or in the park; but you never sleep well, because you have to be able to wake up fast in case someone tries to mess with you. You're tired all the time, and hungry, and pissed off at the world, and you tell yourself that you don't care about anybody or anything, and so you spend your time getting high—"

"I do not!" Edie shouted. "I don't do drugs, so you can keep your superior attitude to yourself, you stupid . . . suit! You think you're so smart and successful, but I see guys like you every single night, driving around where I hang out. They come looking for girls, or boys, or drugs, or whatever they think they need, and we all just laugh at them, wasting their money on stupid shit like that. You think you know me? You're wrong. *I* know *you*."

"No," Max said quietly. "You don't. I was on the streets when I was your age, and someday I'll tell you about it.

Then, you might know me. And maybe someday you'll tell me your story, and I'll know you. But that doesn't matter. The point is that you either care about something or you're dead, Edie. And eventually you have to choose one or the other."

Edie had folded her arms tightly against her chest as he spoke, and hunched her shoulders so that she seemed to be hugging herself. Her face was red, and her chin wobbled. She wouldn't look at Max. "I want to leave," she said.

"Nobody's stopping you," Max said, waving toward the door.

Carly couldn't control herself any longer. "Wait, please don't go. Have some ice cream. We should talk more about the job. I really want you to do this."

"I don't want to talk about it," Edie said, heading for the door.

"Edie." Max's voice cut through the small apartment, and the girl froze. "Do you need a place to stay tonight?"

The girl exhaled wearily. "What is this, National Mentorship Day? No, I don't need a place to stay, or a job, or ice cream, or anything from either of you. I'm fine, so leave me alone."

" 'Sure," Max said, and shrugged. "See you around."

His callousness shocked Carly, and she made a noise of protest. It seemed to her that they had had a breakthrough. Edie had not dropped her defensive posture, but Max's words had clearly affected her. Now was not the time to be cool and casual, it was the time to reach out.

"Edie," she said quickly, "you care enough about animals to go to the library and study veterinary textbooks. You're smart and dedicated, and—"

The girl scowled at her. "I told you that I don't want to talk about it."

"But—" Carly began, then stopped abruptly as Max put his hand on her shoulder and squeezed, warningly. She looked up at him, confused.

"Let her go," he said in a low voice, his words almost inaudible. Carly frowned, about to argue, but his fingers bit into her shoulder. His eyes held hers, and she yielded, reluctantly.

"Well . . . thanks for bringing Nero," she said to Edie. "I'll let you know if I have any luck finding his owner. Otherwise, I'll start looking around for a home for him."

"Okay," Edie said. She hesitated for a moment, looking from Carly to Max as if she were about to say something. But then she turned and opened the door. "See you," she muttered, and slipped out into the night.

They stood, staring at the door, until it became clear that she was not coming back.

Max finally broke the silence. "Interesting girl," he said.

The sound of his voice released Carly. She blew out a long breath of astonishment. "I think I'd better sit down," she said, and collapsed on the couch. "Do you think she'll ever talk to me again?"

"Yes," Max said immediately. He sat down next to her. "In fact, I think that she is giving your job offer serious consideration."

"Are you kidding? She wouldn't even listen to me. How frustrating! I wish there was something I could do."

"You did it. I'll bet you a hundred bucks that she shows

up either here or at your clinic sometime in the next few weeks, wanting to know more."

"I don't *have* a hundred bucks," Carly said, exasperated. "And she wasn't interested. I don't know why you think that she—"

"She was. She was so interested, in fact, that your offer scared the hell out of her. She needed time to think. That's why I told you to let her go. I didn't want you to push her until she said no, because then she might have been too proud to change her mind. But she never did say no, did she?"

Carly stared at him. Stunned, she thought back over the whole episode and realized that he was absolutely right. Her own attempt to push Edie toward the clinic job, using praise and encouragement, was exactly the wrong strategy. She had overwhelmed the girl, and—as Max pointed out—scared her. At some point, positive feedback would probably work, but right now, it was too much. Sensing that, Max had provoked Edie, insulted her and challenged her; but he had never made an obvious attempt to control her. He had handled the situation masterfully.

He was observing Carly's surprise. "You would be amazed," he said dryly, "at how much insight into human psychology you can pick up while going through the New York State foster-care system."

"I . . . guess so," Carly admitted. "That was a pretty impressive performance."

"The years of study are paying off. The same principles apply in the modern business world."

"Have you ever thought about doing this for real? Working with street kids?"

Max snorted. "Me? The girl was right. You are crazy."

"But you're good at it. And your background means that you understand them in a way that most other people can't. It's obviously important to you. You can talk to these kids, Max, I just saw you do it. You know how to make them listen."

"I can honestly say that I've never considered the idea," Max said.

"You should," Carly urged. "I think you would be great at it. You could really do some good for—"

There was a low rumbling sound from the kitchen doorway. Carly looked over and was dismayed to see Nero standing there, growling, his jaws still clamped on the stick. The mop of hair concealing his face made it impossible to see what he was looking at, but she had a bad feeling—from the direction in which his nose was pointed—that he was aiming the growl at Max.

"My God," Max said. "What is that thing? It looks like a giant hedgehog."

"It's a dog. His name is Nero. Edie found him in the park. I told her that I would find a home for him."

Max narrowed his eyes. "She should have left him in the park. He looks like he belongs there. Are you sure it's a dog?"

Nero dropped the stick and sped toward Max. Carly marveled, briefly, that such stumpy legs could move so quickly, but then her amusement turned to horror. The dog's teeth flashed and he snapped at the air in the exact spot where, only seconds before, Max's ankles had been.

"Watch out!" Carly exclaimed, belatedly, and heard Max swear. He had lifted his feet just in time and was now holding them in the air over the small dog's head. Nero sniffed wildly around the empty space, muttering, then gave up and scurried into Carly's bedroom.

Max put his feet down. "You're supposed to find a home for him?"

"Edie said that he doesn't like men," Carly said. "But she also told me that he doesn't bite people."

"One of those things is not true," Max said.

"Oh, dear," Carly said. "I'll go and shut the bedroom door."

She felt Max's gaze on her back as she walked over and pulled the door shut. She turned and saw that he was still watching her. "Max," she said, "were you serious when you told Edie that you used to be on the streets?"

"I bailed out on a few foster homes." He shrugged. "I was not a model kid."

"Where did you go when you ran away?"

"Manhattan. Always. I was underage, so I didn't have much luck getting a paycheck, but there were a couple of restaurants in Little Italy that would feed me if I worked. You know, washing dishes, cleaning floors. I showed up whenever I needed a meal."

"It's hard for me to imagine you cleaning floors," Carly said. She sat down on the couch next to him and tucked her feet under herself.

"I didn't care. It was better than the alternatives."

"How on earth did you get from there to here?"

"You didn't read the *Fortune* article?"

"No. Should I?"

"Don't bother. I gave them a few clichéd quotes about hard work and the American Dream. But what really happened was that I got arrested."

"What?" He was teasing her, Carly thought.

"It wasn't the first time. I'd been in trouble for petty theft, trespassing. But when I was sixteen, I broke into an electronics store and stole a couple of televisions. I had big plans to sell them on the street and make enough money to come to California." He shook his head. "Stupid kid."

"You got caught?"

"Immediately. And when the owner of the store found out that I was a teenager, he came down to the station to see me. Jack Levitsky. He told me that he wouldn't press charges if I came to work for him. I still don't know what the hell he was thinking."

"You sound like Edie," Carly remarked.

"He started me on the lousiest stockroom job that he had. I worked harder for him than I ever had in my life, and for some reason, I liked it. By the time I was twenty-one, I knew the business inside out, and I was basically running things for Jack. I got us into computers, and we started expanding. We started hiring college kids over the summers, to do repairs, and to help customers with their systems. That was how I met Gary. Hell of a programmer, but he was like a baby. He didn't know anything about business, and he didn't want to know. We eventually teamed up to start our company, and the rest is history."

"Where is he now?"

"Retired at thirty-four. He bought a big Perini Navi and now he sails around the world with his wife and kids. He sent me a postcard from Bali a few months ago."

"Unbelievable," Carly said. "What about the old guy, Jack?"

"He died almost ten years ago. We were never really friends, but I respected him. And I made sure that his investment in me paid off. He spent the last years of his life relaxing at home with his grandkids while I turned his business into the biggest chain of electronics stores in the Northeast."

He nodded slightly, to himself, as if he was confirming it. *He has a right to be proud*, Carly thought. Alan Tremayne had started with everything and turned it into nothing. Max Giordano had done the opposite. "Max, do you remember when you came storming into my clinic and I told you—very self-righteously, I'm afraid—that I hoped you hadn't missed your chance to know your grandfather?"

His pale gray eyes narrowed. "Yes. Why?"

"Because now I also hope that Henry will have a chance to know you. I think that he would consider it an honor to call you his grandson."

Max's mouth compressed, and he looked away. "We'll see."

Carly reached out and put a gentle hand on his chest. She could feel his heartbeat under her fingers, and he tensed as she touched him. He glanced back, his eyes meeting hers, then he reached up and took her hand away. He held it for a moment, looking down at it, running his thumb over her palm as if he could read her future there. Then he exhaled and released her.

"I should go," he said abruptly, and stood up.

"Now?" Carly was dismayed. "But you said that you wanted to talk to me."

He shook his head and picked up his suit jacket. "It's nothing. Another time."

"Are you sure?" Carly stood up, too. She thought about throwing her body between Max and the door, then decided that it might make her look desperate. Which she was, but she didn't want him to know that.

She was able to keep herself under reasonable control until she heard the sound of Max's car pulling away from the curb. Then she picked up the spoon he had been using, and—suddenly empathizing with Edie—flung it at the wall. "Damn, damn, damn!"

The spoon clattered to the floor, leaving a sticky chocolate mark on the plaster. Carly looked unhappily at it. "It's nothing?" she exclaimed, out loud to the empty room. "Nothing? What does that mean? *What* is nothing?"

The room did not answer. But there was a growling, scrabbling sound coming from her bedroom, and Carly thought of the beautiful wooden armoire that her parents had given her for her college graduation.

"Okay," she muttered, and walked toward the kitchen. Because of Edie's habit of bringing in strays, she had started keeping a stock of veterinary supplies at home. She had everything that she needed to do a basic physical exam, including the standard vaccinations.

"Nero, my friend," she said. "Tonight is your lucky night. For lack of anything better to do, Dr. Martin is going to give you a rabies shot."

CHAPTER 20

———— •❖• ————

When Max arrived at the mansion on Wednesday evening, Carly's white van—her official house-call transportation— was parked in the driveway. It was quiet in the front hall, and the absence of a mob of dogs skidding forward to greet him suggested that either they were still outside or they were currently being fed. The living room held the usual assortment of dozing cats, some of whom glanced disinterestedly at him from their spots on the velvet-upholstered furniture. One yawned. Max ignored them right back. It wasn't that he disliked cats, he thought, it was just that he didn't particularly like them. It seemed to him that an animal ought to show some gratitude for being housed and fed in royal style, but they seemed to expect it as their due. A dog like Lola at least made an effort to be friendly. When you scratched her head in just the right spot, she would gaze up at you so adoringly that you felt as if you were the greatest person on earth. He reminded himself that he didn't particularly like dogs, either. But he could understand why some people did.

He heard the muffled sounds of Carly and Pauline talking in the kitchen, and the accompanying clatter of dishes suggested that it was feeding time. Instead of walking down the hall to join them, he stood, arms folded, contemplating the staircase. The front hall was dim, even in the yellow light from the grand chandelier. It was a funeral parlor atmosphere, Max thought suddenly, with distaste. He walked over to the row of tall windows and began to pull open the heavy velvet drapes.

Warm evening light flooded the hall and the living room, illuminating the wooden paneling and the rich colors of the carpets. In the sunshine, the rooms appeared shabbier than they did in the forgiving incandescent glow. The fabric on the chairs was threadbare and faded, and although the total effect was that of genteel disrepair, the house suddenly seemed less grandly intimidating.

The cats, annoyed by the disruption, turned as one to glare at him as he walked back through the living room toward the staircase. The huge Persian carpet in the front hall was one of the only things not diminished by the natural light; on the contrary, the soft pinks and purples of the intricate design seemed to glow. Max looked down at it, impressed. His own tastes tended toward the modern, but a piece like this showed by example why so many people were fanatical about antiques.

He frowned as his eyes picked out a discolored spot. It was irregular, about the size of a silver dollar, and it could only be the place where Henry's head had been lying when Pauline had found him. Max squatted for a closer look. Pauline had done an admirable job of getting the blood out of the fragile wool, but you couldn't use strong cleaning agents on a carpet this old and valuable, and the shadow of the bloodstain remained. It was only evident in the light, and even then, only if you were looking for it.

Max ran his hand over the spot, feeling the soft nap of the carpet as he glanced around, searching for the mysterious blunt object. At that point, he would have given his fortune for a decorative bell, or an urn filled with carved fruit, casually placed by the side of the staircase. Anything, he thought, to avoid having to conclude that Henry's "accident" had not been an accident at all. But there was nothing in the hall to set his mind at ease.

The problem with the idea of someone silently creeping up behind Henry and hitting him in the head, Max thought, was that it was almost impossible to creep anywhere silently in this house. He walked slowly forward, and—as if in agreement—the wooden floor creaked loudly under his weight. It occurred to him that he had never asked Carly whether Henry was hard of hearing. If so, then it might have been possible for someone to catch him unawares.

He heard footsteps coming down the hall from the kitchen, then Carly's voice.

"Hello?" she called. "Is someone . . . oh, Max. I didn't know you were here."

"The drapes," Pauline exclaimed, bringing up the rear. She looked disapprovingly at the drawn-back velvet and the tall, bright windows. "That sun will fade the furniture. I'd hate for it to be ruined while poor Henry is away."

In Max's opinion, it was already too late for the furniture. Also, he thought, any man who really cared about his upholstery would not keep twenty-three cats.

"Now, look at that," Pauline said disapprovingly, as she saw some specks of dust exposed by the sunlight. She hurried into the living room to fuss over the polished wood.

"Did Henry have a hearing problem?" Max asked Carly.

She shook her head. "Not that I know of. Why?"

"Hearing problem!" Pauline said indignantly from the other room, demonstrating that she had no such handicap. "Mr. Max, why would you think a thing like that?"

Since Pauline was addressing him, Max turned to her. "Has anything been removed from this area in the past few weeks?"

"I remove the cats every day," Pauline said, casting a dark look over the assemblage of felines. "Every single day. But *someone* always forgets to keep the hall door closed, and so they come right back. It doesn't seem right to me to have cats in the front parlor. There really should be one nice room for guests."

She flapped her hands ineffectually at the cats. Max saw a furtively guilty expression cross Carly's face.

"Well," Carly said, weakly. "I'll . . . remind the teenagers about that. They can be a little forgetful."

"Very forgetful," Pauline said.

Max cleared his throat. "I'm talking about something that would have been on the floor near the base of the stairs. Something that was there on the night of the accident but isn't there now."

"What kind of thing?" Pauline looked blank.

"Something about the size of a tennis ball but hard. Or something that has a piece like that attached to it. A sculpture. Or a doorstop. Or a rock."

Sudden comprehension registered on Carly's face, but

she said nothing. He saw her glance curiously around the entry hall. Pauline continued to stare at him as if he had gone crazy.

"A rock?" she repeated disdainfully.

"What about cleaning equipment?" Max did not personally own a vacuum cleaner, hadn't used one in ten years, and didn't even have a clear idea of what one looked like, but a machine like that might have some kind of protrusion, and if it had been at the foot of the stairs, maybe Henry had tripped, fallen, and hit his head on it . . .

"I do not leave cleaning equipment lying around the house," Pauline said, with finality, and Max had no doubt that it was true.

"Well," he said, "if you think of anything—"

"I'm sure that I'll let you know if I do." Injured dignity suffused the housekeeper's voice. "But I'll tell you right now, Mr. Max, I do not leave *anything* lying around. Anywhere." She shot a final disgusted look at the reclining cats and marched off toward the kitchen.

"Max," said Carl from behind him, "look at this."

He turned. She was kneeling on the carpet, about halfway between the foot of the stairs and the front door, staring down at something. He joined her in two quick strides. Crouching down beside her, he saw it immediately: a rusty spot the size of a pencil eraser. Blood.

This spot had not been washed out, and the carpet fibers were stuck together with the dried substance. It was almost camouflaged by the floral design. Without the improved light, it would have been invisible. Even so, it took sharp eyes to pick it out from a standing position.

"What the hell . . . ?" Max said in a low voice. There was no reason why a bloodstain should be there, more than ten feet from where Henry had fallen. He ran his hands all around the area, feeling for another rough spot, searching with his eyes for another stain. He found nothing.

One single drop. Not a spray, or a smear, but a round drop, as if it had fallen from a height. It was the kind of mark that you would leave every few feet if you cut your finger, then hurried, bleeding, to the kitchen for a bandage. Not a lot of blood, but Henry's injury had produced only a small cut on his scalp, despite the damage it had done to his skull. Max's heart was pounding. He crawled forward, toward the front door, scanning the carpet, and a few feet farther along, he found another drop.

The front door was just ahead, and he rose quickly to his feet and reached for the handle. He pulled open the door and stepped outside, with Carly right on his heels.

Outside the door, the flagstone path was bordered by low ornamental hedges and manicured camellia bushes. Nestled into the greenery, flanking the front door, were the two stone gargoyles, their wide-fanged mouths stretched into grimaces that could be either snarl or grin. They sat on their haunches, their tails tucked up behind them, as if they were ready to spring on any unwelcome visitor. Their tails tucked up . . .

Max swore under his breath. The creatures had been carved with long, swishing tails ending in improbable forks, but the sculptor had attempted to capture a sense of motion by depicting the appendages as if they had been frozen midlash. The result was a protrusion from each gargoyle's backside that resembled the bobbed tail of a Rottweiler. Rounded, fist-sized, and at the height of Max's shin, that lump of stone would deliver a terrible impact to any person unlucky enough to slip and hit his head on it.

Carly saw what he was staring at and made a soft sound of surprise. "He fell out here?"

Max turned to face the front door, calculating the trajectory of a falling body. If Henry had been standing a few feet in front of the door, in the middle of the walkway, and somehow lost his footing, he could indeed have fallen backward and struck his head against one of the gargoyles. He knelt to examine the statue on the left. There were no marks anywhere on the stone, and he was about to turn to check the other statue when, suddenly, his eye caught something. He sucked in his breath in a sharp hiss.

"What?" Carly was hovering over him, trying to see.

He pointed. "Blood," he said. "On the camellia."

It was a small spatter, but it was unmistakable: dots sitting darkly on a few glossy leaves, almost at ground level. The position of the plant, behind the statue and under the eaves of the house, had protected it from the light rainfalls of the past few weeks.

Carly looked at him. "How did you know about this?"

"I didn't. I only knew that he didn't fall down the stairs." Max briefly described what had happened since Thursday.

Her eyes grew wide. "You heard about this last Thursday? *This* is why you were asking me all of those questions? But . . . why didn't you just tell me then?"

"It hadn't been confirmed."

"I see," Carly said slowly. "And when was it confirmed?"

"Monday."

"Monday. But you were at my apartment last night, and

you didn't say anything. No, I take that back. You said, specifically, that it was nothing. This doesn't seem like 'nothing' to me."

She looked hurt, as if he had somehow betrayed her with his silence. Max didn't answer. He was not in the habit of confiding in anyone. *And now*, he thought, *would be a very bad time to begin.* He stared down at the statue, feeling a chill in his stomach.

Carly exhaled sharply. "You know, this may be news to you, but sometimes two people can actually accomplish more than one stubborn loner. I was the one who found the blood, remember? Without me, you wouldn't have figured this out."

Max didn't appreciate the reminder. He was angry with himself for never thinking to search so far from where it seemed Henry had fallen. He had continuously taken the situation at face value, assuming first that the old man had fallen down the stairs, then that he had been injured in the front hall. But the obvious answer was dead wrong in both cases, and his own stupidity had cost him valuable time.

"Max!" Carly exclaimed. "Why is it so hard for you to accept that you just can't do everything alone?"

Can't I? Max thought. *We'll see.* A few tiny drops of blood had just changed everything. Carly hadn't yet realized—or was pretending not to know—that it would have been virtually impossible for Henry Tremayne, an eighty-year-old man with the back of his skull fractured by a nearly fatal blow, to have gotten up from where he had fallen and walked fifty feet into the house to collapse at the foot of the stairs.

CHAPTER 21

———— ◆◆ ————

Carly had long been in the habit of packing her own lunch in the morning before she left home, a moneysaving effort that she had begun in vet school and never quite felt comfortable abandoning. She had a limited repertoire of sandwiches, though, and today she would gladly have fed her peanut-butter-and-banana-on-whole-wheat to one of her canine clients. True success, she thought, as she poked at her carrot sticks, would be a daily delivery of fettuccine Alfredo from the bistro down the street. As life goals went, it wasn't a bad one.

She sighed and stuffed the half-eaten sandwich back into the brown paper bag. It was a relatively quiet day at the clinic, and she was sitting at the table in the break room. Technically, she had an office, a tiny space that barely held her desk and one extra chair, but she found it claustrophobic and preferred the friendly bustle of the staff area.

"Carly."

She looked up. Richard was standing in the doorway.

He looked tired, she thought, and wondered why. He had been working hard, but he had always done long hours in surgery, and they had never seemed to affect his health before. His tanned skin looked dull and coarse, and even his hair seemed lank.

"I thought you had the Martinez cat at noon," he said.

She shook her head. "Canceled."

"When? It was on the schedule this morning. If that lady thinks I won't enforce our twenty-four-hour-notice policy, she's going to be very depressed when I bill her for today."

"Her car broke down," Carly said. "She called at ten to say so. If she were psychic, I'm sure that she would have called yesterday."

"We could have put someone else in that time slot."

"Not today we couldn't. I've only got three appointments this afternoon."

"Great," Richard muttered. "So I'm paying a receptionist and a technician to sit around and do nothing. You!" He pointed at Brian, who was sitting at the lab table, in front of the microscope. "What are you doing?"

Brian started visibly, and his face flushed a dull red that clashed with the yellow of his hair. Carly winced. He was a nice kid, but so shy that he seemed to huddle into himself even when he was standing straight. He was great with animals; but people were another story, and he was no match for Richard. "P-parasitology screen," he stammered.

"Finish it and punch out. Go home."

"I . . . I'm . . . on the schedule until six," Brian said.

"Not anymore. Come back tomorrow when we need you. Dr. Martin is going to do her own lab work today."

"Richard!" Carly exclaimed.

"Don't start. You said yourself that you only have three appointments for the rest of the day. Instead of just sitting around while the kid works, suppose you do it yourself. What a concept."

"I am very familiar with that concept," Carly said through her teeth. "And I am not just sitting around, I am eating my lunch. Are you planning to send Michelle home, too? Shall I also answer the phone and book appointments, or did you want to do that?"

"Spare me the drama, all right? You might have your eye on a millionaire, but I'm trying to run a business." He paused, waiting for her reaction, and looked disappointed when she didn't rise to the bait. "Speaking of millionaires," he added, "how's your friend Henry Tremayne? He still in the hospital?"

"Yes," Carly said. "How did you hear about that? I didn't tell you."

"It was in the *Chronicle.* In the society column—he's rich, that automatically makes him interesting, huh? I meant to ask you about it last week, but I forgot. What happened to him?"

"He fell," Carly said. It was a reasonable question, she supposed, but she would have appreciated a little more sensitivity. Richard had met Henry only once, two years ago, so he probably thought of the old man as nothing more than a regular source of revenue, but he knew that Carly considered him a friend.

"The paper said he's in a coma."

"He was, last week. Now he's waking up."

"He's awake?"

"Not exactly. His eyes are open, but he's not conscious."

"Jesus." Richard shuddered. "If that were me, I'd want them to pull the plug."

"I'll make a note of that," Carly said coldly.

"Seriously. I wouldn't want to live like that. Do they really think he's going to get better? What is he, ninety years old?"

"Eighty."

"I guess we should send some flowers. He's our best client."

"That would be nice," Carly said.

He frowned, considering. "Then again, if he's not going to know, there's no point in sending them now. Maybe later. We'll see how it goes." He nodded to himself, satisfied, then poured a fresh cup of coffee and left.

Carly glanced at Brian, who was staring into the microscope as if he had become one with the lens, pretending that he hadn't heard a thing.

"Sorry about that, Bri," she said. "You didn't know what you were getting yourself into when you signed on with us, did you?"

Brian was still red with anxiety. "I meant to tell him . . . that there was still a lot to do, but I didn't get a chance. Should I really go home? I need the hours."

"I know," Carly said. "It's up to you. He goes into surgery at one, and if you want to stay, I can keep you out of his way until then. Carrie is supposed to be cleaning cages when she comes in, but if you go back and start that now, I'll find something else for her to do."

"Okay," Brian got up, relieved. "Buzz me when you need me."

*   *   *

Hector Gracie was a short, muscular man with sallow skin, gray hair, and a drooping mustache that made him look more like an aged Wyatt Earp than a senior San Francisco police detective. He shook Max's hand and looked him up and down with dark, expressionless eyes.

Max had not called the police directly. In his experience, everything from legal procedures to blind dates tended to run more smoothly when they were arranged through a preestablished network. He had, therefore, called the mayor's office, and the mayor's office had called the chief of police. A short time later, Gracie met him at the Tremayne mansion.

The detective listened briefly to Max's description of what had been happening, then nodded brusquely and squatted to look at the statue. Then, without saying a word, he stood up and walked into the house. Max followed him, but before he could speak, he saw that the detective had already found the drops of blood on the rug. Gracie knelt, squinted at them, then stood up. He fixed his gaze on Max.

"Okay," he said. "I'm going to get an evidence technician out here. We'll check out the blood, and anything else that we find. It's late in the game, though. This area has been cleaned?"

"More than once," Max said.

"That won't help." Coolly, Gracie looked at Max as if he had personally come in with a mop and the intention of destroying evidence.

Max stared right back at him. "Any idea why the cop in charge didn't file a report when he should have?"

The detective shrugged, completely unfazed. "Nope. But I'm going to find out."

Max believed him. Gracie had sharp eyes, he thought, and he was clearly nobody's dupe. It was too soon to say that he liked the detective, but the early signs were favorable.

"You know of anybody who doesn't like your grandfather?" Gracie asked. "Somebody he might have had words with recently?"

"No," Max said. "But I'm not the one to ask."

The detective grinned, unexpectedly. "That's okay. You're not the only one I'll be asking."

It was a crosstown drive to Ocean Beach from the Ritz-Carlton, but Max had gotten into the habit of making a late-afternoon pilgrimage on the days when his schedule didn't give him time for morning exercise. A crack-of-dawn run through downtown San Francisco was a relatively peaceful experience, but the same path at 6 P.M. would have endangered his life. He had made the mistake of trying it once, shortly after he had arrived in the city, and had barely escaped being mowed down by a bicycle courier. Rush-hour traffic, be it automotive or pedestrian, was too much of a distraction to allow him to get into the meditative state that he craved, and using the health-club treadmill was not, in his opinion, an acceptable alternative.

He liked Ocean Beach. It was usually shrouded in a chilly fog by the time he arrived, but there was something powerful and serene about the endless stretch of coastline and the steady crash and hiss of the gray waves. When he ran there he felt wild, solitary, and free, and the harsh cries of the circling shore birds touched an echoing chord inside him. The primal sounds seemed to give voice to the isolation he often felt, but in the anonymity of the fog it seemed only natural, allowing him to relax into himself. He had never, ever considered bringing company.

Until today.

"Okay," he said, as he parked the car, "if you can't keep up with me, I'm not going to wait for you. I'm going to quit and call this a failed experiment. No screwing around. I mean it."

His companion thumped her tail against the leather upholstery and waited for him to finish. He did not even want to begin to think about the fact that he was lecturing a dog, but she really did seem to be listening.

"I don't care if you chase birds," Max continued. "Just don't get lost. And for God's sake, don't *jump* on anybody."

Lola grinned at him, and he regarded her skeptically. He probably should have brought a leash or something, but the idea offended him. His run was about freedom, and he didn't want to be tied to the dog any more than she wanted to be tied to him. It didn't seem necessary, anyway. Lola was timid and tended to stick to him like a burr. It was his hope that the atmosphere of the beach would be as good for her as it was for him.

"Well," he said, pocketing the car key and walking around to the passenger door to set the dog loose, "Here goes. Let's see what we can do."

He knew that Lola had a checkered past, but he hadn't even considered the possibility that a dog raised on the California coast might never have seen the ocean before. She froze on the pavement, sniffing the air, her eyes rolling from side to side with an astonishment that made it obvious that this was a completely new experience for her. She looked skeptically at the soft sand, and Max began to laugh at the look on her face as she stepped cautiously off the concrete. Daintily, she put down one paw, then another, then suddenly decided that this beach was a fine place and leaped forward, kicking up her heels like a colt. She did one exuberant circle around him, then sped toward the water, sending gulls into flight before her as she ran.

"I'll be damned," Max said, suddenly alarmed as her lanky brown body disappeared into the fog. It seemed that Lola's ability to keep up with him was not going to be an issue. For a moment, there was nothing, then suddenly she reappeared, breaking through the fog like a fighter jet. Soaked with brine, she did another joyful swoop around him and tore off again.

"Hey!" Max yelled, and she skidded to a stop, turning to look quizzically back at him. "Wait for me."

She did, more or less. He found his rhythm quickly, and they started down the beach together, Max on the firmly packed surface of the wet sand, Lola bounding through the ankle-deep water. She liked to speed forward to scatter the flocks of birds, then loop back around to regain her place just in front of him, glancing at him as if she wondered why he was so slow.

He discovered that she would respond to a two-note whistle, and practiced calling her to him as they ran. The fog was thinner than usual, and he could see traces of the evening sun shining weakly through the drifting mist. He lifted his face to the sky and took deep breaths of the ocean air. It was the shortest five miles that he had ever run.

CHAPTER 22

◆

Carly was curled up on the couch in her apartment, wearing her favorite peach bathrobe and reading a mystery novel, when the doorbell rang. It was 8 P.M., and she had gotten back from pet duties at Henry's house only half an hour earlier. She had jumped in and out of the shower, and immediately settled down to relax. She was warm, clean, comfortable, and absorbed in her book, and moving was the last thing that she felt like doing.

The bell sounded again and was accompanied this time by an authoritative rapping. Carly groaned and got slowly to her feet, cinching the belt of her robe more modestly around her. She opened the door and stopped short when she saw who was standing outside. "Max," she said, surprised. "What are you doing here?"

"I was in the neighborhood," he said. He looked warily into her apartment. "Where's Nero?"

"Gone."

"You took him back to the park? Good."

"No," Carly said. "I found him a home."

"Not possible. What did you really do?"

"It's true. There is the nicest little old lady three doors down the street, and she met him yesterday morning when I had him out for a walk. The two of them fell in love, can you believe it? He lets her rub his tummy. It just proves what I've always believed, that there's someone out there for everyone." Max's expression made her laugh. "We should all be so lucky," she added.

"Maybe so," Max said. "But if my someone turned out to be a fat, psychotic little dog, I'd want to have a few words with the man upstairs." He brushed past her in the doorway. His hair was damp and windblown, and he was wearing black nylon running clothes and sneakers. The jacket was unzipped, showing a white T-shirt underneath, and she could smell the salt of the ocean on him.

"Where have you been?" she asked. It was dark outside, and the fog was blowing past the streetlights in curling white wisps. His car was parked on the street, and she saw a furry form in the backseat. "Pauline told me that you took Lola and drove off into the sunset."

"We went running at the beach." Max stripped off his windbreaker and tossed it on a chair.

"All this time? It's been dark for an hour!"

"We went out for cheeseburgers afterward."

"Let me get this straight," Carly said. "You allowed a wet and sandy dog to get into the backseat of your Jaguar? And then you took her to a restaurant and fed her a cheeseburger?"

"Three cheeseburgers." Max said. "She was hungry. And what was I supposed to do, make her walk home?"

Carly didn't bother to argue. If someone had offered to

bet her, three weeks ago, that Max Giordano—of the immaculate suits and frosty manners—would shortly be chauffeuring a Great Dane around in his luxury sedan, she would have lost a fortune.

"You'd better bring her inside," she said. "She's steaming up your windows."

Lola, exhausted from the excitement of the day, came in and collapsed under Carly's kitchen table and began to snore. Max didn't show any signs of weariness. He moved around the apartment, touching things. He picked up a photo of her family and set it down again, crooked. He examined the book she had been reading. He ran his hands over the blanket on the back of the couch.

Carly stood, watching him pace, wondering what had prompted his visit. She had the feeling, as she did every time he was in her apartment, that she was caught with a too-big animal in a too-small cage. He gave no indication of what he wanted, so she finally just sat down, and waited.

"Long day at work?" he asked. He did not appear to notice that she was wearing a bathrobe.

Carly shrugged. "Richard had one of his tantrums and tried to send our new technician home. I had to juggle the schedule to keep the poor guy out of Rich's way, so he was stuck in the back cleaning cages for part of the afternoon. Not exactly the work he signed on for, I think." She sighed. "I don't know what's going on with Rich. I swear that he's changed over this past year."

"Don't tell me that he used to be sweet and charming."

"When we were a couple, he had a sense of humor. Well, sort of. He's never been able to laugh at himself, but we had jokes together. Now, I can hardly imagine him laughing, in a genuine way."

"How sad," Max said coldly.

"It is sad. It makes me wish that there was something I could do to help him—"

"*Help* him? That makes a lot of sense." He was standing behind the couch, and his hands were clenched into the crocheted blanket that she had draped over it to hide the worn upholstery.

"What's the matter with you?" Carly asked, exasperated. "Stop it, Max. My mother made that blanket, and you're going to ruin it." She stood up and reached forward, across the couch, and took his hands in an attempt to disengage them physically. He abruptly let go of the blanket, and his fingers snapped around her wrists like manacles. "Ouch," she said, stumbling forward against the cushions. He let go, and she recovered her balance, looking up at him with wide, surprised eyes.

"Did it ever occur to you to be more discriminating about whom you spend your kindness on?" he asked. "Not to be so damn quick to defend every idiot who starts whining about having had a rough life?"

"I don't do that," Carly said.

He looked coolly at her. "No? I heard an interesting story about a Cuban exchange student. What was his name?"

"Luis. How do you know about him? No, let me guess. My family told you. What did they say, exactly?"

"That he almost persuaded you to marry him when he told you that he needed US citizenship to keep from being sent home, where Castro wanted to have him killed because of his pro-democratic beliefs."

"I was *nineteen*! I felt sorry for him."

"Obviously. When he turned out to be a con artist from the Philippines, you still helped him with the immigration forms."

"He wasn't a bad guy, just desperate for a visa. There's not a lot of work in Manila."

"That's not how your family tells it."

"My family," Carly said hotly, "talks too much. What else did they tell you?"

"Enough to give me the impression that you have a regular habit of bringing home charity cases. I found it very enlightening, considering where I was at the time. So, tell me, Carly. Why did you take me to Davis?"

Carly looked at him, dismayed. *Great*, she thought. *Thanks, everyone.* Her family, having been told that Max was just a friend, had probably thought that he would be amused by tales of her past misadventures. Instead, he had drawn the obvious conclusion.

"I took you to Davis because I thought that my family would like you," she said carefully. "And I thought that you would like them. That's all. I told you, we always have guests for Sunday dinner."

Max raised his eyebrows but said nothing.

Carly sighed. "Max, how could anyone think of you as a charity case? You're handsome, and smart, and successful, and rich."

"Damn right," he said.

"But," Carly continued, "like I told you before, I don't think it's good to be alone in the world. When I made you the offer of family, it wasn't because I felt sorry for you—"

"No? Why was it, then?"

"It was because I thought that you might . . . that we could . . . uh . . ." She faltered, trying to find a way to explain the difference between pity and compassion.

Max nodded grimly. "That's what I thought," he said, moving toward her. "Let me be very clear about this, Carly. My grandfather can pick up abandoned animals, pet them and feed them, and make their little lives happy. But I am no goddamned stray cat."

"I know that," Carly said. "But—"

"So don't insult my intelligence by telling me that if I just start coming to dinner with your big, happy family, I'll suddenly become one of you. I won't. That's not the way life works."

"Max, I understand if you don't want—"

"What I *want* has nothing to do with it," he said fiercely. "You just don't get it, do you? It isn't a matter of choice. You didn't choose your life any more than I chose mine. That's just the way the cards fell, and I'm fine with it. You may have been born lucky, but I made my own luck, and I'm nobody's damn charity case anymore."

He stopped, waiting as if he was daring her to disagree, and then he seemed to hear the echo of his own words in the silence. His mouth tightened. "Unbelievable," he muttered, more to himself than to her.

"What?" Carly asked.

"This doesn't happen to me," Max said darkly. "Ever. Except with you. I don't know what it is about you, Carly, that pushes me over the edge."

His eyes moved over her, and something in his expression made her breath catch in her throat. He looked like a stranger, she thought, something that shouldn't have surprised her. In many ways, he still was a stranger. It wasn't that she had been taking him for granted—it would be impossible to take a man like Max for granted—but she had begun to assume that she knew him. Or at least, that she understood him. Who he was, what he needed, how she could help him—it had been clear to her. But, looking at him now, Carly wondered if she had been overconfident. He was right, she thought warily. He was not a stray cat. He suddenly looked much more like a prowling leopard.

"Max . . ." she began, and then stopped as he reached out and put one finger firmly over her mouth. It was a small gesture, but she hadn't expected it, and it sent a jolt through her. She stared at him, her lips parting under his touch. His eyes were shadowed by dark lashes, and she could read nothing in them.

"What do *you* want?" he asked. His hand slid around to the nape of her neck, and her heart quickened.

"What do you mean?" she whispered.

His mouth curved, but it was not humor that she saw on his face. "You and your charmed life," he said. "There must be something that you want and can't have. What is it?"

You, she thought. Her skin was shimmering under his touch like the surface of a pool in the rain. She bit her lip. "I don't know," she said, her eyes meeting his. "Max, please . . ."

His arm tightened, pulling her toward him. "There is a very fine line between wanting and needing," he said, his mouth only inches from hers. "And I'm defining it. I'm going to push you over the edge this time, Carly. Let's see how you like it."

She had no time to question this before he kissed her. It was a slow, hot kiss, demanding but perfectly controlled, and it went on, and on, until her body was taut and her breath was fast and ragged. She slid her hands under his shirt and ran them up his chest, feeling the curves of the firm muscles under his skin. He was hot and damp with sweat, and he felt incredible to her, hard and soft all at once. She brushed her palms over the pebbles of his nipples, then brought them down over the ridges of his stomach to the waistband of his pants.

He sucked in a sharp breath and caught her wrists, stopping her. "My terms," he said, roughly, against her mouth. "Not yours."

He reached for her belt and pulled it loose with one abrupt motion. The edges of the robe fell open around her, letting in a rush of cool air that shocked Carly's flushed skin. Underneath, she was wearing only white cotton panties, and she felt a shiver of purely primal excitement as Max held her by the shoulders, his eyes moving over her body.

Impatiently, she knotted her fingers into the front of his shirt and tugged. "Take this off."

"I have a better idea," he said, and pushed her robe off her shoulders. It slumped around her feet in a soft heap, and before she realized what he intended to do, he had picked her up as easily as if she were a child. She gasped, tensing against him, and heard him laugh, low in his throat.

"What are you doing?" she asked, breathlessly.

"What I should have done last week," he said, and carried her toward the bedroom.

Carly had one brief moment to remember, somewhere in the back of her mind, that she had not made the bed that morning. And then Max put her down in the middle of the rumpled blankets and began to kiss her in a way that obliterated all other thought.

He took his time with her, moving slowly, exploring her with his hands and mouth, until her nerve endings were crackling, and she was tossing restlessly under him. She gripped his shoulders, feeling the muscles flex as his mouth trailed a line of heat down, over her breasts and stomach, to linger on the sensitive skin just under her navel.

Carly moaned, and his arm tightened under her, lifting her slightly as he slipped his fingertips under the edge of her panties. He bent his head, and she felt his breath, hot through the thin cotton. He began to kiss her slowly, brushing his mouth back and forth against her. Carly's head fell back. The intensity of the sensation was dulled only slightly by the layer of fabric between his lips and her flesh, and she could feel the burr of his beard stubble grazing her inner thighs. There was a hot flood rising inside her, and her nerves were so tight that she could feel herself quivering like a guitar string. She thought that she was going to die if she did not have him inside her. It was the most incredibly carnal feeling she'd ever experienced.

"Max," she gasped, her fingers digging urgently into his shoulders. "Please, please. Don't wait. I can't . . ."

He didn't wait. She realized then, from the force of his hands as he pulled the scrap of cotton down and away from her body, that the controlled pace had not been easy for him, either. She watched as he stood and stripped off the rest of his clothes. The bedroom was dark, lit only by the glow from the lamps in the living room, and Max was silhouetted against the bright doorway, dusky and featureless as a shadow as he turned to her.

And then his arms were around her and she was holding him, pulling him down on top of her, feeling the solid weight of him pressing her into the mattress. His mouth met hers again, in a deep, hot kiss, and she heard him groan. He raised his head and looked into her eyes. "Carly," he said, his voice low and rough with passion, "are you sure you want to do this?"

He had something in his hand, and she realized that it was a condom. He must have taken it from his wallet when he undressed, she thought, shocked that it hadn't even occurred to her to use protection. Max was definitely the one in control this time.

"Yes," she said breathlessly. "Yes, I'm sure. Put it on. Hurry."

Moments later, the hard muscles of his legs parted hers, and with one thrust, he buried himself in her. She cried out as he entered her, and tears came to her eyes. She wrapped her legs around him, trying to draw him in deeper, wanting to feel him in the very core of her.

His skin was slick with sweat, and her hands slipped over his back as she clung to him, moving with him, listening to his ragged breath. She felt the flood begin to rise again, surging up inside her, higher, and higher as Max's body pushed roughly against hers. It was filling her skin, she thought dizzily, swelling outward with a pressure that suddenly seemed to drown her mind. For a moment, she couldn't see, couldn't hear. And then everything exploded in a burst of sensation that seemed to go on and on. Her body shuddered as spasms went through her, and she thought that she might have shouted.

She heard Max's voice and felt his hand twist into her hair. He stared down into her eyes. "What have you done to me?" he asked hoarsely, and took her mouth with his own. His body slammed into hers, and she felt him tense.

"Ah, God," he groaned, throwing his head back. And then he collapsed onto her, rolling slightly sideways so that he wouldn't crush her. They lay silently, still entwined, and did not move for a long time.

Carly was the first to pull away. Max's legs were heavy and warm on hers, and she carefully disentangled herself, moving back far enough on the bed so that she could sit up and look at him. His eyes were closed, and his breathing was slow and steady. He didn't move, and she thought that he must be asleep. Curiously, she studied him. His naked body was long and lean, but he had clearly worked for his well-defined muscles. His coloring was lighter than the southern Italians, but darker than the WASPy Tremaynes. With his eyes closed, he looked like a guy from Brooklyn. With his eyes open . . . he looked like Max. The combination of his olive skin and dark hair with the pale Tremayne eyes was, Carly thought with sudden affectionate pride, totally unique.

She reached out and delicately traced the curves of his arm with her fingertip.

He opened his eyes, and she stopped, startled. "Oh," she said. "I didn't mean to wake you."

"I wasn't sleeping." He looked at her with a thoughtful expression, then rolled onto his back and put his hands behind his head, staring at the ceiling.

"Regrets already?" she asked lightly, trying to sound as if his answer didn't matter to her.

He turned his head, and his eyes met hers. "No," he said, as if it surprised him. "Not at all. I feel pretty damn good, actually." He stretched and sat up. "Are you hungry?"

"Yes. What did you have in mind?"

He laughed softly and reached out to brush his fingers over her breasts. "Food," he said. "For now. Put some clothes on, and I'll show you how to make the world's best pasta primavera."

CHAPTER 23

"Excuse me," Max said, wiggling his foot. It was past eleven o'clock on Friday morning. He had been sitting at the desk in his hotel room for over an hour, and he had not moved in all that time. His entire leg had fallen asleep, and he couldn't stand it any longer.

Lola blinked at him and obligingly shifted her head onto his other foot. "That wasn't what I meant," he muttered. It was beyond him to understand why, when confronted with the splendor and comfort of a Ritz-Carlton hotel suite, she would end up wedged into the space under his desk. He obviously did not think like a dog, and he didn't plan to start anytime soon.

They had caused a small commotion in the hotel that morning when he had marched through the lobby with her at his side. Max had had a business call scheduled for 10 A.M., and he had come straight from Carly's apartment to the Ritz.

Lola had kept to a perfect heel all the way through the lobby to the elevator. It was a product of shyness, not training, but the result was that she flanked him as perfectly as a Seeing Eye dog. They moved too quickly to get any reaction other than a few pop-eyed looks from the front desk staff. If Lola had been a Chihuahua, he might have been able to smuggle her in, but it was hard to hide 120 pounds of Great Dane under a coat. He had not been surprised when the phone began to ring as soon as they were in the room.

"Mr. Giordano? Good morning." It was the Guest Services Manager. "I've been told that you have a . . . dog . . . in your room."

"That's true," Max said. "A big one."

"I'm going to have to ask you to remove her, sir. Guests are not permitted to bring their pets into the hotel."

"She's not my pet."

"I beg your pardon?"

"She's not my pet," Max repeated. "I don't have a pet."

There was a short pause. "But you have a dog in your room, sir. This is against our policy. She can't stay there."

"*Stay* here?" Max exclaimed, appalled. "With me? Damn right she can't. There's no way she's staying here." He looked down at Lola, who was asleep and snoring gently. "Absolutely not," he said.

"Yes, sir. I'd be glad to have the concierge find a kennel to board her while you're with us."

"I can't put her in a kennel. She's not my dog."

"Well . . . you can't *keep* her in your *room*, sir."

"I'm not keeping her. She can leave if she wants to—what do I care? But she's asleep, and I'm about to make a call to Buenos Aires, so if you'll excuse me . . ."

"But—but—"

"Thank you," Max said, and hung up.

*   *   *

They had at least had the grace not to bother him while he was on the phone, but the hiatus had not lasted long. Max was shaking the pins and needles out of his newly remobilized foot when the doorbell rang.

"You're certainly *canis non grata* around here," he said to Lola, who was looking suspiciously at the door. Max felt the same way. He was paying enough money to these people, you'd think they would relax. What did they expect her to do, eat the drapes? Even if she did, they had his credit card on file, and they should know by now that it worked. He had every intention of taking Lola back to Henry's house as soon as he had the chance, but he didn't like being nagged.

He opened the door, ready to express his opinion of the "guest services," and felt the words wither and die on his lips. It was not the manager. It was a slim blond woman, dressed in her usual uniform of a black designer pantsuit and three-inch heels. She smiled when she saw him, then pursed her lips and blew him a kiss. "Hello, darling," she said. "Surprise."

Max felt the jarring impact of two worlds colliding. "Nina," he said, "what the hell are you doing here?"

It was not until a few minutes later, after she had inspected the suite, commented on the decor and the view and settled herself on the couch, one tailored leg crossed elegantly over the other, that Max was able to collect himself enough to be even slightly polite.

"Do you want something to drink?" he asked.

"What, from the minibar?" Nina laughed. "I suppose a glass of wine is out of the question, hmm? They don't put drinkable chardonnay in those little bottles. How about whiskey on the rocks?"

"It's eleven-thirty in the morning," Max said, disapprovingly.

She shrugged. "Well, that's almost noon, isn't it? Oh, Max, I just like to provoke you. Give me a seltzer or something—I'll be a California girl. Thank you." She accepted the glass and the bottle and gazed charmingly at him. "Well, you look healthy. Just back from a run?"

"More or less." He was still dressed in running clothes.

"Poor Max, you look somewhere between stunned and horrified to see me," Nina said lightly, but he heard a note of pique in her voice. She had been hoping for a warmer reception. "I should have called. If I had, I could have arrived *after* your shower. Or is this how you always dress now? Have you gone native?"

"What are you doing in San Francisco, Nina?"

"I'm putting together a fifties-themed editorial for winter—a tribute to Kim Novak in *Vertigo*. It's just a quick trip—I'm going back to the City tomorrow morning."

The City, meaning New York City, specifically Manhattan. All Manhattanites believed that there was only one real city on earth, and they considered the word a proper noun that needed no qualifiers. Whether she was in Albany or Milan, to Nina, the City would always be the City.

"I've missed you," she said. "And it's not as if you remember to call me."

"Don't try to tell me that you've been sitting at home waiting for the phone to ring."

She laughed. "That would be boring, wouldn't it? Max, I know that this is hardly an exclusive relationship, but you really could phone and say hello every now and then. It's been over a month since I've heard from you."

"I've been busy."

"Out here? What's to do? There's no real theater, and not much of a gallery scene. I suppose they must have restaurants, though. One of the photographers was telling me about a place that serves only raw foods . . . it sounds very cleansing."

"Actually," Max said, "there is theater. And art. There are also a lot of very good restaurants, but I haven't been going to them. I've been working."

"Too hard, I'm sure. Let's dress up and go out on the town tonight. Oh, don't frown at me like that." She stood up and came toward him, reaching out to caress his chest. Her hair tickled his chin. He could smell her perfume, a strong floral he had once found appropriately glamorous but now seemed cloying. "Come on . . . I know you've missed me. We'll stay out late, and then come back here and . . . talk. Or something."

Max stood still as her arms twined around him, and she tilted her face up to his. Nina had been a model, so she was tall for a woman, and in her high heels, she was almost as tall as he was. Her lips parted invitingly, and her hands tightened on the back of his neck, urging his mouth toward hers.

Max reached back and gently disengaged her hands. Irritated, she pulled out of his grasp and stepped back. "I'm getting the feeling that I'm not welcome here. Is there something I should know?"

From the other room, there was a sudden creak of bedsprings. It was quiet but distinct, and Nina's eyebrows rose. She looked curiously at the double doors, which stood ajar. "Aha," she said. "Now I understand. Did I arrive at an awkward moment?"

"No," he said.

She smiled. "Such a poker face. You should have said something. Do you think I'm so tacky that I'd make a scene? Or is your new friend just shy?"

"She is shy," Max said. "She ran and hid in the bedroom when I opened the door. Before that, she was under the desk."

Nina's mouth dropped open, and Max gave his two-note whistle.

"Oh, my God," Nina exclaimed, as Lola came bounding out. "What *is* that? A pony?"

Lola did not greet Nina in her usual bipedal fashion, which was probably a good thing. Instead, she skidded to a halt just behind Max and craned her neck around his legs. She sniffed at Nina, then sneezed vigorously.

"Ugh," Nina said, staring at Lola, then at Max as if he had just grown a second head. "I didn't know that dogs could be so big. How did this happen?"

"She eats a lot."

"No, I mean, how did *you* end up with a pet?"

The distaste on Nina's face raised a fierce protectiveness in Max. It was too bad, he thought, that some people had such bad attitudes toward animals. Lola had already been kicked around by one human, and as long as he was on duty, she wouldn't be sneered at by any other. He reached down to rub her head. She whined softly, and he said, "Are you a good dog? Yes, you are."

"Well," Nina said valiantly. "This is nice. I love dogs. I shared an apartment once with a woman who had a dog.

One of those little furry ones. It was white and really very sweet. It didn't shed much at all. Or smell. She took it everywhere, in a Louis Vuitton carrier."

She picked up her glass, looking as if she wished for something stronger. She was really very beautiful, Max thought, with the same kind of aesthetic admiration that he would have had for a fine piece of art. Everything about her was meticulously controlled and groomed, from her expensively highlighted hair to her pale pink nails to her toned body. She was everything that a rich, successful man should want, and at one time, that perfection had pleased him very much.

He had never been particularly passionate about her, nor she about him. That wasn't the point. They looked good together at charity events and business dinners. Other men stared at her and envied him, and that had been enough for him. He liked Nina. He appreciated her drop-dead elegance and her attitude, and her rich-girl sense of entitlement had always amused him. She was everything he had always thought that he wanted—not just in a woman, but in a life.

"Max," Nina said, "don't you dare tell me that you need to work tonight. There's something very important that we have to talk about."

"What?"

She tapped one polished nail on his chest. "Not now." Her smooth smile returned. "I have to run—you're not the only busy one, you know. So, dinner? I'll meet you here at seven." She handed him the empty glass. "*Ciao*, darling."

* * *

When Carly arrived at the clinic, Michelle was already at her desk. "What's on my schedule today?" Carly asked after greeting the receptionist.

"Routine stuff. Exams this morning, then you've got surgery all afternoon. Two spays and some dental extractions. The surgery patients are already checked in, except for the Anderson dog, who gets here at noon. I pulled all the charts and put them on your desk. Dr. Wexler left this morning for that conference in Florida. Can you believe he locked his office? What does he think I'm going to do, go through his desk and peek at his dirty magazines, or whatever it is he keeps in there? Like I care."

"He does take his privacy seriously," Carly said.

"Well," Michelle said smugly, "he's not as clever as he thinks he is. There are two keys to that lock, and I have one of them in my drawer. I've had it since this place opened, and it's a good thing, too. The way he was rushing around this morning, he's probably locked up something we'll need, and he won't be back until next week. You should have seen him. He never used to be nervous about giving seminars, but he was jittering around like he'd had ten espressos. His eyes were bugging out. I just stayed out of his way."

Carly could imagine it, and she was glad not to have been there to witness it. Absently, she shuffled through the stack of mail sitting on Michelle's desk.

There were a few personal letters and postcards in the midst of the usual junk advertising, and she picked one up. "Look at this—Tiffany stationery with an embossed blue pawprint. It can only be . . ."

"Gigi Beeson!" Michelle crowed. "And Percy the Pug. Who ever heard of a dog with his own stationery?"

Carly slit open the envelope and pulled out the sheet of paper. "Dear Dr. Martin," she read out loud. "Just a little note to tell you that I am feeling much better, thanks to your quick work. Mama is glad to have her earring back, and I am much more careful now when I kiss her. Yours truly, Percy."

"Awww," said Michelle. "That's cute."

"Here." Carly handed her the enclosed photo. In it, Gigi was holding Percy up to the camera, at an angle that distorted the pug's already squashed features, making his flat nose look enormous. Dog and owner wore matching green sweaters. "Tack this up on our celebrity wall."

In her office, Carly glanced through the day's client folders. They were all stuffed with papers, and they made a precarious pile. It would be great when they had the office completely computerized, she thought, although at the current rate, that was most likely to happen sometime long after she had gone. None of the clinic staff were thrilled with Richard's plan that they should spend their spare time doing data entry, and work was proceeding slowly.

To give Richard the credit he deserved, he had asked them to do no more than he had done himself. Client histories didn't particularly interest him, but money did, and he had been spending evenings and weekends bringing the clinic's accounting into the twenty-first century. That much, at least, was finished. He had made a few offers to sit down with Carly and teach her how to use the new software, but she had gone to the computer store and bought a book instead. She was looking forward to studying the manual, then shocking Rich with her sudden proficiency.

Through the open door of her office, Carly could hear

subdued rock tunes coming from the lab, where Brian and Pam were working. She smiled. Richard disapproved of music in the office, on the grounds that it was "unprofessional," but Carly had never minded, and the staff knew it. The clinic was officially hers for a week, and it was nice to see everyone lightening up a bit.

CHAPTER 24

———◆———

Among the messages on Max's voice mail that evening was one from Tom Meyer, reporting that the initial background checks on Carly Martin and Pauline Braun had turned up nothing of note in either case. No credit problems, no criminal records. Carly's worst offense, it seemed, was a habit of picking up speeding tickets. Max was not sure how she managed that, considering the state of her car. Tom reminded him that it would take longer to get more detailed information on Carly's finances, but he expected to have it by the end of next week.

Nina was waiting for Max when he walked into the hotel bar, which was a first in his acquaintance with her. She liked to be fashionably late and had a fondness for making dramatic, breathlessly apologetic entrances, so he had expected to have at least fifteen minutes to sit and relax before she arrived.

"You're on time," he said, and kissed her on the cheek. "This must be important."

She was wearing a black cocktail dress similar to the one that Carly had startled him with. She was much thinner than Carly, though, with fashionable angles where Carly had flesh, and the effect was stylish, but not erotic.

"I hope you don't mind eating here at the hotel," she said. "It's more private. I'm not in the mood for one of those loud, trendy places, and I know that you don't really like them. This will be more comfortable."

Privacy? Comfortable? This was a new side of Nina. Max raised his eyebrows but didn't argue.

Whatever it was that she had on her mind, though, she didn't disclose it in a hurry. They ordered dinner and made light conversation through three courses. Max found himself tuning out as she filled him in on the latest news about her friends in the City.

"You're not listening to me," Nina said reproachfully.

"I was listening." He picked up a cube of sugar and stirred it into his coffee.

She raised her eyebrows at him. "So what do you think about Sergio's vacation?"

"Sounds fine."

She exhaled impatiently. "I just told you that he was kidnapped by aliens."

"Really," he said dryly. "What did they do to him? That, I'd like to hear about."

Nina looked startled, and he realized that she was unaccustomed to hearing him joke. Hadn't he had a sense of humor in New York? Surely he had, but he couldn't remember laughing much. He had always been working, and when he wasn't working, he had been performing the obligatory social duties. None of it had been particularly joyful.

"*Joyful*." He frowned. Why the hell had he chosen that word? Joy was not something that he had ever associated with his life, or even sought. Joy was a word for hippies, a peace-and-love word, a concept that had little place in an upwardly mobile lifestyle.

"It's been hard not having you around, Max," Nina said suddenly. She reached across the table and took his hand. "But it really has given me a chance to think about some important things."

The idea that she had been sitting around pining for him and reevaluating her life in his absence was a little too much for Max to swallow. He knew her too well. Nina's idea of introspection involved figuring out which shoes suited her mood on any given day.

"I see," he said.

"What I'm trying to say is that I've been wrong," she said. "Do you remember when you wanted me to stop seeing other people? I should have done it. I wish I had. I just wasn't ready to settle down then. I know that it hurt you, and I'm sorry."

Max blinked at her. "That was a long time ago, Nina."

"I know. And just think where we might be now if I'd done what you asked."

Max preferred not to. In his opinion, rather than making apologies, she should be taking credit for averting a disaster. He doubted that her unwillingness to commit to him had anything to do with an understanding of their basic incompatibility—rather, she had disliked the idea of having her options limited. The cynic in him reminded him that at that time, he had also had a lot less money.

"It doesn't matter," he said, meaning it.

"But it does!" she exclaimed, squeezing his hand and

looking warmly into his eyes. "I'm ready for a different kind of relationship now. When you come back to New York, we'll get a place together. I was thinking about something on the Upper West Side ... maybe a penthouse."

"What if I don't come back to New York?" Max asked.

"What?" She stared at him as if he had just announced that he planned to live in Tibet. "Stay here? You're not serious."

To Max's own surprise, he was. He did not want to go back, he realized. It was not something that he could rationally explain, but it seemed to him that the New York part of his life—the drama that had begun in Brooklyn thirty-eight years ago—had somehow ended with the sale of his company. Whatever lay ahead would take place here, in California.

"Why would you want to live here?" Nina demanded. "I mean, it's pretty, but ..."

"I like the beach," Max said.

"We'll get a house in the Hamptons."

"Not that kind of beach," Max said. It wasn't rich small-town clapboard and exclusivity that he wanted, it was the mysterious fog, and the smell of cold salt air, and the towering sand cliffs. It was the endless stretch of coastline, and the endless sense of freedom.

Nina frowned. "Well, there's the Caribbean. St. Bart's ... Mustique ..."

"Not that kind of beach, either."

She let out a short breath of frustration. Max could see that she was thinking hard. He waited. Finally, she squared her shoulders and looked straight at him. "I want to have a baby," she said.

It was the last thing in the world that Max would have expected to hear from her, but somehow, oddly, it made sense. "I see."

"Do you?" she asked plaintively. "I think we should get married, Max. I'm tired of my life—it's too crazy. I want something new."

Max didn't answer. He didn't know exactly how old Nina was—she had never told him—but he guessed that she was about thirty-five. Maybe everyone reached a point where the things that they had always taken for granted began to stir like boats in a rising tide.

"I'm sure you never thought you'd hear me say that," she said. "I couldn't have done it before—I was establishing my career. But now . . . Max, we could hire lots of help, and it wouldn't be so bad at all. And there are the cutest things out there for babies, you wouldn't believe it. Little Gucci booties . . . so adorable."

Max sipped his coffee. She had not relinquished her hold on his other hand, and he felt the edges of her nails digging into his skin. He wondered how she intended to diaper a baby without jabbing it with those beautiful, perfect nails.

"I know how much this idea of family means to you," Nina continued. "You'd come back to New York for that, wouldn't you? For a family? Our family?"

He shook his head. "No."

Her lips parted in shock. "What?"

"I'm not going back. I'm sorry."

"But . . . but I don't want to live *here*," she exclaimed, then stopped. "Oh," she said slowly. "You're not asking me to, are you?" She released his hand abruptly. "Well, this is hardly how I planned it. God, Max, don't give me that stony look. I'm not going to fight with you in the middle of a restaurant. Please. *C'est la vie.* Should I assume that we're finished, then?"

Max set down his coffee cup. "I'll get the check."

"Thank you, but I wasn't referring to our dinner, darling. I do think that you've just answered my question, though."

The lobby was busy, though not as crowded as it should have been on a Friday night. The lounge was half-full, and the sound of live piano music mixed with the clinking of glassware and the background murmur of voices. Nina linked her arm through Max's as they walked, making bright conversation. Any casual observer would have thought that they were on the best of terms, and for all Max knew, they still were. Nina had a veneer of poise so well tempered that it would take more than the blow he had delivered to crack it.

She was telling him an anecdote about a well-known photographer, and he was listening politely, his eyes roaming over the crowd as they walked together toward the entranceway. He didn't know which happened first: the slowing of Nina's stride or his own sudden shock of recognition. He stopped in his tracks, with Nina still clinging to his arm.

"Who is that?" Nina asked, but Max barely heard her. The stream of anonymous faces continued to flow past, but he saw nothing but Carly. She was standing just inside the entrance, looking from him, to Nina, to him again, her expressive face marked with surprise and pain.

CHAPTER 25

———— •◆• ————

Carly was as easy to read as a tabloid newspaper. Max heard Nina chuckle softly, telling him that she had guessed the basics of what was happening. Nina had a great love of dramatic scenes and obviously foresaw a good one, but Max had no intention of allowing either himself or Carly to be anyone's entertainment for the evening.

Carly stepped forward. "Hello, Max," she said, with simple dignity. He could hear a slight tremor in her voice. She turned to Nina and extended her hand. "Hello. I'm Carly Martin."

Nina smiled and offered Carly her fingers, elegantly limp, as if she were more accustomed to having her hand kissed than shaken. "Nina Blackwell."

Carly nodded. "Yes, I know. Welcome to San Francisco."

"Why, thank you," Nina said. "Max is such a wonderful host. I suppose we should have gone out for dinner, but staying in the hotel was so much easier." She looked Carly up and down, her eyebrows slightly raised. "And how did you say that you know Max?"

"I'm his grandfather's veterinarian," Carly said.

"Pardon me?" Nina looked blank. Max had never said a word to her—or to anyone else in New York—about Henry Tremayne.

"A veterinarian is a doctor who takes care of animals," Carly said coolly.

"Yes," Nina said, irritated. "I know that. Max, did she say something about your grandfather? I thought that you didn't have any family."

"I do now," Max said.

"Why, that's such good news," Nina exclaimed. "He lives here, in San Francisco? And you've become close?" She looked at Carly. "He must be very old. What a comfort for him to have Max here."

"I hope so," Carly said. "He's in the hospital."

"Oh, I'm so sorry." Nina put her hand back on Max's arm. "Darling, what a stressful time for you. We should have picked a better night to talk about marriage and children." She tossed a smile at Carly. "It would be a mistake to rush into a decision about something so important, don't you agree?"

"Hold it," Max said sharply, "We were not—"

But Carly interrupted him. "I absolutely agree," she said in a strange, tense voice. "Decisions about marriage and children are the most important ones that you'll ever make. So I'll let you two get on with it. Good luck."

She turned and fled before Max could react. He had a glimpse of her disappearing through the front door of the hotel, into a throng of tourists who had just disembarked from an airport shuttle van.

"Dammit," he said, incensed, and went after her. The tourists, and their luggage, were clogging the entrance. He pushed his way through the doors, ignoring the exclamations of protest. He stopped on the pavement outside, looking left and right. The half circle of driveway was filled with cars, valets, bellmen, and luggage carts, but there was no sign of Carly and no indication of where she had gone.

The doorman noticed him. "Can I help you with something, Mr. Giordano?"

"There was a woman here just a minute ago. Reddish hair, wearing a dark . . . something." Max didn't know what she had been wearing. He only remembered her face. The doorman shook his head and apologized. Too many people. He had been dealing with luggage and hadn't seen anyone of Carly's description.

"Have someone get my car," Max said.

"Right away, sir. Two minutes to bring it around."

Nina was waiting for him when he walked back into the lobby. "Aren't you chivalrous?" she said brightly. "Did you find her?"

"No."

"Too bad. That girl—poor thing—is absolutely in love with you, can you imagine? I suppose you've noticed. And now I've probably made her cry. I know I shouldn't have teased her like that, but—"

"Drop it," Max said sharply.

"Excuse me?" She stared at him, comprehension dawning on her face. "Well," she said slowly. "This is very interesting. I did wonder for a moment if you could possibly . . . but then I thought, no. Max and a *veterinarian*?"

He clenched his hands at his sides. "Get your car, Nina. Go home."

She began to laugh. "I don't believe this! This is too funny. *This* is why you won't move back to New York? This is why you broke up with me? For her? The girl wears her hair in a braid, for God's sake. Who does she think she is, Holly Hobbie?"

Max said nothing, but the look on his face must have warned her that she had gone too far. She opened her purse and pulled out her valet ticket. "All right," she said. "I'm leaving. If you ever come to your senses, you know where to find me, but I think you might be a lost cause. You look at that girl like an alcoholic looks at a bottle of gin."

"What?" He stared at her.

"You heard me. It's pathetic, Max. I never thought that you of all people would get caught like this. Do you *need* her?"

"No," Max said, but he felt a sudden chill, deep in his gut.

The doorman entered the lobby. "Your car is out front, Mr. Giordano."

"Oh, this is priceless," Nina exclaimed. "You're rushing out to find her. You're so contemptuous of anyone that you consider weak; but you're not very strong yourself, are you? You're the one who told me that love is just another kind of addiction, and now here you are, hooked."

Max turned to leave, and she caught his arm. "This is why we're so good together," she insisted. "You don't need me, and I don't need you. Be realistic, Max. I can give you everything that you ever wanted."

He shook off her clinging fingers. "Not everything," he said, and left her standing there in the crowded lobby.

"Carly! Are you all right? What happened?"

Carly hadn't looked in a mirror since she left her apartment to find Max at the Ritz, almost two hours ago. From the horrified expression on her sister's face, she guessed that she didn't look good. After she had fled the hotel, she had locked herself in her car, parked just around the corner, and cried for half an hour, with the uncontrolled belly-deep sobs of a small child. When she was too exhausted to cry any more, she had driven to Jeannie's house in Berkeley. It was almost ten o'clock, and her sister was wearing her bathrobe, her hair up in a clip and her face shiny with moisturizer.

Jeannie fumbled at the latch on the screen door, opened it, and enfolded Carly in a night-cream-scented hug. Then she pulled away, held Carly at arm's length, and looked her over.

"You're a mess," she said. "You've been crying. Your mascara is all over your cheeks, and your face is swollen up like a muffin. Did Richard do something? I'm going to call Dad and Josh. And Mom, too, God help him—"

Carly burst into a fresh flood of tears. "Not Richard."

"Not Richard? Then who . . ." Jeannie stopped, dismayed. "Carly! You aren't crying about . . . Max? Are you?"

"Max Giordano is a horrible person," Carly sobbed. "I hate him."

"Oh, this is not good," Jeannie exclaimed. "This is very bad. Are you sure?"

Carly stopped crying and looked suspiciously at Jeannie. "Am I sure about what?"

Jeannie waved her hands in agitation. "I don't know. Are you sure that he did whatever you think he did? Maybe there was a misunderstanding."

"Jeannie, you don't even know what happened!"

"You'd better tell me right away. There has to be some kind of mistake. Maybe we can work it out before it gets any worse."

"I can't believe this," Carly said. "I'm your sister, I show up at your door crying, and you're defending Max?"

"We all liked Max. We were hoping that he would come back."

Carly scowled at her. "There used to be loyalty within our family."

Jeannie sighed. "Honey, come inside and tell me everything. Do you want some cocoa?"

"Yes," Carly said, and followed her sister into the house. It didn't take her long to go through the whole story, although she was slightly put out by Jeannie's reaction. Instead of clucking with the appropriate amounts of sympathy and outrage, her sister listened quietly and intently, frowning in concentration like a Supreme Court judge.

"How do you know that they were talking about getting married and having children?" Jeannie asked. "You weren't there during dinner. Who told you that?"

"She did. She was very smug."

"Maybe she was trying to intimidate you. What did Max say?"

"I don't remember the details. I was upset, and now it's all a blur. But I don't think that he said anything."

"Hmm," Jeannie muttered. "This is very strange."

"She said that it was a very serious decision, getting married and having children. He seemed angry with her. I think he must have been asking her to marry him over dinner, and she turned him down. I remember him telling me that she didn't want to live out here in California."

"Oh, dear." Jeannie was beginning to look less confident, which set Carly off again.

"I should never have gone there to see him," she sobbed. "No, I take that back. I'm glad that I did. I would never have known, otherwise. He slept with me, then, the next night, asked her to marry him! Am I that bad in bed?"

"I hope not," Jeannie said, and handed Carly a tissue.

"Very funny," Carly said, and blew her nose. "Well, fine. He can go ahead and love that horrible woman for all I care—he deserves her. I hope they do get married and have lots of horrible children." She buried her head in her arms.

"Oh, dear," Jeannie said again, anxiously. She got up and came around the table to rub Carly's back.

"Why am I so stupid about men?" Carly asked, her voice muffled. "I don't understand why this keeps happening to me. I think I need a psychiatrist."

"No, you don't," Jeannie said soothingly. "You're fine. Well, some of your choices have been a little off, but . . . hush, Carly, never mind. Forget I said that. This time, who knew? We all thought Max was . . . in fact, I still just can't believe . . . You should at least talk to him."

"I don't want to."

"You have to. At least give him a chance to tell you what happened tonight. You deserve that much, and so does he."

"I'm not going looking for him," Carly said stubbornly. "Ever again."

"Well, you can't avoid him, either. Not unless you're planning to abandon Henry's animals and hide in your apartment. Just don't do anything crazy. It's possible that your feelings about Max may be making it hard for you to see the situation clearly."

"But what if I am seeing it clearly?"

Jeannie sighed. "Well, then, don't be too hard on yourself. Remember Dad's motto."

"Which one?" Carly asked. Their father had Latin mottos for most occasions. "*In vino veritas*?"

"No, no. You know the one I mean, the one he always quotes when things like this happen. Remember? 'Even a god finds it hard to love and be wise at the same time.'"

When Max arrived at the Tremayne house on Saturday morning, he was greeted by the sight of a pack of sleeping dogs, scattered around the floor of the solarium and kitchen like lumpy bags of laundry. It was only 8 A.M., too early for them to have finished their breakfasts, but their dozy disinterest in him was a sure sign that they had already been fed. Pauline confirmed it: Carly had come and gone.

"She's supposed to be here at eight," Max said, annoyed. "She's always here at eight."

"Well, Mr. Max, it was as much a surprise to me as it is to you. When I woke up, I was expecting to have a chance to drink my tea in peace before the kitchen was filled with dogs, but she was just finishing when I came downstairs, and she barely bothered to say hello before she ran off again."

"I see," Max said.

"She was acting *very strangely*, in my opinion," Pauline continued. "She looked nervous. She nearly jumped out of her skin when I came into the kitchen and found her there. And then she said something that made no sense."

"What?"

"She said, 'Oh, Pauline, it's you.'" The housekeeper shrugged. "As if she was relieved. I asked her who else it could possibly have been but me, but she didn't answer. I can't imagine what she was up to."

"I can," Max said. He had gone to her apartment last night, looking for her, and found it empty. She did not answer her phone, and she had not returned the message that he left on her answering machine.

"Damn her," he muttered. Lola, who had joyfully attached herself to his hip upon his arrival, whined anxiously. "Not you," he said, and rubbed her ears.

"Are you still having trouble finding Miss Martin?" Pauline inquired. He had awakened her last night when he came to the house. She had answered the door wearing a pink quilted bathrobe with a matching turban, and brandishing a large can of Mace.

"Yes," Max said flatly. He felt like a fool, chasing after a woman who did not want to be found, and he resented it. He wondered where she had gone last night. No doubt she had run off to cry in the arms of her family, telling them everything she thought she knew. Davis was too far away, but there were Martins and Martin affiliates all over the Bay Area. Her sister, he recalled, lived somewhere in Berkeley. By now, they all would have heard about what a bad guy he was—the latest loser in Carly's life.

"Well, if you ask me," Pauline said, "Miss Martin has something on her mind. She is behaving—in my opinion—like someone might behave if they had a *guilty conscience*."

Max exhaled sharply. He was in no mood to deal with innuendo. "You don't like Carly very much, do you?"

Pauline gasped. "Mr. Max!" she exclaimed. "That certainly isn't true. I've been very thankful for Miss Martin's help ever since poor Henry's accident, and I know I've said so. She's been very kind, which is why I never even told you about seeing that van. I knew it would be wrong to say anything, since I really wasn't sure about it . . ."

"What van?" Max asked. "What are you talking about?"

Her lips compressed. "I don't think I should say."

"You already did say," Max growled. "What about a van?"

"Well . . ." Pauline said, looking more uncomfortable than he had ever seen her before, "on that evening when poor Henry fell . . ."

"What about it?"

"Miss Martin says that she left here at six-fifteen."

"That's right. So?"

"I'm sure that's the truth, and now I suppose that you'll think I'm just making this up to be spiteful—"

"Pauline," Max said, ominously. "Tell me what you saw."

The housekeeper's eyes rounded at his tone. "The van. Miss Martin's white van. I can't be absolutely sure—my eyes aren't what they used to be, you know—but when I was coming home, I thought I saw it driving away down the street. That would mean that she left here at seven, Mr. Max. But if she did, why would she lie to you?"

"All clear, sir," said the bellhop in a dramatic sotto voce. He held open the door to the service corridor, and Max hustled Lola out into the dim and silent hallway of the Ritz-Carlton. With the help of a few well-placed bribes, he had created a dog-smuggling route into the hotel that involved entry through the loading-dock door and a trip up in the service elevator. He had his key ready, and they quickly reached his suite.

"In," Max ordered. "Hurry up. No sniffing."

Lola scurried inside, and Max hung out the DO NOT DIS-TURB sign and locked the door. It was dark. A single lamp burned next to the bed, throwing a faint pool of yellow light through the open double doors into the living room. The evening housekeepers had long since come through, and the bed was covered by crisp white sheets, invitingly turned down, which seemed to please Lola. Before Max could say a word, she galloped forward and leaped onto the middle of the duvet. She grinned at him and began to investigate the wrapped chocolate sitting on his pillow.

"Oh, no," Max said. "Absolutely not. I will run with you. I will feed you. I will even accept that you are my dog. But I will not sleep in the same damn bed with you. Get down right now."

It took significant persuasion—and a packet of peanuts from the minibar—to convince Lola to settle down on the rug, but she finally, grudgingly, did so. Max sat down at his desk and made a halfhearted attempt to catch up on his e-mail, but his mind kept returning to the conversation with Pauline. At first, the housekeeper had insisted that she hadn't told anyone else about seeing the white van. But then, as Max questioned her, she had "remembered" mentioning it to Detective Gracie when he interviewed her.

Max had had to make an effort to control himself. "Why would you tell Gracie about this two days ago, but not tell me until now?"

"Well, Mr. Max! He is a *police officer.*"

"I appreciate your sense of civic duty," Max said, "but that doesn't answer my question."

Pauline pursed her lips. "I certainly don't want to be accused of trying to stir up trouble between you and Miss Martin."

Max hadn't even attempted to respond to that.

Pauline wasn't the only one who was being reticent with information. Max had just spoken with Gracie that morning, and the detective hadn't said a word about any sighting of a van. Of course, that was probably because there was nothing to say. With only Pauline's unconfirmed possible sighting, there was no valid reason to doubt Carly's story.

Max wondered if Pauline actually believed that Carly had been involved with Henry's injury. He had asked her that, straight out. She'd had the nerve to look shocked by the question, then she had given him the kind of evasive answer that he had expected. It wouldn't have surprised Max very much to hear that when the woman was alone with Carly, she dropped hints about how he himself might be a villain. God knows, Henry's trust gave him the same motive for murder that it gave Carly.

Or did it? He and Carly had roughly equal shares in Henry's estate, a fortune in either case. But wouldn't money mean more to someone like Carly, who had none? Henry's money would not change Max's own life in any significant way, but Carly was another story entirely. Upon Henry Tremayne's death, she would suddenly become a rich and powerful woman.

But try as he might, Max simply couldn't believe that Carly was capable of premeditated murder. If she was, then she was an actress of a caliber that put any Academy Award winner to shame. What, then, of the van?

Several things were possible, he thought. One was that Pauline had made the whole thing up. Another was that she had seen a van that was not Carly's. Another was that Carly had indeed left the house at seven and lied about it. It seemed impossible, and yet . . .

What if Henry's fall had indeed been an accident, and Carly had witnessed it? Max considered the scenario. While saying good-bye to her at the door, Henry had— somehow—slipped and fallen backward, hitting his head on the statue. It was an improbable notion, but for the moment, he tried to imagine that there had been a freak accident. Carly was physically strong enough to move Henry's body from the front door to the foot of the stairs, but why would she do such a thing? She was a medical professional, and she knew not to move a person with a head injury. The only thing to do at that point was to call an ambulance.

But no ambulance had been called. Whoever had dragged Henry into the house had not had his recovery in mind. They must have believed him to be either dead or moments from death. The only possible purpose for leaving him at the foot of the stairs was to make the cause of his injury—and death—seem obvious, avoiding any investigation. It had almost worked.

Max steeled himself, trying to be objective. Even if Carly did not have the capacity for premeditated murder, was it possible that—having seen the accident—she had decided to take advantage of the opportunity? She had claimed surprise when he first told her of the terms of the Tremayne trust, but she had also admitted that she and Henry had discussed it. She might well have known what Henry's death would mean to her.

It made sense. Didn't it?

"No," Max said, aloud. It did not. If Carly had been involved with the accident, something in her manner would have already shown it. Nobody could handle almost four weeks of stressful uncertainty without starting to crack around the edges. When he looked into Carly's eyes, he saw nothing but unwavering honesty. If eyes really were the windows to the soul, he thought, then Carly Martin's soul was as clear and luminous as a summer sky.

And if eyes were sometimes just another part of a beautiful, deceptive facade? Max frowned down at the computer. Nobody was that good a liar, he told himself. It simply wasn't possible. Was it?

CHAPTER 26

———◆———

Coward, Carly said to herself, as she parked outside Henry's house on Sunday morning. It was just past 7 A.M., much earlier than she usually arrived. The dogs were delighted to be fed at any hour, but it was not a desire to accommodate them that had gotten her out of her bed at sunrise on a weekend. She had changed her schedule around yesterday as well, and had managed to avoid Max completely.

"You're early again," Pauline said, as Carly walked into the kitchen. The housekeeper was wearing a blue-and-purple-flowered caftan that made her look like a slip-covered armchair. "Do you want a cup of tea?"

"No, thank you," Carly said.

"Oh, I know that you prefer coffee, of course, but you can't expect me to have any made at this hour. If I'd known that you were coming at seven, I would have had time to brew a pot. I'll put it on now, but you'll have to wait."

"Really, I'm fine without. Please don't go to any trouble."

"It's no trouble," Pauline said, with a deep sigh. "I'll put it on."

The feeding procedure had become routine, and Carly was adept at going through the motions in her usual semiconscious early-morning condition. Once the dogs had gobbled up their breakfasts, she hustled them out the back door into the yard.

"Yes," she said to Samson, the old spaniel, who lingered by the door, looking entreatingly up at her. His rib had healed, and he no longer had special dispensation to sleep on the sunroom couch all day. "You, too, sir. The fresh air will be good for you."

Carly ignored a loud sniff from Pauline and turned her attention to the cats. The hall door was closed—she had been trying to remember to keep it so—and many of the cats were in the solarium, tucked into various nooks and crannies. There were six chairs at the breakfast table, and on each seat, without exception, was a cat. Carly made the rounds, checking the group, occasionally capturing a feline who needed to be brushed or medicated. It was almost eight by the time she finished, and she was getting increasingly edgy as the clock hands crept forward. There was no reason to think that Max would come to the house at all; but if he did, she didn't want to be there. She walked back into the kitchen to wash her hands.

"Your coffee is ready," Pauline said.

"Oh." She had forgotten about the coffee. "It is? I need to be going, actually . . ."

The housekeeper drew herself up. "I made a fresh pot," she said. "Just for you."

"I . . . oh. Okay, thank you. I guess I will have some."
It was still before her usual arrival time. One cup of coffee should be safe.

Pauline took Carly's usual cup out of the cupboard: a special-edition porcelain mug, hand-painted with a Noah's Ark scene. She peered into it and frowned. "Humph! Spotty," she announced.

Carly watched curiously as the housekeeper walked to the sink and began to scrub the offending mug. She made a long show of washing, drying, and inspecting it before deeming it clean enough to be used. Then, with great care, she poured the coffee.

"Sugar?" she asked, still holding Carly's mug.

Never, in two years of visiting Henry, had Carly put sugar in either her coffee or her tea, as Pauline knew perfectly well.

"No," Carly said. "Thank you."

"Milk?"

"Please." Carly always put milk in her coffee. And in her tea. Pauline also knew that.

Pauline set the mug on the counter, out of Carly's reach, and walked to the refrigerator. She opened it, pulled out a quart-sized carton, and sniffed suspiciously at it. "My goodness. This milk has turned sour. I wonder if there's more in here. I know I bought two cartons."

She stood, staring into the refrigerator, which was not large or crowded enough to obscure any object the size of a carton of milk. Carly fidgeted in her chair.

"It's fine," Carly said, finally, unable to stay silent any longer. "I'll drink it black. It's not a problem."

"I'm sure that I bought another carton when I was at

the store. It must be downstairs in the other icebox. I'll go and get it."

"Black coffee is fine," Carly insisted. "Really."

Pauline picked up the mug again, holding it possessively as Carly reached for it. "Certainly not," she said. "I won't be the one to keep you from drinking your coffee the way you prefer it. I'll just be a minute. Or two. The other icebox is down the stairs in the cellar, you know. My hip has been bothering me, so it may take a little longer . . ."

"I'll go," Carly said. "If you just tell me where—"

"No, no. It would take much too long to explain, and you don't know where to find the light switch. And the icebox handle is very tricky. You have to close it the right way, or else it doesn't seal properly, and all the cold air leaks out. I'll go. It'll take me only a few minutes."

"Please." Carly was feeling slightly desperate at the thought of being trapped there while Pauline waddled down to the cellar and back. "Let me do it. I'm sure that I can find the light switch. I'll—"

She stopped. Pauline wasn't listening to her. Instead, the housekeeper had cocked her head slightly, an expression of barely disguised relief on her face. There were footsteps coming down the hall, getting louder now as they approached the kitchen, and the firm stride was unmistakable. Carly's stomach clenched, and she cast one brief, panicked look at the back door, but it was too late to flee. The hall door opened, and Max appeared.

He was wearing his running clothes, and he did not look happy. He nodded to Pauline, then turned to Carly, his mouth set in a forbidding line. She was too startled by his sudden appearance to do anything but glare back at him. Her temper rose quickly. How dare he come charging in, she thought, scowling at her as if *she* had done something to offend *him*! If anyone in the room had a right to be mad, she did. He should be launching a fleet of apologies. And what was he doing here in the first place? It was too early.

Pauline swiftly answered that question. "I called as soon as she arrived, Mr. Max. And left you a message."

"Thank you," Max said. "I got it."

Carly looked from one to the other. She didn't know what was happening, but she knew that she didn't like it. "Excuse me," she began, indignantly. "What—"

"I've been stalling her," Pauline added. "I think that if people would keep to a schedule instead of coming and going on a whim, it would be less trouble for everyone, don't you agree?"

"Yes," Max said grimly. His arms were folded against his chest, and he hadn't taken his eyes off Carly for a moment, as if he thought that she might vanish if he looked away. "It would be much less trouble."

"Would you like some coffee, Mr. Max? There are blueberry muffins, too. I baked them last night because I thought you might be coming over."

"Not right now," Max said. "First, I need to have a talk with Miss Martin." He took Carly by the arm. "Let's go."

Carly balked. "What is this, a KGB arrest? I'm not going anywhere with you. Let go of me!"

"No," Max said. "We're going outside. Either you walk with me, or I'll carry you. Your choice."

Pauline gasped, and Carly began to blush hotly. "Leave me alone," she said, through her teeth. "I don't want to talk to you."

"I don't care," Max said. "I've been looking for you since Friday night, and I am getting pretty damn tired of being avoided. What were you planning to do, sneak around forever and think that I wouldn't figure out what you were doing?"

"I have not been *sneaking* around," Carly exclaimed. "I have a very busy life. If you haven't seen me, it's because I have important things to do. Do you think I'd go to the trouble of changing my schedule just to avoid *you?*"

"Yes."

"Ha! You have a lot of nerve. I don't know what you're doing here, talking to me, when you have such important issues of your own to work out. Marriage and children—"

"That does it," Max said. He bent down, and, before Carly knew what was happening, he had hooked one arm under her arms and one under her knees, and lifted her into the air, knocking over her chair in the process. Carly squawked in surprise and alarm, seized a handful of Max's shirt, and kicked the air as he half slung her over his shoulder. "What are you doing? Stop it!"

"Mr. Max!" cried Pauline, raising her hands in astonished horror.

"The back door, please," Max said, walking forward. He stopped, and the housekeeper scurried to open it. "Thank you."

Accompanied by a few curious dogs, he carried Carly out into the yard and down the steps toward the stone bench by Henry's small pond. In her undignified position, Carly was almost too embarrassed and overwhelmed to breathe, much less to speak. But when he set her on her feet, and she regained her balance, she felt the hot blood pounding in her face, and she exploded.

"Max Giordano, how dare you use these macho tactics on me! You have no right to haul me around like a sack of dog food, or to make a scene in front of Pauline, or do anything except apologize to me for . . . for . . ."

"For what?" Max asked coldly.

"For *what*?" Carly repeated, outraged. "Oh, excuse me. I didn't realize that it was acceptable behavior to spend the night with one woman, then propose marriage to another the next day! My mistake. And believe me, I mean that."

"Oh?" Max said. "Sleeping with me was a mistake?"

"A huge one," Carly said. "And it won't happen again. I've wasted too much time in relationships with men like you."

"Men like me." Max's voice was dangerously calm. "And so, once you figured out that I was a rotten bastard, you rushed off to tell your family about it, so that they could sympathize."

"What makes you think I rushed off to see my family?"

"Didn't you?"

"Well . . . so what if I did? I went to Jeannie's."

"Of course you did. You Martins would defend each other to the death. You're an exclusive little club, and it's a good thing that I didn't take you up on your offer of membership. If I had, where would I be right now? Tossed back out onto the street, wondering what had happened, right?"

Carly looked warily at him. "I don't know," she said.

"I do." His face was hard. "And now maybe you'll understand why I don't want you patronizing me by telling me that your family 'adopts' people like me. It's a nice idea, but it isn't true. I'd rather be surrounded by strangers than by false friends."

Carly's anger was quickly being replaced by irritation. "If you'll stop feeling sorry for yourself for a minute," she said tartly, "you might be interested to know that Jeannie spent most of Friday night defending you."

"What? Why the hell would she do that?"

"I have no idea," Carly said. "For some bizarre reason, the Martins like you. They're trying very hard to convince me that you really don't *seem* like a rotten bastard, and that I should give you a chance to explain what happened."

Max folded his arms against his chest. A thoughtful frown touched his forehead, but he said nothing.

"I knew it," Carly said. "I told them that it wouldn't do any good. I was there, after all. I saw what you—"

"Actually," Max said coolly, "you didn't."

"Didn't what?"

"Didn't see a damned thing. Were you standing there, listening, when I made this marriage proposal to Nina? No? Then how do you know what happened?"

"You said—"

"I didn't say anything," Max exclaimed. "Nina was the one talking about marriage and children. I told her that I wasn't interested. You found us in the lobby about five minutes after we agreed that the relationship was over."

"But . . . but she said—"

"She was being catty. Obviously there was something about you that made her feel like bringing out her claws."

Carly sat down on the stone bench. She did not have a clear recollection of exactly what had happened at the hotel. The stress of the moment had overwhelmed her, and in retrospect the whole encounter had a hazy, slow-motion feel, like the memory of a car accident. But it was possible that Max was telling her the truth. Very possible. In fact, the more she thought about it, the more sense it made.

"That woman is awful," she said, finally. "Why would you date someone like that?"

"I could ask you the same thing about Wexler."

"Richard wasn't always so bad. He's . . . complicated."

"Everybody's complicated. Nina's no exception. She can be very charming when she wants to be." He met Carly's skeptical look with an even one. "Things were different when I lived in New York. She fit into my life very well then."

"That's hard to imagine," Carly said. "Were you so different, then?"

"Apparently so."

Carly took a deep breath. "Well. Hmm. This is very awkward, isn't it. I'm . . . glad that you aren't getting married."

"That makes two of us," Max said. He was looking down at her with an impenetrable expression, and Carly could still feel the tension standing like an invisible wall between them. She decided to take a risk.

"Listen," she said. "This might be a bad idea, but . . . it's Sunday. If you're not doing anything for dinner, why not come to Davis with me? Then you can watch my whole family give me smug we-knew-it-all-along looks when they see you. I won't enjoy it, but you might."

"Carly, for God's sake," Max began, and then stopped himself. He exhaled hard and looked away. "You're right. It is a bad idea."

"Not really," Carly said, in her most persuasive voice. She stood up and stepped forward to stand right in front of him. He didn't look at her, so she tapped him lightly on the chest. "We'll do it your way," she said. "No offers of anything but a good meal and the company of a lot of strangers. In fact, we won't even be nice to you. You can bring Lola, and we'll talk to her while you wash the dishes."

Max made a strange sound that fell somewhere between a choke and a laugh. "Unbelievable," he muttered. "You aren't going to drop this, are you."

"No," Carly said. He suddenly seemed more exhausted than annoyed, which she took as a positive sign. She thought—she wasn't sure, but she thought—that he was going to give in. His eyes met hers then, and in them, she saw a spark of reluctant humor that confirmed it. "Max," she said gently, "this is how strangers turn into honest friends. There's nothing false about it. And if you want to belong somewhere, you have to start by showing up."

CHAPTER 27

————◆————

On the way to Davis later that Sunday Max said something to Carly about his one-sided conversations with Henry, and she surprised him by suggesting that he read aloud during the visits.

Initially, Max dismissed the idea. "I can't do that," he said.

Carly feigned surprise. "You can't read?"

"You know what I mean." He rarely read for pleasure, and the last time he remembered reading out loud was in the third grade. "I can't do it the way he would want to hear it. And if he can hear it, he deserves better. I'll hire someone."

But Carly insisted that it would be better for Henry to hear Max's voice, and he finally gave in.

The following morning in the Tremayne library, Carly led him to a stack of books she had pulled from the shelves. It was Max's first encounter with most of them, although he recognized all the titles. He vaguely remembered some from high school, although at that time in his life, he hadn't considered a classical education—not to mention class attendance—a priority. Reading had always seemed frivolous to him, something that replaced action and used up energy to no real effect, like a car spinning its wheels in the snow.

Henry had been of a different mind. He apparently read for the sheer pleasure of the experience. Max approached the books curiously, wondering what clues they held about his grandfather. In the absence of Henry's own voice, Max found that his books could speak for him. Henry loved stories of struggle and redemption, dramatic adventure and great odds overcome. He was no snob; his taste ran from *King Lear* to *Treasure Island,* and covered a lot of ground in between.

Max decided that if he was going to do it, he would do it right, and chose a new translation of Homer's *Odyssey.* Several days later, they were well into the epic poem, and while the lyrical language made progress a little slow, Max became completely absorbed in the trials of the beleaguered warrior Odysseus, fighting his way back to his home and family.

The hospital visit had become the most relaxing part of Max's day, and he had been finding himself increasingly reluctant to close the book as noon approached. Yesterday's session had left Odysseus and his men imperiled by the Cyclops, a savage one-eyed monster who had trapped the sailors in his cave with the intention of eating them all. Max had been looking forward to continuing the story, but he was having trouble concentrating. Every few pages he had to stop and remind himself to pay attention. His eyes and voice were dutifully working their way through the text, but his mind kept drifting away.

He had finally begun to relax into the rhythm of the prose when he heard Henry groan.

He glanced up. Henry's eyelids fluttered and opened sightlessly, as Max had seen them do many times over the past few weeks. His head turned in a convulsive movement, and his hands rose to push at the air, as if he were warding off an invisible foe.

Max set down the book. "Grandfather?"

The old man's swollen lips moved. "No . . ." he whispered.

Max rose to his feet, and the Odyssey clattered to the floor. "Grandfather?" he said again, quickly. "Can you hear me?"

Henry gave no sign that he understood. His pulse rate had risen suddenly, and he was more agitated than Max had ever seen him, moving weakly from side to side on the bed. "No . . ." he said, more clearly this time. "Help."

Alarmed, Max pressed the button to call the nurse. "It's all right," he said, though his own heart was pounding, and he didn't know what was happening. It seemed to him that Henry, trapped in twilight sleep, was having a nightmare. Max took his grandfather's hand. "What's wrong? Can you tell me?"

Henry groaned again, and his fingers gripped Max's with surprising strength. His brow was furrowed, but his eyes were unfocused, staring blankly at some point beyond Max's shoulder. His body flexed slightly, as if he were trying to sit up, then fell back against the bed. His mouth worked, and he mumbled something. The sound was distorted by the nasogastric tube in his throat, but

Max understood it, and the hairs on the back of his neck prickled with sudden shock. It was a name.

"Carly," his grandfather had said.

"Do you have any idea why he would be calling out her name?" Max asked Bill Sheaffer half an hour later. They were sitting in the doctor's office, and Max was nursing a cup of cafeteria coffee, still shaken from the encounter in Henry's room.

"No," Dr. Sheaffer said. "And frankly, you shouldn't read much into it, Max. This is all good. Your grandfather is making better progress than any of us could have hoped."

Max wasn't convinced. "He's upset about something, Bill. He seemed as if he wanted . . . needed . . . to tell me something."

Dr. Sheaffer nodded. "I'm sure it did seem that way. But this is a normal stage of recovery. The agitation, the confusion—it's completely by the book, and it doesn't mean anything other than that the brain is healing and trying to recalibrate itself."

"So you don't think that he's trying to communicate something about the accident?"

"At this point, I don't think he's *trying* to do anything at all."

"But even if he's not aware of what he's saying, there has to be some reason for it," Max argued. Henry had continued to mumble for some time after the arrival of the nurse and Dr. Sheaffer. Most of it had been unintelligible, but they had all heard him repeat Carly's name several times. "When I was alone with him, I heard him call for help. He was moving his arms as if he was trying to protect himself. It may be unconscious behavior, but so is a dream, right? And dreams generally reflect real-life issues."

"He's not dreaming. This is completely different. At this point, there's no reason to think that there is any meaning to what he's saying."

"If it were random, I might agree," Max said. "But I don't understand why he's focused on Carly."

"Well, she has been here many times over the past few weeks."

"So have I," Max pointed out.

Dr. Sheaffer gave him a strange, thoughtful look. He steepled his fingers on his desk. "Max," he said, "what you saw today would have upset anyone who isn't accustomed to seeing brain-injured patients. I think it would be a good idea if you made an appointment to talk to Joanna."

"Why?"

"You two are on good terms, and she's very experienced with the issues that come up within families under these circumstances. Feelings of guilt. Helplessness. It's all very normal."

Max frowned. "Are you suggesting that I consult her in her capacity as a rehabilitation therapist or as a psychologist?"

"You've shown admirable devotion to your grandfather, Max. If he were able, I'm sure that he would tell you how grateful he is for everything that you've done. The fact that he's talking about Carly Martin doesn't reflect in any way on his relationship with you—"

"Wait a minute," Max interrupted. "You think that's

what this is about? That I'm upset because he was calling out Carly's name and not mine?"

Dr. Sheaffer looked uncomfortable. "Joanna really would be a better person to—"

"For God's sake, Bill. I don't need a shrink! This isn't a case of jealousy. I'm trying to understand what happened to put my grandfather in that hospital bed."

"Of course. I'm sorry. I know that there have been some new concerns about the circumstances of your grandfather's fall. I already spoke with the police. There was a detective here a few days ago."

"Gracie?"

"That was the name. Tough guy. He took the clothing that Mr. Tremayne was wearing when he was admitted."

"Fine," Max said stiffly. He was starting to feel as if he had turned a key and started the motion of a giant machine, one whose heavy gears were grinding forward with no regard for his intention or direction.

"Max, I don't mean to pry, but from the questions that the detective was asking me, and now from some of the things you're saying, I can't help getting the impression that you think Carly Martin could have . . . that she might . . ."

"What?" Max asked.

Bill Sheaffer laughed nervously. "Well, you know . . ."

"Carly Martin might what?"

The neurologist took one look at Max's stony expression and quickly sat back in his chair. "Uh . . . nothing, really. It was just a crazy thought. Not one that's worth discussing."

Max's face did not soften. "I agree."

CHAPTER 28

———◆·◆———

Professor Martin raised his glass of homemade wine. "Your attention, please," he said, to the assembled group.

The babble of voices continued without so much as a pause, and he began to scowl. He cleared his throat. "Your attention!"

No one listened. It was another perfect Sunday evening in Davis. The spring air was sweet and warm, and the late-day sunshine poured over the surrounding fields like warm syrup. Carly had never been to Tuscany, but she didn't think that the rolling hills of the Italian countryside could be any more fertile or beautiful than the oak-studded grasslands around her parents' home. But there was trouble in paradise, as evidenced by the look on her father's face. There was nothing that Professor Martin hated more than being ignored.

Carly sighed, picked up her spoon, and began to tap it on her water glass at approximately the same moment that her father began to thump the tabletop with his free hand.

"Silence!" he thundered.

That did it. The seventeen people—including babies—seated at the long outdoor table turned to look at him. He smiled benevolently. "Thank you," he said.

Max, on Carly's left, looked quizzically at her. She leaned toward him. "He's going to make a toast," she whispered. "It will probably take a while."

There was other murmuring up and down the length of the table, but even that stilled as Mr. Martin looked over his clan with an eagle eye. "First of all," he said, "let me officially welcome our guest, Professor Arthur Zimmerman, whose seminal work, 'Phylogenetic Classification of Spatially Aggregated Wildflower Metapopulations,' has been both a challenge and an inspiration to me." He nodded and gestured with his glass toward the short, balding man seated on Carly's right.

Professor Zimmerman had already consumed several different varieties of the Martin homebrew with his dinner. "George, you flatter me," he said modestly, and hiccupped. "But I'll gladly take compliments from the man who redefined the role of the protoxylem lacuna."

"Ah, yes," Professor Martin looked misty for a moment. "So I did. Those were the days, Arthur. Graduate school, what a wild and free time it was. Do you remember?"

"Do I remember? Like it was yesterday, George. Those nights with the mustards . . . pollinating, pollinating, until our fingers were numb."

Max poked Carly under the table. "What the hell is he talking about?" he whispered.

"They went to school together," Carly whispered back. "Dad's doctoral dissertation had something to do with the genetics of wild mustard plants. Don't ask me for details."

"I wasn't planning to."

"They do this every time they get together," Carly continued, "which, lucky for us, is less than once a year. In a minute, they'll do the poem."

"Poem?"

Carly didn't have a chance to explain before Professor Zimmerman began to giggle. "We always knew you'd go far, George," he said. "You remember the limerick, don't you? Catherine! Catherine, have I told you about the limerick we wrote for George?"

"Poor Mom," Carly said.

Professor Martin was making a show of looking stern, but he was obviously delighted. "Oh," he said unconvincingly. "Not that old thing."

Arthur Zimmerman took another slug of his wine. "We came up with this when George was an undergraduate," he explained to the group, most of whom looked politely resigned. "Little did we know that his thesis would turn out to be the foundation for a life's work! Catherine, dear, you need to hear this. It's a hoot."

"Really," Mrs. Martin said dryly. "I can hardly wait."

"It goes like this." Professor Zimmerman cleared his throat and began.

> *"When George was a senior in college, he*
> *was studying mustard biology.*
> *He thought it terrific*
> *to continue specific*
> *with a master's in ketchup ecology!"*

"Well, now," Professor Martin exclaimed. "I'd forgotten all about that!"

Both men began to howl with laughter, and Mrs. Martin rolled her eyes skyward. Carly glanced apprehensively at Max, and was relieved to see that he looked amused. He had been behaving strangely for the past few days. He seemed distant and distracted, and he had developed an unsettling habit of watching her when he thought that she wasn't aware of it. It should have pleased her, but something in his face made her uneasy. She thought that he was probably worrying about Henry, but it was hard to know for sure. Over the past week, Max had gone from reticent to almost totally silent on the topic of his grandfather and the police investigation, and she had tried not to add to his stress level by asking him about it.

Most of what she knew about the investigation—which was almost nothing—had come from her own conversations with Detective Gracie. He had interviewed her twice so far, once last week to take her statement about the night of the accident, and then again on Wednesday, when he had come by the clinic to ask her for a few more details. Carly had liked the detective immediately. He was taciturn, but he listened intently to everything that she said, and his careful questions told her that he didn't miss much.

"A toast," said Mr. Martin, raising his glass. "To friends and family. Present and future." To Carly's horror, he winked at Max. Max nodded back and raised his water glass. Carly did the same, gritting her teeth. She loved her father, but sometimes . . .

"Such a lovely family," Professor Zimmerman said with a sigh, draining his glass. Under the table, his other hand landed on Carly's bare knee. She jumped. She turned to look at him, and he smiled froggily at her. The hand began to creep up her thigh.

"Good grief," Carly muttered, and reached down to seize it. "Professor Zimmerman."

"Call me Arthur, my dear." He squeezed her hand, apparently under the impression that she was holding it affectionately. "What a lovely young woman you've become."

"Thank you," Carly said sternly. "We're all very sorry that Mrs. Zimmerman couldn't join us this year. You said that she was traveling with a friend?"

"Yes. A friend. In . . . in Alaska."

His hand was pushing steadily upward. Gripping it firmly, Carly pushed back. "How fascinating," she said. "It's early to be traveling so far north, isn't it? I thought that the tourist season there didn't really begin until July."

His hand suddenly went limp. "I'm not fooling you, am I?"

"What?"

"I can tell," he said mournfully. "It's no use." He released her and tried to grab a nearby bottle of wine. It was just out of his reach, and his arm collapsed like a wet sock onto the table. "She's gone. Gone!" He slumped forward, and his shoulders began to shake.

"What?" Carly said again. "Who, your wife?"

"Darlene. She left me. She went to Alaska with Bill Bayette. Do you know what he does?"

"No . . ." Carly said.

Professor Zimmerman shook his head bitterly. "He's a dolphin researcher! How could anyone compete with that? Women, damn them all . . . fickle . . . damn them." He reached again toward the bottle and promptly knocked it over. Wine splattered in every direction. Carly jumped up and began to blot the bloody-looking puddle with her napkin, and Professor Zimmerman moaned and buried his head in his hands.

"Oh, my," said Mrs. Martin in surprise. "Arthur?"

"Here, now," exclaimed Mr. Martin. "Carly, what have you done?"

"Me? I haven't done anything," Carly said indignantly, mopping. Max, standing next to her, leaned in with his own napkin and finished the job. Carly looked gratefully at him, and noticed that his shirt was covered with a fine spray of red droplets.

Mr. Martin hurried around the table. He clapped Arthur Zimmerman jovially on the back. "Well, Arthur," he said. "Well. Whatever it is, it can't be that bad." He paused, frowning. "Can it?" He looked at Carly.

"Darlene," Professor Zimmerman lamented into his hands. Max was watching in amazed fascination, and Carly thought that it would be very unwise to tell him that this sort of thing happened regularly at her parents' house. It would be better, she thought, to let him figure that out on his own. Slowly.

She looked at her father. "Dad, do something."

He looked unhappy. "Me?"

"I was so sure that this time it would be forever," moaned Professor Zimmerman.

"Yes, Arthur, we were too," Professor Martin said awkwardly, patting him on the shoulder. "They do say 'third time lucky.' Guess not, though."

"Dad!"

"Hmm," said George Martin. "Come on, old boy. Dessert can wait. Let's go for a walk in the meadow. I'll show you a new variety of *Campanula prenanthoides* that I brought back from southern Oregon last fall, and you can tell me what happened and get it all off your chest."

They walked off. Mrs. Martin began to direct the clearing of the table, and Carly turned to Max. "Sorry about that," she said. "Never a dull moment around here."

"I'm getting that impression."

"You look as if you were attacked by a swarm of mosquitoes," she said. "We'd better put your shirt in the laundry before the stain sets. Come with me."

Max followed Carly to the little laundry room in the back of the house. It was about the size of the bathroom in his hotel suite, but it had a window overlooking the olive grove, and the clean, comforting smell of soap and cotton. Carly pulled a folded sweatshirt out of a wicker basket next to the dryer and handed it to him.

"This should fit you," she said. "More or less. Dad's smaller than you are, but it'll do."

"Thank you."

She smiled mischievously at him. "May I help you with that?" She reached out and began to unbutton his shirt. Max felt a stirring of desire, despite their surroundings. Carly had a way of making domestiticity seem attractive. He shrugged out of his shirt. She took it, looked at it, and frowned. "This doesn't have a care label."

"It's custom-made."

"Shouldn't it still have a label? Don't people who buy custom-made shirts wash them?"

"No. We wear them once, then throw them out."

She looked horrified. "Not really."

"No, not really," Max said, and grinned, in spite of

himself. His dark mood had eased slightly in the warmth of the Martin atmosphere. "I don't know how it's supposed to be washed. I always send it out." He shrugged. "It doesn't matter."

"It does," Carly protested. "It's a nice shirt. I don't want to ruin it."

"It's already ruined."

"That's true. Okay, I'll put it in warm water and we'll see what happens. Promise not to sue me."

She turned to drop it into the washing machine, and Max eyed the curves of her body. She was wearing a navy blue cotton sweater and snug, faded jeans. He stepped behind her, putting his arms around her waist, and began to kiss the nape of her neck. He felt her shiver, and she leaned back against him.

"You have wine on your sweater," he said.

"I do? How can you tell?"

"I can tell. You should wash it."

She began to laugh, and he caught the hem of her sweater, tugging it up, over her head, and off. He threw it into the machine on top of his shirt. She was wearing a lacy white bra, and her breasts rose enticingly out of the low-cut cups. Max ran his hands up to caress them, feeling their weight in his palms, rubbing his thumbs over her nipples, firm under the thin fabric. He kissed her neck, drinking in the scent of her.

She sighed with pleasure and turned within the circle of his arms to face him. "I feel like a teenager," she said. "Messing around in the laundry room. What if someone comes in?"

Max glanced at the door. "Does that lock?"

"Yes."

"Lock it."

She did, then came back to him, eager but uncertain. "The window . . ."

"Doesn't have a view into this corner," he said, pulling her with him as he stepped back against the far wall, where built-in shelves held orderly piles of folded sheets and towels. Max felt their softness against his back and the fragrant warmth of Carly against his chest. He kissed her until she seemed to be melting against him, and his own body ached with longing for her. There was something about her that seemed to turn off his brain, and at the moment, it was a relief. He did not want to think; he simply wanted her.

He unbuttoned the top of her jeans and felt for the zipper pull. Metal rasped as he lowered it, and Carly moaned against his mouth as he reached into her jeans. The denim was rough over his fingers, and tight enough to press his hand against her. He slipped his hand into her panties, his fingers quickly finding her most sensitive spot. Her knees buckled, and her nails dug into his shoulders, stinging slightly, but he didn't care. The pain was an indicator of how unaware she was of anything but what he was doing to her.

"Oh, Max . . ." she said. "Oh, my God."

"Sssh," he murmured. "Don't let anyone hear you."

Her eyes were wide and dazed with desire. "This is crazy," she whispered, and gasped softly. "Don't stop."

He could feel an instinctive rhythm taking control of her body as he touched her, sliding his fingers slowly back and forth in the wet, hot core of her, feeling her tremble and tense. Her eyes closed, her lips were parted, and her breath was fast and shallow. He watched her intently. The sight of her, helpless in his hands, completely abandoned to the pleasure that he was giving her, was the most erotic thing that he had ever seen.

He slipped one finger inside of her, then another, slowly, carefully, loving the heat and the tightness of her. She cried out, muffling the sound against his shoulder, and bit him gently. He felt the muscles of her thighs clench around his hand, then she sagged against him. He held her as shudders wracked her body, and her breathing gradually slowed.

"That," she said finally, into his chest, "was amazing. But it doesn't seem quite fair . . ."

Max had already resigned himself to waiting. They were already well beyond the limits of hospitality, in his opinion, and much as he wanted to push down her jeans and drive himself into her, right there against the laundry room wall, he had no intention of doing it.

"I think we can find a better time and place to continue this," he said.

"I suppose so," Carly agreed reluctantly. She looked him up and down, and a conspiratorial smile touched her mouth. "I see that it isn't a lack of desire that's stopping you, so it must be good manners. Very admirable."

"Give me a minute," Max said.

"Take your time. Here, toss me that other sweatshirt. We're lucky that Dad lives in these things." She put it on and smoothed down her hair, looking flushed.

The doorknob rattled suddenly, and they both jumped. There was a knock. "Carly? Are you in there?" It was Anna, Carly's littlest sister.

"I'm here, sweetie," Carly said quickly. "What is it?"

"Why is the door locked?" There was a pause. "Where's Max? I can't find him."

"He's here, too." Carly went over to unlock the door. She opened it, and Anna peered in suspiciously.

"What are you doing?"

"Laundry," Max said, pointing to the machine, and saw Carly suppress a smile.

"Laundry?" Anna said disdainfully, and rolled her eyes. "Give me a break. I'm thirteen, not three. I know how these things are. So, are you coming out for dessert, or should I tell everyone that I can't find you?"

CHAPTER 29

———◆———

We feasted through the day 'til sundown, but when the sun had set and darkness was upon us, the men laid down to sleep by the cables of the ship . . .

Max stopped, and looked up from the text. He had been reading out loud for half an hour and had only a vague idea of what he had said in all that time. It was Monday morning at the hospital, and he had a heavy, dark feeling in his chest. Something had been nagging at him for days, lurking on the edges of his consciousness, teasing him, then slipping away when he reached for it. And then, late last night, clear as a bell, it had come to him.

What about the dogs?

He had no idea why he hadn't caught it earlier. He remembered his first time inside the Tremayne mansion, when he and Carly had been flooded by a rush of dogs, with Lola in the lead. "Meet your grandfather's security system," Carly had said. Where had the dogs been just one day earlier, when some stranger had dragged Henry

Tremayne's body into the house and left him at the foot of the stairs? No sane intruder would enter a house filled with dogs. Either the dogs all had been in the backyard that evening, or . . .

Or the intruder had not been a stranger.

Max put the book facedown on the bed. *Too many coincidences*, he thought darkly. *Every time I turn around, I'm blindsided by a new one*. Individually, none of them meant much, and each one could be explained away. But they were beginning to add up. At what point did volume create significance?

He had always believed that his judgment would never allow him to be duped or manipulated by anyone. There was no person on earth wily enough to fool him for more than a very short time. No person except—perhaps—himself.

Could he have fallen into some kind of pit of self-deception? Could he have been deceived not so much by Carly as by his own longing for family, for connection, for the love and security that Carly had come to represent?

He had seen firsthand how easy it was to convince yourself that something was harmless when it was actually destroying you. He remembered himself at nine years old, confronting his mother with tremulous courage.

"Mama, it's bad to drink so much. It makes you sick. Gramma says—"

"Gramma!" His mother rolled her eyes. "Always Gramma. You two just get together and talk about how bad I am, don't you."

"No—"

She leaned close to him, her long black hair tickling his face. He could smell her musky perfume and the sharp tang of gin on her breath. "Baby, she just talks bad about me because she wants you to love her and not me. She's jealous because she never had a son. But you still love me best, don't you?"

He nodded silently.

"Aren't you going to say it?"

"I love you best, Mama. But—"

"Butbutbut . . ." she said, mimicking him in a squeaky voice. She laughed and ruffled his hair. "How did I get such a serious kid? You and your gramma, always worrying. It's just fun, baby. It makes me feel good. It's no big deal, so quit nagging me."

She had still been beautiful then. But Max could now take the child's memories and reexamine them through an adult's eyes, seeing the slight puffiness of her features, the thickening waist, the increasingly sallow skin. A dying woman, digging her own grave with her eyes squeezed shut. It made him sick to think about it.

Was it possible, Max asked himself slowly, that his own desire to believe in Carly's innocence had blinded him to the truth? Perhaps the most important question to be asked was not whether he trusted Carly Martin, but whether he trusted himself.

Did he?

Yes, dammit, he thought fiercely. *I know what I know.* Twenty million dollars would challenge the morals of many people, but Carly Martin was not one of them. He couldn't be wrong about her. He exhaled slowly and picked up the book again.

The Sirens, Odysseus was told, were demon-women who sang a song so sweet and thrilling that any sailor who heard it would go mad with the desire to rush to them. To do so, however, was death. The Sirens sat in a meadow heaped with the rotting bones of thousands of men. But Odysseus longed to hear their forbidden song, and he told his sailors to seal their own ears with wax but lash him to the ship's mast so that he could listen safely as they sailed past.

It seemed to Max to be a daring but foolish proposition. How could Odysseus be so sure that the influence of the song would fade as his ship sailed away and left the Sirens behind? What if, once heard, the song and the longing stayed in your blood forever? What if miles of sea and land between you and the danger were not enough to erase the memory of the desire? If so, it would be like a wound that could not heal, and nothing would ever be the same again.

He felt his mood growing blacker. He was angry with Odysseus for his recklessness, and he had to remind himself that it was just a story, an ancient Greek soap opera.

Henry had been much less agitated that morning, which was both a relief and a disappointment to Max. He had hoped that his grandfather would utter something—anything—that might serve as a clue. But the turbulence of the previous week was gone, and the old man had been quiet all morning. Henry generally drifted in and out of sleep several times over the course of a visit, and now, as Max paused in his reading, he realized that the old man had been silent for some time. He glanced up, expecting to see Henry sleeping, and was mildly surprised to see that his grandfather's eyes were open.

He looked down again, about to continue, then it hit him like a wave of ice water.

Henry was looking at him.

Max had no idea how he knew it, but the difference between this moment and all of the others before it was like the difference between life and death. His grandfather was awake.

He rose to his feet. "Grandfather?" he said hoarsely. "Can you hear me?"

Henry lifted his hand weakly, his gaze fixed on Max's face. His swollen lips moved, and a faint sound came out, like the rustle of a brown paper bag, or the whisper of dry leaves in the wind.

"What?" Max asked. "What did you say?"

He leaned over the bed. Henry's hand reached for his shoulder and landed there, light and fragile as a bird.

"I can't hear you," Max said, frantically trying to figure out what the old man wanted. Water, painkillers, his doctor? He knew that he should call for the nurse, but his grandfather was holding his shoulder, and at that moment nothing could have induced Max to pull away. He leaned closer so that his head was right next to Henry's. He hardly dared to breathe. A lump had formed in his throat, and his eyes were burning. With fierce concentration, he listened as the old man began to whisper again.

This time, he understood.

"I dreamed," his grandfather said, "of the Sirens."

Several hours later, Max phoned Carly. She gasped when he told her the news, and then promptly burst into tears.

"I'm sorry," she sobbed, and he heard her rummaging around for a tissue. "I'm just so glad. Wait, will you hold on for a minute? I'm going to go into my office and close the door."

Moments later, she was back on the line, sounding a little steadier. "Oh, Max. I knew it, I knew that he would be all right. Thank God. Tell me everything. Does he remember anything about the accident?"

She was asking because she wanted to know the truth, Max told himself. Just as he did. Her reaction was everything that it should have been, but still, there was a dark seed of doubt within him that he could not cast out.

"No. He doesn't remember anything about that night, or even the few days before it. He's still very weak, and disoriented."

"Oh," she said, and was silent.

"The doctors told me that memory loss surrounding that kind of accident is very typical. It might all come back, and it might not. So I'm afraid that our star witness is not going to be much help right now."

"It doesn't matter," Carly said, and he listened carefully for nuances in her voice. Did he hear relief? He did, but surely that was for Henry's recovery, not for his lack of memory.

"How is he otherwise?" she asked, anxiously. "Does he seem . . . normal?"

"Yes. They warned me to expect anything: personality changes, strange behavior, confusion. But he seems rational. As far as I could tell, at least. I'm obviously not qualified to judge whether he's his old self or not."

"How long did you talk?"

"Almost an hour. It was very slow, but he's definitely there." Just thinking about that conversation made Max feel unsteady. He swallowed hard and regained control of himself. "He knew who I was. He apologized for not contacting me."

"Yes," Carly said softly. "He would."

"He wanted to know what happened, and how long he had been in the hospital. Then he asked about the animals—if they were all right. I said that you had been taking good care of them, and that everything at the house was ready for him to come home."

"Did the doctors say when that might be?"

"Not anytime soon. They'll be doing a lot of tests over the next few days, and then we'll know more. He's having some muscle-control problems on his left side. They tell me that it can be improved with physical therapy, though."

The phone crackled briefly. "Where are you?" Carly asked.

"In my car, headed back to the hotel. Then I have a meeting in Santa Clara."

"Do you want to come over for dinner tonight? I'll be home by seven-thirty."

He didn't answer right away. He was tired, bone-tired, and it was only three o'clock in the afternoon. But he wanted to see her, wanted it badly enough to repress the disquiet in his mind. When he was with Carly, the bands of tension that held him upright and walked him through his days seemed to loosen, and he felt as if he could breathe freely. With her, the possibility of a different kind of life rose before him, like the first pale light of dawn on the horizon.

He thought of Nina and her mocking smile. *Do you need her, Max?*

He'd had a quick answer then, but he did not have one now. He didn't understand how one woman could represent both storm and shelter. *And if I do need her?* He thought of making love to Carly, crushing her to him, always feeling as if he couldn't hold her closely enough to satisfy the desire that he felt for her. A long time ago, when he had told Nina that love was just another form of addiction, he had meant that it was powerful enough to overwhelm and destroy you if you were weak enough to let it. But what if destruction was not the inevitable outcome? If Carly really was who she seemed to be, then anything might be possible, even the things that he had never allowed himself to hope for.

"Max?" Carly said, her voice scratchy in the static on the speakerphone. "Did I lose you?"

"No," he said. "I'll see you at seven-thirty."

As Max walked through the lobby of the Ritz-Carlton, he was so wrapped up in his own thoughts that he passed right by Hector Gracie without seeing him.

"Mr. Giordano."

Max stopped and turned around. Gracie was sitting in one of the baroque armchairs that peppered the lobby. Afternoon tea was being served in the lounge, and the delicate trickle of harp music flowed through the air. The detective rose to his feet.

Max had no idea how the man had known that he would be at the hotel in the middle of the afternoon, and he didn't care. He had been wanting an update from Gracie and had tried several times over the weekend to reach him, to no avail.

He nodded briefly. "Detective. Did you get my message?"

"Messages," Gracie said. "I got them."

"You take weekends off?"

Gracie gazed expressionlessly at him. "I took a weekend off once. In 1985, when my mother died. This past weekend, I was busy. If you're interested, I thought that we could sit down and talk about some things. Okay?"

They took the elevator up to Max's suite. The detective looked around the large outer room and nodded. "Nice," he said, and sat down on the couch.

"Thanks. Do you want something to drink?"

Gracie accepted a Diet Coke. He drank thirstily, then blotted his mustache with a paper cocktail napkin. "A couple of things. There were scraping marks on the backs of your grandfather's shoes. Hard to put marks like those on your own heels, so we can confirm that someone dragged him inside after he fell. Not a big surprise."

Max nodded. It was not. "What about the house?"

"Not much there," Gracie said. "Or too much, is another way to put it. Let people walk all over a crime scene for a month, let a bunch of dogs play on it . . . you get the idea? Not too useful. We're checking out a couple of things from the sweep of the area, but . . ." he shrugged. "We'll see."

"Too bad your patrol officer didn't do his job a month ago," Max said.

"He's not my officer. But I've been asking about him. He has a reputation for being a little too eager for his own retirement, and I'm thinking he'll get his wish after this." Gracie grinned.

Barely missing a beat, and without changing the conversational tone of his voice, the detective added, "I've got a neighbor lady across the street who says she was walking her dog and saw a white van coming out of the Tremayne driveway at seven o'clock on the night of the incident." He sipped his Diet Coke. "She said it was driving too fast."

Max felt as if a giant hand had just clenched around his stomach. He was still standing, leaning on the back of the armchair facing Gracie, and he didn't speak for a moment. "Did she get a license?" he asked finally.

"Nope. But with the housekeeper's statement, that makes two witnesses who saw a white van at seven. Interesting, eh?"

Max said nothing.

"Carly Martin tells me that she left the house no later than six-fifteen that evening."

"There are thousands of white minivans in this city," Max said. "It could have been anyone."

"Sure," Gracie said laconically. "Anyone. But let's talk a little more about Carly Martin. She seems like a nice young lady. You've known her for about a month? Not too long."

Until that moment, Max had neither liked nor disliked the detective. Suddenly, he found himself fighting a feeling of absolute loathing. "Carly did not attack my grandfather. You're looking at the wrong person."

"Maybe it was an accident."

"No. Not possible." The detective's eyebrows raised slightly at his tone, and Max realized that he was gripping the back of the chair. He forced himself to relax.

"Did she know about your grandfather's trust?" Gracie asked.

"I don't think so."

The detective jotted something down in his small notebook. "That nice young lady stands to make a lot of money from the Tremayne estate," he remarked.

"So do I," Max said.

"That's true, but in your case, Mr. Giordano, I have five people who were sitting in a room with you until 8 P.M. that night. The meeting went late, eh? I heard that you ordered out Chinese for dinner."

"Carly did not attack my grandfather," Max repeated. "She isn't a violent person. And she loves him."

The edges of Gracie's mustache curved up. "I'd love anybody who wanted to give me twenty million dollars. You know for a fact that she isn't violent? You ever see her get mad?"

"No more than anyone. Do you have proof that the white van was hers?"

Gracie shook his head. "I'm still looking around."

"Then you're wasting your time," Max said. "And mine. Whoever attacked my grandfather is still out there, and you should be looking for him."

"That's what I'm doing. And no offense, Mr. Giordano, but you're the one who asked me to do it. I'm not trying to get you upset, you know? I realize that this is difficult for you. You and Carly Martin have a personal relationship, isn't that right?"

"Yes," Max said.

"Love is a beautiful thing," the detective said. "My wife's name is Angela. She and I have been married for thirty-two years, how about that?"

"Congratulations."

"Thank you. Now, if I ever thought that Angie was in some kind of trouble, I would do anything I could for her. So I understand about that, okay? And if it turns out that Carly Martin had something to do with the incident, you're going to want to help her in any way that you can, right?"

When Max said nothing, the detective continued. "So you can start by helping me, eh? Like I said, she is a very nice young lady. If there was a problem at the house that night, some kind of accident, we need to get it straightened out fast so that we can keep her out of trouble."

"I've told you everything I know," Max said. "I'm not protecting Carly, or anyone else."

"Okay. Good." Gracie nodded. "So did she ever talk to you about her business?"

"Not much."

"Clinic is doing well? Lots of clients?"

"I have no idea," Max said. "She seems busy."

"She had a previous relationship with her business partner, Richard Wexler. Did she tell you about that?"

"Yes," Max said coldly.

"Do you think that they could still be involved?"

Max recoiled. "What the hell kind of question is that? No, of course not. And what does that have to do with anything?"

Gracie made a few more notes. "Okay," he said. He finished his drink in a long swallow, set down the glass, and stood up. "I know you have my phone number. If you think of anything, give me a call."

"Where are you going?"

"Everywhere. I've got a lot to do." Gracie chuckled suddenly. "And if I get it all done, maybe I can take next weekend off, eh?"

After the detective left the room, Max picked up the phone and called his lawyer.

"Max, good timing," Tom Meyer said. "My people got back to me late on Friday regarding the Martin check— that's why you're calling, I assume?"

"Yes. What have you got?"

"Some interesting stuff about her financial situation. It hasn't shown up on her personal credit report yet, but it will. You know that she owns a stake in this veterinary clinic where she works, right? About 30 percent. The other 70 percent is held by a guy named Richard Wexler."

"I know all of that," Max said shortly. "What else?"

"Well, it turns out that those two are mortgaged to the hilt. Their primary assets are the clinic building and the medical equipment, but they have loans out on everything."

"*What?*" It was the last thing that Max had expected to hear. "Go on," he said.

"They've got two mortgages on the building," Tom continued. "As far as I can see, they've managed to borrow more than their assets are worth. It's pretty ugly. And they're months behind on their payments. The bank is about to start foreclosure proceedings."

"Jesus Christ," Max said in a low voice.

"Yeah, no kidding," Tom said. "Charlotte Martin does have a little bit of savings in the bank, but believe me, it doesn't add up to anywhere near the 30 percent of the debt. She's looking at bankruptcy when this house of cards collapses."

Max gazed down at the surface of the desk, his eyes picking out imperfections in the polished surface. It was interesting, he thought clinically, that he wasn't angry. He wasn't even upset. He was simply numb.

"Listen, Max, this is the woman that your grandfather wants to put in charge of his foundation, right?"

"Yes."

"Well, to state the obvious, that doesn't seem like a very good idea. I don't know who counsels him, but his people really should have told him about this when he was setting up the trust. Not to sell myself short, but this kind of information is not all that hard to get. When your grandfather is back on his feet, you might want to have a talk with him about finding a better legal team."

"Thanks, Tom."

"No problem. Call me if you need anything else. Even at 3 A.M."

Quietly, Max put the phone down. He sat for a long time, not moving. There was a strange tightness in his chest, similar to the way he felt when he passed an accident scene on the freeway. The twisted metal and shattered glass were there, right there, just beyond the edge of his vision, and as much as he did not want to turn and look, he did.

He looked with hard eyes, and he saw betrayal. To think that only a few hours ago, he had been wondering about the point at which a string of coincidences added up to significance. *How about now?* he thought, and almost laughed, despite the sick feeling in his chest. *Is this enough?* The terms of the trust hadn't been enough. Pauline's sighting of the van hadn't been enough. Henry's unconscious groans, the question of the dogs, even the *second* sighting of Carly's van hadn't been quite enough to make him accept what had always been there, right in front of him. After a few more weeks of this, even a video of Carly dragging Henry's unconscious body would probably just make him insist that the tape's resolution wasn't clear enough for a positive ID.

He felt as if someone had taken a dull knife and gouged a furrow through his heart. But what right did he have to be so stunned? He had known, all along, that he was playing a dangerous game. Only a fool would build his house on a fault line, then announce that he was shocked—shocked!—when the earth moved and his walls came tumbling down.

You gambled, Max said cruelly to himself. *And you lost. Deal with it.* He had come too far and fought too hard to let himself be sidelined by something like this. Carly Martin hadn't lied to him any more than he had lied to himself. He had put blinders on his own eyes, but finally he was beginning to see things very clearly. Rigid self-delusion might have killed his mother, but he was smarter than she had been, and not so easy to destroy.

CHAPTER 30

◆——◆——◆

"Carly," Michelle said over the clinic intercom. "There's someone here to see you."

Carly turned her head so quickly that her nose bumped into the side of the kitten sitting on her shoulder. The kitten squeaked and dug in her tiny claws. Carly grimaced and reached up to disengage the small, sharp creature.

"Who is it?" she asked. She handed the kitten to Brian and reached up to smooth her shirt. *It's Max*, she thought, relieved. *It has to be. Thank goodness.*

Something strange had happened last night. She had come home to find a phone message saying that he would not be coming to dinner. He had made no excuse, and his voice had been as cool and impersonal as a stranger's. She had immediately phoned the hospital, afraid that something terrible had happened to Henry, and had been relieved to hear that everything was fine.

Max was not at the hospital or his hotel. Finally, Carly had tried his cell phone but reached only the voice mail. She left a message and waited up until one in the morning for him to call, but he never did. Finally, puzzled and tired, she had fallen asleep.

She had tried again that morning, with no luck, and had gone to work with an anxious feeling in her stomach. Something important had come up, she told herself, and he hadn't gotten back to the hotel until very late. He had not called her because he hadn't wanted to disturb her. He hadn't realized how curt his message had sounded, and he didn't know that she was worried.

"She won't tell me her name," Michelle said. "Or anything else. She says that she needs to talk to you."

"She?" Carly's rising hope slumped. It was not Max. *Well*, she thought. *Fine*. Whatever was going on with him would certainly be straightened out soon, and as for now, it was time to stop thinking about it.

To her surprise, it was Edie in the waiting room. The girl had not taken a seat, although there were several available. She stood, hovering halfway between Michelle's desk and the door, as if she thought that she might need to make a break for freedom. Her arms were folded against her chest, holding the edges of her leopard-print coat closed around her.

"Edie," Carly said, "how did you know where to find me?"

"You're in the phone book," Edie said, as if she were speaking to an idiot. She hugged herself more tightly. "I thought your place would be bigger."

Carly smiled. "You should see the size of my office. Since you're here, would you like a tour? I have a few minutes before my next appointment."

Edie shrugged. "I guess."

The girl was mostly quiet as they walked down the hall,

stopping to see the exam rooms, the lab, and the treatment room. They looked into the surgery, which was not being used that day. Tuesday was normally one of Richard's intensive workdays, but he was still at the conference in Florida and was not due back until the next morning.

Edie looked impressed, in spite of herself. "It's like a real hospital."

"It is a real hospital," Carly said. She pointed out the various monitors, the dental cleaning equipment, the anesthesia machines, and Richard's surgical laser. Next door was the X-ray room, and beyond that, the cat ward. At the sight of the animals, Edie suddenly came alive. She began walking up and down the length of the small room, looking into the rows of cages, talking to the cats and peppering Carly with questions.

"What's wrong with him?" she asked, stopping at one cage to look at a gray tabby who was lying quietly on a folded blanket. The fur on his abdomen had been shaved, and there was a catheter sutured to the outside of his body. "Is he sick?"

"He's improving," Carly said. "He was very sick on Friday. He had a urinary obstruction, which means that there was a mix of inflammatory cells and mineral crystals clogging up his urethra and preventing him from going to the bathroom when he needed to. He was vomiting and feeling really terrible."

"Would he have died?"

"Probably. But he's going to be okay. I cleared out the blockage, and he's getting a lot of fluids, to clean out his body and help his kidneys recover."

"How do you know that he's drinking enough?"

"We don't depend on him to do it. He was on an IV

over the weekend. Now he's getting an electrolyte solution subcutaneously, which means that we use a needle to put it right under his skin so that he can absorb it quickly."

"Doesn't that hurt?"

"Not much, and it's making him feel a lot better. He's due for another round, in fact. If you want, I'll teach you how to do it, and you can sit with him while he gets the fluids."

"Me?" Edie looked astonished by the idea.

"I think you could do it. You seem smart enough." Carly thought that she might finally be learning how to talk to the girl. She did not tell Edie that she often taught clients how to administer fluids to their own pets at home. In the later stages of some illnesses, it could be necessary to hydrate an animal daily, and it was quite easy to do, once you got the hang of it. "Of course, you don't have to. If you think that it might be too complicated—"

"No, I can do it," Edie said immediately. She looked defiantly at Carly.

Carly suppressed a smile. "Okay, if you're sure. Why don't you come back to the staff room with me, and I'll get you some scrubs to wear. You can change in the bathroom. This way."

Carly introduced Edie to the rest of the staff, and asked Brian to come and help her demonstrate how to give fluids. Edie learned quickly, as Carly had thought she would. She left them there together, suggesting to Brian that when they were finished, he take Edie back to the kennel runs. They had two dogs who needed some basic grooming, and it seemed to Carly like a good next step. She wanted to give Edie as much hands-on work with the

animals as possible, partly because she knew that the girl
was good at it, and partly because she thought that such
work had a better chance of holding her interest.

Her next two appointments ran long, and it was an hour
before she had a chance to go and see how things were
going. She found Brian and Pam in the lab, but Edie was
nowhere to be seen.

"Where is she?" Carly asked. "She didn't leave, did
she?"

"No, she's out back," Brian said. "Smoking."

"She found a pack of Dr. Wexler's cigarettes and asked
if she could have them," Pam announced, looking up from
the sink where she was washing slides. "I wasn't going to
stop her. I thought if I said no, she might stab me."

Carly sighed and looked at Brian. "Is she okay?"

"Yeah, she's okay. She isn't too friendly—"

"She sure isn't," Pam cut in. "What's her problem?"

Brian ignored the interruption. "But it's just an act. She
talks tough, but she isn't really mean."

"Oh, excuse me," Pam said. "I didn't know you two
were such good friends. What's with all of that eyeliner?
She looks like a hooker."

"Don't be a jerk," Brian said sharply. "She's a run-
away."

Pam's mouth dropped open, and she stared at him.
Carly was equally taken aback. In the few weeks that the
young man had worked at the clinic, he had been as quiet
and meek as a mouse. Apparently, he had shocked himself, too, because he turned bright red and hunched his
shoulders. "She wants to learn," he muttered. "And she
asks smart questions."

"Is she going to work here?" Pam asked.

"I hope so," Carly said. "Look, you guys. I know that she can be difficult, but she's had a tough time, and she needs our help. It would mean a lot to me if you would try to ignore her attitude for now. I think she'll turn out to be worth it if we all invest a little effort. Will you do it for me? Please?"

"Oh, all right," Pam grumbled.

"I'll work with her," Brian said. "I don't mind. She's not that bad, and she really loves animals."

Edie was standing in the small yard behind the clinic, leaning against the wall. When she saw Carly, she dropped the butt of her cigarette and stepped on it. She looked younger and smaller in Carly's light blue scrubs, like a child dressed up in her mother's clothes.

"How's it going?" Carly asked.

Edie wouldn't look at her. "I have to leave," she said.

"Now? But—" Carly stopped herself, remembering Max's strategy. "Well, okay. Thanks for coming over."

The girl gave a slight shrug, still staring at the ground.

"I saw the dogs that you worked on," Carly said. "They look good."

"Thanks."

"So . . . do you think you might come back sometime?"

Edie raised her head, and Carly was surprised to see that her eyes were red and swollen. "I can't work here," she muttered. "I just waited around to tell you that."

"Oh," Carly said, surprised. "You know, if there's any problem with Pam, I'll talk to her and make sure that—"

Edie snorted dismissively. "You think I can't handle her? I don't care about her. It's that other guy, the one in the picture. I don't like him."

Carly was totally mystified by this. "What guy?"

"That's his car," Edie said, pointing. "Right?"

"That's Dr. Wexler's car," Carly said. He had left his Porsche sitting in the private driveway behind the clinic while he was away, because he did not have off-street parking at his apartment in Sausalito.

"I didn't know his name," Edie said. "I didn't know he was a vet, either."

"Edie, what are you talking about?"

"I just told you. I saw his picture inside, and that girl Pam told me that he works here. I know him because he comes to my friend's house to meet this guy named Darius, who supplies a lot of the rich guys."

"I don't understand," Carly said slowly.

Edie threw her an angry look. "Moron," she snapped. "Wake up. Your friend is a cokehead. He snorts that stuff like he's got no bottom in his wallet. He's one of Darius's best customers, and he's been coming around as long as I've been there, which is more than a year. How can you not know that? The amount he buys, he must be messed up all the time. How can you let him do surgery on animals?" She sniffled and kicked furiously at the ground. "You make me sick."

Carly felt as if her heart had just stopped in her chest. There was a roaring sound in her ears, and she put one hand against the brick wall to steady herself. "Are you sure?" she asked in a choked voice.

"I should have known that you wouldn't believe me," Edie said. "Who cares. I'm getting out of here." She turned, about to leave, but Carly reached out and grabbed her by her bony arm.

"What are you doing?" Edie demanded. "Get off me!"

"Edie," Carly exclaimed, looking the girl right in the eyes. "Answer me right now. Are you absolutely sure? Are you *positive* that my partner, Richard Wexler, is the man who you saw buying drugs? If you say yes, I'll believe you."

Edie stopped pulling. "Yes," she said sullenly. "It's not like it was just one time, okay? I told you, he's been coming around for a while."

Carly let go of the girl's arm. She closed her eyes and ran her hands over her face like a sleepwalker awakening from a dream. "My God. It's true. I *am* a moron."

She couldn't believe that she hadn't seen it herself. The mood swings, the secretiveness, the marathon surgery sessions—she had known for a long time that Richard's behavior was not exactly normal, even for him, but she had never considered anything like drugs. How could she not have known what was going on? The signs had all been right there, in front of her face, for months.

She swallowed hard. "When did you last see him there?"

"I don't know. About two weeks ago. Are you okay? You don't look very good."

"I don't feel very good," Carly said.

"You believe me?"

Carly nodded. "Yes. I do. Thank you for telling me the truth, Edie. I hope you'll change your mind and stay, but it's up to you. I understand if you'd rather leave."

Carly walked numbly back into the building, passing through the workrooms without making eye contact with anyone. She would have to come up with a plan of action, she thought. And fast. Richard was due back in the office tomorrow morning, and he had a full day of surgery scheduled. Obviously, she couldn't stand aside and allow him to work. But how could she stop him?

The most obvious choice was to go to the police, but what would that mean to Richard? Cocaine possession was a felony, wasn't it? Carly didn't know much about the drug laws, but even the thought that Richard might be sent to prison gave her pause for thought. His use of cocaine did, technically, make him a criminal, but did he deserve such a draconian fate? He was also a brilliant and talented surgeon, and someone who could—if he turned his life around—do twenty more years of useful work. Perhaps if she confronted him and told him what she knew, she could convince him to take time off from the practice and check himself into a rehabilitation program.

It wasn't as if he could refuse. Even if he denied everything, he would never pass a drug test. She could probably force him to get treatment by threatening to report him; but the idea of confronting him, even with the intention of helping him, sent a shiver of apprehension through her.

And what about her own situation? She was no longer ignorant about what Richard was doing, and that put her in a very vulnerable position. If she didn't report him to the police and to the Veterinary Board, she could lose her license on ethical misconduct charges.

She was wondering whom to call for advice when she saw Hector Gracie standing at the reception desk. It was as if he sensed trouble in the air, she thought, hurrying forward to greet him.

"Dr. Martin," said the detective when he saw her. "Day going well?"

"I've had better days," Carly said. "Are you here to see me?" She wondered if he had spoken with Max recently, but she didn't ask.

Gracie nodded. "I need to clear up a couple of things with you. Do you have a few minutes?"

"Sure. Let's go back to my office." She started down the hall, but the detective didn't budge.

"Actually, I thought we could go down to the station. If you don't mind."

Carly frowned. "I have three more appointments today. And wouldn't it be easier to talk here?"

"It's up to you, ma'am," said the detective. "You aren't required to come with me. But I thought that you might want to go somewhere more private."

"Oh." Gracie sounded very serious, as if something important had happened. Maybe, she thought suddenly, this was the reason why Max had never returned her call. If there had been an arrest, or some other major development in the case, maybe he hadn't been allowed to say anything until the police did what they needed to do.

"I understand," she said quickly. "We should probably go right now, shouldn't we?"

"If you wouldn't mind."

"No, no, of course not. This is important. I'll just go and get my things."

CHAPTER 31

———— ◆ ————

Carly collected her coat and bag, apologized to her waiting client, and asked Michelle to reschedule her remaining two appointments.

Gracie drove her to the district station. She had passed by it many times but had never actually been inside. They walked in through the back entrance, and Gracie ushered her into a small room that was empty except for a table in the middle, surrounded by mismatched plastic chairs. On the far wall, Carly noted with fascination, was a mirror. She felt as if she were in a movie, and wondered if anyone was looking at her from the other side of the glass.

"Have a seat," Gracie said. "Can I get you a cup of coffee?"

Carly nodded. "Thank you."

"Cream? Sugar?" In the harsh fluorescent light, the detective looked sallow and weather-beaten. Carly could see from her own reflection in the mirror that the lighting did not flatter her, either.

She winced and instinctively reached up to smooth her hair. "Just milk, please."

He seemed to be gone for a long time. Carly sat, waiting, listening to the hum of the lights, and the faint sounds of the room from behind the closed door. She thought about Max and wondered if he had left a message for her. She had called to check her answering machine at lunchtime, but there had been nothing.

Gracie finally came back, carrying two styrofoam cups. A manila folder was tucked under his arm, and he was accompanied by a trim, pleasant-looking blond woman in a navy pantsuit. "This is Detective Roberts," he said. "Okay if she joins us?" He handed Carly one of the cups.

"Sure." Carly nodded.

Detective Roberts smiled at her, set a tape recorder on the table, and sat down. "Call me Lori," she said. "Do you mind if we record this? It's routine."

"That's fine," Carly said. "I don't mind."

Gracie closed the door and joined them. Lori Roberts pushed the record button on the machine and looked at Gracie.

He sipped his coffee. "Okay," he said. "We'll get the basics out of the way. You know, Carly, that you are not in police custody, and you are free to get up and leave at any time."

"Yes, of course," Carly said, puzzled. "I know." It seemed strange to her that he kept saying that. Why wouldn't she be free to leave? He was probably just being considerate. No doubt most people were very intimidated by the police. She wasn't, though. She liked Gracie. He was polite, and he seemed trustworthy.

"Okay," Gracie said. "I have a written statement,

signed by you, Carly Martin, that describes your actions on the night that Henry Tremayne was critically injured. Let's go over it again. You arrived at the Tremayne house at approximately 5:30 P.M. You were alone in the house with Mr. Tremayne. You gave medical care to several of his animals, then you and Mr. Tremayne had a short conversation. You left the house just after 6 P.M. and drove away in your van no later than six-fifteen. You went home, cooked dinner, read a book, then went to bed. You did not see anyone after you returned home, and you did not make any phone calls that night."

He looked up at her. She nodded.

"Is there anything in your statement that you want to change? Anything that could be made more accurate?"

"No, I don't think so. That pretty much covers it."

Gracie took another sip of his coffee, and Carly remembered her own cup. She tasted it and waited for Gracie to continue.

"Carly, let's talk about your relationship with Henry Tremayne. He's a nice guy, eh?"

"He's wonderful," Carly said. "I've known him for two years."

"He left you a lot of money in his will. That was generous of him. Did you ever think that maybe he would change his mind? Rewrite it?"

"I didn't know about it in the first place," Carly said. "They only told me when he went into the hospital."

"You didn't know?"

She shook her head. "No. I was shocked when Max told me."

"According to Mr. Giordano, you told him that you and Mr. Tremayne had discussed the foundation."

"Oh. Well, yes, we did talk about that, but . . ."

"You just told me that you didn't know about it. If you talked about it with him, then you knew about it. Right?"

"Well . . ." Carly began, flustered. "Yes. But we only talked about the foundation as an idea. He never said anything about putting me in charge of it, so I didn't know about that. And he never mentioned the house."

"Never?"

"I mean, he never mentioned the idea of giving it to me. He might have told me that he wanted to use the house for the foundation."

Gracie nodded and didn't speak for a few moments. He looked through the papers in front of him. Carly shifted uncomfortably in her chair. She was starting to get an uneasy feeling, and she didn't understand why Gracie had suddenly become so confrontational. He hadn't told her anything new about Henry, and he was asking her the same questions that she had already answered last week.

Gracie looked up. "How's your business doing, Carly?"

It was an abrupt change, she thought, surprised. "The clinic? Fine."

"You've been pretty busy there? Lots of clients?"

"Yes, very busy."

"It's good to own your own business. You have 30 percent of it, right?"

"Yes," Carly said slowly. "That's right. My partner owns the other 70 percent." She hadn't expected him to know the details of her financial situation. Why had Gracie been investigating her? She suddenly wondered if this strange interview could have anything to do with Richard and his drugs. But that made no sense. Why would Gracie care about Richard's coke habit? It had nothing to do with Henry.

"So everything is fine at work. You're making money, you're saving up for a nice vacation, a new car maybe . . . something like that. Do you do the books yourself, Carly?"

"No. My partner does them."

"You pay attention to how things are going, though."

"Of course," Carly said, slightly offended. Did he think that because she was female she ignored the finances? She had regularly examined the books until Richard had computerized everything a few months ago, and as soon as she had a chance to learn how to use the software, she would continue to do so. "We're doing well."

"Okay. Let's talk about your car. You drive a white Chevrolet van?"

"Only for clinic business. I use it to do errands and to make house calls."

"You take it home with you sometimes, though."

"Sometimes. It depends where I am when I finish my house calls, and whether I need to stop back at the clinic or not before I go home."

"Did you take it home with you on the night of Mr. Tremayne's accident?"

"I . . . don't remember. Probably. I usually do on Wednesdays."

"Are you certain that you left the Tremayne house no later than six-fifteen that night? Take as long as you need to think about it."

"I have thought about it," Carly said. "Yes. I'm sure."

Gracie's face was expressionless as he looked at her. "Carly, I have two witnesses who saw you driving away from the Tremayne house at 7 P.M. that night. Can you explain that to me?"

Carly sat back in her chair. She stared at the detectives, looking back and forth from Gracie to Lori Roberts, so stunned that she didn't know what to say. "No," she finally said. "I can't. Who said that?"

"That doesn't matter. It's true, isn't it? You left the house at seven. Why didn't you tell me that before, Carly?"

Carly began to feel frantic. It was all becoming suddenly, terrifyingly, clear. Gracie's request that she come to the station, the other detective, the tape recorder, the unexpected interrogation. Gracie thought that she had been involved in Henry's accident. How could he believe that? Who would have lied about seeing her there? She couldn't imagine who would do something so malicious.

Tears came unexpectedly to her eyes. She had been on edge ever since the scene with Edie, and she wondered how all of this could possibly be happening. "It's not true," she said. "I know that I left just a few minutes after six, because the television was on, and the six o'clock news had just started. That's when I said good-bye to Henry."

Silently, Lori Roberts handed her a tissue. Carly took it, clenching it in her hand.

Gracie was shaking his head. "I don't buy it, Carly. I think you had an argument with Henry Tremayne. You lost your temper, pushed him. Forgot that he was just an old man, eh? And then you moved his body into the house to try to fool everyone into thinking that he fell down the stairs."

"No!" Carly exclaimed, horrified.

Gracie slammed his hands down on the table, and Carly jumped. "Do not lie to me, young lady," he exclaimed, shaking a finger at her. "You—"

"Hector," Lori Roberts cut in, sharply. "Cool down, okay? You're overreacting. I think you should go outside and take a break."

Gracie shot Lori a baleful look from under his thick eyebrows, but he did not argue. He muttered something under his breath and stood up. He narrowed his eyes. "Okay. I'm going. But I'll be back."

The door slammed behind him. Carly, trembling, turned to Lori Roberts. "I don't understand what's happening," she said in a small voice. "Do I need a lawyer?"

Lori reached out sympathetically and patted Carly's hand. "Listen to me. You are not under arrest. Remember, you can leave at any time, and I wouldn't blame you if you did. Hector shouldn't talk to you like that. It isn't helpful. Do you want to go? I'll drive you back to your office right now."

"No," Carly said quickly. "I don't want to go. I want to make him understand that I would never do anything to hurt Henry. There's been some kind of awful mistake."

"Hector's a very suspicious guy. He always imagines the worst. He forgets that sometimes bad things can happen—just by accident—to good people."

Carly nodded. She blew her nose and tried to compose herself.

"You really care a lot about Henry, don't you?" Lori asked. "I can tell."

"He's been a very good friend," Carly said shakily. "I guess some people would think that it was strange for me to enjoy spending time with an eighty-year-old man, but we always found things to talk about."

"I don't think that's strange at all," Lori assured her. "Age doesn't matter when you have interests in common. Carly, look. I'm worried about you. Hector's determined to pin this on you. I think that he really believes that you tried to kill Henry Tremayne."

Carly's eyes overflowed. "But I didn't."

"I know. I believe you, and I'll do everything I can to help you. But I need you to be honest with me. It was an accident, wasn't it? You were there when he fell. I'll bet that you tried to carry him into the house to protect him—to help him. Right?"

"No," Carly protested, shaking her head violently. "He was sitting in his chair when I left. He was fine."

Lori Roberts looked sad. "Please, Carly. I need to hear the truth. I can't help you unless you tell me what really happened."

"But I didn't . . ." Carly began passionately, then abruptly fell silent. On the table, the tape machine was still recording. She looked at it, then looked up at Lori Roberts. It had taken her long enough, she thought numbly, to recognize the oldest trick in the book. She took a deep breath and stood up. "I was not present when Henry Tremayne was injured," she said quietly. "And if I'm not under arrest, I would like to leave now."

Carly hurried up Fillmore Street, huddling her coat around her. She was cold, despite the gentle warmth of the late-afternoon sun, and she was still shaking. Detective Roberts had done a good job of concealing her disappointment over her failure to get a confession, but

Carly had seen the blond woman's lips tighten briefly in frustration when Carly had announced her intention to go. Hector Gracie was nowhere to be seen as Carly walked quickly out of the building. She wondered if he had been watching her conversation with his colleague from behind the two-way glass.

Carly had refused Lori Robert's offer to drive her back to the clinic. She didn't want any more contact with either of the detectives until she had spoken with a lawyer. It was a long walk, but she could always catch the bus if she needed it, and she was in no hurry to get back to the clinic, anyway. At some point, she would need to pick up her car, then go to Henry's house to feed the pets, but she wanted to wait until Michelle and the rest of the staff had gone. She didn't have the energy to pretend to be normal when she felt as if the world were collapsing around her.

She thought about calling Jeannie and decided against it. How could she possibly explain to her sister that the police suspected her of trying to kill Henry Tremayne? Jeannie would immediately get upset, and Carly didn't want to have to soothe her. There was really only one person in the world who she wanted to talk to, and he was nowhere to be found. Where was Max? She desperately wanted to hear his voice, to be comforted and reassured, and to feel his strong arms around her. This was more than she could bear on her own.

She reached into her bag for her cell phone and called her answering machine, but there was only one message, from her mother. Misery swelled in Carly's chest, and she stopped walking. She stepped back, away from the crowded sidewalk, and leaned against the brick wall of a storefront, fighting tears of exhaustion and anxiety. Where *was* Max? What had happened? He had completely vanished, and she didn't understand why.

And then it came to her, in a rush of comprehension so cold and powerful that she almost dropped the phone. She knew why he had left her such a terse message yesterday and why she had not heard a word from him since. He had not vanished . . . no. He had simply cut his ties with her. Because it was not only the police who believed that she was guilty of attacking Henry Tremayne. Max believed it, too.

CHAPTER 32

W̲hen Max heard the knock on his hotel-suite door, he assumed that it was room service. He had called them an hour earlier, then again fifteen minutes ago to ask why it was taking them so long to produce a salad and a steak sandwich. In truth, he didn't care about the sandwich. He wasn't particularly hungry, and he had ordered dinner more from force of habit than from any desire to eat.

He had been trying all day to go about his business as if everything was fine, but his black mood had communicated itself quickly and completely to everyone he encountered. By the middle of the afternoon, he was fed up with the way people were tiptoeing around him, casting skittish looks at him out of the corners of their eyes as if they thought that he might explode at any moment. The nervous deference just made things worse, and Max began to think that he might prove their fears correct. He had canceled his last meeting of the day and left the office, thinking that he should take himself someplace where he would not be a danger to anyone but himself.

He had, of course, ended up at the beach. Even his run had felt wrong, though. He had pushed himself through all five miles, but it had been as plodding and painful as if there were sandbags tied to his legs, and he had been unable to drop into the mindless state that he craved.

The knock came again, and he got slowly to his feet. He had been lying on the bed, reading the newspaper, still wearing his running clothes, and he knew that he looked as coarse as he felt. *It's about time,* he thought darkly, as he walked to the door. The thought of eating actually made him feel nauseous, but dinner was a normal daily ritual, and he was damned if he was going to let his current state drag him down so far that he couldn't even eat. That would be a personal failure.

He opened the door and stopped short.

Carly was wearing an old brown coat buttoned up to her chin, and her hands were jammed into her pockets. Her eyes and nose were red, and she looked as forlorn as a lost child, but there was also something steely in the way that she held herself. There was a moment of shocked silence as they stared at each other, then she nodded.

"I thought you would be here," she said. "I need to talk to you."

Max did not move aside, and he did not invite her in. He had known that he would have to confront her sooner or later, and he had known that it would be difficult, but he had not expected to be assaulted by a mixture of emotions so intense that they left him weak and speechless. How, he wondered angrily, could he want her so much, even now? Knowing what he did, how could he feel anything but coldness when he looked into her face? And yet, it took every bit of self-control that he possessed to keep himself from reaching out to her.

And if he did that, he thought, he would be lost. He didn't even know what he would do if he suddenly found her in his arms. He wanted to seize her, to kiss her, to hurt her, to hear her beg him to believe that despite everything, she really had loved him all along. He wanted to take her beautiful face in his hands and hold her there until he could see the truth in her eyes.

He shook his head. His fingers tightened on the doorknob. "This is not a good time."

She didn't seem to hear him. "Why didn't you return my calls?"

"You know why."

She recoiled as if he had slapped her. "No, I don't. I would like you to tell me, please. I want to hear it from you."

"Christ, Carly," Max began, then lowered his voice. "I'm not playing this game anymore. It's over. We have nothing to talk about."

"Wrong. You owe me an explanation." There were tears in her eyes, but she looked defiantly at him. "Max, do you really believe that I tried to kill your grandfather?"

He let his eyes move over her. He knew every detail of her face, from the way that her eyes crinkled when she laughed, to the way that her lips parted when she waited for him to kiss her. He had believed that he also knew her soul, arrogantly dismissing the possibility that he could be fooled by a false front. But he had been fooled, and he did not know her at all. Even now, even confronted with all the damning evidence, he simply could not believe that she would have hurt his grandfather. It ran counter to his every instinct. And that told him exactly how deeply this woman had affected him and how dangerous that made her.

"Yes," he said.

A tear ran down Carly's cheek, and Max looked away.

"You really think that I would do that?" she whispered.

He found it hard to speak. "Yes."

"But why?"

It was more than he could take. Max knew that he had to end the conversation quickly. "Look," he said. "I know about the loans."

She looked blankly at him. "Loans?"

"Stop it. I had you investigated. I know about the clinic finances, about the mortgages, and the debts."

Her face seemed frozen, suddenly. "Debts?"

"I'll admit that you had me fooled. All that talk about not being able to leave the clinic because you were protecting your investment. That wasn't true, was it? You and Wexler have just been delaying the inevitable disaster as long as you can. And now that the bank is about to foreclose, you must have been desperate to find a way to keep from losing everything."

Carly said nothing. Max knew that he was talking too much, but he couldn't stop himself. "If it makes you feel any better," he added coldly, "I don't think that you would have done it if you hadn't been desperate."

She inhaled sharply, in a strange kind of gasp, and turned so white that he was sure she was about to faint. Instinctively, he moved forward to steady her, but she recoiled, raising her hands. He stared at her. He had never seen an expression like the one on her face. Her eyes looked huge, and bruised, and stunned.

"Carly," he said, "What—"

Her hands stayed up like a barrier, keeping him back. "I have to go," she said, in a trembling voice. "And I don't ever want to see you again. Ever. You are not the person I thought you were."

She took a breath. "I will give you credit for one thing, though," she said bitterly. "You were absolutely right about Richard."

She turned and left him standing in the doorway, staring after her. Her stride was purposeful, as if she was on her way to do something very important. Max watched her until she turned the corner and disappeared. She did not look back.

It was past six by the time the taxi dropped Carly off in front of the clinic. It was only a short drive from the hotel, but there had been enough traffic to add ten minutes to the trip. She had spent the ride sitting numbly in the backseat, staring through the window, barely seeing the city around her, barely hearing the rock station on the radio.

How's your business doing? Gracie had asked. Now she understood why. Gracie knew, Max knew. Richard certainly knew, damn him. *She* was the only one in the dark. Loans, mortgages, debts—Max had spoken of them in plural. How bad was it? And how could she not have known? Richard had managed to conceal the truth, but perhaps it hadn't taken much effort. She would be the first to admit that she had not paid as much attention to their finances lately as she could have. But she hadn't been ignoring them, either. He had obviously been keeping a false set of books, because if things were really as bad as

Max had made them sound, then this charade had been going on for a long time.

She could hear Edie's scornful voice. *He snorts that stuff like he's got no bottom in his wallet.* On the contrary, it sounded to Carly as if he finally had hit bottom, and she was right there with him. How bad was it? How bad? The question played in her mind like a discordant musical refrain. The clinic had almost a million dollars in assets, including the building and all of the equipment they owned. If Richard had secretly taken out loans, using their assets as collateral, he could have come up with a staggering sum to squander. Was it really possible to use up so much money on drugs? She couldn't believe it. If they really were in danger of losing everything, then Richard must have been channeling their money—*her* money—into all kinds of personal expenses.

Fury gave Carly back her stamina. How dare he do this? He had the right to ruin his own life, but to casually and carelessly destroy hers as well? That did it. She had been self-indulgent and stupid with her insistence on trying to see the good in people. She hadn't been noble, she had been naive, and look where she had ended up. Well, that unfortunate aspect of her personality was now officially dead, laid to rest next to any residual sympathy for Richard Wexler. It was time that she started protecting herself, because it was suddenly very clear that no one else would do it. Not even Max.

Especially not Max. Carly's strength faltered for a moment, shimmering around her like a mirage. He was gone. She couldn't think about it. If she let herself think, then the pain would swallow her, and there was no time for that.

She pulled her keys out of her bag and unlocked the front door of the clinic. Even if Richard had been showing her false accounting, he couldn't have created such a financial morass without leaving a trail of genuine paperwork. If all of this was true, then somewhere in his office there had to be loan papers and accurate bank statements, and with the help of Michelle's spare key, Carly intended to find them. And when she found them, she thought grimly, she would photocopy them. And then, first thing in the morning, she would find herself the meanest, toughest bulldog of a lawyer she could afford. The world was about to see a very different Carly Martin.

CHAPTER 33

————————◆————————

The clinic was dark and silent, except for a light burning down the hall in the staff room. They had several animals staying overnight in the wards, a first for the clinic, as the patients who needed extended care were usually transferred to a twenty-four-hour hospital nearby. But the hospital had been having power outage problems since the weekend, and so Brian had volunteered to do "night nurse" duty, sleeping on a cot in the staff room and making periodic checks of the wards.

Carly went back to say a brief hello and to tell him that she had stopped by to pick up some files. He was so involved with his science-fiction novel that he barely looked up, which was fine with Carly. She did not know if she looked as wild-eyed as she felt, and she did not want to find out. It didn't particularly matter that Brian was there. He would not question her even if he found her on her hands and knees shredding client files behind the front desk.

She found the key in Michelle's drawer and let herself

into Richard's office. It was more of a mess than she had ever seen it. Richard had never been neat in his personal space, but there had always been some general order to it. Now there was no order apparent at all. Several months ago, Richard had complained about their weekly cleaning service and forbidden them to go into his office when he wasn't around to supervise, which basically meant never. It showed, Carly thought. Dirty coffee mugs littered the room, and the wastebasket was overflowing. Deep piles of books and papers obscured the surface of the desk, and the shelves were stuffed with files, books, stacks of photocopied articles, and several years' worth of accumulated veterinary journals.

His file drawers were behind the desk. Carly slid each open in turn and flicked through the files without finding much of interest. She hadn't expected to. Judging from the state of his office, Richard's world was rapidly destabilizing, and Carly thought that she would be unlikely to turn up a neat folder labeled "Mortgages, Debts, and Other Cold-Blooded Deceptions." Where, then, should she look? If Richard was smart, she thought, he wouldn't keep those documents in the office at all. But he wasn't smart, and he would have no reason—yet—to expect her to be suspicious. She opened the top drawer of the desk and found it full of miscellaneous office supplies, most branded with the names of pet food or pharmaceutical companies. The next drawer held notepads, professional stationery, and a half-eaten bag of pretzels. The bottom drawer was locked.

"Damn," Carly muttered, rattling it. It was an old metal desk, and she could feel the locking bar hitting against the inside of the drawer as she pulled. It was not a sturdy lock, but it was effective enough to keep her out. Or was it? She narrowed her eyes, studying it. Maybe not, she thought. She had a screwdriver in her office, left over from putting up some storage shelves. If she just slipped it into the lip of the drawer and pulled . . .

Moments later, she was back with the screwdriver in hand. If she was successful, it would be obvious to Richard that someone had broken into his desk, but what did that really matter? It wasn't as if she needed to maintain good working relations with him at this point.

She wedged the blade of the screwdriver down into the narrow space between the desk frame and the lip of the drawer, and pried it back, pulling as hard as she could. For a moment, nothing happened, and then the metal groaned and the lock broke with a sudden, loud crack. The drawer gave way, and Carly sat down hard on the floor.

She put down the screwdriver. "Not bad," she said, surprised.

The drawer was haphazardly stuffed with papers, and at first, all that Carly saw were the bills. There were overdue notices for everything from the utilities, to the telephone, to the payments on their newest medical equipment. Many of the envelopes had not even been opened. It looked as if Richard had just been tossing every new notice into the drawer, then locking it up again.

Gradually, the paper trail began to come together. It was a sickening story, and almost exactly as Max had said. Six months after she joined the clinic, Richard had had their building appraised and had taken out a second mortgage for the staggering sum of four hundred thousand dollars. A more recent document from the bank showed another loan, this one against the total value of their medical equipment.

So much money, Carly thought, suddenly feeling weak. It was more than she could imagine having, much less spending. Could it really be gone? How could so much money just vanish? Judging from the letters from the bank—increasingly terse in tone—Richard had not made any loan payments in months. The most recent letter, which had been shoved into the middle of the pile, stated the bank's intention to begin foreclosure proceedings against the clinic building.

Carly felt hysteria bubbling up inside her. It really was true, then. Everything was gone. The clinic, her savings, her credit rating, her reputation. It was too much, she thought. All of this, the loans, the debt, the drug use—had been going on for so long, and she had known nothing. Nothing. What was the matter with her? How could she have been so stupid? She closed her eyes for a moment, trying to calm down, reminding herself that she could stand up and scream as loudly and as long as she wanted to, but it would not make a whisper of difference. All she could do for the moment was to make copies of everything and take them to someone who might be able to help her.

She reached into the drawer to grab the remainder of the pile, then noticed something that she hadn't seen before. A single, folded sheet of notepaper; thick and elegantly ecru-toned, it stood out from the mass of cheap commercial paper like a leather-bound book in a newsstand.

Carly immediately recognized the stationery, because she had her own collection of polite notes penned on that very paper. Frowning, she picked it up, unfolded it, and saw Henry Tremayne's familiar spidery handwriting. But why would Henry have written a letter to Richard? They barely knew each other. Puzzled, she sat down on the floor and began to read.

You were absolutely right about Richard.

Carly's words, and the expression on her face, had engraved themselves into Max's brain. He found himself mentally replaying that moment over and over again as he sat in his hotel suite, staring down at his untouched dinner.

The cliché that kept coming to him was that she had looked as if she'd seen a ghost. It had been a look of utterly horrified comprehension, as if something that could not possibly exist had suddenly popped up in front of her and forced her to believe in it.

He picked up the television remote, turned on CNN, and tried to focus on the news. He couldn't. All he could see was Carly's face. How, he asked himself, could anyone—no matter how skilled an actress—fake a look like that? He had expected one of a variety of possible reactions when he confronted her, and nothing that she had said or done had matched anything that he had imagined. She had not shown guilt, or fear, or defiance. She had not confessed, or begged him to listen to her side of the story, or tried to seduce him. It was as if his statements had shocked her so completely that she had stopped thinking about him—and Henry—at all. What had she said, finally? *I have to go.*

What the hell was that about? It made no sense to Max. Carly's reaction had been that of a woman who was absolutely stunned to hear that she was a month away from

bankruptcy. It really seemed as if she had been totally unaware of the mess she was in.

But that was insane. How could you not know something so fundamental? Although . . . He frowned, considering. Wexler owned the major share of the
business—that was a fact, confirmed by Tom Meyer. And
that meant that Carly's signature would not have been required on the loan agreements. If Wexler had taken out the
loans on his own and concealed the truth from Carly, then
she could, possibly, have been unaware of the true situation.

Max shook his head. It was almost inconceivable to
him that anyone could own—or even partially own—a
business without scrutinizing every detail of what was
going on. He had done all of the accounting for his own
company for years, until the job became so huge that he
was finally forced to delegate it. Even then, he had obses-
sively audited his own accountants and executives. If you
didn't pay attention to these things, he had always believed, you inevitably got screwed by someone.

An idea came to him. He stood up, walked to his desk,
and a moment later, he had Tom Meyer on the phone.

"Max," said the lawyer. "It's only ten. You're slipping."

Max didn't waste any time. "You told me two weeks
ago that Carly Martin's personal credit was fine?"

"It was. She's got one charge card and some student
loans, all paid up to date. She owns her car, so no payments there. If you overlook the business disaster, she's
got the credit rating of the average schoolteacher."

"Did you check out Wexler? Her business partner?"

Tom snorted. "Five cards, maxed out. All overdue. Car

payments . . . well, let's just say that if I were him, I wouldn't be parking the Porsche in the same place for two nights in a row. I know homeless people with better credit than that guy."

"I'll be damned," Max said slowly. It was not proof that Wexler had been the only one behind the problems at the clinic; but if a pattern of behavior counted for anything, this certainly supported that possibility.

He thanked the lawyer and hung up, his mind moving quickly. Even if Carly hadn't known about the state of her business, he thought, that still didn't explain any of the other indications that she had been involved with Henry's injury. And yet . . .

And yet, before he had been given that final piece of damning evidence, he had been ready to write off everything else—except for the strange question of the van—as coincidence. Hope and caution mixed uneasily inside him, and he thought of the way that Carly had looked at him when she told him that she never wanted to see him again.

Be careful, he thought. *Very careful.* He would do himself no favor by rushing back into this.

> *Dear Mr. Wexler:*
> *I have recently become aware of the unfortunate fact that your business is in serious financial trouble because of your nonrepayment of several large loans. While I do not consider your accounts to be any of my affair, I want to emphasize that I do have the greatest interest in the welfare of your partner, Carly Martin . . .*

Carly read slowly, her astonishment growing as she gradually deciphered Henry Tremayne's elegantly looped handwriting. It had Henry's style, she thought, but the voice in the letter was far sterner and more formidable than the gentle old man she knew.

> . . . *while I do not believe that an honorable man would have behaved as you did in the first place, I feel that it is my duty to give you one last chance to do the honorable thing before I involve myself further . . .*

He was threatening Richard, Carly realized. Not overtly, of course, but his meaning was clear. She read on. Richard was to immediately tell Carly the truth, then liquidate all of his assets, business and personal, to pay off the loans and return Carly's investment. If Richard did not do so, Henry wrote, he would be forced to go to the police with a report of his "full knowledge" of Richard's "various unlawful activities." He did not specify what those activities were, but Carly had no doubt that Richard knew exactly what the old man was talking about. His drug use? Maybe. Or anything else that Henry had managed to turn up. He had obviously had someone investigating Richard, although Carly couldn't imagine why he would have done such a thing. Perhaps he had started with her, she thought, when he was setting up the trust. And then he had turned up the muddy finances just as Max had. *Am I the only one around*, she wondered, *who doesn't employ a full-time private eye?* Too bad she hadn't. It would have saved her a lot of grief.

Carly stared at the letter. Richard would have panicked

when he read it, she thought. A cold feeling began to seep through her body, and for the first time, she took notice of the date on the top of the page. Sunday, April 20. Henry had written the letter three days before the accident. Allowing for time in the mail, it had very likely landed on Richard's desk on Wednesday morning, the day that someone had confronted Henry Tremayne outside the front door of his house.

Then Carly realized something so important that she could not believe that it had ever slipped her mind. She jumped to her feet, grabbed the phone, and began to dial. By now, she knew Max's hotel phone number by heart. "Please be there," she whispered as she listened to the ringing. "Please."

When she heard the sickeningly familiar message on his voice mail, she almost started to cry. She swallowed hard and waited for the beep. "Max," she said urgently. "Please listen. I wasn't driving the white van on the day that your grandfather fell. It was in the shop. I had my own car. Nobody asked me anything about the van until today, or I would have remembered. But then the police were firing questions at me, and I got so rattled that I wasn't thinking clearly . . ."

She took a quick breath. "It was Richard who picked up the van that afternoon. You can check the records at the dealer—I'm sure that he must have signed something. But there's another thing. I just found a letter from Henry in Richard's desk. I didn't know about the loans, but Henry did, and he was threatening Rich with—"

With a gasp, she stopped. There was a figure standing in the office doorway, and it took her almost a second to realize that it was not Richard. It was small and silent, and wearing a leopard-print coat. Edie. Carly breathed out. Her heart felt as if it were about to jump out of her chest.

"Max," she said into the phone, "I'm taking Henry's letter home with me. Please come over as soon as you get this message. I want to talk to you before I go to the police." She hung up and tried to compose herself.

"What's going on?" Edie asked suspiciously.

"Nothing," Carly said. "You surprised me, that's all. What are you doing here?"

"Brian said that I could come and help him. Why are you here? It's late."

"Not that late. And I'm about to leave. I just came to pick up some papers." That was certainly true, she thought, as she bent down to gather up the scattered loan documents and dunning letters. She decided not to bother to photocopy them, and slid the whole pile into her bag. *To hell with Richard*, she thought. *If he wants his papers back, he can talk to my lawyer.* She tucked Henry's letter into the inside pocket of her coat.

"You don't care if I'm here tonight, right?" Edie asked.

Carly did not have the energy or patience to choose her words carefully. "I'm glad you're here," she said, picking up her bag. "It would make me very happy if you would come to work every day."

"With your cokehead friend? Great."

"He's not my friend. And I'm afraid that this clinic won't be around for much longer. But I'll promise you something, Edie. If you really do care about this work, and you're willing to show up and do it well, I'll make sure that one way or another, you will always have a job. Okay?"

Edie shrugged and said nothing.

"Think about it," Carly said wearily. She slung her bag over her shoulder and walked past the girl, turning off the lights in Richard's office and pulling the door shut behind her.

She was at the front door by the time Edie finally spoke.

"Carly."

Carly stopped. It was the first time that she remembered ever hearing the girl say her name. She turned. "What?"

Edie stood awkwardly, silhouetted in the light spilling down the hallway from the staff room. As Carly's eyes adjusted to the darkness, the dim glow of the streetlights coming through the front windows was just enough to illuminate the girl's face.

Edie smiled at her. It was a tiny smile, tentative and hopeful. "Okay," she said.

CHAPTER 34

———————◆◆———————

Max was toweling himself dry after his shower when the phone rang. There was an extension in the bathroom, right next to the toilet, which was more connectivity than anyone needed, in his opinion. Some spaces should be sacred. It had also been ringing earlier, while he was standing under the cascade of hot water, trying to rinse some clarity back into his brain. He had intentionally ignored it then, and did not feel inclined to answer it now. The hospital had his cell phone number, they would call it if there was any problem, and as for everyone else . . .

He shook his head. Everyone else could go to hell.

The rings bounced insistently off the marble walls, and he thought of Carly. She never wanted to see him again, he reminded himself. Therefore, she would not be calling him. And even if she was, he was in no shape to talk to her. He felt as if he had been hollowed out in the middle, and he didn't trust himself to make any decisions.

The phone kept ringing. How long did it take before the voice mail picked up? The sound was obnoxiously loud in the small space, destroying the warm relaxation he had found in the shower, and setting his nerves on edge again.

"Goddamn it," he muttered. He dropped his towel and grabbed the receiver. "What?"

There was a silence on the other end, and just as he was about to hang up, an unfamiliar female voice said, "Who is this?"

"If you don't know that," Max growled, "then you have the wrong number. Good-bye."

"I want to talk to Carly's friend Max."

Max, who had been about to hang up, stopped. He frowned. The voice was not actually unfamiliar, he thought. He recognized it, but he could not place it. "Speaking," he said.

"You sounded different," said the voice accusingly. "Look, you need to go over to Carly's house right now, okay? I think she's in trouble."

"What?" Max said. "Wait a minute. Edie? How did you get this number?"

"I didn't," she said. "I pushed redial. Carly called you half an hour ago before she left. Look, this is serious. I'm at the clinic, and that guy she works with was just here—"

"Richard Wexler?"

"Pay attention, genius." She sounded agitated. "That's what I just said. He came in to pick up his car. Carly broke into his desk and took some papers, and when he saw what she did, he went crazy. We didn't say anything, but he knew it was her. He just drove off, and I think he's going to her house."

Max had absolutely no idea what the girl was talking about, but her alarm transmitted itself clearly. "Did you call Carly?"

"Yes! We've been calling her, but she's not answering. You have to go over there. There's going to be trouble. He's really mad, and he's all coked up—"

"He's *what*?"

"Just shut up and go, okay? Now!" Edie hung up.

Stunned, Max replaced the receiver. Carly had broken into Richard's desk? Richard was on drugs and going to her house? What the hell was going on? It was as if everything had just fast-forwarded around him and left him standing six frames behind. It made no sense, but that didn't matter. If Carly was in danger, he would act first and ask questions later. He strode into the bedroom, grabbed pants and a shirt out of the closet, and threw them on. He could be at her house in fifteen minutes if he drove fast. Wexler did not have much of a head start. And if he laid so much as a finger on Carly, then that California rich boy would learn more than he had ever wanted to know about how things worked in Brooklyn.

It had taken Carly longer than she had planned to get home. Halfway there, she suddenly remembered that Henry's pets still needed to be fed. She had gone cautiously to the mansion, unsure of her welcome after the events of the day, half-expecting Pauline to slam the door in her face. But Pauline had not been there, so Carly quickly fed the animals and left, glad to have avoided any confrontation.

Outside her apartment door, she could hear her phone ringing. She fumbled for her keys, feeling the reassuring crackle of Henry's letter in her coat pocket, then unlocked the door and hurried into her dark apartment.

It took her only a few seconds to realize that she smelled cigarette smoke in the air, but even so, the awareness did not come fast enough to help her. Someone slammed the door shut behind her. Carly gasped, dropped her bag, and whirled around.

The lights went on, and she saw who was standing there, between her and the door. "Richard," she said, her heart pounding so hard that she could feel it throughout her body. She was briefly relieved that it was not a stranger, but the look on Richard Wexler's face did not make her feel very safe. "What are you doing here? I thought you were in Florida."

"My flight got in an hour ago," he said. "Then I went to the clinic to pick up my car and found that somebody had been in my office while I was gone. Any idea who that might be, Carly?"

Carly ignored the question. "How did you get into my apartment?"

"With this." He held up her spare key. "You've had a key in that flowerpot for two years."

"You had no right to let yourself in here."

"And you had no right to break into my goddamned desk!" He was wearing a black leather jacket, and even in the dim light, she could see that he had a tan. He was sweating, and his face looked creased and oily. His eyes were strangely bright.

"Look," she said, trying to sound calm, "I've had a long day, and I'm tired. I think you should go home now, and we'll talk about all of this tomorrow. Okay?"

"You think so?" He smiled. It was not a nice smile, and Carly felt a stab of fear.

"Richard, I want you to leave. Now."

"I'll bet you do, but I don't give a shit what you want, Carly. Where's the letter?"

"If you don't go right now, I'm going to call the police."

He moved so quickly that she was barely able to step back before he grabbed her. His hands knotted into the front of her coat, lifting her. She had forgotten how strong he was, she thought wildly, as he propelled her backward. He threw her up against the wall, knocking the wind out of her, and pinned her there, breathing hard. She kicked at him, gasping.

"You are not in charge here, Carly," he said, his face inches from hers. His pupils were dilated, she realized. That was why his eyes looked so strange. "I am. Get it? You broke into my desk. You took my papers. I want the letter back. You better believe that I am not going to jail just because some lame old man can't keep his balance. Where is the letter? If I'd known that you were so good with a screwdriver, I would have gotten rid of it a month ago."

He started to laugh. He was talking too fast, and for the first time, Carly was truly afraid. This man with the crazy face was a total stranger. She thought she knew Richard, but she was wrong. The drugs had changed him, or the stress had pushed him over the edge. Either way, she had no idea what he was now capable of.

"It's in my bag," she whispered.

He released her abruptly, and she staggered forward, sucking in deep breaths of air, her pulse pounding in her temples. He grabbed the bag and threw it at her. It thumped to the floor at her feet. "Find it," he said.

She knelt and began to shuffle through the stack of

bank papers, pretending to search for Henry's letter. Her head was throbbing, and she felt dizzy. She needed just a moment to think . . . Max had said that Henry had no memory of the accident or the days surrounding it. Had he also forgotten sending the letter to Richard? If so, and if she gave Richard the letter and he destroyed it, then she would have nothing to prove that Richard had had a motive to attack Henry. Without that letter, her own fate might depend on whether or not the Chevy dealer had any record of Richard's picking up the van that afternoon, and that was more of a risk than she was willing to take.

As she fumbled inside the bag, her hands shaking, her fingers brushed against her cell phone. Hope seized her for a moment, before she realized that she could not possibly dial 911 without Richard realizing what she was doing. Even if she was able to get the call through before he stopped her, it would take the police too long to arrive. It was too risky. She didn't think that he would seriously hurt her, but she was not sure enough.

"Carly," said Richard, "you are pissing me off. What are you doing? Where is it?"

"Just a minute," she said sharply, stress putting an edge on her voice, and, to her shock, she felt his hand close around her hair, yanking her head back. He hit her across the face, hard, with the back of his hand, and she tasted the coppery tang of blood in her mouth.

"You have developed an attitude problem," he said. "You were better when you were younger. Remember how well we got along? You were so sweet then, but now you have this bitch mouth. Does your rich boyfriend like being argued with all the time? I don't let women talk like that to me. You'd better apologize before I get mad."

Carly blinked tears out of her eyes and glared at him. "Richard," she said through her teeth, "do you want me to find your goddamned letter, or not?"

He backhanded her again, and she cried out, as much in rage as in fear. The side of her face was burning, and she could feel her cut lip beginning to swell. "Say it," he said, bending over her, his fingers still knotted into her hair. "Say, *I'm sorry, Richard, darling. Please forgive me.*"

He moved her head up and down in a parody of a nod, and Carly tensed, breathing hard. She was trembling with anger and adrenaline, and she looked up at him through the hair that had fallen around her face, wanting to launch herself at his throat like a pit bull. But she was no physical match for him. If only she could distract him for a moment. Just long enough for her to get out the cell phone and call for help. Even if she couldn't talk to the 911 operator, the call would be recorded, and someone would eventually come to help her.

And then an idea shot through her, sharp as an electric shock, and she dropped her head, afraid that Richard might see the sudden excitement in her expression. It was crazy, she thought, so crazy that it should have been impossible, but there was a chance that it might actually work.

She took a shaky breath, trying to make her face absolutely neutral, and looked up again. "I'm sorry, Richard," she said, in as steady a voice as she could manage.

He looked surprised by her sudden compliance, and then he began to laugh. "Great," he said. "I love this. But you didn't finish. I said 'Richard, darling,' remember?"

Carly steeled herself. "Richard, darling."

"And?"

"Please forgive me," she murmured.

"Beautiful. See how easy that was? Remember how nice you used to be?" He let go of her hair. "Now, give me my letter, babe, and let's finish up here."

Carly ducked her head and reached into the bag. Feeling Richard's eyes on her, she made a show of shuffling through the papers with one hand. With her other hand, she reached under them, feeling around in the cavernous bottom of her bag until her fingers touched the cell phone again. Quickly, she found the send button and pushed it.

Please work, she thought. She was almost positive that the last call she had made had been to check her own answering machine. She held her breath, and then, as if by magic, the phone on her desk began to ring.

She looked toward it, then at Richard. He shook his head. "Don't even think about it," he said. Feigning meekness, she obeyed. After four rings, Carly heard her machine click as it answered and silently began to record.

CHAPTER 35

◆◆◆

"Richard," Carly said, raising her voice slightly, "I can't find the letter. It's not in here."

Richard's eyes narrowed. He grabbed the bag from her and dumped the contents onto the floor. The papers fell into a ruffled heap, her lipstick rolled under the couch, and the cell phone landed next to a paperback novel under a shower of loose change. He swept through the papers with one hand, spreading them out farther.

"You're right," he said. He did not look pleased. "It isn't here. So what the fuck did you do with it?"

"I . . . I don't remember." Carly braced herself. She couldn't give him the letter. Not yet. Not until she made him talk about Henry.

Richard stared at her. "You don't remember? Do you think I'm playing around here, Carly? I'm not. And I'm not going to ask you again. What the hell is the matter with you?" He stopped. "Or do you like this? Maybe that's it. Should I have tried this with you a long time ago, babe? I never would have guessed."

He reached out and ran his fingers over her swollen cheek, then raised his hand, feigning another blow. She flinched, instinctively closing her eyes, and heard him laughing.

She opened her eyes. "Is this what you did to Henry Tremayne?"

"I didn't do anything to Henry Tremayne. I went up there to talk to him. I wanted to have a civilized conversation. Actually, I wanted to tell him to mind his own goddamned business."

"You tried to kill him."

"I did not! I was trying to make a point. I got pissed off, maybe I shoved him a little. It was an accident."

"You tried to cover it up by dragging him inside and leaving him at the foot of the stairs."

"What the fuck else was I supposed to do? Go to jail over something that wasn't even my fault? I hardly touched him. I did worse to his dog than I did to him."

His dog? *Samson*, Carly thought, suddenly. *Of course. The old cocker spaniel with the cracked rib.* And Richard's hand, bandaged the day after Henry was injured. She remembered that she had sent the other dogs out to play in the yard that evening, since Pauline was not around to protest the inevitable mud. But the old spaniel always stayed inside, and he had probably gone to the door with Henry when Richard rang the bell. Richard must have kicked him when he tried to defend his master.

"Samson bit you." For some reason, perhaps hysteria, she found that very funny. Richard's eyes narrowed, and Carly realized her mistake when he seized her by the arms, dragging her to her feet.

"You're laughing at me? You think this is a joke?"

"No," she gasped. "I don't."

"Don't condescend to me, Carly, or I'll make you sorry." He had pinned her arms to her sides, his fingers biting into her flesh with bruising strength, and his words were hot against her face. "Or maybe that's what you want me to do. Maybe you do like this."

The cold, heavy syrup of horror flooded Carly's belly as she saw the look on his face. His mouth came down hard on hers, grinding her lips painfully back against her teeth. She cried out in furious protest, wrenched her head to the side, and bit him hard on the corner of the mouth.

Richard yelled and jerked his head back, swearing, and Carly saw, with brief satisfaction, that there was blood on his cheek. She twisted away, but he grabbed her, lifted her entirely off of her feet, and slammed her back against the wall. Her head hit the plaster with an impact that flashed stars in front of her eyes, and the air rushed out of her lungs in a huff.

He had her pinned between him and the wall, his solid, square body crushing hers, and she could feel his chest moving with quick, shallow breaths. He reached for the neck of her shirt and ripped downward, tearing the thin cotton halfway down her chest. Carly took a deep, sobbing breath and screamed at the top of her lungs.

Richard hit her, and she screamed again, and again, her voice smothered against the hand that he clamped over her mouth and nose. And then, like a miracle, she heard someone pounding on her door. The knob rattled, then the pounding started again. "Carly!"

It was Max. His voice was muffled through the wall, but she would have known it anywhere. She struggled for breath, frantically trying to suck air through Richard's fingers, and getting almost none. Everything around her seemed to be glowing weirdly, and her pulse was pounding so loudly in her head that she could barely hear anything else. She couldn't breathe, she thought, and panicked, thrashing wildly against Richard's heavy body. He was going to suffocate her, she thought, terrified, and she would never see Max again. A strange buzzing warmth was creeping through her, and she suddenly felt as if she were floating. She heard a loud crash, then another, but the sounds meant nothing to her. It was as if they were miles away.

Richard released her suddenly, and she felt herself falling for what seemed to be a long time. Then the floor was under her, and she was drinking in deep breaths of air, and the fog in her brain started to clear.

She lifted her head shakily and saw Max—standing tall as a titan from her perspective—put his fist into Richard's jaw with a force that snapped Richard's head back and seemed to lift him inches into the air. He flew backward into Carly's end table, knocking over a lamp and a stack of paperback books, all of which crashed down on top of him as he crumpled to the floor and lay still.

And then Max was kneeling beside her.

"Carly?" He helped her into a sitting position, cradling her gently. "Talk to me. Are you all right?"

"You broke down my door," she said, wonderingly. It was standing open, and through the empty rectangle, she could see the faces of curious neighbors peering in at them.

"Damn right I did," Max said. "Tell your landlord that I'll pay for it."

"And you knocked Richard out with one punch?"

"I wanted to hit him a few more times, but it didn't work out that way."

"I had no idea that you had such a serious right hook," she said, and, inexplicably, burst into tears. He held her, stroking her hair, murmuring things that made her cry even harder. She had never been so happy to see anyone in her entire life, and she thought that she never wanted to leave the protective circle of his arms.

He put his fingers carefully under her chin, turning her face, and swore under his breath at the sight of her bruised cheek. "I'm going to kill him," he said grimly, and to Carly, he sounded as if he meant it. Startled, she stopped crying and took a deep breath, trying to get control of herself. She was about to ask him if he had gotten her message, but there was a sudden clatter of feet on the stairs outside.

Hector Gracie and a uniformed patrol officer appeared in the front doorway, and Carly stiffened, her fingers instinctively clutching Max's shirt. "What is he doing here?" she asked fearfully. Had he come to arrest her? *The letter*, she thought. *I have to give him the letter.*

"Sssh," Max said. "It's all right. I called him. I heard your message on the way over."

Gracie motioned the officer toward Richard, who was beginning to stir. "She okay?" the detective asked, looking at Carly.

"I'm fine," Carly said. She reached into her coat pocket, pulled out Henry's letter, and held it out toward Gracie. "This is from Henry Tremayne. I found it in Richard's desk. And if that isn't enough to clear me, I think—I hope—I have Richard's confession on my answering machine."

At the detective's uncomprehending look, she explained.

"You taped him? Through a cell phone?" Gracie's eyebrows went up, and he shook his head. "That's a new one for me, Miss Martin."

He picked up the cell phone from the floor and put it to his ear, listening for a moment, then shrugged. He pressed the end button. "Where's the machine?"

Carly pointed to her desk. Gracie walked over and scrutinized the old answering machine. He fiddled with the buttons, and a few moments later, the tape was playing. Carly's voice was small and muffled behind all of the foreground noise, but her words were clear enough to understand. *Richard, I can't find the letter.*

"I'll be damned," Max muttered, as the recorded conversation continued.

I hardly touched him. I did worse to his dog than I did to him . . .

Gracie stood listening, his arms folded against his chest, his face expressionless.

Maybe you do like this, said Richard's voice.

Carly shuddered, and Max's arms tightened around her. He made a sound, low in his throat, that sounded like a growl. There was a dull thud on the tape that Carly recognized as the sound of her own body being thrown against the wall. Her scream, remote and tinny as a neighbor's teakettle, was abruptly cut off as the tape ended.

The machine beeped and began to rewind. The sudden silence in the room was broken by Richard's groan, as he struggled to sit up under the watchful eye of the police officer.

"Well," Gracie said, and began to chuckle. "Not bad,

Miss Martin. Not bad. I always did think that you were a nice lady."

"Thank you," Carly said. The scene at the police station was still a little too fresh in her mind for her to feel much warmth toward the detective.

Gracie looked down at Richard. "So, guy, how about that? Beating up on old men and young ladies make you feel tough?"

"Fuck you," Richard mumbled groggily, holding his face in his hands. He glared up at Max, who glared right back at him. "You! You broke my jaw. I'm going to sue you for every—"

Gracie cut him off. "Sue him? I don't think so. You're going to be too busy to sue anybody, guy, because you are under arrest for assaulting this nice lady. And that, I think, is only the beginning of your troubles. You have the right to remain silent. Anything you say can and will be used against you in a court of law. You have the right to an attorney . . ."

Richard listened sullenly as Gracie read him his rights. The patrol officer pulled him to his feet, snapping handcuffs on him, and Carly turned her face into Max's chest, not wanting to see any more.

"Can you stand up?" Max asked her. She nodded, and he helped her to her feet and led her into the kitchen. He pulled out one of the chairs. "Sit down. I'm going to get some ice for your face."

"I don't have any ice," Carly said, watching him as he opened the freezer and looked inside. She never wanted to take her eyes off of him again. Having him there, warm and solid, was like a miracle.

"You're right," Max said. "No ice. Not a problem,

though. This will work." He pulled out a bag of frozen peas.

Carly eyed it dubiously. "You must be kidding."

"Brooklyn special. Hold still."

He sat down facing her, so close that his legs were on either side of hers, and leaned toward her, applying the cold plastic bag to the side of her face.

"Ouch," Carly said, although she hardly felt a thing. He was looking into her eyes, and the pounding in her swollen cheek was nothing compared to what her heart was doing. "Max, did you say that you heard my message in the car, on your way over here?"

"That's right."

"But why were you coming over, if you hadn't already heard it?"

"Edie called me to warn me that you were in trouble. She was there when Wexler saw that you'd broken into his desk."

That made no sense to Carly. "But if you hadn't heard my message, then you had no reason to think that anything had changed. So you came to help me, even though you still believed that I had tried to kill your grandfather? Why would you do that? I thought that you hated me."

"I tried to hate you," Max said. He put the peas down, to Carly's relief. "I kept telling myself that you'd been lying to me, that the fact that I was in love with you had made me completely insane, that I couldn't see the truth—"

She inhaled sharply.

"What's wrong?"

"Say that again."

He frowned. "I thought I couldn't see the truth—"

"Not that." Tears of a very different kind were suddenly hot in Carly's eyes. She could feel a huge happiness rising inside her like a helium balloon, but she needed to hear him say the words again. "The love part."

Max's expression cleared, and he reached out, his hand stopping just before he touched her, as if he thought that he might hurt her. She leaned her face into his palm and felt his fingers curve gently over her bruised cheek. "I love you, Carly," he said, his voice rough with emotion. "My God, you have no idea how much. When I heard you through that door . . . screaming . . ." He tensed at the memory. "I went crazy. Nothing could have kept me out. Nothing."

"When . . . did you know?"

"That I loved you? Almost from the first day that I met you."

Carly sniffled. "It couldn't have been that very first day."

"No," Max agreed dryly. "It was definitely not that very first day. It was the day you yelled at me in the car and stormed off into the park." He nodded, remembering. "That did it."

"Because I yelled at you? That's a very strange reason to fall in love with someone."

"It wasn't because you were yelling, it was what you said. I remember looking into your eyes . . . It was a hell of a shock, Carly. You were everything that I had never believed in until that moment. I knew it then, but it took me a lot longer to admit it." His face darkened. "And then, when the evidence kept piling up . . . pointing to you . . . I started to question myself."

His hands clenched into fists in his lap, and he stared

down at them. "I'm sorry," he said, in a voice that Carly had never heard before and never wanted to hear again. "By all rights, it's you who should hate me. I don't know how to find the words to—"

"Stop," Carly said, alarmed. "Max, no. How could I ever hate you?"

"Easily. I'm not the person you thought I was."

"I didn't mean that! Just like you didn't mean what you said to me. Max, look at me, please." She stood up and reached for him, holding his shoulders, looking down into his eyes. "I love you," she said softly. "Don't you know that already? I've loved since that day in the olive grove when you kissed my hand. I told you that we wanted to make you an honorary member of the Martin family, but the truth was that I wanted you to be all mine. My own family. The rest of them can get in line."

His eyes held hers. "That's the truth?"

"Yes. You're everything that I've always believed in. I just never found it until I found you. And I'll never leave you, not for as long as you want me." She smiled tremulously at him. "Um . . . do you have any idea of how long that might be? Just so I know?"

"Always," he said fiercely. And then his arms were around her, and he was pulling her down to him. She fell awkwardly into his lap, laughing as he kissed her, holding him tightly.

"You want a family of your own," he said, as if he was confirming it. "With me."

Carly nodded. "You would be a good start."

"And then?"

"Then we'll expand. Anytime that suits you."

"Now suits me. How long does it take to plan a wedding?"

"No time at all," Carly said hopefully, "if we elope."

Max shook his head. "Can't do that. The Martins want a party."

"What?" She straightened, dismayed. It was true, and she knew it, but she didn't understand how Max could be so certain. "How did you—"

"Your father told me."

"*What?* When?"

"Last week. He took me aside and talked to me about your ex-boyfriends and what losers they were—"

"Oh, my God."

"And then he clapped me on the shoulder and told me that you've always secretly dreamed of a huge wedding, and that he and your mother want more grandchildren, and that someday, somehow, who knows? Maybe it would all work out that way."

"This is unbelievable," Carly said indignantly. "I'm going to kill him. I'm surprised that you didn't get up and run screaming down the road."

Max shrugged. "I didn't."

"I never wanted a huge wedding," Carly grumbled. "They want one. They've probably got it all planned, hoping that *someday, somehow,* I might bring home someone who isn't a loser."

"Took you long enough," Max said.

"Very funny," Carly said. "You're starting to sound more like a Martin all the time. You'll eventually get tired of them and their wiseacre remarks, believe me."

Max suddenly looked very serious. "I look forward to

being around that long," he said. "And just for the record, I don't have any problem with doing it their way."

In truth, Carly didn't either. It would be some time before Henry Tremayne was strong enough to leave the hospital, and they could hardly have a wedding without him. And maybe the pets, as well. Yes, she thought, nodding to herself. Definitely the pets—all of them. The Martins wanted a big wedding, didn't they?

She looked into Max's face, imagining their own children, gray-eyed like the Tremaynes, playing in the Martins' meadow, watched by Max, and Henry, and a dog named Lola.

Max must have seen something in her expression. "What do you think?" he asked.

She smiled at him. "I think," she said, "that we can work something out."

ABOUT THE AUTHOR

———— •◆• ————

MELANIE CRAFT does not have a houseful of pets at the moment, but shows early signs of becoming a cat lady in later life. She studied archaeology at Oberlin College and the American University in Cairo, Egypt, and now lives near San Francisco. For information on her next novel, please visit her website at www.melaniecraft.com.

More
Melanie Craft!

Please turn this page
for an excerpt
from
MAN TROUBLE
available soon
from Warner Books.

CHAPTER 1

———— ◆ ————

"The Captain's boy be no boy at all," snarled Delancey. "And I'll prove it to ye!"

Angeline gasped, stumbling as the first mate's thick hand jerked her forward before the assembled crew. "No!" she cried. "He's a liar—"

"Liar, am I?" With one cruel motion, Delancey ripped her tunic from collar to hem, exposing the tight wrapping of bandages that disguised her bosom. She struggled, spitting and swearing at him, but he made short work of the strips of cloth. A rumble of astonishment ran through the crew at the sight of her milk-white breasts.

Delancey leered at her, close enough for Angeline to smell his stinking, rum-laced breath. "What do you say now, wench?"

"Very brave, Professor Shaw," said a voice just behind Molly. "Are you finally throwing caution to the winds, or are you just getting sloppy?"

Startled, Molly jumped, her leg knocking against the underside of the cafeteria table. Next to her laptop, a cup of lukewarm coffee sloshed into its saucer. In a well-practiced move, her fingers hit the key combination to activate the computer's screensaver, and the page of text was instantly replaced by a bucolic scene of blue water and gently cruising tropical fish. Outside the student union, the view was somewhat different. It was snowing again, not an unusual event in Belden, Wisconsin, in early December. Through the tall windows, Molly could see a row of bicycles lined up haphazardly in a rack. Frosted with white, they were slumped together as if huddled for warmth.

"Carter," she said, without turning around, "didn't your mother ever teach you that it's rude to read over someone's shoulder?"

Carter McKee came around the table and sat down opposite her. He was a small man, with rumpled brown hair, a rumpled brown jacket, a blue bow tie, and a crooked grin that made him look more like a naughty schoolboy than a journalist. It was a look that women—he claimed—found irresistible. Molly herself had never had any trouble resisting it, which was one reason why they were still friends after so many years.

"My mother taught me to salsa dance," Carter said, picking up Molly's coffee cup. He sipped, grimaced, and quickly set it down again. "She also taught me to mix a mint julep, and to rationalize the kind of behavior that might otherwise make me question my morals. I don't recall anything about shoulders, though."

"You're a snoop."

"Me?" Carter said innocently. "You'll feel terrible for

saying that when you realize that I was being helpful. Think what might have happened if one of your students had strolled by and seen his history professor madly typing 'milk-white breasts' into her laptop."

"I wasn't typing *madly*," Molly said with dignity. "I was typing *steadily*. That's different. You make me sound like some kind of crazed spinster."

"Either way, I assumed that the mysterious Sandra—"

"Shhh!"

Carter lowered his voice. "I assumed," he repeated, "that the mysterious Sandra St. Clair didn't want to be unmasked by a nosy freshman in the Belden College student union."

"You've got that right," Molly said. "We both know what would happen to me if the administration found out about this."

Carter's grin returned. "That would shake things up in this fossil pit."

"Not funny! This is my career we're talking about."

"You think that your dean wouldn't be happy to learn that one of his elite faculty members wrote the novel that the *New York Post* just called . . . what was it? A sleazy saga?"

"Swashbuckler," Molly said grimly.

He chuckled with delight. "That's it. 'A sleazy swashbuckler, soaked with sin and shipwrecked by schlock.' I love it."

Molly groaned. "Do we have to talk about this?"

"Not the greatest review," Carter said. "But you have to admit that it was an impressive use of alliteration."

"There's something very bizarre about having the *New York Post* accusing *me* of writing sleaze," Molly said.

Carter shrugged. "Don't tell me you were hoping for a Pulitzer," he said. "You want credit for your brains, write an academic book."

"I did! *Maritime Wives:* a feminist analysis of the role of sea captains' wives on eighteenth-century merchant ships. I lifted it straight from my dissertation, and it sold forty-two copies, ten of those to my mother. I didn't make a dime." She paused, reconsidering. "No, actually, I probably did make a dime."

"I have a copy," Carter said. "Your mother gave it to me. But I thought that money wasn't the point with you professor types. Aren't you supposed to survive on the fruit of knowledge and the milk of reason?" He quirked an eyebrow at her. "Or something like that?"

"That's after I get tenure," Molly said. "Which will never, ever happen if anyone links me to *Pirate Gold.* They'll take away my library card. I'll be out on the street, holding a sign that says 'Will deconstruct social theory for food.'"

Carter looked exasperated. "Why do you need tenure? You wrote a best-selling novel, for God's sake. Quit. Go buy a castle somewhere and write another one. Enjoy your life. What's so great about this place?" He gestured contemptuously around the half-empty cafeteria.

"Are you serious? Do you know how hard it is to get a position at a school like this? I'm lucky to be here." She paused and couldn't help adding, "And despite what everyone says, I earned it."

"Are people still grumbling about that? It's been three years. They should drop it."

"Academics never drop anything," Molly said. "There are feuds on this campus that go back to the 1940's. When

I'm seventy and hobbling across the quad, they'll be whispering, 'There goes that Shaw girl. She had a very *influential* father.' "

"That," Carter said, "is a chilling thought."

"I agree. Which is why I'd like to distinguish myself in something other than the trashy novel field."

"I meant that it was chilling to think that you might still be here when you're seventy."

"My father is seventy," Molly said. "And he's still here."

"Exactly," Carter said. His sour expression betrayed his opinion of Molly's father, who—she knew from experience—returned the sentiment. "And how is the great Stanford Shaw these days?"

"Fine," Molly said. Her father, currently Belden's emeritus professor of history, was the top god in the college's academic pantheon. He was the author of *The Chronicles of Civilization,* a dry nine-volume series considered to be among the finest scholarly works of the twentieth century, and although he no longer taught regularly, he was a regular sight on campus. One glimpse of his noble white head was enough to raise the heart rates of impressionable freshmen and to give everyone else the uneasy feeling that they were not living up to their potential.

"Everyone here is holding their breath, waiting for me to fail," Molly said. "I'm damned if I'll give them that satisfaction. I would rather be run through with a cutlass."

"Cheers," Carter said. "I salute your determination. Just one question, though."

"What?"

"Do you like it here?"

"What do you mean?" Molly felt an upwelling of anxiety in her chest. "That's a silly question. This is my job. I worked very hard to get it. Why wouldn't I like it?"

Carter shrugged. "Just asking."

"No, you weren't. You were making a point. I can tell by that smug look on your face. But you can forget it, Carter. I am not a trashy novel writer. I'm a professor and a historian. I have an excellent academic reputation, and I'm not going to throw it away just because my *hobby* accidentally turned into something huge!"

He gazed at her, unfazed. "But do you like it here?"

Molly scowled at him. "You know," she said, "every historical detail in *Pirate Gold* was one hundred percent accurate. You could learn as much from that book as from an introductory text on the eighteenth century. Just because there was a little bit of sex in it . . ."

"A *lot* of sex."

"Well, a reasonable amount of—"

"Molly," Carter said, "it was a lot. And then there were the kidnappings, and the keelhaulings, and the torture scenes, and that rather . . . stirring episode in the waterfront bawdy house with André DuPre and the two ladies of the evening."

"Oh, all right," Molly grumbled. "Whatever."

"Don't try to explain to me why your novel has academic merit," Carter said. "I don't care. But I'd love to know why you want to stay at a place where you have to hide the fact that your book was on the *New York Times* bestseller list."

"I like it here," Molly said. "I *like* it here. Okay? Satisfied?"

"If you say so."

"I do! I have an office. I have students. I like teaching."

"So come and live in Chicago, teach writing at the community college, and quit panicking when someone reads over your shoulder."

"Leave me alone!" Molly exclaimed too loudly. People turned to look, and she blushed, avoiding the curious stares. On her laptop screen, the tropical fish meandered through their virtual ocean, electronically bright and perpetually placid. "I really don't want to talk about this."

He held up one hand. "I didn't drive an hour north just to argue with you. I do have another reason for being here."

"Good," Molly said. "What?"

"My new project." Carter reached for her coffee cup again and began to fiddle with it, turning it round and round in his fingers. He flashed her his most charming smile, and Molly noticed that the tips of his ears were reddening. "It's big. Very big. But it hinges on a couple of things. One thing, actually, in particular." He took another swallow from the cup and made the same face.

"Carter," Molly said, "would you like me to get you some new coffee?"

He shook his head. "No, listen, this is important. The project hinges on you."

"Me?"

"I need your help."

"What, as a consultant? You're doing a historical piece?" It seemed out of character. Carter's writing style was aggressively commercial, the kind of work more likely to be published in *Esquire* than *American Antiquity*. It was hard for Molly to imagine being any help to him on the kind of project that he would consider "big."

"Not exactly," Carter said. His ears were getting redder. He frowned. "I'm not sure how to put this."

Molly hadn't seen him look so uncomfortable since their senior year in high school, when he had tried to talk her into telling Kara Swenson that he had already asked Becky Lipinski to the prom.

"Out with it," she said. "What's the project?"

"Okay," he said. He put down the cup and stared meaningfully at her. "Two words. Jake Berenger."

Molly nodded. "And?"

Her lack of reaction had clearly disappointed him. "You do know who he is," he said reproachfully. "The hotel mogul? The resort developer? The *billionaire*?"

"Of course I know who he is," Molly said. "I read the papers. But what's so new about this? You told me a year ago that you were doing a profile on him. You said that the *Miami Herald* wanted to run it in their Sunday magazine. Last I remember, you were busy interviewing all of his former girlfriends."

"Not all of them," Carter said. "That would have been physically impossible if I wanted to publish in this decade. Anyway, it was getting redundant. They all said some version of the same thing. 'Jake was always a gentleman, but I could tell that underneath it all, deep emotional wounds were preventing him from ever trusting me with his heart.'" He rolled his eyes. "Yawn. Spare me, please, from the pop psychobabble of a bunch of models."

"You never showed me the article," Molly said. "How did it turn out?"

"It didn't. He wouldn't talk to me. Not in person, not on the phone, not even by mail. And then I found out that he never gives interviews."

"Never? But he's always in the papers. There are pictures of him everywhere."

"Yes," Carter said. "People take pictures of Jake Berenger. People write stories about Jake Berenger. But he never gives interviews. He may be the world's most publicly private person."

"How strange," Molly said. "Doesn't the CEO of a major corporation have to talk to reporters sometime?"

"Oh, sure, he does the earnings reports," Carter said. "Very tightly controlled by the Berenger corporate PR office. But he's never done a single personal interview, not that every magazine and newspaper on earth hadn't been trying to get to him. Word on the street is that he hates the press." He chuckled evilly. "Can't imagine why, when we love him so much."

"I hope you didn't waste too much time on him."

"It wasn't a waste. There's no shortage of market for articles about this guy. The fact that he won't talk only makes people more obsessed with him. But there's only so far you can go with an outside-observer piece. The usual tabloid trash about the girls, the race cars, the wild parties . . . you know the tune. I can do better. A lot better. I'm going to write . . ." He paused, for dramatic effect. "A book."

"A *book*?"

"The one and only authorized biography. Jake Berenger's story in his own words. He doesn't know it yet, but he wants to work with me. I can feel it."

"He sounds like a shallow playboy. Why don't you pick someone more worthy to write about?"

Carter grinned. "He's worth one point one billion dollars on a good stock day. That's worthy enough for me."

"You're unbelievable," Molly said.

"Share the wealth, Molly! This book will sell. It'll get my name into the mainstream. When they write about him, they'll quote me. If I can make this happen, it'll be the coup of the decade."

"Great. All you'll need to do is get the man who never even gives interviews to agree to help you write a book. Or did you forget about that small detail?"

"No," Carter said. "I didn't forget."

"So," Molly prompted, "how do you plan to succeed where a hundred other hungry journalists have failed?"

"The approach," Carter said. He nodded. "Yes. I truly believe that it's all in the approach."

Molly smiled. "Oh, you're going to ask him *nicely*?"

"In a sense, yes. When you want to break through someone's armor, you look for the weakest spot, don't you?"

"I guess so."

"Right," Carter said. He had a determined look on his face. "Okay. Molly, when we were in college and your car broke down on our way home from the Dells, who walked eight miles in the snow to get help?"

"You did. You were very brave."

"And who covered for you when we were sixteen and you were dating Greg Ackerman? You couldn't admit to your father that you had a crush on a football player, so you told him that you were studying at my house every Saturday night. And then you went home slobbering drunk that time, and Stanford was sure that I'd done it to take advantage of you."

Molly frowned. "I wasn't slobbering."

"He's hated me ever since," Carter said. "But most

recently, who convinced you to send *Pirate Gold* to my agent in New York when you were barely willing to let it out of a locked dresser drawer?"

"Carter, I agree that I owe you a favor," Molly said. "But I don't see how I can help you with this Jake Berenger project. What do you want from me, a letter of recommendation assuring him that you're a decent guy? That you won't do a hatchet job on his life story?"

"You could include that when you talk to him," Carter said thoughtfully. "It might help."

Molly stared at him. "Hold it. Talk to him? Are you saying that you want *me* to ask Jake Berenger if he'll do this book?"

"That's the plan," Carter said. "But first, you'll need to seduce him."

THE EDITOR'S DIARY

Dear Reader,

Whether it's a matter of knowing when to be bad, or knowing when to trust, both of these elements can play a hand in bringing two people together. As Delilah Montague and Carly Martin will discover in our Warner Forever titles this November.

Janet Evanovich exclaims, "When life gets tough, read a book by Leanne Banks." Nothing could be truer than while reading **Leanne Banks's** WHEN SHE'S BAD. Delilah Montague is a self-made woman who manages an exclusive spa in Houston, TX. She garners a bad girl reputation due to her supposed establishment by a married tycoon, though they were never romantically involved. Delilah uses her bad rep to keep people at a distance. She is one tough cookie who likes to be in control and live a quiet life . . . until a certain brainy stud moves in next door. Benjamin Huntington begins upsetting her calm existence by renovating in the middle of the night and playing opera music. But her world is about to be turned completely upside-down when a baby appears on her doorstep . . . and Delilah may need a little help from her handsome neighbor *and* Cupid!

Going from sizzling guy-next-door to brooding alpha male, we offer **TRUST ME** by **Melanie Craft**, a wonderful new voice in contemporary romance. Veterinarian Carly Martin has a soft touch for stray animals and vulnerable men, so she is shocked when a stranger barges into her clinic one day and accuses her of being a gold digger. The stranger is Max Giordano, the illegitimate grandson of an eccentric millionaire, whose menagerie of animals is under Carly's care. With his grandfather on his deathbed, Max has to inform Carly that she will inherit the Tremayne mansion and the animals. At first, Max is suspicious of her, only he begins to see she's a guileless and gentle person that he is rapidly falling for. Now if he can just get Carly to trust him after getting things off to such a bad start . . .

To find out more about Warner Forever, these November titles, and the authors, visit us at www.warnerforever.com.

With warmest wishes,

Karen Kosztolnyik

Karen Kosztolnyik, Senior Editor

P.S. With the holidays approaching, Warner Forever presents two titles that are perfect gifts—and perfect indulgences! **Lori Wilde** pens a fun-filled tale about a female private eye helping her drop-dead gorgeous client dodge bullets and goons on their tail when they end up creating sparks that could ignite Las Vegas in **LICENSE TO THRILL**; and **Edie Claire** makes her mainstream romance debut in **LONG TIME COMING**, a captivating novel about a young woman who returns to her hometown to confront her childhood memories of her best friend's tragic death, and falls in love with the man she held responsible.